HOUSE OF THE PATRIARCH

HOUSE OF THE PATRIARCH

Barbara Hambly

Severn House Large Print
London & New York

This first large print edition published in Great Britain and the USA in 2021 by Severn House, an imprint of Canongate Books Ltd, 14 High Street, Edinburgh EH1 1TE.

First world regular print edition published in 2020 by Severn House, an imprint of Canongate Books Ltd.

British Library Cataloguing-in-Publication Data
A CIP catalogue record for this title is available from the British Library.

ISBN-13: 9781780291741

MIX
Paper from responsible sources
FSC
www.fsc.org FSC® C013056

Typeset by Palimpsest Book Production Ltd., Falkirk, Stirlingshire, Scotland.
Printed and bound in Great Britain by TJ Books Limited, Padstow, Cornwall.

To Harry and Laura

One

'Our daughter is missing.' The tall Englishman spoke quietly, but Benjamin January, sitting opposite him across the empty fireplace, saw his long fingers twitch as he drew out a letter, and an octavo-sized square of what looked like brown cardboard, from his breast pocket. His wife, short and snub-nosed, with the air of a woman supremely in charge of her life, turned her face away quickly, and January saw her tears.

As January held out his hand his eyes met, for a moment, those of his own wife, standing beside her. Rose always looked collected, but behind the lenses of her spectacles he saw the same painful division of mind and heart that he knew she saw in him.

He had just come back from another journey – another job – that had nearly cost him his life. The bullet graze in the muscles of his back was barely healed.

And they really, really needed money.

Damn it, thought January. *Damn it, damn it . . .*

He took the papers. He was to spend the next seven weeks kicking himself for doing so.

From the couch on the other side of the parlor, Henri Viellard spoke up. 'I told Mr Russell of the remarkable success you had in finding our friend Mr Singletary in Washington City a few years ago.'

1

January was tempted to mutter, *Ibn al-harîm*, his first wife's favorite indelicate expression when annoyed. But, mindful that he was speaking to a white man, he only inclined his head and said, 'You're very kind, sir.'

And in fact he was.

January's relationship with the Viellards – Chloë Viellard sat next to her husband, like a bespectacled schoolgirl in her plain gray dress – was one of those arrangements impossible to explain to anyone not born and raised in New Orleans. When the Viellard family corporation had forced Henri to marry his cousin Chloë, Henri had already been the 'protector' of January's lovely youngest sister Dominique; making Henri, in a sense, January's brother-in-law. Or brother-*out*-law, given the fact that Louisiana law forbade Henri to marry even the fairest of crème-café quadroons like Dominique, no matter how much he loved her.

Henri's note earlier that morning had said that English friends – connections of the private bank with which the extremely wealthy Viellards did business – had need of the kind of assistance that January might be able to render; would it be convenient for him to bring them to January's house?

January unfolded the letter.

New York
Thursday, 11 June, 1840
Paget,
    My poor cousin . . . there's no way to say this except to say it.

2

Eve has disappeared. She spent a week with the Delapores in King's Point, and was returning by way of the steam packet on Monday with not only Lucy, but Andy, the Delapores' coachman . . .

January guessed that Lucy must be her maid, since young ladies of the Russells' class didn't undertake journeys alone.

He glanced up from the shaken scrawl to meet Paget Russell's grief-racked blue eyes. 'She disappeared while staying in New York, then, sir?'

The Englishman nodded. 'Eve wouldn't – that is . . .'

Mrs Russell, hovering at his shoulder, put in, 'Eve asked if she could remain in New York with my cousin's family – the Winterinks, they're related to the Brevoorts, you know – rather than traveling with us to New Orleans. We saw no reason why it should not be so. Eve was a *great* success in New York society.' She pressed her kid-gloved hand quickly to her lips, as if to still their sudden unsteadiness. 'Why, she was invited to stay with the Ganesvoorts in Saratoga County, and one of the Livingston boys stood up with her – *twice!* – at the Brevoorts' ball!'

She spoke the names of the wealthy New York families with the same reverence January had heard in the voice of Henri Viellard's mother, when she referred to the aristocratic French families who ruled New Orleans society, the Mandevilles and Metoyers and Blanques. 'And Mrs Livingston told me—'

Her husband reached back to touch her hand gently, silencing her. 'We received this letter only yesterday,' he said. 'I have no idea what my cousin's family has done so far, or what the police might have learned. But I cannot . . . *we* cannot . . .'

Three weeks for the letter to get here, thought January. *Anything can have happened in that time . . .*

He returned to the letter.

> When the time came to disembark, Lucy and Andy waited for Eve to rejoin them (she had gone to the rear of the steamboat to view yachts sailing off College Point). When she did not come, they searched the whole of the vessel, asking questions of everyone they saw. No one recalled a girl of Eve's description, either on-board or getting off. Of course we notified the police at once, and they sent a 'detective' officer to question the captain and crew, but to no avail. In four days now we have heard nothing, either of a demand for ransom, or of any girl who could be Eve brought in to any hospital . . .

January glanced again at the strained faces of the girl's parents. Their eyes on his, begging him to make things well.

Their correspondent – he glanced at the foot of the letter, saw it was signed by Charlotte Winterink – didn't mention searching the city morgue. Given the girl's disappearance off a steam packet crossing Long Island Sound that would have been the first place the police would inquire. But some things, he knew, you couldn't write.

Beyond the parlor's French doors, open on to the Rue Esplanade, the distant clang of steamboat bells could be heard from the wharves. Closer, axles creaked down the center of the wide street, drays hauling freight back to the canal basin. It was ten in the morning and already the wet heat was insufferable.

'How old is your daughter, sir?'

'Seventeen.'

'She turned seventeen in March,' amplified Mrs Russell, blinking back tears and presenting the information as if it were a bouquet. 'She was brought out at a ball at her aunt's house, my cousin Caroline, Lady Emsworth – her husband is Lord Emsworth of Parclose, one of the first families in Sussex. She was presented at the Queen's Drawing Room in April, just before we left for America – cream-colored silk gauze, with a pelerine of point-d'esprit and three flounces that picked up the design of the train . . . I was *devastated* that Eve could not have a full Season this year, but it would have looked worse, had we waited until—'

Her husband laid a finger on her wrist again. January, whose first wife – whom he had never ceased to grieve – had been a dressmaker, noted that the woman's dress had been re-cut – he could see where the ruffles popular three years ago had been removed – and estimated the cost of her simple pearls. The superfine of Mr

5

Russell's coat was too sturdy to show wear, but the lapels of his waistcoat, and the colors of its silk, were also several seasons out of date.

'Why would anyone kidnap a young woman for ransom, sir, if her parents are known to be three weeks away in New Orleans?' he asked

'That's just *it*, Mr January!' the mother wailed. 'It isn't as though my husband and I are wealthy! We'll be able to dower Eve respectably, of course, when the time comes, but if someone wished to kidnap a girl for ransom, why not Georgiana Ganesvoort? Or Aemilia Drew, whose uncle owns all those steamboats and is making so much money . . . Why not one of the Roosevelt girls? Why—'

Her voice caught on tears, and Rose put gentle hands on her shoulders, and tried to lead her to the couch where the Viellards sat.

'In any case,' her husband said matter-of-factly, 'I cannot see how even the cleverest gang of bravos could remove a girl from the deck of a crowded steamboat in broad daylight.'

January was silent, considering the more obvious of several possibilities. Considering, too, what he – as a man of African descent in New Orleans – could be heard to suggest about a well-bred white girl to her parents. The English in general weren't as likely to take violent umbrage if a black man asked, *Might your daughter have run off with someone?* And the Viellards, as good Creole French, were both inclined, if pushed to the wall, to admit that a spade was in fact a spade.

But you never knew who would talk to whom,

and January had observed that with the bank crash three years ago – and the increase in slave runaways due to the growing efficiency of the so-called Underground Railroad – American whites had become touchier about keeping free blacks like himself 'in their place'. With more and more Americans coming into New Orleans every year, he had no desire to be waked up some night by having his windows broken or his house burned.

So he said, as tactfully as he could, 'You say your daughter asked to remain in New York, sir? While you and Mrs Russell came on here to New Orleans? You wouldn't know if there was anyone that she met . . .' He let the sentence trail off into a gesture as tactful as it was non-committal.

'Good *Heavens*, no!' Mrs Russell pulled away from Rose's solicitude and bustled back to the hearth. 'Why, Eve was only just out! And I'd certainly have known – Lucy had *strict* instructions to tell me if Eve received *any* cards or notes or presents . . .'

January kept his eyebrows firmly level at this insight into the relations between mother and daughter, but he did wonder how Eve felt about having her maid set to spy on her.

'And in any case' – the little woman leaned forward confidentially – 'Eve is *far* too well bred to even *conceive* of anything that smacks of the clandestine! Indeed – although as I said she made *quite* a stir, both in London and in New York, this season, I would never have said that she favored any young gentleman above another.

Though in London she received bouquets from Viscount Mannering – the most beautiful pink roses! – and even from the Earl of Selby, though of course His Grace is quite too old for her. Still, he did single her out to dance the quadrille at—'

January caught Mr Russell's eye again, and again saw the shadow there.

To Rose, he said, 'My nightingale, could you perhaps see if there's tea – or ginger water perhaps' – the clammy warmth of the morning was giving way to yet another day of sticky heat – 'for our guests? Mr Russell, might I beg the favor of a few words with you in private?'

With a look of stricken anxiety, Mrs Russell made as if she would catch her tall husband's sleeve as he stood, but January saw, in Paget Russell's eyes, the look of relief.

Whatever it is, he doesn't want to speak of it where his wife can hear.

'You will help us?' Mrs Russell turned pleading brown eyes towards January. 'Chloë tells me that you know *just* what to do in these cases, how to find . . . How to find what has happened . . .'

Chloë Viellard looked on the point of observing that there was no reason to suppose that M'sieu Janvier would be able or willing to travel with the couple back to New York – a quick glance at the rest of the short letter told January that its final paragraph consisted only of a plea that the Russells return to that city by the first available vessel. But her husband, a bespectacled mama's-boy who had remained uncomfortably silent in his chair through the interview, rose now like an embarrassed blancmange and took Mrs Russell's

8

hand in his own big pudgy one. 'Of course he will, madame! Madame Viellard and I had already made plans to travel to New York with my mother next week, and we can easily put forward our arrangements, to accompany you, and include M'sieu Janvier in our suite.'

Rachel Russell whispered, 'Thank you,' and clung to Henri's hand. Tears flooded again from her eyes. 'Oh, thank you!'

'You will come' – Henri turned his cow-like, short-sighted gaze on January – 'won't you, Benjamin? Please.'

With a rich man's disregard for money, it would never have occurred to Henri Viellard to mention – or even think about – the fact that with the departure of the last pupils from Rose's school at the end of April, there was a good chance that he would be lending January money to live on before the wealthy of the town began to return in November. But January was aware of it.

And he was aware, too, that a payment for his trouble from Mr Russell would make such a loan unnecessary.

January was fond of Henri Viellard, and had a deep regard for the tiny, fragile, bespectacled Chloë. Having been emotionally blackmailed by his mother for much of his life, he wanted very much to keep finances out of their friendship, which was complicated enough. He guessed, too, that Henri – or more probably the ruthlessly efficient Chloë – would arrange payment for his services as an unofficial 'detective policeman' (as they were beginning to be called) before their departure for New York. Even without students at the boarding school which Rose kept in their house, Rose would be free of worry for the summer.

So though everything he had heard about New York was shouting, *Don't do it you idiot!* he inclined his head, and said, 'Of course.'

Rising, he added, 'But there are a few things that I need to know about your trip to America, Mr Russell.' And crossing to the door of his little office, he gestured the Englishman to precede him, while Rose excused herself and went in quest of tea.

Two

Closing the door, January asked quietly, 'What do you think happened?'

The Englishman met his eyes. Not defiantly, nor angry at the implications of such a question, as many Americans would have been.

Just not sure how to speak of his daughter to a stranger.

Maybe not sure how to speak of his daughter at all.

More gently, January asked, 'Was your daughter happy?'

As he spoke he gestured the man to the simple bergère chair in the corner of the little room. By the traditions of the Caribbean creoles, this chamber would have been the bedroom of the master of the house, and it was through its long

10

French windows – rather than those of the parlor – that January had welcomed the Viellards and their guests, when they'd mounted the high steps to the gallery from the street.

After a long time, Russell said, 'I don't . . . I don't think so.' He rubbed his eyes, as if to clear his thoughts. January wondered how much sleep he'd gotten, since he'd received that letter. 'But I can't think of any reason that she would not have been so.'

He folded his tall form into the much-worn brocade, while January took his seat at the desk. 'With girls sometimes it's hard to tell, you know.'

'I know.' For four years – since an unexpected windfall had allowed them to purchase the old Spanish house on Rue Esplanade – he and Rose had taught girls there, boarding some, opening the classes to others whose mothers lived in town. Girls of color, the daughters of *plaçeés* like his sister Dominique by their white protectors. The daughters, too, some of them, of the *sang-melée* craftsman who made up so large a proportion of the population of the old French Town. Girls that had shared their house, eaten meals with them, absorbed – or simply sat through – his lessons in the art of music. He often wondered what they dreamed.

'Do you think there might have been a young man, sir?' It was not something he could have said, with Mrs Russell in the room. He suspected Mr Russell was as glad as he was, to speak privately.

The father's sparse, fair brows sank over his eyes. He had a narrow face, dominated by a

11

jutting nose and close-set, sky-blue eyes. January had the impression of intelligence without much imagination, the sort of man who is very good at what he does but doesn't ask why he's doing it. He was a banker, Henri had said, with Thelwell's, a large private banking firm in the Midlands. The firm had thought sufficiently well of his judgment to send him first to New York, then to New Orleans – where his wife had relatives – to meet with private banks desirous of re-establishing their credit after America's disastrous National Bank debacle of 1837. He wondered if the missing girl had taken after her father's intense intelligence, or Mrs Russell's feather-headed chattiness.

'I don't think so.' Russell's long, spindly fingers twisted at a sleeve button. 'As Mrs Russell said, Eve was invited to . . . to balls and routs and all the other things people of consideration attend. I didn't particularly notice her being neglected. She was asked to dance, and never ended up standing in a corner with the chaperones, that sort of thing. Mrs Russell would have spoken of it, if she had. I don't think she favored one young man above another . . . But then I had my own concerns at these events, you see. And Mrs Russell tells me I'm . . . that I don't see the things she sees. I daresay she's right.'

He touched the rectangle of brown cardboard that he'd handed January with the letter. 'That's her,' he explained. 'We had it done at a place on Broadway.'

Unfolding the cardboard cover, January exclaimed, 'It's a daguerreotype!'

12

He moved the slip of glass-covered metal back and forth in its cardboard holder, the image of the girl queerly luminous – now a strange black-and-white portrait, now a ghost-like pattern of darkness and light. 'I've read of such things, but I've never seen one.' He angled the picture so that the image was a true one – a very pretty, round-faced, snub-nosed young lady with fairish curls clustering under a crown of small white roses.

'Fellow on Broadway said he was the first in this country,' affirmed the banker. 'There's only one man doing them in London. Though I should imagine there'll be a dozen by the time we . . .' His voice faltered a little. 'By the time *we* get home.'

'She favors her mother.'

'Yes.' With the factual statement, the iron reserve was back in the man's tone. 'Very much so.'

January studied the image in a kind of amazement. Not even masters like Da Vinci and Titian that he'd seen in Paris, not the finest Americans like Peale and Stuart, had ever touched this type of reproduction. The closest he'd seen to this humanness, this *realness*, had been in the portrait busts by the Romans, and even they had the perfection of something produced by consummate craft. The reality of the human features had been reproduced, however accurately, by another human being.

But nothing had stood between *that girl*, that single person – Eve Russell, soul and flesh and upbringing unlike anyone else created since time began – and the image resting in his hand. This was *her*. Not a painter's view of her. No choice of colors, not the smallest trace of opinion as to what that small, reserved smile meant. No sense whatsoever of future or past. Impersonally transmitted, without error or judgment, the product solely of chemicals and light.

Rose would be fascinated.

'This will help me very much, if I may keep it for a time.'

Looking deeper into the ghostly depths, he saw the differences, too. Or was it, he wondered, his imagination, that read Paget Russell's intelligence in those wide dark eyes? That saw troubled pensiveness in the mouth that in her mother's face beamed when she spoke of her daughter's social accomplishments? Why was he so certain that the upright needle scratch between the plucked and groomed eyebrows was thoughtfulness – anger, even – rather than concern about the circumference of her corseted waist, or the number of posies sent to her after a ball?

'I rather thought she was impatient with them, you know,' Russell went on. 'The young gentlemen. Mrs Russell would bring her the cards that came for her to the house – not only in New York, but back in London at the beginning of the Season – and she'd have to urge her to look at them. She's said to me several times, "I don't know what I'm going to do with the girl."'

January looked from the girl's face to the father's, hearing the puzzlement in his words.

'They . . . They don't get on,' Russell explained,

14

as if the words were being forced from him at knifepoint. 'I don't know why. Monsieur Viellard assured me that anything I say will remain in the strictest confidence, and I must ask you not to speak of what I say even to my wife—'

January shook his head. 'I can see,' he said tactfully, 'that Mrs Russell wants only the best for your daughter, sir. But perhaps she and her daughter have different ideas of what "best" means.'

'I think . . .' Again Russell paused, and January guessed that like many well-off men – black and white alike – Russell had barely spoken with his daughter through most of her life. Barely knew her, save as a child brought out from the nursery once a day for a little desultory catechism about the day's events before the nanny – or later the governess – took the girl back to the schoolroom.

Yet something struggled in his eyes.

'Was there anything,' asked January, 'that your daughter *did* seem interested in, in New York, sir?'

'Lectures.' Russell replied at once, and with the appearance of relief.

Lectures.

'By anyone in particular?'

'No.' The Englishman shook his head. 'That is, she attended a lecture at the New York University, on abolitionism, and came home with, I gather, a number of tracts and pamphlets which she apparently concealed from her mother under the mattress of her bed. One of her aunts took her to a lecture on the rights of women – for

15

which my wife roundly scolded the aunt, since eccentricity is the last thing a young man wants to see in a girl . . .'

Again a thought fleeted unspoken across the back of his eyes.

'But in the main,' he went on slowly, 'she went to religious lectures, when she could get one of our friends to take her. I went with her once. Terrible tosh, I thought it. We're C of E, of course,' he continued, 'and she was instructed very properly and received into the Church. And she's always been very good about attending.'

His words slowed as he went on, as if he were trying to fit events together into a pattern that he for the life of him could not see. 'But she never showed much interest in it, you know, until she came to New York. I don't know if you're aware of it, Mr January, but New York State is a . . . a sort of hotbed of some very odd forms of belief. And now they have the Canal dug, and the railroads going through, and all sorts of goods coming in from the western parts of the state, and trade going out there . . .'

He spread his hands, a little helplessly. 'A lot of these . . . these backwoods preachers come into New York, and rent lecture halls or set up in churches as . . . well, as messiahs. As if the Bible isn't good enough, and they all have some new revelation. Lunatics, I thought them. Like that fellow Miller, who's gathered followers around him claiming that – er – Jesus Christ is going to return and end the world in – 1843, I think it is. Or the man in Wayne County

16

who claimed that Jesus Christ came to America after his resurrection and preached to the Indians. Or all those communities – Quakers and Shakers and Swedenborgians, and followers after the Divine Economy, whatever that is. All claiming they're living like the early Christians and holding their property in common and all that sort of thing.'

He shook his head again, like a horse with a fly buzzing at his ear. 'Well, after that abolitionist business, Mrs Russell had Lucy – that's our maid – search Eve's room, and for a while we thought she was only going to the lectures to keep herself amused. But then we discovered that Eve was hiding these . . . these tracts, these broadsides, all over the house. I read some of them, and they were every bit as mad as the lecturer I'd heard.'

His eyes lost their focus for a moment, searching the distance past January's shoulder for some familiar landmark. Grieving, perhaps, thought January, for things said or things done, that might have prevented this situation – had he only known what to do or say.

'And her explanations of them were no saner. She ended by crying that we didn't understand, that we *couldn't* understand – to which I responded that if Mrs Russell and I *couldn't* understand there was no sense in her getting angry at us for not doing so. I don't suppose that helped much,' he added remorsefully. 'I ended by sending her to her room and having Grislock – our butler – burn the lot.'

He looked down at his hands, folded upon his bony knees.

17

He still couldn't speak his thought, so January spoke it for him.

'Do you fear she's run off to one of these religious communities, sir?'

He nodded. Again January had the impression of a man forced to yield up secrets he would sooner have taken to his coffin.

'I don't see why she would have,' he added, after a long stillness. 'But you're quite right, Mr January. You see, it seems impossible that she could have been taken off the steam packet, in broad daylight, against her will.'

January considered again the round face in the daguerreotype, with its childishly short nose and its crown of roses. She looked barely fourteen, though there was little of the child in her eyes.

What had she thought of Rachel Russell's too obvious schemes to introduce her to the 'best society' in London and New York, to make her courted and fêted? To marry her into a family 'of consideration'?

What did she think of her father, who *had other things to think about . . .*'?

What did she think of the world she'd been born into, the world that January himself had observed in the homes of the students he taught? He and Rose struggled constantly on the edge of poverty, because Rose had chosen to teach in her school subjects with real meat to them – history, Latin, chemistry, the wondrous mechanics of the stars. Most parents, men and women alike, wanted their daughters to learn dancing, deportment, sketching, fancy needlework.

. . . eccentricity is the last thing a young man wants to see in a girl . . .

He thought of all those ornate parlors where he gave piano lessons, with issues of *Godey's Ladies' Book* on the marble-topped tables and not a book or newspaper in sight.

'Do you mind my asking, sir, why your daughter didn't accompany you and your wife to New Orleans?'

Again the frown of a man trying to puzzle out something he couldn't quite understand. 'She told us – told her mother and myself – that our cousins had asked her to stay on. She said she understood that New Orleans would be horribly unpleasant this time of year. She'd been invited to the Roosevelts' place in Oyster Bay, and to visit the Delapores in the country. But Lucy told my wife later that Eve said she had no desire to go into a country where – er – slavery was prevalent.' He pronounced the word apologetically, as if he hated to bring up the fact that January was black and might possibly have relatives in bondage.

Something not to be spoken of. Something that polite people – especially well-bred young ladies – weren't supposed to see.

A little defensively, Russell added, 'But there's slavery in New York, you know. Southern visitors bring their slaves with them all the time. And she'd never said a word about this before.'

And to whom, January did not ask, would she have said one?

'These cults,' he said, 'these sects . . . Do you know if she favored one above the others? If she spoke of one, or had more of their tracts?'

19

Russell's face skewed with thought. 'I honestly don't recall. There were dozens of tracts, and I didn't notice any names in particular. Harmonites? Universal Society for Something-or-Other . . . Latter-Day Saints . . . Children of the Light . . . Convention of the New Jerusalem . . . Something about the Second Advent . . . All of them perfectly absurd.'

'Your daughter doesn't seem to have thought so, sir,' pointed out January.

'No.' The man's breath went out of him in a sigh. 'And of course, Mrs Russell won't hear of it, you know. She's convinced Eve was kidnapped, though why anyone would kidnap a girl whose family isn't wealthy . . . not to speak of *how* it would have been managed. I've had to stop her from writing to every influential man in whose house we dined – urging them to offer rewards, to hire men to search – until we know more . . . It's hard to know what to do, because in fact she may be right.'

In spite of himself, January flinched at the possibility that crossed his mind at the words.

'The worst of it is not knowing.' Russell's voice sank almost to a whisper. 'By the time we return she'll have been gone for almost *seven weeks* . . .'

'And we may get there to find her returned already,' pointed out January. 'Having gotten bored with religious ranting or vegetarian meals or studying the secret spiritual structure of the planetary planes . . .'

'Do you honestly think that will be the case, Mr January?'

January was silent for a long moment. 'No,' he said quietly. 'But she may very well have sent a letter explaining herself, and asking your forgiveness. One that you simply have not yet received.'

He closed his mouth on the other possible outcomes of the situation. Mr Russell brightened a little – not being a man of imagination – and January let the matter rest. The man had grief enough for the present.

Three

'Does that all sound as odd to you as it does to me?' asked Rose, as he came back in through the French doors of his study, from seeing the Viellard carriage on its way down Rue Esplanade.

The sweltering July morning outside was beginning to cloud over, as it did nearly every morning of summer, for the inevitable mid-afternoon rainstorm. Like the rattle of tambourines, cicadas droned in the trees along the neutral ground, the sound rising and falling, waves blown by an impalpable wind.

'She may have sent word explaining herself, which didn't reach Mrs Winterink until after she wrote to the girl's parents.' He glanced at the notes he'd made when reading the letter through a second time. 'Though four days seems ample time – and Mamzelle Russell has to have known that her hostess would write to

21

her parents, if she didn't have some kind of notice herself.'

'Unless the girl is a monster.' As a schoolmistress, Rose had dealt with adolescent monsters in her time.

She propped her spectacles higher on to her nose, a tall, slim woman, from whose white father she'd inherited a tendency to freckle, and the hazel-gray eyes often found among the fairer quadroons. 'And girls sometimes take to religion that way. I don't know how many of my students, at one time or another, have informed me that God wishes them to become nuns. Even the Protestant ones, presumably those who have read Mrs Radcliffe's *The Italian* too many times. And then, of course . . .'

She paused, and January finished for her, 'Yes. But I doubt a girl could fling herself off the steam packet in broad daylight without a dozen people seeing her.'

Both were silent. January recalled Gertrude's lines in *Hamlet*, speaking of another young girl's suicide: how the air trapped in Ophelia's skirts bore her up, mermaid-like, before the saturated fabric dragged her down . . .

Ophelia, too, he remembered, had lived among people who seemed not to have regarded what she thought or felt.

But how would anyone not have seen?

Rose went to the dining room's sideboard, took out a japanned tray and began gathering up cups and plates. Distraught as Madame Russell might have been, January noted that only a crumb or two of his nephew Gabriel's very excellent

22

pralines remained on the plate closest to where she had been sitting.

'Why kidnap – or lure away – a girl whose parents couldn't pay a large ransom?' he asked. 'Whose parents are three weeks away? That's laying yourself open for a terrible amount of trouble without much to show for it.'

'Whoever took her may not have been terribly rational—'

'Maybe,' agreed January slowly. 'She couldn't have gotten off the boat without a confederate, to provide her with a change of clothing, and possibly – probably – transportation away from the wharves. That seems like a good deal of trouble to go to, simply to gain one more convert who can bring nothing to a religious community but a pair of willing hands. And a great deal more trouble to go to, to gain, possibly . . . What? Mr Russell is merely the representative of his bank, not an owner. A bank, moreover, that's in England, and only just beginning to establish connections in Louisiana. What information or advantage could kidnappers have hoped to achieve?'

'*She* could have lied to *them*.' She set the plates down on the dining table. 'The parents may be lying about what life is like *chez* Russell.'

January considered that possibility, while the rattle of a carriage in the street, and the curses of the draymen, came loud through the open French doors. The older of his two sisters, Olympe – the voodoos called her Olympia Snakebones – had told him things about families, white and black, that made the childhood he'd shared with her in slavery seem an innocent idyll. And what little Olympe hadn't heard of, Rose had, in her years of teaching school.

'Then why hire someone to find her?'

'Really, Benjamin,' she said, with only half a smile, 'do you honestly think Mrs Russell would let the world start saying that her *great* success of a daughter, who was presented to the queen only a few months ago, would flee from her parents and go into hiding with a pack of backwoods utopians?'

He said, 'Hmn.' And then, 'Of course, it could just be that the *Don't-Follow-Me-I'm-Perfectly-Safe* letter went astray. They do, you know.'

'Do you believe that?' Rose opened the bottom of the sideboard, took out a once-handsome Queensware basin with a chipped rim, and a couple of clean towels.

'No.' As January said it, he felt – as he had felt when he'd given the same answer to Paget Russell – as he would have felt if, opening the door into a pitch-black room, he had heard stealthy movement in the dark.

'Will you go?'

January said quietly, 'I think I'll have to.'

Together they passed through the French doors on to the house's rear gallery, across its shade and down the steps to the dense heat of the yard. Even from the base of the steps, January could feel the heat that radiated from the kitchen, in its little semi-jungle of banana plants and resurrection fern. Closer to the open French doors of that miniature Gehenna the heat was enough to knock a man down. Flies droned under

24

the rafters, and upon the open hearth, two heaps of coals glowed like the sullen fires of Vesuvius. A pot of stew for dinner was buried under one. A pot of beans and rice, under the other. From the aqueous gloom among the banana plants outside, Plutarch the cat regarded them with the remote pity accorded a pair of lunatics.

'We'll get by somehow,' said Rose, but by the careful tones of her voice he knew that she wasn't thinking of the money they didn't have.

In May, with the wealthy of New Orleans already deserting the city before the rank heat of the fever season, January had returned from the Republic of Texas with a bullet scar across his back and seven hundred and fifty dollars' worth of debt, incurred when he'd gone to rescue another missing girl. Selina Bellinger, too, had run away – in her case, with a blackguard who had sold the love-struck young octoroon as a slave.[1]

Selina's white planter father had wept to have his daughter restored to him, and had immediately reimbursed January for the money he'd borrowed – at short notice and high interest – to undertake the rescue. But planters lived on credit, from harvest to harvest, and the most he'd been able to give January over and above that repayment had been seventy-five dollars. And January knew, as surely as he knew his name, that both repayment and reward had been raised by the sale of one of Roux Bellinger's slaves.

[1] See *Lady of Perdition*

He wished he'd had the courage to tell the planter not to pay him back at all. Not at the cost of taking a father from his children – as January's own father had lost his wife and his children. Not at the cost of taking a woman from her husband, or sweetheart, or family and friends.

But he had not had that option. All that he had – all that Rose had, and his tiny sons – was the house. With the whole country still laboring under the aftermath of Andrew Jackson's fiscal policies, he could not – dared not – remain in debt. If something else happened – and something else *always* happened – and they lost the house, they would be lost indeed.

Olympe had said to him once, regarding him with those night-dark voodoo eyes, *You can't save everyone, Ben.*

About half of that money was already gone.

And it wasn't only that.

. . . *urging them to offer rewards*, Russell had said, *to hire men to search . . . in fact she may be right.*

Thinking of the men who would jump at those rewards, who would jump at the chance to search houses along the Canadian border, January shivered again.

In silence, he dipped a pannikin of water from the simmering boiler within the fireplace, and in silence Rose picked up the gourd of soft soap from beside the sink. They crossed the yard again as the first huge drops of the afternoon's rain splatted down, and in the dining room once again, January emptied the hot water into the basin. Rose's mother – a plaçeé, as January's had been in her salad days – had been of the old school which believed that no servant was to be trusted to wash the good dishes.

In time Rose remarked, 'It's three weeks up to New York. When you get there, you may find the girl safe and sound. Or married to someone unsuitable after all and living in ecstatic destitution in Brooklyn.'

'Good,' said January. 'I will weep with gratification and take the first vessel back.' He dried the cups, aware of the swift sidelong glance Rose gave him, at the dryness of his reply. For a time he said nothing further, while Rose handed him the delicate china-ware with the mechanical efficiency which she otherwise devoted to her chemical experiments, and to the manufacture of fireworks for the Opera House.

At length he went on, 'But even if Mademoiselle Russell tires of spiritual meditation and vegetarian rations, many of these congregations and communes of Millerites and Swedenborgians are in the western counties of the state, along the lakes and the border with Canada. That's a long way to come back, for a girl of seventeen.'

'It depends on the girl.'

January hid a smile. Rose herself was perfectly capable of traveling to Oregon and back unaccompanied . . . and he wouldn't have taken bets against his mother, or Olympe, making it home safely from China.

The beautiful Ayasha, he remembered, had escaped from her father's harem at the age of fourteen, rather than marry the man's middle-aged business partner, and had traveled all the way to Paris disguised as a boy. Within two years she'd been operating her own dress shop and employing three other girls.

The memory – the thought of Ayasha – as always, warmed his heart. He could well imagine what she would have had to say about the Russell family.

But his smile faded, as he thought of all the things that could befall a girl that young on the road.

And of other things. Reasons beyond money, that whispered to him that he had to travel to the border of Canada.

The voice of his niece Zizi-Marie came faintly from the storerooms under the house, calling 'Fi, fie, fo, fum! You can't hide from me . . .' And a moment later, the high-pitched laughter of his sons.

The rain was now coming down in earnest, violent gray sheets of it, and rivers pouring from the deep overhang of the eaves. The primal softness of the air breathed through the house, and it seemed to him, for a time, as if the whole of the house were cut off from the fever and filth of New Orleans, from the bitter horrors of slavery and greed and poverty. As if, for that time, there was only his family – Rose and three-year-old Professor John, and baby Xander, and Gabriel and Zizi-Marie (and Plutarch the cat, now crouched beneath the couch) – safe within those gray walls of water. Safe within the quiet moment, before the rain ceased, and the outside world became real again.

28

This was the world where he wanted to live, forever, and he drank the time as he would have drunk clean water before setting forth across a desert.

Then he sighed, and went to the little mahogany secrètaire in one corner of the parlor. From its drawer he took two sheets of notepaper, and began to write.

Shortly after the rain ceased, when – as they said in New Orleans – *the rocks were burning* with the steam that rose under the newly uncovered afternoon sun, a Viellard groom arrived with a note from Chloë Viellard. Accommodations had been booked on the *Marengo*, leaving for Havana and points north the following morning. Ostensibly the Viellards were accompanying Henri's formidable mother to New York, to consult a specialist about her swollen toes which she swore were not due to gout.

('You should hear my mother on the subject of Madame Viellard's ailments,' remarked January, folding the missive and stowing it in a pocket. 'And Dominique, every time Madame requires Henri to remain at the town house and look after her . . .')

The groom also brought the livery of a servant, of an old-fashioned cut which would mark January as somebody's property, since slave badges weren't used in New York. He tightened his lips at the sight of the uniform, but packed it all the same, in the small wicker valise that was all he would carry with him on the voyage. He hated masquerading as a slave, but knew the clothing might very well mean the difference between life and death.

Giving the two notes – folded and sealed with wafers – to Zizi-Marie to deliver, he set forth along the Rue Esplanade for the marshy *ciprière* along Bayou St-John. The cathedral clock was sounding four as he circled through the 'back of town', among vacant lots, shanties built of old flat-boat planks, cheap bordellos and cheaper saloons, watching behind him and around him.

At this time of day it was more or less safe for a black man to venture into 'the Swamp', as this part of town was called: the ruffians, river pirates, and sailors who frequented its dives were either still at their work, or not drunk enough to think it worth their time to beat up a man forbidden by law to raise his hand against whites.

Still, January walked carefully.

He had found, more and more, that he hated leaving the French Town, hated it with an uneasy dread that compounded itself like interest from month to month. He'd been raised in the French Town from the age of seven, and knew almost everyone there. A hundred respectable white men would step forward and say, *Sure, I know Ben! Of course he's a free man! Teaches piano to my daughter . . . played at my sister's wedding . . . see him in the orchestra every ball I go to, during Carnival . . .*

Courts would listen to a white man.

As he came out of the straggly cypress trees beyond the Charity Hospital he saw a young man, a sailor, light enough of complexion that

30

he could have been a Spaniard or Italian, but for the African shape of his lips and nose. January noticed him because of the way he looked around him at the grimy saloons along Marais Street. *Just off his ship*, January guessed.

He was about fifty feet from January on the other side of the street, gawking in surprise and distaste at the frogs (*and worse things, probably*) that swarmed the ditches. A black girl wearing little but a chemise called to him from the gallery of the Blackleg Saloon, and the young man hastily backed away. January quickened his pace to overtake him, but a tall, loose-limbed man emerged from the Salt River Tavern and crossed the lot to reach the young sailor first. January heard him call out, 'You look like you need a guide 'round here, friend!'

The young sailor turned with a grateful expression and a rueful grin. 'I do, that, sir!'

Damn it, thought January . . .

The young man looked at the semi-desolation around them. In the blasting slant of the late falling light it looked dreary and sordid – and stank like the cesspits of Hell – but didn't seem particularly dangerous. A couple of dogs scratched on the gallery of Broadhorn Sal's; from a shanty among the weeds and cypresses, the shrill voice of a woman rose in anger, cut off sharply, as by a blow. 'What I need mostly is where a man can get a drink.'

The tall man draped a friendly arm around the sailor's shoulder. 'You is wise to ask, brother. White men 'round here, they'll beat you bloody if you walk through the door of the wrong place—'

Damn it, thought January again, and quickened his steps. He dug in his pocket, but the only things he had were his silver watch and a couple of silver fifty-cent pieces. But he had to hold up something, so he held up two of the coins and called out, 'Hey, sailor! You drop this?' and prayed the tout's friends weren't nearby.

The young man looked startled, patted his pockets – the tall man leaned close, and whispered something in his ear. The sailor's eyes flared with shock and fear, and as January started towards them, two white men appeared out of Broadhorn Sal's (*DAMN it!*) and came to him. At the same time the sailor said hastily 'Uh – no, no sir, I ain't drop nuthin' . . .' and January guessed what it was that the tall man had said.

I know that man . . . he works for the slave-catcher gangs . . .

The two whites – greasy hair, dirty beards, knives at their belts – closed in on him as the tall man hustled the young sailor away down the street and into a dirty shack made half of tent canvas, half of old flatboat planks. The heavier of the two whites said quietly, 'Maybe you better mind your own business, Sambo.'

At six-foot-three and muscled like Hercules, January could have taken on both men – had he not known for a fact that at least ten other white ruffians would have emerged as if by magic from every saloon and whorehouse along the street, to 'teach him a lesson' in 'respect'.

As it was, he put on his most innocent expression and backed up – naturally enough, since the man's knife was now in his hand – and held up the money. 'I just saw that young sailor done drop these coin, sir. I didn't mean nuthin' by it.'

He knew they'd take the money from him and they did ('We'll give it to him.'). When he walked off, heart pounding – and listening behind him, to see if they followed – he was glad to get out of the situation with nothing more than their scornful laughter, and some tobacco-imbued spit on his face and his back. He felt almost sick with rage and fear.

The young sailor, he knew, was never going to make it back to his ship. He was going to wake up tomorrow with an opium headache in a barracoon or a slave jail someplace, naked and without his free papers. He would be sold, almost certainly, within days.

And January was well aware of how close he'd come to waking up beside him. And of how stupid he'd been to even try to meddle.

You can't save everyone . . .

And every time he tried, he ran the risk of leaving Rose, and their sons, and Gabriel and Zizi-Marie, adrift in a world where such events wouldn't even draw comment.

But I can't not try.

He felt the eyes of the two white men on his back for some time, as he hurried away through the tropical heat.

Four

Hannibal Sefton was sitting up in his shabby pallet, in one of the shacks behind Kate the Gouger's bathhouse on Perdidio Street, looking like a dead elf and playing the larghetto from Vivaldi's 'Concerto in A for Guitar' on his violin. Crossing the shaggy groves of swamp laurel that backed Kate's establishment, January rejoiced to hear the music, sweet and lilting and unbearably sad. A week ago he had feared that his friend's hacking cough was turning to pneumonia, and knew that would finish him.

As always, the music soothed him, and helped him set aside the sickened hatred that the encounter on Marais Street had stirred to life.

'There was nothing I could do,' he concluded, when his friend had listened to his account of the young sailor's kidnapping. 'I know that. I told myself that, every step of my way here.' He looked aside, not wanting Hannibal to see what was in his eyes; that it was hard not to hate all white men, this dilapidated Irishman with the others. 'I just sometimes wonder when the Hell there is going to be something I *can* do.'

'And there is.' Hannibal coughed, pressing his hand to his side. 'You can find this girl before her parents offer a reward for her that will have every scoundrel and slave catcher combing through all the Quaker farmhouses and utopian

34

communes in western New York State. Given how close that area lies to the Canadian border, they may not find Miss Russell, but they'll certainly find a score of runaways – and the people who hide them, and feed them, and send them on their way. That's the main reason you're going, isn't it?'

January nodded, and sighed. 'I can't very well not. Her mother thinks she was kidnapped . . .'

The coffee-dark eyes sparkled wryly. 'Who'd kidnap a girl whose parents aren't rich?' He picked up the daguerreotype that January had laid on the threadbare sheet which covered him. 'There are places that specialize in virgins.'

'Hiring a good fake is cheaper.' Hannibal shrugged, and reached back to shift the pile of sacks that did duty for a pillow. 'Especially when the girl's parents are just rich enough to cause trouble. You couldn't sell her, not even to Havana or Cartagena. How old did you say she was?'

'Seventeen. Sixteen, when that was taken.'

'They could pass her as off a twelve-year-old at the Queen's Fancy in Kingston. *O formose puer, nimium ne crede colori* . . . She *might* have given kidnappers the impression that her parents were indifferent, but I don't know a pimp in the business who'd take that kind of risk.' The fiddler gathered his long, dark hair away from his face and began to braid it – fingers trembling – into a shaky queue. 'Not when they can get German or Irish girls for five dollars apiece on the wharves.'

January handed him the wine-red velvet ribbon that lay on the packing crate beside the pallet,

35

and then a gourd cup of ginger water that stood beside it. The shack was the smallest of the four behind the bathhouse, the other three of which did service for the whores who worked the place. The only furniture, besides the pallet, was a couple of crates which had once contained liquor bottles.

'I know.' Kate the Gouger, he had heard, had brought all of three dollars to her family when she'd been turned out, and he couldn't imagine any pander in his right mind paying as much as a nickel for such Perdidio Street harpies as Kentucky Williams and Railspike, even in the days of their virginity. 'Yet it sounds like somebody went to a lot of trouble to spirit her away.'

He reached across and took the fiddler's wrist in his hand, fragile as bird bone but with a pulse strong and steady. Through the long wooden tube of his stethoscope, his friend's lungs sounded as well as they ever did.

'*Pessisimus transiit*,' Hannibal assured him. 'In a week I shall stand ready to imitate the action of the tiger. Pearlie – the young lady in the next villa' – he nodded in the direction of the broken-down crib immediately river-ward of his own – 'comes over between customers to see if there's anything I need. She's grown very maternal. God only knows why.'

'Probably because you're the only man in years who hasn't hit her.' January felt the glands in his friend's throat, caught the hot light from the half-open door in a fragment of shaving-mirror to look into his eyes. 'Students won't be arriving at our house until October, you can—'

'I can scandalize the entire French Town by living under the same roof with Rose – *and* with your niece! – and put paid to any chance that anyone will send their young daughters to be educated by such an *impiissima et meretrix* ever again – to say nothing of what it will do to *my* reputation. And don't tell me every single one of your neighbors isn't capable of putting the most scandalous interpretation on even the briefest and most innocent episode of cohabitation . . . *Nihil est autem tam volucre, quam maledictim . . .'*

He stretched out a hand like a bundle of desiccated twigs. 'I am grateful beyond what I can say, *amicus meus*, to you and to the beautiful Rose. As for the young man you didn't die trying to rescue, there was nothing you could have . . .'

The sound of cursing came through the shack's open door, and Woze – who worked for Kate the Gouger in exchange for opium and food – emerged from the rear of the bathhouse and limped across to the rain barrels, to prepare for the cleaner side of the evening's business. January knew it was time to go. Far off, he had heard the cathedral clock chime five some while ago, and if he remained longer he ran the risk of being beaten up, when the girls' clients began to arrive. Of the whores who worked out of the other shacks, one was black and another Mexican, but the keelboatmen who patronized Kate's place would beat any man of color they even suspected of lying where they had lain. (*Every white man in the Mississippi*

37

Valley and the seven seas, yes, reflected January wearily. *But a black man . . . There are some things that cannot be borne!*)

The weariness returned. And the hate.

'Watch out for yourself,' said Hannibal quietly.

January nodded, almost absently. 'Jesus said, *Love your enemies*,' he said after a time. 'Pray for them that persecute you. I can't do that. I don't even know if Jesus would have wanted men in my position to do that.'

'Well,' said the fiddler reasonably, 'God didn't give Moses any instructions on the subject in his dealings with the Egyptians, so it would be difficult to arrive at consistent guidelines. ζῶμεν γάρ οὐχ ὡς θέλομεν, ἀλλ ὡς δυνάμεθα, as Menander observes. And at least, having talked to so many Israelites, I'm sure God will understand your feelings. I'm only sorry I won't be able to accompany you north.'

'It's nothing. The Viellards should prove a stout defense.'

'Well, Henri should, anyway—'

The pun on M'sieu Viellard's *avoirdupois* made him grin.

'When you're on your feet again,' he said, 'would you do me a great favor?'

'*Quod tuum'st meum'st; omne meum* – such as it is' – his gesture took in the books heaped on the packing crates – '*est autem tuum*. Name it.'

'Make excuses to scrounge dinner off Rose every day or so.' He made his voice deliberately gruff. 'Just to see her and make certain all is well.'

His brusque tone fooled neither himself nor the

38

fiddler, but it wasn't meant to. Hannibal replied meekly, 'It shall be as you say, *amicus meus*. And fetch water to wash the dishes besides.'

'See that you do.' He leaned down, to grasp his friend's wrist in parting, and used the gesture to hide his other hand as it slipped his last fifty-cent piece under the flat excuse for a pillow.

When he reached the market, just downriver of the Place d'Armes, most of the vendors of vegetables and fish had closed up their stands and departed, though the last of the summer daylight still brightened the sky. The worn brick pavement beneath the arcades was dotted with wilted spinach leaves, fragments of baskets, strawberry hulls and roses dropped from the trays of the flower sellers; the dimness stank of the coal smoke of the nearby steamboat wharves, and of the overwhelming reek of staling fish.

Life and movement still stirred along the levee, and with the cooling of the day's brazen heat, men and women had come out to the Place, simply to promenade before the mosquitoes became unbearable. A vendor wailed the melismatic virtues of brooms for sale. A cat fished for crawfish in the gutter.

Close beside La Violette's coffee stand a couple of *marchandes* in the tawny brightness of cheap calico sat at one of the rough tables, their tignons like gaudy cushions on their heads and their baskets on the pavement at their sides. At another table a steamboat captain in a peaked cap sat drinking coffee and staring out across Rue de Levée; nearby, three boys whom January recognized as cargo thieves sipped coffee, smoked cigars, and planned the evening's work. Nearest the archways that opened on to the levee itself, and the black forest of smokestacks beyond, a man whom January recognized as a lawyer named Harshaw was reading a news-paper. As January was promising eventual payment for a tin cup of scalding brew the lawyer lowered his paper and called out sharply, 'Ben!' and January turned with a manufactured start.

Harshaw beckoned peremptorily and January hastened to the little table. 'Mr Harshaw, sir . . .'

The lawyer pulled a notebook from his breast pocket and flipped it open on the table, prodded the page with an impatient forefinger. January bent down to look more closely, his head close to the white man's.

The page was blank – as had been the note that January had sent to him via Zizi-Marie that forenoon. The three wafers that had sealed it meant: *we need to meet.* The time and the place were prearranged, and changed from day to day. In an undervoice, Harshaw murmured, 'What's afoot?'

'An Englishman named Russell hired me to find his daughter in upstate New York,' said January. 'He thinks she's run off to join one of the religious groups that you find up there. Her mother thinks she's been kidnapped, and talks of offering a reward.'

Harshaw said, 'Damnation.' The hard eyes that glanced up over the tinted lenses of his spectacles were a peculiar golden hazel, almost yellow, like a wolf's.

His real name was Bredon. For eight years he had coordinated the activities of the Underground Railroad in New Orleans, including the runaways whom January periodically hid in the storerooms beneath his house. Like January and Rose, he knew all about what was likely to happen if the New York river pirates and black-birders thought they had an excuse to go poking around among the Quaker communities between New York and the Canadian border.

'We leave in the morning. I'll be traveling with the Viellards' – Bredon knew all about them, too – 'they're friends of the Russells, who'll be on the same boat. Who do I need to speak to in New York?'

'David Ruggles.' Bredon flipped a blank page in his notebook. Nobody seemed to be noticing, but January nodded anyway, as if he were being lectured about something. 'He's got a house on Lispenard Street, west of Broadway. If you can't find him, go to the Reverend Theodore Wright. His house on White Street is only a few blocks from Ruggles.' His eyes flicked sidelong as the youthful thieves finished their coffee and departed. The pilot had already gone. La Violette poured herself a well-earned cup of her own coffee and padded to one of the vacant tables to drink it.

The shadows in the market's arches deepened.

'These days there's two separate vigilance committees working in New York, putting up posters, warning people when the slave catchers are coming through. And of course they're quarrelling with each other. But either will help you.'

'Anybody you know in the western counties?'

'About a dozen. But they're scattered all along the Canal. And I haven't been in that area for about three years. Ruggles or Wright will have a better idea of who to go to, once you know a little more about where this young lady went . . . if she went upstate at all.'

'I've thought of that,' January said. 'But I have to check.'

'God, yes! There's more blackbirders in New York than ever, and of course the city police force abets them. If there's a New York policeman who wouldn't sell a total stranger to the dealers – or his sister, if he thought he could pass her for black – for the price of a glass of gin, I've certainly never heard of him. I'll try to get you some money tonight.'

'Thank you,' said January. 'That'll help. Anything else I need to know?'

'Stay away from Five Points,' whispered Bredon. 'It's the neighborhood where the old Collect Pond used to be, around the Bowery and Anthony Street, just north-west of the wharves. Six years ago the whites – mostly Irish – rioted and drove out most of the blacks, burned their churches, their shops if they had 'em. The gangs run that part of town. And stay clear of the Colonization Society—'

'I thought they wanted to emancipate us?'

'They want to get black people the hell out of the United States,' Bredon grunted. 'They've started more than one riot outside abolitionist meetings; claim that abolitionism is "diverting" public attention from the *real* solution to the problem. Imbeciles,' he growled. 'If you get into real trouble, head north of the city to Seneca Village. It's a sort of colony where the free blacks own property, three, maybe four miles north of the center of town. Anything you need me to do here?'

'Just keep an eye on Rose. And on Sefton.'

'How is he?'

'Better,' said January.

Bredon nodded. 'Glad to hear it.' His pleasure, January knew, was genuine, and not simply because of Hannibal's adeptness in forging slave passes and freedom papers. 'I'll look in on him, and do what I can.'

They parted, for it wouldn't do for them to be seen too long in conversation, and January made his way home through the damp heat of the evening. When he reached Rue Esplanade, he crossed it to call on Virginie Metoyer, who lived opposite his own house and had been *plaçeé* to a banker named Granville. Granville was there – that had been January's second letter that morning – and affirmed that an officer of Thelwell's Private Bank in Coventry would have no access to information that would assist even the cleverest ring of New York rogues to gain either cash or credit.

'Couldn't be done, Ben.' The white man puffed his cigar, blew a line of smoke through the tall French windows of Virginie's parlor in which they sat. 'And I can't see someone in Russell's position making enough to interest kidnappers, no matter who his wife's related to. Thelwell's just isn't that big a bank.'

43

So what is actually going on? January swiped at the mosquitoes that hummed around his ears, as he returned over the wide neutral ground in the center of the street and made for the glow of the smudges burning on his own house's tall gallery. *If she wasn't kidnapped, why didn't she send a note? And if she was, why didn't they send one . . . ?*

There was something about the whole business that simply didn't fit.

As he was packing that evening a parcel was dropped off at the house by a cab driver whom he knew slightly, containing twenty-five silver dollars and five gold half-eagles. Not a great deal, he guessed, if he had to get himself out of trouble in New York State and back to Louisiana in an emergency. Within an hour of that event, Reinette – one of Madame Viellard's housemaids – appeared on the gallery with a draft on the Bank of Louisiana for a like sum. Chloë Viellard, reflected January, though cold-blooded as a lizard, could always be relied upon to know what was the most important element in any situation. And making sure that Rose and his family had money to survive until her students returned in the fall was, to him, more important than anything that might be happening to young Eve Russell.

With that slight degree of reassurance he went to bed, and rose before daybreak, to make his way through the gluey darkness, along the wharves to the downstream side of the market. In the iron gloom before him, the lights of the ocean-going ships burned like cressets lighting the way to Hell.

Five

From New Orleans to Havana, from Havana to Nassau, and on up past the wet flat green line of the Florida coast to Charleston and points north, January made it his business to befriend Alfred Grislock and bypass his reluctance to admit that the Russell family was anything but an exemplar of virtue and happiness. In between helping Leopold, Henri Viellard's Austrian valet, nurse the young planter through devastating *mal de mer*, January assisted the butler with ironing in the minuscule servants' cabin, with shifting the mountains of luggage to make sure Mrs Russell always had the right gloves, shoes, reticule and jewelry to dine with the Captain, and respectfully admired his touch with boot-blacking, razor-stropping, and the care of brushes and combs.

In response to Mr Russell's instructions, the handsome butler – who could have been cast as Malvolio in a production of *Twelfth Night* – answered January's questions with civil standoffishness. Yes, Miss Russell had asked her mother if she might stay on with the Winterinks. Yes, at Mr Russell's request he had burned a quantity of pamphlets, broadsides, and cheaply got-up books that Lucy had found in Miss Russell's room. Grislock's attitude had all but screamed that he did not consider it his place to speak about his employers – or, that he did not care to have it thought of him that he would do so. The Delapores, with whom Miss Russell had gone to stay before her disappearance, were a very well-spoken-of and respectable New York family – French Huguenots, he believed – connections of the Winterinks through two marriages. No, he was not aware of Miss Russell forming any sort of attachment, either to one of the Delapore sons (there were three: the youngest, Grislock understood, was at West Point, the older two attended Princeton College) or to anyone else. She was not, he said, so inclined.

But January, well aware that he was the only other servant on board who spoke English, patiently cultivated the man. He'd got up a game of whist, acting as a translator between Grislock, the Captain's man (who spoke only French), and Leopold (who spoke only German – neither Madame Aurelié Viellard's butler, Visigoth, nor her footman, Jacques-Ange, played). This gave Grislock the chance to see that both the other men – white men – treated January with friendly camaraderie. When they'd reached Havana, he'd suggested to Henri and to Mr Russell that they allow their servants a night onshore, during which he'd guided the butler around the more respectable posadas of that beautiful city and translated what went on around them.

Strolling back along the Calle San Ignacio toward the harbor in the dense tropical darkness, Grislock had remarked, 'It is an adventure, isn't it?' speaking for the first time as man to man.

46

'Quite different from America. What was that we had for dinner, again?'

After that, as they steamed stolidly through the turquoise rim of the Caribbean, and then the sapphire-black swells of the Atlantic, January listened with genuine interest to the man's endless minutiae concerning the running of a London household ('You need *two* cloths to clean brass – I cannot *tell* you how some of these girls are so lazy they'll pour the *polish directly on to the cloth* . . .!'), and eventually worked the conversation around to the Russell family's stay in New York.

'Bless me if I ever saw such a farrago!' Grislock shook his slickly pomaded head, and poured out some of the tea which January had had the forethought to bring along for consumption in the servants' cabin. 'The things you Americans believe, out in the west of the state! Magical golden tablets – new gospels in the Bible – new prophets that can't hardly read or write, getting new revelations from God . . .'

'I've heard stories,' groaned January encouragingly.

'Lord!' The butler flung up his hands. 'There was one woman who went into trances and preached sermons in her sleep – a woman! And who claimed to be able to speak with the dead! And another fellow who claimed he'd met an angel who gave him a magic staff that let him travel to the planet Saturn and talk to the Saturnians, who'd heard the Gospel from Our Lord Himself, who'd gone there by means of that selfsame staff! And people *believe* this!'

47

January carefully refrained from recounting the number of clergymen – both Protestant and Catholic – who had at one time or another pointed out to him that nowhere in the Bible did anyone say that slavery was against God's will, a favorite topic preached from Southern pulpits. And a discussion of the Puritan belief in predestination would, he knew, lead nowhere useful. So instead, he put on his most fascinated expression and asked, 'And Miss Russell saw all of these . . . these prophets?'

'She did. I don't understand what she saw in them. Queer, they were, and not at all the thing.'

'But she did see something?'

'Well . . .' The high brow furrowed beneath the shiny cap of pomaded hair. As if, January thought, this man was putting together for the first time what he himself had already guessed about Eve Russell. That she was looking for something.

As, January recalled, his sister Olympe had been looking, when she rebelled against their mother's attempts to have her taught the social accomplishments that would attract a wealthy white protector, and had run away with the voodoos.

As his beautiful Ayasha had rebelled, when she'd fled her father's house in Algiers.

In their way, all the girls in Rose's little school were rebelling as well, hungering for real learning – literature, science, history, mathematics – beyond what young girls of color (or white girls, for that matter) were customarily taught.

'That's just it, Mr J.' Grislock sighed at last.

'Mrs Russell . . . Well, she does push, you know. It's her way, and I perfectly understand it. But I've known Miss Russell from a child, and that was never the life she wanted. Not really. A perfectly sweet and well-brought-up young lady, but . . . It's different for a boy, you know.'

January allowed that it was.

'She was always asking questions of her governess, you know, that poor Miss Nutley couldn't answer, nor anyone, I shouldn't think. Things like, why was there slavery? And, would God really condemn just and moral people like Homer and Socrates – and heaven only knows where she heard about *them*! – to Hell just because they'd been born too early to hear the true word of God? She asked all about these monster skeletons that people were digging up in Germany and even in England, and why weren't *they* mentioned in the Bible? And wasn't it unjust for landlords to call the Irish peasants stupid when they did nothing to provide schools for them, and how on earth could Uncle Theodore – that's Mr Russell's brother – put children eight and ten years old to working in his mills, when Mr Theodore and Mr Russell would cry out with horror if somebody tried to put *her*, or her cousins, working for twelve and sixteen hours a day? And, what happens to souls after they die?'

The lantern overhead swung with the steady roll of the ship, plowing north through darkness and warm Caribbean rain.

'And she wouldn't take "no" for an answer,' he went on, and added a chunk of sugar to his tea. 'She was always coming back to, why couldn't she go to school, like her cousin Teddy, and learn about these things? And when poor Mrs Russell told her that girls didn't go to school, it was always, "why not?" I mean, how could you even *think* of sending a girl to a bear garden like Rugby or Eton?'

How could you even think of sending a girl to work sixteen hours a day in a cotton mill? reflected January. Or set her to chopping the weeds from around cotton plants, from the darkness before dawn until it was too dark again to see?

'She was like that even before her little friend died,' added Grislock, with a little, disapproving frown. 'In fact worse.'

'Who was her friend?'

'Oh,' said the butler, 'that was years ago. She wasn't but nine or ten. But she was cut up over it. Cut up very badly.'

And, when January cocked his head with a look of inquiry, Grislock shrugged. 'Belle, her name was; Isobel Martin. She had lessons with Miss Russell, their mothers being neighbors and good friends. Little Miss Martin and her baby sister both took with the scarlet fever, and Mrs Russell immediately took Miss Russell away into the country, lest she be exposed. I remember Miss Russell cried a great deal, though she never took with the fever herself. Miss Martin died of it, and her little sister was never the same.'

The butler frowned into the distance for a time, reviewing the memories, as if with disapproval. Leopold entered, with a small jug of water from the kitchen, which he set on the spirit lamp where

50

the tea had been brewed. Stout, stolid, fair and middle-aged, he had been nursing his master like a mother since they'd passed the mouths of the Mississippi. Certainly, January reflected, more assiduously than Henri's own mother, or his wife, neither of whom experienced the slightest twinge of sickness and who had been playing piquet in the Ladies' Cabin with Mrs Russell for the whole of the voyage.

'For months after that Miss Russell would ask about people who were dead,' Grislock went on, 'and whether they were happy? Were they already in Heaven, she asked, and if so, what happens on Judgment Day? Miss Nutley – Miss Russell's governess, you understand – told her that it was something she'd have to take on faith – she being a parson's daughter and brought up to a strict view of things. When Miss Russell would ask her mother after it, I'm afraid Mrs Russell only said, "Heavens, child, to think of you asking such questions!" and passed her back to poor Miss Nutley. I didn't think much of it at the time, you know, and she stopped asking, after a few months. But looking back, I think she was much cut up indeed. You wouldn't think it, a little girl like that.'

Well, thought January, *obviously SOME people wouldn't think it . . .*

'But it did come back to me,' said the butler, 'when she lied to her mother about going – three times, it was! – to hear those people who claimed to speak to the dead.'

There were two, Grislock went on, who specialized particularly in speaking to the dead.

One was a boy of fifteen or sixteen, who would look into a crystal and claimed that the spirit of a 'Red Indian sachem' came on to the dim-lit stage and told him what the spirits of the dead thought and said.

The other was a young woman called the Shining Herald. She would go into a trance, and spirits would enter her body, and speak through her lips; sometimes angels, describing Heaven or pronouncing God's will and commandments. Sometimes the souls of those who had died.

'All nonsense, of course. Like they have nothing better to do, up in Heaven, than hang about chatting with people on Earth. But Miss Russell was very taken with the whole matter.'

January, who had encountered Swedenborgian doctrines in his years in Paris (to say nothing of being familiar with the events described in the First Book of Samuel, Chapter Twenty-Eight), asked, 'Were these the tracts and pamphlets she had hidden in her room?'

'Well, it started with the abolitionists.' Grislock moved his chair a little, to let Leopold get past. Moving carefully in the tiny space, the Austrian had taken from his dressing case a small porcelain teapot, a caddy of peppermint tea, and a single cup, all of which he bore from the cabin with the air of the Grail procession carrying cup, krater, and spear to the Fisher King. 'Miss Russell had read in the papers back home about abolition – though what a young lady wants with newspapers in the first place I have no idea.' Grislock clicked his tongue. 'But all these other religious people who came 'round the door of the hall as well. They do all seem to swarm together, like bees.'

Grislock recalled seeing at least five tracts in Eve Russell's surreptitious collection headed by the title of the Shining Herald, or the Children of the Light (which seemed to be the same group). It wasn't long after that, he said, that Miss Russell started going out with her Winterink cousins several nights a week. 'And of course, Mrs Russell thought it perfectly all right. They are Family, you know.'

'And it was to see this woman, this Herald?'

'Now, that I don't know,' said Grislock. But it was shortly after this, that Lucy had discovered the tracts in Miss Russell's room – pamphlets and books about abolition, about Judgment Day, about conversations with the dead, about the intervention of angels in everyday life. Mrs Russell had been outraged – 'And quite rightly, I thought . . .' – and Mr Russell had had a fearful row with his daughter, and had ordered the offending literature burned.

'Then when it was time for the family to go on to New Orleans, Miss Russell said she'd been invited to stay with the Roosevelts, and the Delapores, and Mrs Russell was pleased that she'd made friends in proper society. As any mother would be, who had her daughter's welfare to her heart. For you must admit,' he added, 'proper society – the *best* society – is to be found in New York, though of course there are some very prominent families in New Orleans as well. But most of them are – well – *French* . . .'

Meaning, January guessed, Catholic. He

nodded and said, 'There is that.' Though he guessed that it was just as likely that a society gentleman in New York would take a white mistress the minute he was married (if he didn't have one before) than it was that a prominent New Orleanean would have a quadroon *plaçeé*.

After a moment he asked, 'Would you say Mamzelle Russell was the kind of girl who would run away like that, without sending word to her parents?'

Again, the butler wore the expression of a man who'd never thought of such a question before. 'I really couldn't say,' he replied. 'I mean, I wouldn't have said so, but then I'd never have said she was the kind of girl who'd run off at all. On the other hand, she didn't know where her parents would be staying in New Orleans. I mean, she knew they'd be with the Truloves, but not any specific direction in town, and she may not have remembered the name of their country place. Or she may have written down the direction wrong. All sorts of things can go amiss with a letter in this country, you know. It's not the same as back home.'

No, reflected January. The man might be an ass, but he was right about that.

And a letter from the Winterinks with the news, *We've heard from your daughter and she is well* . . . might still be on its way from New York, and his entire journey, to New York and back, was a waste of time.

Still, he thought. *Still* . . .

54

Six

The Viellards and the Russells took two cabs from the New York wharves up Broadway to the Dominion Hotel in Union Square; their servants followed in a wagon with the luggage. Perched precariously behind twelve steamer trunks and twenty portmanteaux and valises – which included his own modest wicker grip – January looked out across what seemed to him a fulminating swarm of brown faces and white, of sweat smell and shouting, and the hair prickled on his head.

The New Orleans wharves were crowded. He was used to that. Since he was seven years old, he had known those mazes of boxes and barrels, of work gangs and wagons; penned pigs, scavenging dogs, half a dozen different languages all shouted at the top of peoples' lungs. He'd darted among the sacks and bales, dodged the hooves of horses, his lungs full of the rags of pipe smoke and coal fumes and the drifting steam of coffee sellers' barrows.

But not crowded like this.

There were more men, more vendors, more barrels and boxes and crates being unloaded. A forest of masts lined the eastern flank of Manhattan Island under a hard, hot, cloud-puffed sky. A wall of buildings faced them, brick warehouses and shabby wooden taverns swarming with men in shirtsleeves, men in frock coats and plug hats, whores in tattered calico or grimy silk. Boys waved newspapers and shouted, or pursued with shoeshine boxes anyone who looked like he might have a penny to spend. Little girls sold hot ears of corn from makeshift carts, barefoot and in rags. Irish carters in the togs that January recognized from their New Orleans brethren – gaudy shirts, Conestoga boots, hair slicked down in long soap locks under top hats and the inevitable Long Nine cigar. Muscles glistening, half-naked stevedores – black and white – sweated as they wrestled sacks of coffee, bales of cotton, hogsheads of sugar from the ship cranes. Men more slickly dressed loitered in tavern doors.

January didn't like the calculating glint of their eyes.

The noise was like being beaten with hammers, far worse than the clamor of the New Orleans wharves. Vendors bellowed the merits of the wares in their baskets: pies, fruit, phosphorous matches. Carthorses and cabhorses whinnied in terror or pain. The stinks of tar and coal smoke, the sullen reek of the city beyond, was choking after weeks at sea: horse shit, privies, tanneries and breweries and knackers' yards.

The New Orleans waterfront was dangerous, for white men as well as for blacks. River pirates, slave stealers, confidence tricksters and pickpockets mingled with the crowds there looking for victims, as they did in any port. But there was something deeply frightening about the size, and the cruel coldness, of New York.

Beyond the wharves the streets were choked. Broken-down wooden houses swarmed with men, women, children; the flagways lined with barrows of fruit, of old clothes, of sacks of potatoes. Girls hawked fish and milk and day-old buns, boys darted among the crowds with nimble feet and watchful glances. January saw a lad of six or seven whip an apple from a handcart: the lad wasn't quick enough to avoid the grab of the cart's owner. The big man knocked the child to the ground with the butt of his cart whip and was beating him where he lay as the Viellard luggage wagon jolted around the corner of Pearl Street, and the scene was lost. But January didn't see a single person register surprise or anger, or offer to help the screaming child. A little further on, they passed a man flogging a dying horse between the shafts of an overladen dray. No one glanced at that, either.

It was nothing that January hadn't seen in New Orleans, in Havana or Galveston. But as well as turning him sick, it filled him with a kind of shaken dread. *No one here cares.*

No one.

Pigs rooted unconcerned in the mud-clogged gutters. New Orleans was dirty, but January had never seen the number of dead rats, dead dogs, dead cats lying in the road. When they passed a garbage pile at the end of another street January saw that it moved with women and children in rags, picking through the old newspapers, clinker-coal and kitchen waste for anything which could conceivably be eaten or sold. He was reminded of the poor in Mexico City, who had barely scraps to cover their nakedness.

And they all watched, all around them, all the time.

For predators more hungry than they?

No one dares to care. Every single one of them is afraid.

For a distance Broadway was like that, too: crowded with foot traffic, with wagons and drays, lined with barrooms, tawdry theaters, and shops. A second lining crowded the sidewalks: barrows, brass-lunged hawkers crying fruit, old clothes, mousetraps and chairs to mend. Even at two in the afternoon, men and women milled around the doors of the public houses – the Nanny Goat, the Gullet, the Ruins – and the dancehalls stood open, jangling music only barely detectable above the yammer of the street. The stink of raw sewage in the gutter mixed with the pong of stale beer. Outside the gaudy theaters, signs shouted the bills of the evening's performance: *The Bengal Tiger, The Fate of a Bushranger, The Nun's Revenge.*

All-New Musical Minstrel Review!

Monster Freak Child – Is it Human? Is it a Fish? – See in the Flesh, 10¢!

Singing Waiter-Girls!

See the Ugliest Woman In The World – only 10¢!

Rat-baiting every night $1.50.

Bright-colored signs protruded at all heights, the druggist's mortar and pestle creaking beside the trumpets and violins of instrument

58

vendors, the horrifying gold grin of a dentist's shingle.

'Here's clams, here's clams, here's clams today, They lately come from Rockaway . . .'

And next to that man, bellowing in competition to be louder yet, 'Old rags, old rags, any ol' rags . . .'

The noise lessened. The saloons grew fewer as they moved north, and alternated with larger and flashier theaters. Comfortable-looking beer gardens stood behind wooden fences. Niblo's Garden. The Argyle Room. Carriages mingled with the commercial vehicles. Among the throngs on the sidewalk January began to see women respectably dressed and gloved, bosoms covered and hair undyed. Nursemaids walked with children. Boys rolled hoops. The black men he saw – fewer and fewer of them, as they came into the neighborhood where houses were more expensive – often wore the discreet livery of servants.

The Dominion Hotel stood on what was called Union Square, an open space of long grass and trees surrounded – like a London residential square – with iron palings, and faced with scattered brownstone houses of what were clearly the more affluent sort of people. As the wagon drew into the hotel's rear courtyard another dray was being unloaded there, hotel servants assisting three men and a woman whom January guessed, by their clothing, to be the slaves of another southern guest. Like a good servant he helped the hotel's men in unloading and carrying the trunks upstairs – some to the hotel attics, some to the Viellards' suite – before reporting to Chloë Viellard.

'The Russells have just now gone on to the Winterinks, where they'll be staying.' As usual, Chloë Viellard looked as if she'd been freshly unwrapped from cotton wool and silver tissue paper, her great round spectacles gleaming in the afternoon window light like a spider's eyes. 'They should all be back here just after dinner, including the Winterinks' eldest daughter, who I understand went about a good deal with Miss Russell. I suggested that they bring the maid, Lucy Palmer, as well. Would you prefer to be introduced as a member of our household, or as a colleague of my husband's with experience in the finding of missing persons?'

January bowed. 'Thank you for asking, m'am.' He wondered if Henri, who had had to be almost carried from the ship to his cab, would be sufficiently recovered to be present at the interview at all. 'I think the Winterinks would be more inclined to respect – and confide in – a free man.'

The immense, crystal-blue eyes narrowed. 'If they can be got to understand that you *are* free. Madame Russell never did seem to grasp that notion. It won't harm your investigation in other directions, if these people blab to their servants about you?'

'The only people that would make a difference to is kidnappers.' Though he tried to keep his voice light, January was aware of its grim edge. 'For which reason,' he added, 'I would appreciate it, if you'd be so good as to write up a

60

pass for me for this afternoon. And if I'm not back by dark, could you send someone out to look for me?'

The chef in charge of the Dominion's kitchens was a Frenchman, but most of his staff were free blacks, who lived in the cheap lodging houses along the waterfronts or far up above Twentieth Street, in the community of free blacks that Bredon had called Seneca Village. The assistant chef, Shakespeare Chapman, gave January a questioning glance when he asked for directions to Lispenard Street. 'You a friend of Mr Ruggles?'

'We have some of the same friends.'

Chapman – a medium-sized man heavy through the shoulders, with classic Ashanti features and January's *beau noire lustré*, as the slave dealers called that ebony, African complexion – studied him again from beneath heavy eyelids, as if matching the implications of his words with his maroon-plush livery.

'Then you and I share friends as well,' said the cook at length. 'Lispenard Street's down below Greenwich Village, just off Broadway. Mr Ruggles lives on the corner of Church Street. Here, I'll draw you a map. He has a bookshop, and a library, as well as taking in . . . boarders.' The slight movement of his eyelids indicated that some of those who stayed beneath the Ruggles roof paid no board . . . and came and went by night. 'You may want to take someone with you, if you don't know the city. Maybe even if you do. It's a long walk.'

January had seen brightly colored streetcars

61

on Broadway, and guessed that they weren't for the likes of himself and Mr Chapman. The summer days were long, but he would have to step lively, if he wanted to be back by dark. And, he remembered Bredon's warnings, and what he'd heard about the 'slave catcher' gangs that worked the New York streets like farmers worked a wheat field. 'I'll bow to your experience, sir.'

Chapman leaned through the back door of the kitchen, called out 'Bill!' to a stout little man in shirtsleeves, who was helping a couple of carters unload sacks from a dray. 'I got a message that needs be took down to Mr Ruggles.'

Bill paused in his work, and raised his brows in cautious inquiry.

'Ben here says he'll walk down with you.'

And, when Bill disappeared into the stables to find his jacket, 'You should be all right.'

He studied January's old-fashioned attire again as he took a carpenter's pencil from a drawer, and scribbled on a scrap of paper. 'But don't push your luck. They've gone into schoolrooms and snatched children – *and* got certificates on them as runaways. Remember that in this town, men gets put on the police force 'cause of their politics, not 'cause they give a rat's ass about right or wrong. The chief constable works with the blackbirder gangs – he boasts he can have any black man in town put on the auction block in Baltimore inside twenty-four hours. Ben,' he introduced, as the stocky little hostler stepped in through the kitchen door, 'this is Bill. He's your new best friend.'

'I cannot tell you,' said January, shaking Bill's

big, damp hand, 'how pleased I am to make your acquaintance, Bill.'

'And I cannot tell you how pleased *I* am,' returned Bill, as he shoved Chapman's note into his pocket, 'to get out of washing down the harnesses this afternoon.' He led the way out into the yard, around the corner of the hotel, and down the wide, bricked drive toward Union Square. 'You're up from New Orleans?'

January nodded.

'Hope you like the attic where they put the Southern guests' slaves?'

'Better than having to sleep at the foot of Michie's bed like a dog,' pointed out January gravely.

The hostler rolled his eyes. He was young, January guessed, not more than twenty-two, and bustling with energy. 'I know there's some that actually ask for that, but I've *never* understood it.'

'What?' January flung up his hands in affected shock. 'You'd make a white gentleman grope around under the bed for his own thunder mug?'

'Forgive me.' Bill bowed his head contritely. 'I just didn't think. Livin' here in New York has corrupted me—'

'Sounds like if you stay much longer you'll be as corrupt as your police force here—'

'Oh, hell,' returned Bill. 'The police is little white lambs, compared to some. For years the *city recorder* worked with the slave catchers. He'd have a certificate on you before you could get a message out to anybody you knew. The gangs have their boats standing ready, all the time, at the wharves.'

'Remind me,' said January, 'to stay under my bed until Michie an' M'am Viellard ready to leave for home.'

Bill clutched his breast in mimed astonishment. 'You got a *bed*?'

Both men laughed.

The crowds thickened as they went down Broadway, and January found himself grateful that he wasn't alone. He had learned the hard way that six-feet-three was of very little use against a lead sap. Now and then, among the posters and handbills that smeared every fence, gate, and vertical surface below Eighth Street, he glimpsed placards that said:

BEWARE OF KIDNAPPERS.
The Madison Street Gang of
Kidnappers is at large and has been
seen on Mercer Street, on Lafayette in
the neighborhood of Bond Street, and
on Allen Street in the neighborhood of
the Italian Garden Dance Palace.

Someone had smeared ink on two or three of these. Others had been roughly torn.

Vigilance committees, Bredon had said.

'Watch yourself.' Bill put a hand on January's elbow and steered him away from the wall of one of the tall, flat-fronted, brick 'tenant houses' that more and more frequently broke the line of shabby wooden gable ends. 'Don't get too near the wall. Slave catchers'll have a woman in one of the upstairs rooms with a bucket of ashes. She'll get the signal from a watchman down the street, dump the ashes on your head, and while you're still pawin' around at your eyes, two stooges'll grab an' hustle you down the nearest alley. The gangs work that trick, too, only if it's the Shirt-Tails or the Forty Thieves that grab you, the most you'll be is robbed, stripped, an' kicked to a pulp, not sold . . .'

A thousand dollars split four ways, calculated January, with a glance up at the windows above him. *Not bad for ten minutes' work . . .*

But the anger tapped like a little red pulse in his temple.

Several of the Vigilance Committee handbills had been plastered over with advertisements for shows and exhibitions: 'The Ugliest Woman In the World' (again); 'You Will Split Your Sides Laughing – every night at Jackson's, the Bowery'; and 'See the Cannibals of the Feejee Islands – The Egyptian Dance Hall, Water Street'. The usual price to view these so-called 'freaks of nature' seemed to be ten cents.

'Those are nothing.' Bill sniffed with contempt. 'Five years ago, some bastard got hold of a poor old woman who should have been left in quiet with her family, bought her from her master over in Pennsylvania – illegally – and advertised her as George Washington's mammy.'

His grin was sour, as he saw January trying to estimate how old the mammy of the Father of the Country would have to be in 1835.

'A hundred-and-sixty-one years old she was, he said. Cleaned up a fortune, letting people come gawk at her at ten cents a peek at Niblo's

65

. . . And I will say, old Joice had the wits to come up with tender memories of Little Georgie's childhood, not that she ever saw a nickel of the take. Guessed the scoundrel would sell her to the blackbirders if she didn't, I'm thinking.'

Bill grimaced, and stepped out of the way as a man was slung, sobbing, out the door of a dram shop in their path. January made a move to kneel at the man's side, but Bill pulled him quickly back. The proprietress still stood in the barroom door, meaty arms folded and eyes like brass in a face like a bleached ham. Two men stood behind her, likewise watching their victim as he lay weeping on the cobblestones. 'The Roach Guards,' whispered Bill, nudging January away down the street. 'See the blue stripes on their trousers? They killed two of the Dead Rabbits in a fight at the Burnt Rag Thursday night. Don't cross 'em.'

At the sound of cursing behind them January glanced back. A carter pulled his horse aside to keep from running over the prostrate drunkard, but made no effort to drag the man out of the street. It was the first act of mercy January had seen in New York.

He said softly, 'That's cold.'

'You want to see cold,' replied Bill grimly. 'When poor old Joice died – George Washington's hundred-and-sixty-one-year-old mammy – this Barnum bastard wouldn't let her rest in peace, but had her autopsied – cut up! – in a local saloon, and charged fifty cents for whoever wanted to come watch! Then he took out advertisements saying what a fool he'd been because she was really barely eighty . . . And just about tripled the take at his "Variety Show" after that. It's a cold town,' he added. 'A cold town.'

Seven

David Ruggles was younger than January had thought he'd be, barely thirty. He was thin, and dressed with almost foppish care in a mustard-colored coat that was, despite its relative newness, slightly too large for his wasted frame. Behind thick spectacles his eyes had the uncertain intensity that told January that the man was losing his sight. He guided Bill and January to the back room of his bookstore without hesitation, as if he knew every stick of furniture and every rag rug by heart. 'Will you have lemonade? If you've come all the way down from Union Square—'

'I'll get it, sir,' offered Bill, and ducked through a doorway into a gloomy kitchen barely larger than a cupboard. He brought in a couple of glasses, cool from being stored, January guessed, in a larger vessel of water, then scooped up a copy of *The Mirror of Liberty* from a small stack of them on the table, and retreated to the kitchen once more.

Ruggles seated himself beside the cold, tiny hearth, and asked, 'How may I help?'

He listened to January's account of Eve Russell's disappearance, and his face set in wary anger. He didn't need it spelled out to him, what would happen if the girl were not found, and found soon. 'Damn it,' he said, 'the black-birder gangs would pay *Russell* to give them good reason to bypass the local sheriffs in the western counties, and go through every Quaker farmhouse and religious community along the Canal.'

'That's what I thought myself, sir.'

'*Damn* it.'

Every window of the parlor was open, but the surrounding buildings were constructed so close that they blocked what little breeze might have drifted from the North River, and the room was stifling. The neighborhood was a poor one, many of its two-story wooden houses rickety with age and neglect and spilling over with tenants: Irish or German immigrants, to judge by the shouting that came over from Church Street. Iron wagon tires clattered noisily on the brick pavements, and the dreary see-saw of a chimney sweep's cry carried above the clamor of other vendors and a German oompah band.

'Have you heard of the Shining Herald?' asked January. 'Or these Children of the Light?'

'Oh, yes.' Ruggles propped his spectacles up on to his nose. 'About a year ago their patri-arch, the Reverend Serapis Broadax, founded a community out near Syracuse, based on the preaching that the Herald claims has been given her by angels, in her sleep. Broadax has helped about twenty fugitives from slavery get across

68

the border to Canada, some of them under the very noses of the blackbirder gangs. The house – the central residence – of what they call the Blessed Land is well suited for it: it was built as a fort by the British, before Mr Madison's war, and was afterwards added to by a smuggler named Teasle, for bringing in guns to sell to the Iroquois. It's a huge, rambling place with more wings to it than the seraphim of Ezekiel, and tunnels down to the river where they'd bring in contraband goods.'

Startled at the description, January said, 'This Shining Herald must make decent money, communicating with the dead.'

'Well,' said Ruggles, 'she does. But they also get donations. The Tappan Brothers' – he named two of the wealthiest philanthropists in New York – 'have contributed a good deal to their efforts at helping runaways, and a number of groups have given the Patriarch – and the Herald – money, to further their translation of a lost gospel of the Bible, which Broadax found on an expedition to the Holy Land.'

'Do you believe she's able to speak with the dead?' January asked curiously.

The young man was silent for a time, considering the question. At length he said, 'I don't – I'm not really sure what to think. I've heard her preach. And I've seen . . . things I can't really explain.' His brow pulled down, and he turned the thick glass between skeletal fingers.

'According to Broadax, the Herald appeared to him in a dream, while he was somewhere in the Holy Land – I think he was searching for

Noah's Ark, to refute the claims Lyell makes in the *Principles of Geology*, that the Earth is far older than the date the Bible gives for Creation. In the dream the Herald told him to go to the ruins of Babylon, and while he was there, she appeared to him again, in a waking vision this time, showing him where the scroll was hidden. It's a book written by James the Lesser – the stepbrother of Our Lord – giving revelations that He spoke after His Resurrection. Of course Broadax couldn't read it, but when he returned to this country, the Herald sought him out – they'd never met before – and offered to help him translate it, with the help of her spirit voices.'

January said nothing. He remembered a novice at the convent of St-Souffrance near Paris, whose hands and forehead had bled with spontaneous wounds on Good Friday. Recalled, too, what Ayasha had told him of a dervish she had seen in the marketplace of a village she had passed through near her home, who drove rusted nails into the flesh of his arm and, withdrawing them, left no wound.

It is the love of God which lets me do this, he had said.

'"Your sons and your daughters shall prophesy," says the prophet Joel,' Ruggles went on slowly. '"Your old men shall dream dreams, your young men shall see visions." But as to who might be sending those visions and dreams . . .'

He shook his head, gazing into the distance with troubled eyes. 'My parents were deeply devout, Mr January. My father would hear

70

nothing, but what was in the Bible – what he had been *taught* about what was in the Bible. But out in the west of the state, men – and women, too – *do* see visions, and dream dreams. There was a man near New Lebanon not so long ago, who claimed to live as the prophets lived, eating nothing but gruel and wearing nothing but leather and bearskins – his followers, too. He told them that the Lord had forbidden them to wash or shave, and to practice polygamy as the ancient Patriarchs did . . . something which doesn't sound likely to me, but how can I say?'

She was always asking questions, Grislock had said of his employers' daughter.

And, *It was all nonsense, of course . . .*

'These days,' Ruggles went on, 'it's as if everything about faith is being remade. As if, like the Quakers, people are getting their faith straight from . . . from wherever, instead of from the Bible or the churches. Backwoods preachers go through the farms, and the new communities that have sprung up along the Canal, saving souls and preaching a new type of salvation – plastering the towns they go through with handbills like politicians running for Congress, preaching in the woods and demanding that everyone be saved. Others found communities, congregations, like the Shakers and the Church of the New Jerusalem . . . "In my Father's House there are many mansions," the Lord says. Who am I to judge?'

Including the young gentleman who was taken up to the planet Saturn by means of a magical staff?

71

They are drunk with new wine, pious Jews had sniffed, seeing the Apostles in the ecstasy of Pentecost . . .

January thought of that childlike face in the daguerreotype, the trace of sadness in those too-intelligent dark eyes. How could even a wise man judge, much less a girl of seventeen?

'And this Community of theirs,' said January. 'Do *they* live the way the ancient patriarchs did?'

'Well, different groups claim different things,' said Ruggles. 'The Children of the Light don't practice polygamy, if that's what you're asking. They do hold their land in common. The Teasle land – with the house, and about two hundred acres of farmland – was owned by a man named Jared Ott. He donated it to the Community after the Herald had a vision of his dead wife. About thirty families in that area have done the same: signed over their acres to form the Blessed Land, which they farm in common. The congregation is much larger than that, though. A number of very wealthy New Yorkers – men of great integrity and probity, I might add – take the train out to Syracuse to receive spiritual guidance from the Herald, and they've donated a great deal of money as well.'

Which presumably paid for the printing costs of the pamphlets Grislock had burned . . .

'Do you think they would have lured a seventeen-year-old girl away from her family to join them?'

'Absolutely not!' The abolitionist looked startled at the very idea. 'Why would Broadax do such a thing – or *need* to do such a thing? They

72

have no need of money. Although I'm sure,' he went on drily, 'that it will be *said* of him, by the members of the more conservative churches, that he's done exactly that. And by men who're looking for an excuse to search the property for fugitives.'

January nodded slowly. He was remembering, too, the passionate uproar there had been some sixteen years ago, when a Virginian named Morgan had disappeared, supposedly murdered by the Freemasons for violating their secrets . . . He had been in France at the time, but it had been much discussed in his own Lodge, and the hatred for the Masons had gone the length of engendering a political party dedicated to their downfall.

And there hadn't even, in that case, been the encouragement of monetary rewards for captured fugitives.

'Could you make arrangements for me to go to the Blessed Land?' he asked after a time. 'Not as a representative of the Russells, but as a fugitive, on my way to Canada. I won't know for certain until I've talked to the Winterinks, and to Mamzelle Russell's maid, but it sounds as if these Children of the Light were the ones to whom the young lady was drawn. If indeed she left New York at all – and there's still the possibility that she didn't.'

'I can't imagine Broadax permitting a girl that young to simply turn up on his doorstep without communicating with her parents.'

'No,' said January thoughtfully. 'And yet her disappearance sounds well organized. Wherever

73

she went, whatever happened to her, I don't think she could have disappeared like that without accomplices. But kidnappers would have to have known it would be weeks before her parents could even get a ransom note. And if there were kidnapping to be done, why didn't they take her friend Miss Winterink, whose parents really are wealthy?'

'Maybe they thought they had. Maybe she was the one deceived – she thought whoever she ran off with were indeed the Children of Light, when in fact they were . . .'

'Were what?' asked January. He didn't elaborate on what he surmised would happen to a girl, abducted by mistake, when her kidnappers discovered they had the wrong victim, and the abolitionist had no answer for him.

Nor did he speculate on why a seventeen-year-old girl might lie about her family situation, to reach sanctuary elsewhere.

Or on the possibility that the girl seeking sanctuary might not have been lying at all.

'I don't know what's going on,' January said at last. 'Or who might be lying to whom. But it's the best lead I have so far. It's why I want to go there without connection to her family, or to any sheriff or representative of the law. Can you arrange that? I want to see the place. To see, first off, if she's actually there. And then to see who these people are, when they're not in their Sunday best.'

A smile flicked across Ruggles' face at the metaphor, the gouges of stress and care dissolving for a moment. He was a man infinitely tired,

January thought, yet he could see in him still the fierceness that had led him to confront would-be kidnappers on the streets, to fight battles in the courtrooms and to elude several attempts on his life.

'I'll find someone to introduce you.' Ruggles rose from his chair. 'It'll probably be Byron Spring, who preaches at one of the churches in Seneca Village – he's taken cargoes up to the Blessed Land before.' 'Cargo' was one of the code words used on the Underground Railway, meaning, fugitives, to be left at the 'station'. 'Nobody's ever caught those who Broadax has helped. He's good. But I'd suggest you have this Mr Viellard of yours travel by the same boat, in case there's trouble. The blackbirders work the boats as well – and the railway line. They watch for men of color traveling alone. It's too damn easy for a man to disappear in transit, and his family to think, "Oh, he just missed his train . . ." And by the time they realize he's gone, it's too late.'

'Yes,' said January quietly, thinking of the young sailor on Marais Street. Did his captain just shrug him off with: Ah, he's probably just drunk some-place . . .? He'll be along tomorrow . . .

The chief constable boasts he can have any black man in town put on the auction block in Baltimore inside twenty-four hours . . .

'Would your Mr Viellard be willing to do that?'

'I think he would, yes.' January mentally weighed Chloë Viellard's steely efficiency against the juggernaut that was Madame Viellard. 'Unless I learn something definite, and different, from

75

the Winterinks this evening, I'll speak with him tonight, and try to make arrangements to leave for Syracuse on Saturday. I'll send you a note as soon as I know anything definite.'

'Good.' The abolitionist went to a corner cupboard and took out pencil and paper, called out, 'Bill!' And, when the stocky young hostler appeared in the kitchen doorway, said, 'Would you be willing to take a note up to Seneca Village?'

When he wrote, January noticed how he turned his head, as if he could see better with peripheral vision than straight on, and how huge and straggling were the letters on the page. Without being asked, Bill fetched a lamp from a cupboard's upper shelf and kindled it, though daylight of a sort still trickled through the windows despite the narrow gap between the house and the tenant house next door. 'You'd best be starting back,' Ruggles added, returning his glance to January, 'if you're going to get to Union Square before dark.'

'Thank you for arranging the introduction,' said January. 'And the escort – all the way down Broadway I was hanging on to Bill's sleeve like a little girl.'

'You hold Spring's hand all the way to Syracuse, if you know what's good for you,' replied Ruggles grimly. 'The line runs from Albany clear out to Auburn, but it's two or three separate lines, really. You'll have to change trains at Schenectady and again at Utica. Watch yourself on the platforms. I'll tell Byron about your supposedly being just a fugitive, but

I still can't picture Broadax admitting a girl that young to the Community of the Blessed Land without asking questions, or writing to her parents, or to *someone* . . .'

'And I can't picture a girl who looks like Mamzelle Russell convincing anyone that she's as much as sixteen, much less that she's of age. But at least,' January concluded, 'we'll know where she *isn't*. And we won't have the Russells offering a reward for an all-out search of every house in the countryside. And that's something.'

'Truthfully,' observed Chloë Viellard, later that evening, 'which is a manifestly silly figure of speech, for what could possibly be gained by me lying to you in the circumstances? Truthfully, I think it best if Henri should go with you, rather than myself. People respond so much more quickly when a man barks an order, than when a woman does. Isn't that so, Henri?'

Her husband, amply filling an armchair in the private sitting room of their suite, responded obediently, 'Whatever you say, madame.' He was still pale from the voyage, but had – by the look of the trays that servants had carried down the backstairs as January had ascended – made a substantial dinner of vol-au-vents, green goose with peas, Scotch tartlets, glazed carrots, white soup, and two kinds of trifle.

In justice, January reflected that his sister's protector had probably shared the gargantuan repast with his mother – no mean trencherwoman herself. Even so, it was impressive for two people, one of whom had been prostrate at two that afternoon.

'I'll inquire of the concierge about what boats leave on Saturday. I do hope this Reverend Spring of yours will be able to find another minister to take his sermon Sunday . . .' Chloë produced a Morocco leather notebook and jotted a reminder to herself. 'That will give us time to purchase tickets and visit the bank tomorrow, and to get your mother settled, Henri, and make arrangements for me to take her to this Dr Fiedler – and presumably for you to make whatever arrangements you need to, m'sieu?' She turned inquiringly back to January.

'I'll be traveling with someone who can introduce me to the Reverend Broadax,' said January.

'Excellent,' she approved briskly. 'I'm sure the concierge will have information about a hotel in Albany for Saturday night as well. And for one in Syracuse . . . I shall write to both establishments this evening and make arrangements. Your railway ticket will be through to Auburn, Henri, but find some plausible reason to get off at Syracuse – does one succumb to *mal de mer* on steam trains? Well, I'm sure you'll find that out . . . Keep your papers concerning M'sieu Janvier ready, but don't produce them unless you have to.'

'No, madame,' replied her husband meekly.

'M'sieu Janvier, I understand that the New York Central railway line has a separate car for people of color, which is just as— Yes?' She turned, as her mother-in-law's tall, gray-haired butler appeared in the doorway and tapped gently on the panels.

'The Winterinks are here, m'am.' He bowed deeply. 'And the Russells, waiting in the lobby. Shall I show them up?'

'By all means. Is coffee ready? Thank you, Visigoth. And comfits? Very good. Thank you.'

January got to his feet and stood, hands folded, beside Henri's chair. Slavery might have been outlawed in New York, but he knew to the marrow of his bones that wealthy, white New Yorkers were not accustomed to come into rooms to find a black man – no matter how neatly dressed and cleanly scrubbed after his excursion downtown – occupying a chair. 'Amalgamation' – that nightmare accusation that whites leveled at abolitionists – didn't mean solely the horror of black men marrying white women (*as if white men haven't been raping their female slaves on a regular basis for the past hundred and fifty years*), but the equally unspeakable possibility that 'rude, illiterate, and odiferous' persons of color might rub elbows with whites in public venues and private parlors. Angry as this made him, he was well aware that the less that people were put off their stride – by uncertainty, or dismay, or even the annoyed sense that things weren't quite as they should be – the easier it would be to get them talking.

And that, he reminded himself, was his goal. Not changing their opinions, or asserting his own.

His first seven years had been spent

in life-and-death subjection to a volatile and suspicious drunkard. For all his massive build and great height, January had spent a good deal of his early life practicing the art of being invisible.

Charlotte Winterink bore a physical resemblance to her cousin Mrs Russell – taller and slimmer, but with the same round, almost child-like face, the same wide-set dark eyes and short upper lip. Like her cousin, she dressed in the height of style, her pink-striped silk frock an amazement of pleatings and tuckings above which a wide, white pelerine collar spread like a snow field on a mountainside. Fashionable clusters of curls, several shades darker than her cousin's, dangled above her ears. Her eyes shifted with the burden of guilt and anxiety; her husband – a middle-sized stout gentleman clearly descended from the island's original Dutch settlers – wore an expression of suspicious anger. Their daughter clearly took after him, her broad-shouldered sturdiness ruthlessly corseted and her straight, fair hair already sinking limply away from its burnt-in ringlets.

The elderly woman – strikingly beautiful despite the iron gray of her hair – who brought up the rear must, by her style of dress, be Lucy Palmer, thought January. The woman who'd been on the steam packet with Eve Russell when she'd disappeared.

Questioning Lettice Winterink in the presence of her parents, and the parents of her vanished friend, wasn't easy, and January didn't learn much that he hadn't already guessed. The girl kept glancing at her mother, and at Mrs Russell, as if asking whether she'd answered aright. No, Eve had never said anything about being unhappy. No, she'd never gotten the impression that her friend had had anything troubling her, except that one time when they'd gone to Weehawken on the ferry for a picnic and Eve had broken the strap on her shoe . . . No, as far as Lettice knew there was no man. 'At least,' said the girl, 'Eve was very popular – she was always coming in from balls with a dozen nosegays, and people were always sending her flowers. Just, I never heard her speak of anyone special.'

'Nonsense!' protested Mrs Russell. 'There was Art Livingston! One of the most eligible young gentlemen in New York! And there was Nicholas Brevoort, and Schuyler Pettis . . .'

'Yes, m'am,' agreed Lettice quickly. 'Of course.'

'But I cannot imagine anyone objecting to their attentions,' put in Chloë smoothly, in her excellent English. 'Nor can I picture any of them resorting to anything clandestine in the least. So I think we can eliminate them from our field of enquiry. There was no one that you knew of, who would be considered *un*suitable?'

'Oh, no! That wasn't – Eve isn't like that.'

They had attended the lectures of the Shining Herald four times. Three of these had been at a private home belonging to a family named Rankin. 'And I wish I'd been struck dead before I'd lied to you, Mama! But Eve begged me, and we got Cousin Violet to go with us once,

81

and Cousin Maria . . . Eve said she'd take all the blame if we were caught!'

'Oh, but the Rankins are perfectly respectable people!' exclaimed Mrs Winterink. 'They're related to van Santvoorts!'

Mrs Russell subsided. 'That's still no excuse for two girls of that age to attend, even if they did talk an older cousin into going with them.'

'She – the Herald – can speak with the souls of the dead.' The girl wiped tears from her eyes at the rebuke, and her voice was now barely a whisper. 'She lies on a couch and falls asleep, just like that. She said, "I see them thronging into the room, like the stars in the Milky Way . . ." She asked if there was somebody named Anne there, because there was a tall man with a beard asking for Anne, saying he was sorry for whipping her, when the cat had spilt the milk . . . And a woman burst into tears and said, "Papa, Papa, it didn't hurt! You could whip me again, if it would mean I'd see you once more!" And that was Anne, you see . . .'

Recalling what Olympe had told him about how the voodoos got to know everything in town, January wondered who 'Anne' had spoken to over the years, about Papa and the cat and the milk . . .

'Sometimes the Herald will talk to angels, and the angels will speak through her lips, about what it's like on the Other Side, in the Summer Land—'

'That's the most ridiculous—'

Chloë reached over and touched Mrs Russell's wrist, to January's infinite gratitude, since he

82

himself could scarcely have put his hand over the woman's mouth to shut her up.

On their third visit, said Lettice, the spirits had spoken to Eve.

'They knew her name,' whispered the girl. 'And I . . . I saw it. Her. I saw *her* . . .'

'What did you see?'

'Lettice, you know that's simply—'

'Please,' whispered Chloë urgently, and taking Mrs Russell by the hand, dragged her away to the other end of the parlor. Mrs Winterink looked as if she might have jumped up and gone with them to find out what was being said, but evidently decided that it would be the greater sin to leave her daughter – even though still in the same room – in so scandalous a *tête-à-tête* . . .

'A shape.' Miss Winterink's voice was so low that January had to lean close to hear. 'A little girl, it looked like. It shined – it held out its hand. I could see the wallpaper, and a chair, straight through it.' She faltered for a moment, bit her lip. 'I'm not making this up!'

'No,' said January gently. 'I know you're not.'

'The Herald spoke, and her voice changed to a little girl's voice. She said, "Eve? It's me, Belle . . ." And Eve started crying, right there in the parlor. She grabbed my hand so tight I almost cried out myself. And Eve said, "Are you all right?" And the Herald said – or I guess Belle said – "Oh, I'm so happy here! I'm so happy! There isn't anything to be afraid of! But I love you, I love you and I miss you! If only you could see how wonderful it is!"'

After the session was over – and a half-dozen

others had been spoken to by those they knew, some of whom had manifested as shining shapes, like the child, infinitely far away – Eve had hurried to the front of the parlor to speak to the Patriarch and the Shining Herald. She'd come away with pamphlets, including those passages from the Lost Gospel of James the Lesser in which Jesus assured the disciples that the souls of those who had passed beyond could – and longed to – continue their relationships with those they had loved on this earth.

'We went once more,' said Lettice, 'after Eve's parents left for New Orleans. We got another of my cousins to go with us, and I . . . I told Mama we were going to a lecture about Rational Dress for Women.' She blushed. 'Belle spoke to her then, too. After the lecture, the Reverend Broadax – the Patriarch, he's called – told us all that this was the last time they'd be able to speak to us for months. They were going back to this Community they had, out in the west of the state, where he works at translating the rest of the Lost Gospel, and everyone works so that everyone may live in harmony and comfort, like the Apostles did. When Eve heard this, she cried all the way home.'

Eight

About the day of Eve's disappearance itself, the maid Lucy Palmer had little to add. 'Miss had been to stay for a week with the Delapores, across the Sound at King's Point,' she explained, in a soft alto every bit as educated as that of her employers. 'A very quiet, genteel place. We were going back to the Winterinks' in the city on the Thursday. No, Miss Winterink' – she glanced towards the fireplace at the other end of the parlor, where Mrs Winterink, her daughter, Mrs Russell and Chloë were engaged in a soft-voiced blood-bath of recrimination and defensiveness – 'hadn't come with us to the Delapores' owing to a visit from one of Mr Winterink's sisters at that time.'

The steam packet back to town had been crowded, she went on: peddlers and ladies, Negroes and Jews, and gentlemen going to work in the city. But when Miss Russell had asked to go to the back of the boat to watch the sailing boats, Lucy had given her leave. What harm could a girl come to, on a boat? 'And Andy went with her, of course, Mrs Delapore's coachman, who'd come along to manage the luggage and see to the tickets, and make sure we got back to Waverly Place all right.'

From beside the fireplace, Charlotte Winterink's querulous voice shrilled in protest, 'Of course I wrote to Clemmie Delapore! Three times – the woman is an absolute nincompoop and doesn't read her mail for weeks at a time!'

Lowering her voice still further, Lucy went on, 'When the packet put in at the Battery I looked about for Miss Eve a little, then made my way to the back of the boat. Andy asked me, first thing, where was Miss Eve? He said she'd said she needed her reticule, which she'd left on the bench beside me at the front of the boat. He'd

85

been waiting for the better part of an hour, for her to come back to him, and had decided that she'd forgotten . . . which isn't like her, and even *he* knew it wasn't like her. But he hadn't liked to leave where he was, he said, because when she *did* come back she'd be looking for him there. By that time most of the passengers were off the boat.' Her moth-wing brows pulled together in distress at the memory.

'You say she spent a week at the Delapores.' January called back to mind the account that Bill the Hostler had given him, on their walk downtown, of the little communities of the Long Island shore, with its woodlands, its neat small farmhouses and fishing shacks, and the new stone mansions of New York's rich. 'Coming back, did she keep any pieces of her luggage with her on the deck?'

'Oh, goodness, no! She had but the trunk and the two valises, and either of them too heavy to carry far. Andy had to bring a hand truck.'

'So the reticule was all she had with her.'

'It was indeed. And she did leave it, on the bench beside me, and never came back for it. Poor Mrs Russell has it now. And when we returned home, finally, after dark and after hunting all over the pier, and never finding a trace of the child, Mr Kingsmill – Mrs Winterink's butler – had a look through the reticule, thinking there might have been a note or something to tell us what might have become of her, but there was nothing. Only a handkerchief, and a little packet of pastilles, and her little sewing things in a pretty wallet . . .'

'No ticket?'

She looked startled at the realization. 'No. Well, she couldn't have got off the boat without one.'

'No,' said January thoughtfully. 'No, she couldn't. What was she wearing, madame?'

'A medium-blue cotton frock sprigged with darker blue,' returned the maid, with professional promptness. 'Wide puff sleeves with two falls of white lace and a darker blue undersleeve, and a white bertha trimmed with black and blue braid. The sleeves – and the back of the bertha – had a big cloverleaf on them, in black and white braid.' Her hand sketched the trefoil design in the air. 'Blue kid walking shoes. A close bonnet, blue with wide, black, velvet ties, and silk ruffles inside, of several different shades of blue. Blue and white silk flowers on the bonnet.'

'And none of these items were found on the boat afterwards? Or found washed up out of the river?'

'No. And – well . . .' She hesitated, with another glance back at her employer, still engaged in altercation with Mrs Winterink. 'Mr Kingsmill and I went to the city morgue next day, and again three days later. It was terrible.' She winced at the recollection. 'But . . . well . . . there was nobody that could have been her.'

But the garments had to go somewhere. And a frock with a distinctive design on sleeves and back would be hard to miss.

As the other women made their way back to the table, January said, 'It sounds to me as if Mademoiselle Russell changed her clothes on the packet – the boat does have a ladies' cloakroom or something of the kind, doesn't it, Mrs Palmer?'

Both mothers looked horrified that such a thing should even have been mentioned, much less by a man and a black man at that, but Lucy replied, 'It does. It's barely a cupboard, tucked away below decks, with a pallet in case a lady should be taken ill.'

'Lucy,' gasped Mrs Russell, 'are you honestly suggesting that my daughter . . . how on *earth* would she have done such a thing? And *why*? It's absurd . . .'

'As long as you keep saying that your daughter would never have done this, and that it's absurd,' pointed out Chloë, fixing her with her wide, aquamarine stare, 'we're not going to get any further toward finding her, madame. One reasonable hypothesis seems to be that your daughter had someone else meet her on the ferry with a change of clothing' – she lifted her hand against the horrified protest – 'probably far less stylish than what she was wearing when she left the Delapores', and that they simply packed up her original dress and bonnet (and shoes, if they were being careful) into whatever they'd brought the substitute garments in . . .'

'Someone . . . *Who?* I refuse to believe it! She was kidnapped—'

'She was undoubtedly lied to, madame,' said January. 'By whom, or for what reason, we don't know. But I think I need to . . . to at least have a look at this Blessed Land, this Community near Syracuse where the Shining Herald, and the Children of the Light, are to be found.'

'But if—'

Chloë again laid a silencing hand on Mrs Russell's wrist.

'Even if she isn't there,' he continued quietly, 'it's a place to start. I may be able to get word of her intentions, or some account of what *she* thought was going on. It sounds to me – from what I've heard this afternoon, and this evening from Mamzelle Winterink and Madame Palmer – as if she could well have been lured into believing that she would be safe, and maybe even justified—'

'She wouldn't do such a thing!' insisted the mother. 'She wouldn't! She wouldn't!' And, collapsing suddenly into a chair, she began to weep, desperate racking sobs as she buried her face in her hands. Lucy sprang immediately to her feet and took a crystal phial from her pocket; Mrs Winterink sank to her knees beside her cousin, wrapping her arms around the heaving shoulders, while Chloë calmly ordered Lettice to fetch some water.

When the girl scurried to obey, Chloë drew January aside and asked quietly, 'You'll be going, then? I'll tell Henri.'

'Thank you.' His glance went to the weeping woman, and something twisted inside him, not only pity, but a dread he shrank from speaking. A fear of shadows, the sense that there was something askew about all this. 'It may be a waste of my time, and of M'sieu Viellard's; from what M'sieu Ruggles told me this afternoon it doesn't sound as if these Children of the Light would deliberately kidnap anyone. But it's clear

89

she had an accomplice. I'll feel better if I can see the place, and these people, for myself. It may tell me something about all this that simply isn't evident from here. It shouldn't take more than a few days.'

'Well, at least Henri won't be bored.' The little lady sighed, and folded her lace-mitted hands. 'I understand there are four types of wood beetle and at least half a dozen species of butterfly in the western counties unique to that area. And he has been reading the tracts that were thrust into our hands by our cab driver, and has spent much of the afternoon looking up references in the Bible to ascertain whether those people who claim the Last Judgment will take place in October of 1843 have their arithmetic correct. Excuse me.'

She hurried to Mrs Russell's side, as the two Winterink ladies and the maid helped her to her feet. January heard Chloë murmur, 'Yes, she'll be much more comfortable . . .' as she preceded them to the door of her bedroom. This she opened, standing aside to let them support Mrs Russell past her.

When she came back to him, January asked, 'Shall I go downstairs and fetch Mssrs Viellard and Winterink?' For the men had departed – at Chloë's suggestion – before he had begun to question the girl Lettice; 'to make the room look a little less Inquisitorial,' Chloë had said.

'Yes, please do, if you would. I wonder if this hotel has a directory of public accommodation available in Syracuse?' She straightened her spectacles. 'Personally, I should be interested to

90

interview one of the dead that this Shining Herald summons. I'd be most curious to find out how the Last Judgment is going to work, if the dead can be called out of their graves now to chat with the survivors . . . not that I should wish to have even the briefest of conversations with either of my parents. If you have the chance while you're in Onondaga County, please do remember to ask.'

A pity we can't have Madame's spirit with M'sieu's body, he wrote to Rose that night, in the sweatbox garret chamber allotted to himself, Visigoth, and the young footman Jacques-Ange. (Leopold, being white, had the sweatbox next door all to himself, with only the rats for company.) Though Chloë Viellard was infinitely more practical than her fat, scholarly husband, January recognized the fact that a man – and particularly a planter, in a state whose trade was so dependent upon the South – would be listened to far more readily than a woman. Both the Viellards were brilliantly intelligent, but *should I need rescuing*, he wrote, *Madame Chloë will react more quickly . . . and be listened to less. Madame Chloë sends her love to you, and to Dominique.*

The sentiment was genuine. Chloë was fast friends with her husband's lovely mistress.

As it happened, the entire matter turned out to be moot.

The following day – every bit as clammily hot as the worst of New Orleans summers – was spent in the dispatch of hotel messengers to purchase tickets and arrange for hotels, and by

January in discreet coaching from Shakespeare Chapman and Bill the Hostler concerning places he would have passed through and things he would have seen, had he in fact been a runaway on his way north. But when January descended to the hotel yard on Saturday morning, with only a few shaving things and a change of linen shoved in a canvas satchel, it was to find Chloë, not Henri, just getting into the cab that would take her to 'Peck's Slip' whence the Albany steamboat would embark. She made an excuse to her maid Hélène, already in the vehicle, and under that rawboned Frenchwoman's disapproving stare, hurried to where January was emerging from the kitchen door.

'It is Madame,' she explained, meaning her queenly, formidable mother-in-law, whom January had barely glimpsed during the whole of the journey and all of the previous day (and didn't want to). 'She spent an indifferent night last night, and insisted this morning at breakfast that Henri remain with her – and in fact began by demanding that I remain as well. No one but her son, she says, can understand and care for her properly.'

Meaning no one but her son would scramble as meekly to do her bidding, reflected January. *Certainly not her daughter-in-law*. He himself wasn't the only one who recognized that a man's requests would be more speedily granted than a woman's. *Though God help the New Yorker, man or woman, who doesn't scramble to obey Madame's commands . . .*

'Thank you' – January inclined his head – 'from

92

the bottom of my heart, for holding out against her demands.' Privately, watching the three trunks of his protectress's luggage being strapped to the top of the cab, he could only marvel at the lady's speed in repacking for the journey.

'Madame was all for sending word to M'sieu Russell to accompany me,' continued Chloë, drawing on her gloves. 'But that would mean his wife would join us also – though Madame couldn't comprehend why a woman who has possibly lost her daughter should mind being deprived of her husband as well – and I will *not* have the pair of them on my hands. But I could not – she said – travel without a male protector, and my suggestion that Hélène and I both don trousers and call ourselves Ganymede and Aliena was not met with favor. In the end – the breakfast coffee being quite cold by that time – Henri made the heroic sacrifice and has assigned poor Leopold to accompany us, leaving Visigoth and Jacques-Ange to look after both him and his mother. I have your papers here.' She patted the slim leather valise which matched the silvery gray of her dress.

'I suspect part of Madame fears also that if Jacques-Ange were to go with me, he might fall into temptation and not come back.'

'What's likelier,' said January grimly, 'is that he'd go for a drink with some plausible stranger, and not come back.'

He walked back to the cab with her, and helped her in. Hélène, who knew all about Henri's relations with January's sister, looked down her nose at him as he shut the door.

The steamboat *Empress of the Hudson* wasn't slated to leave its berth at Peck's Slip until nine. As January walked from Union Square down to Water Street, he found himself looking over his shoulder a dozen times at the raucous crowds on Broadway that surrounded him.

Certain that he was in danger, and not knowing from which direction it would strike.

He was on foot now, and without a companion. Every time he passed one of the Vigilance Committee's warning handbills, or caught one of the soap-locked *b'hoys* of Five Points or the Bowery sizing him up as he walked by, he felt a desire to run.

Only in this overcrowded, hammeringly noisy, filthy city, where could he run to?

They watch for men of color traveling alone, Ruggles had warned. *It's too damn easy for a man to disappear in transit . . .*

Men gets put on the police force 'cause of their politics, Chapman had said. *Not 'cause they give a rat's ass about right or wrong.*

The feeling grew on him the farther down Broadway he went. Carts and drays replaced the carriages of the well-to-do, and in addition to pushcarts and black-clothed Jews hawking umbrellas and gingerbread, he had to pick his way around livestock, foraging chickens and pigs. He remembered how men and women – children, even – had walked around the beaten man lying weeping in the street, and shivered at the thought that no one would raise a hand to help him. When he turned toward the waterfront his pace quickened – *Surely they won't jump out of an alleyway in broad daylight and thwack you over the head . . .*

But in fact, slave catchers would do exactly that. Could do so here, with impunity. He was no longer dressed in the livery of a servant, but in the rough clothing of a vagabond, suitable to his role as runaway. If men stepped out of an alleyway and grabbed him and said, 'You're the fellow escaped from Virginia last week . . .'

In his pocket he fingered the pass Henri had written for him, the papers that supposedly proved him a slave on a legitimate errand. 'No, sir, I'm Ben from New Orleans and my master's Michie Henri Viellard, that's staying at the Dominion Hotel . . .'

He realized his heart was racing.

And in that moment of his fear, he hated white men: Henri Viellard, Hannibal Sefton, and Abishag Shaw along with all the rest.

Movement in the bustle along the street, five men walking together, looking around them as if searching. Plug hats, soap-lock hair, the blue stripe down the side of their trousers that marked them as a gang. What had Bill called them? The Roach Guards?

Moving like hunters. Scanning the flagways around them. Two carried heavy, knotted walking sticks. A third openly wore a brass knuckleduster on his meaty hand.

Looking for someone.

Last night he had studied the sketch map that Shakespeare Chapman had given him, of this part of Manhattan. Now he ducked down Anthony Street, where the press was less, taking

95

landmarks on a broken tenant-house porch, a bearded Jew selling boot polish, as in childhood he had oriented himself with strangely shaped trees and cypress knees in the bayous. He could smell the fish market, above the mingled reek of horse manure in the street and a pigsty in some yard close by. In a doorway a woman was being sodomized by a sailor. January quickened his pace, and heard – or thought he heard – the feet of men behind him.

He turned again, glanced at his map, oriented himself with the blink of sun on water between two ramshackle warehouses. Crates were stacked outside the door of one, surrounded by a muck of muddy cobblestones and broken glass; someone had dropped a crate of liquor bottles and the whole alleyway stank of them. Behind him he heard a man call out, 'He went down this way—'

Damn it . . .

January ducked behind a crate, and almost tripped over a man already hiding there. A big man, crouched impossibly small and panting for breath. Blood trickled from one swollen cheekbone and glistened in his dark, thickly curled hair. The man stared up at him with such desperation, such shock, that January stepped back out from behind the crates even as two more Roach Guards came around the corner ahead of him . . .

January pointed back up the alley. 'He went that way, the bastard,' he said, all the aggrieved fury of his fear in his voice. 'Feller in the blue coat?'

The two pursuers stepped closer, and two others, from the other end of the alley. He saw now that both the knuckleduster and one of the sticks were smeared with blood.

Spitefully, January added, 'Run right into me, he did, the white bastard, and broke all my bottles.' He nodded at the ruin of glass and spilt liquor in the mud nearby.

One of the men spat. For a moment of panic he feared that they would turn on him instead. But they all ran in the direction he pointed.

January stepped back around the crates as the quarry was scrambling to his feet. Without waiting for him to speak, January stripped out of his own scuffed brown corduroy roundabout and threw it to him. 'Gimme your hat,' he said. 'And that coat – they'll be watching for a blue coat.' He pulled off his cap and tossed it on to one of the crates. The fugitive – burly like January and nearly as tall – was already pulling off his blue frock coat, which January took, wadded into a ball, and shoved into his satchel. He put on the hat, which smelled of cheap pomade. 'You go get you some shoe-black and black up your face,' he instructed. 'There's a peddler selling it, round that corner. And you walk – you don't run. They lookin' for someone running in the crowd.'

'Thank you,' gasped the white man. 'I—'

'Don't talk. Git.' January turned on his heel and strode away, disgusted with himself, the white man's plug hat on his head.

For all I know he could be a slave taker himself. And the man lying drunk and weeping yesterday afternoon in the muck of Broadway could have been a rapist, a cheat, well deserving of the beating he'd taken at the hands of the thick-faced Guards.

Who the hell am I, to let him off?

In the back of his mind he heard the gentle voice of Père Eugenius, his confessor: *Inasmuch as ye have done it unto one of the least of these my brethren, ye have done it unto me.*

Our Lord might well have changed his mind about that, reflected January sourly, *if He'd ever been to New York.*

Then he let the thought go, as he emerged into the cleared space of cobbles around Peck's Slip, a long rectangle of water let in from the East River, like the turning basin at the end of the Canal in New Orleans. Two small sloops were moored at one side of the slip, and at the other, almost too large for the narrow waterway, the little steamboat the *Empress of the Hudson*, stevedores just carrying sacks of coffee and sugar up her gangway.

A slim young man in a green jacket – the garment described in the note Bill had slipped him that morning – stood among the crowd of passengers at the stern, leaning on the rail. He saw January and raised his hand in greeting.

It was like seeing the door of Heaven open on a stormy night. January crossed the cobbles, reflecting that at least he hadn't been the Roach Guards' quarry. And he'd gotten a blue frock coat out of the encounter – better than his own – and a sorry-looking plug hat that stank of lime pomade.

Nine

Byron Spring strode to the gangplank as January came up it. He asked, 'Are you the doctor from Paris?' – a signal that had also been in Bill's note.

'I am.' January grasped his extended hand. 'Ben January.'

'Byron Spring.'

'You look young to be a reverend.'

'Living in New York,' replied the young man gravely, 'I'm told I'll age fast.' He spoke like a man of Massachusetts, therefore free born. Seeing January looking around him at the boat, he added, 'How does she compare with the Mississippi boats? I understand they're taller . . .'

'Taller and cram-jammed with cotton bales.' January turned toward the bow, where, beyond the big side wheels, stairways led to the upper deck. The 'Ladies' Reading Room' (according to the sign) situated there seemed to admit both gentlemen and ladies, as long as they were white and well-dressed. He caught a glimpse of Chloë Viellard's diminutive form, severe in her pearl-gray silk, Hélène stalking like a Gothic specter in her wake. He wondered if Leopold were permitted up in that select venue as well.

'We're welcome in the common cabin.' Spring indicated a long saloon that occupied most of the lower deck. He was of medium height, and like David Ruggles he bore a hint of the Fulani bone structure. His eyes, like those of many of the New Orleans *sang melées*, were a striking turquoise-hazel, and he clearly had more white ancestors than black ones. 'If you don't mind the smoke, and the noise. There's card tables, if that's your pleasure, though they separate by race – I expect it's the same in the South . . .'

'Most boats in the South wouldn't even let us in the cabin, these days.' January tilted his plug hat forward, and scratched his short-cropped hair. 'And I can't afford to get fleeced by either white men or black ones, so I think I'll sit out here on the deck, if you don't mind. And you can tell me – again, if you don't mind – everything you know about the Reverend Serapis Broadax, the Blessed Land, and the Shining Herald.'

This didn't differ greatly from what Ruggles had already told him. Spring, like Ruggles, attested that the Reverend Broadax was uncannily skillful at slipping 'cargos' down the Oswego River to Lake Ontario, and so across to Canada, seemingly under the noses of both the Onondaga County sheriff and the blackbirder gangs that would periodically pass through the area. 'He's never had anyone caught, so far as I know.'

Spring, like Ruggles, had gone in April to hear the Shining Herald preach at the hall attached to Scudder's American Museum, and had been left uncertain and a little troubled at what he had seen. 'She speaks in her sleep,' he said. 'Or, rather, in a trance. When she speaks, a light shimmers around her – the stage was quite dark.

Sometimes I saw – or thought I saw – shapes appear, beyond or near the divan where she lay: pale shapes, glowing shapes, that moved and gestured – nothing like magic-lantern shows.

'I've seen magic-lantern shows,' he went on quietly. 'And you can tell that what you're seeing is an image, painted on a slide. These were animate. These were real.'

They sat on a bench, against the wall of the great cabin, where the stairway to the deck above gave a little shade. The August sun was baking hot, but the breeze that came across the water provided some coolness, and carried away the smoke and the soot-smuts that drifted down from the boat's tall stacks. Once they were clear of the city, it brought the heavy green smell of trees and cut hay.

'Seneca Village lies just there, over on the other side of the island.' Spring pointed toward the woodlands and meadows of upper Manhattan. Great gray rocks showed through the trees, and here and there the air was smudged with the smoke – and if the wind set over, the stinks – of the shanty towns that had taken root in the waste ground north of the city. 'If the ground were a little flatter – or if we could go up on the upper deck – I could show you my house, and my church.'

'I hope you were able to get a substitute, to take your congregation tomorrow?' said January, and Spring nodded with a smile. 'Mr Ruggles says Seneca Village is a regular little town . . .'

'It is.' There was love in the young man's strong, clear-toned voice. 'Not like the shanty

101

towns that squatters have thrown up elsewhere in the woods. It has streets and churches and frame houses on numbered lots. Six years ago, after the anti-Negro riots in Five Points, those who could afford it moved up there, though it's three or four miles walk to one's work in town. But it's one of the only places on Manhattan where people of color can buy land – which means we can vote.'

January raised his brows. 'What do the city fathers have to say about that?' In Louisiana, even the property-owning free people of color – who, like January's mother, carefully distinguished themselves from 'blacks' – had been systematically stripped of what rights they had, once Louisiana had become part of the United States.

Spring replied drily, 'I expect we're going to find that out. When New York rewrote its constitution about twenty years ago, they gave all white men the right to vote. Our vote they limited to property owners – and that disqualified about ninety-nine men in a hundred.'

January leaned back on the bench, watched the forest slip past. Raised as he had been in the flat, endless, dark-green of the bayous, where cane fields merged into the ciprière broken only by the plantation houses – blocks of bright color where the French Creoles had their holdings, blocks of whitewash where the Americans had set up shop – the variegated gorgeousness of the Hudson valley filled him with delight.

'And those farmers Mr Ruggles told me about,' he remarked at last, 'the ones who signed their

102

farms over to the Blessed Land – they're still able to vote because they're white. Are they considered to still own their farms?'

'Oh, I think they are,' replied Spring. 'I understand the Reverend Broadax's secretary – Mr Teems – specified that when they wrote up the contracts. The Patriarch wants the Community to continue beyond the lifetime of any single person in it, he says. All those who joined are assured of having a place to live – land to work, a home for their children – for life.'

They passed the inlet of the Harlem River, and left Manhattan behind. The western bank of the Hudson rose up in a glory of bluffs, exquisite woods draping their feet and shoulders like costly velvet. January tried to jot in his notebook what he saw – as Rose had asked him to do – but felt he wasn't doing justice to either the beauty, or the sense of unlimited, peaceful space.

In New Orleans, the long ghastly heat of the fever season had begun. It had been not only the recentness of his journey to Texas, or his aching love for his wife and his sons, that had made him unwilling to undertake this search for Eve Russell. Summer in New Orleans was the time of the cholera, of yellow fever, of the poisonous miasmas that seemed to rise from the gutters every night with the whining of the mosquitoes. It was not unreasonable to fear that he would get home to find them all dead. The reflection that even were he there, he would be able to do nothing, was of no comfort.

At least Rose has fifty dollars . . .

Along with his impressions of the Blessed

103

Land, Spring spoke of New York, of the horrific slums of Five Points and the waterfront; of the riots, six years ago, which had targeted the free blacks with unreasoning hate and of the convoluted, occasionally violent, conflict between the American Colonization Society and those who wanted to abolish slavery in the United States altogether. 'The colonizers claim to want to "help" *Africans*, as they call us, by sending us back to Africa . . . where we won't compete with white men for jobs in the factories. Already it's damn hard for a black man to find anything that pays. More and more white men are refusing to work alongside black ones. They don't want bosses thinking of their jobs as "something a nigger would do".'

He made a gesture of frustration, almost theatrical for all it was fueled by genuine anger; January guessed he was dynamic in the pulpit of his church. 'Have you ever met *any* black person, slave or free, who wants to go back and live in Africa? I'm an American. I was born in America, like my parents and my grandparents – which is more than can be said about half the men in their damn society.'

'I fought for America,' said January slowly, 'at the Battle of New Orleans. Even though I knew jolly damn well I'd have to go to France, to learn to be a surgeon.'

'They don't want to hear that. Diverting the *proper* course of how to deal with slavery, as they call it, into *the wrong channels*. During the riots, they encouraged the men who burned down the meeting hall of the American Abolitionist

104

Society. And then instead of banding together to work against them, the abolitionists are fighting among themselves, about should we try to get rights for black men in the north, or just concentrate on ending slavery? Like *that's* going to happen, with every senator from the south owning slaves.

'It drives me about crazy,' he added bitterly. 'I go to meetings and listen to the heads of committees arguing about temperance, and if a black man should use violence to protect himself from the slave catchers, or whether women should be allowed to join, and will that chase away prospective members who don't believe in rights for women, and I want to scream at them, "We're all on the same side! We'll accomplish nothing unless we work together!"'

He clenched his fist suddenly, as if aware that his voice had risen, and for a time fell silent, while the great paddle wheels sloshed the green waters of the Hudson, and the wooded hills crowded close to the river.

Then in a quieter voice he went on, 'And the white New Yorkers themselves don't care. All they want is to keep *their* jobs, and not to have anyone interfere with the saloons and bagnios and *their* parades on the fourth of July.'

'Is it true,' asked January after a moment, remembering the posters outside the tawdry theaters of lower Broadway, 'that some white man sold tickets to an old black woman's *autopsy*, on the grounds that she'd been George Washington's mammy?'

Spring made a face. 'That's New York,' he

105

said bitterly. 'They'll pay to see anything, if it's different and new.'

'Including conversations with the dead?'

Spring's brow drew down, and a look of trouble clouded his eyes. 'My wife thinks it's a hoax,' he said. 'Those whites who claim that Africans are superstitious about ghosts should try to have a conversation with Mrs Spring. But I don't see how it could be done – and who am I to judge, if the Patriarch – and the Shining Herald – have opened the door to nearly a score of men and women seeking freedom?'

The *Empress of the Hudson* reached Albany just after dark. Chloë, attended by Leopold and Hélène, took rooms at the North River Hotel, on Broadway; Spring and January sought out cheaper lodgings on Center Street, near the basin where the Canal began. The following day – Sunday, the second of August – they took the Mohawk and Hudson Railroad to Schenectady, whence they transferred to the Utica and Schenectady line, and thence on to the Utica and Syracuse Railroad in the afternoon. Chloë, Hélène, and Leopold traveled in the first-class cars – Leopold escorting his master's wife as solicitously as if he were her husband with Hélène like a Spanish duenna at her elbow. Spring and January, on all three lines, were relegated to what were generally called the 'dirt cars' at the end of the trains, sharing the smelly and dilapidated benches with sailors, bargemen, laborers headed for work on the Canal's branch lines, prostitutes, drunkards, and anyone who visibly had so much as a drop of African blood in his or her veins.

And each time they changed trains – with the bells of the Protestant churches chiming in the distance – January saw that Ruggles had not lied. Unshaven, steely-eyed roughnecks loitered on the platform, taking note of every black man or woman as if calculating their potential price against the trouble it would take to secure them. He could well imagine how the Five Points *b'hoys* as well as the professional slave catcher gangs would react to the prospect of a reward for searching the houses of Quakers and utopians.

Inside the dirt car on the Schenectady line a couple of sailors were leaning on the end of one of the uncushioned benches, nudging and pawing a black woman and her daughter, and smelling of liquor and stale cigar smoke the length of the car. January walked down the narrow center aisle as the train lurched into motion, stopped beside the bench and said politely, 'Sorry we were so late getting on, m'am – your husband's holding a seat for you down there . . .'

He pointed to Spring.

Though forbidden by law to strike a white man under any circumstances, January towered over the sailors (in the most respectful manner possible), and they lurched away down the aisle to address a couple of brass-haired white girls in over-colorful frocks. January hoped they'd make the men pay dearly for their attentions.

The woman murmured, 'Thank you,' and got nervously to her feet, her daughter clinging close. January was about to follow them down the car to where Spring had half-risen, when he noticed, two benches away, his own shabby tweed cap and frayed corduroy coatee, worn by a man who had clearly had boot polish on his face at some point in the recent past and had discovered its propensity for staining the skin.

The man met his eyes, startled; with a glance over his shoulder at the woman and her daughter, taking their places across from Byron Spring (who would, January guessed, soothe her fears in moments), he turned back and said, 'May I join you, sir?'

'Please!' The fugitive gave him a bright, sudden grin. 'You'll block the view of anyone in the aisle – and I must say, this blacking isn't at all convincing close-up. Would you like your hat back?'

'There's a gang of toughs on the platform,' said January, sitting beside him on the bench. 'And there will be, when we change trains at Utica.'

'Damn it. They'll have my description from Uncle Geogehan – the gentleman to whom I owe a hundred and fifty dollars. I wouldn't want to lead them to my friends in Syracuse. I never thanked you.' He held out his hand. January noted that he'd been careful with the blacking, and had left his palms pink. 'In fact, I *can* never thank you sufficiently. I know of at least two of Uncle Geogehan's – um – *clients*, who didn't survive the request for payment for his debts.'

January said, 'Keep the hat,' and clasped his hand.

'Thank you. I wouldn't want you to think me cowardly,' he went on. 'It isn't my way to welch on a debt, or to run from conflict. But—'

'You behold in me, sir,' responded January gravely, 'a man ready and willing to take to his heels whenever the situation calls for it. And I'm fairly certain that my circumstances have called for it oftener than yours.'

'Ah.' His new acquaintance thought about that for a moment, the broad baby face suddenly somber. 'Yes. I daresay. Smith,' he introduced himself, a patent lie. 'Lemuel Smith.'

As the train flew through the woodlands of the Mohawk Valley, Smith spoke of the seedier side of New York, of the commingling of poverty and money there, always present and now, with the whole of the Lakes country opened up to trade and profit by the Canal, increased tenfold. He was a ready and fluent talker, and January was hugely entertained by his conversation.

When he spoke of the theaters and dime museums along Broadway and the Bowery, it was with the knowledge of intimate familiarity, which prompted January to ask, 'You ever heard of the Shining Herald?'

'Lord, yes! Woman who talks to the dead?'

'And has them answer,' amended January.

'Ah, well, yes – as Hotspur says to Glendower, that's the trick, isn't it?'

'You think it's a trick?'

'Of course it is.' His companion sounded surprised. 'Given that this "Patriarch" of hers has gotten wealthy churchgoers to give him money for his "translation" of this new Gospel, or whatever it is, on the strength of her heavenly help . . . Easier than learning Babylonian, I daresay.'

'So you think it's about money.'

'Isn't everything?' The bright brown eyes sparkled for a moment. Then Smith seemed to hear his own words, and frowned, as if at himself. 'It is and it isn't,' he said at length. 'I don't know about this Shining Herald and what's his name—'

'The Reverend Broadax.'

'Hmn . . . If that's really his name. When I went to see their act – sorry, their *lecture* – she entered what looked to me like a perfectly genuine trance to "reveal" what she's been told by angels . . . and there are any number of people who can really put themselves into trances, or fall asleep at will, and preach in that state. They usually claim to have no knowledge of what they said. That's certainly not anything new. But I also know that trances are easy to fake – I daresay the Oracle of Delphi knew it, too. And does it matter?'

'That this woman is telling people made-up hogwash, and claiming it's the word of God?'

The man's thick eyebrows quirked. 'People want to believe, my friend,' he said. 'I don't know what she tells them, or where she thinks – or this Broadax thinks – it comes from, but I don't think it's doing anyone any harm. And if he's making up this "translation" of those ancient scrolls from Babylon or wherever they're supposed to have come from, might not at least some people gain spiritual comfort from their message? Or spiritual enlightenment?'

He turned his head for a moment, watching a woman guiding cows across a pasture still dotted with tree stumps, pausing to let her tiny daughter catch up with her.

'People not only want to believe,' he said quietly. 'They *need* to believe. If they believe that Uncle Fred is taking the trouble to speak to them from beyond the grave – to tell them that he remembers them and cares for them still – what harm is there in that? Well,' he added with a grin, 'as long as he doesn't come from beyond the grave to tell them to hand large quantities of money over to the Reverend Broadax—'

'Have you ever heard of that happening?'

The fugitive shook his head. 'Doesn't mean that it hasn't,' he added.

Smith dropped off the train as it slowed to enter the station at Utica – literally dropped off, going to the door of the dirt car with his satchel in hand, and springing down before they entered the station. As January and Spring escorted Mrs Pilsner and her daughter across the station to the street door past a loitering knot of unshaven, soap-locked toughs ('Knock-Out Nash's outfit,' whispered Spring. 'Kidnappers, I've seen them in New York . . .'), he understood Mr 'Smith's' precaution.

As they were hurrying back to the Utica and Syracuse platform to catch the next train, Spring glanced up at January and asked, 'You know who that was you were talking to?'

Damn it, Smith IS a slave catcher. Or a pimp. Or . . .

'That's the bastard you asked me about,' said

111

the preacher. 'The man who "leased" that poor old lady from her master in Pennsylvania, and exhibited her for twelve hours a day as George Washington's nursemaid.' His mouth curled as if he'd bitten rotten fruit. 'And charged fifty cents a head for people to watch her body being cut up, after she died.'

'Birnham?'

'Barnum.' Spring leaped up on to the end coach of the new train. It was less crowded than the Utica-Schenectady line had been, but by the smell of it, the straw on the floor hadn't been changed in weeks. 'P. Taylor Barnum. What was he doing on that train?'

'Fleeing from his creditors, it sounds like.'

Spring grunted. 'Serve him right.'

January nodded his agreement – but in fact, there were few men he would have turned over to the brutes he'd seen in the saloon doorway on Broadway. Just as the train was moving off, Smith – Barnum – sprang nimbly through the door, and took as inconspicuous a place as he could in a corner of the car. January settled on the bench beside Spring as the preacher opened his satchel and brought out a lunch of hard-boiled eggs, ginger beer, bread, and cheese, bland American fare that made January think wistfully of his nephew Gabriel's gumbo and jambalaya.

And of his own house to eat them in, and his beautiful Rose to share them with.

He turned his eyes to the variegated beauty of the woods and farmsteads, and, in time, dozed.

112

Ten

'Welcome, brother.' Serapis Broadax's hand, closing firmly around January's, was large, smooth, and white beneath a dusting of brown hair, like the leftover fabric from a beard that Moses would have envied. 'And thank you, Brother Spring, for bringing our friend here. For giving us the chance to prove again to the Lord that He has done right, in prospering our family here.'

'If the Lord still needs proof at this stage of the proceedings,' returned Spring, in his turn shaking the Patriarch's hand, 'He isn't paying attention.'

Broadax laughed, white teeth gleaming in the gray-shot chestnut ocean.

Getting off the train at Syracuse, Spring and January had lingered only long enough to observe Chloë – veiled to conceal the fact that she could no more counterfeit sickness than she could counterfeit sentimental attachment to small children – being assisted from the first-class car. She would, it had been agreed, establish herself at the Western Empire hotel on Washington Street, and pursue enquiries in town concerning newcomers to the Blessed Land; she had studied the daguerreotype of Eve Russell with interest. After a night spent at an establishment on Water Street which catered to bargemen and

113

'navigators' on the Canal's many enlargements and branch lines, the two men followed the road along the eastern shore of Lake Onondaga, making for the Blessed Land.

They walked for most of the morning, eight miles through marshes and meadows and the smoke that rose from the myriad of little factories where salt was extracted from the region's brine springs. In their impersonation of runaway slaves, they stayed off the road itself, skirting the village of Liverpool on the lake's shore. A peaceful country, reflected January, sufficiently isolated to make the comings and goings of fugitives inconspicuous. Beyond Liverpool, the road dwindled to barely a trace along the Seneca River, and beyond the trees through which they made their way, he glimpsed fields and pastures that spoke of prosperous land well-kept.

'We're on the Blessed Land itself now,' Spring had said as they walked along. 'As I said, it used to be over a dozen farms, along the river and westwards on the other side of the oxbow that the river makes yonder; good farming land, and more valuable now than ever, with the railroads going through as well as the Canal. Fruit picked in these orchards' – he'd gestured towards a small farmhouse, closed up and surrounded by cherry trees – 'can be in New York in two days. And the New York businessmen who belong to the Community can travel out here to hear the Herald's word, even when she doesn't go to the city itself.'

Not a possibility, January had reflected, open to a girl of seventeen, aghast to lose so quickly the only people who understood her search for truth.

The central Residence – as it was called – of the Blessed Land had come into view shortly after that, and January could see that, despite the addition of extra stories in places, of a large kitchen and gable roofs on some of its wings, it had definitely started its existence as a fort. Orchards surrounded it, fenced off both from the depredations of deer from the woods and from the immediate grounds of the house itself. Beyond, January had had an impression of a number of buildings which could have been stables, barns, and workshops. Around one side of the building, men had been unloading hay from a wagon.

'I should warn you,' Spring had added, 'not everyone in the Community knows about the Patriarch's dedication to helping runaways. There are half a dozen Colonizers in the group, and more than that, among his New York business supporters, who feel that Southern planters have a right to keep their so-called *property*. He'll probably ask you to stay in one of the stone cottages in the orchard, until it's dark enough to slip across to the Residence quietly.'

Studying the sprawling octopus of wings, ramifications, stumpy towers and minor courtyards around the Residence's central block, January had no doubt that the Patriarch could have marched a platoon of fugitives into the place through one door without anyone on the other side of the house being even aware of it.

It had been easy enough to get over the low fence which divided the orchard from the woods.

115

Spring had left January in one of the little two-story shelters and had gone on, through a gate in the higher westward wall, to the Residence itself. January had resigned himself to a long wait, but after only a few minutes he'd seen the gate open again, and Spring – and the Patriarch – return.

'We usually put "guests"' – the Reverend gave him a twinkle and a wink upon the word – 'in one of the rooms in the east wing, where I have my quarters. There's four or five of them, windowless cells tucked away in corners, Heaven only knows what they were originally used for. Nothing respectable, I fancy, but deucedly handy now.'

In his character as a fugitive, January replied, 'Believe me, sir, after sleepin' in a pig hutch in North Carolina an' a pigeon coop in Virginia, I'll take any nice, clean, dry, non-stinkin' windowless room you cares to put me in.'

Broadax laughed. 'Good man! We'll have to wait until nightfall to take you across to the Residence, as Brother Spring will have explained. Five of our families live in the west wings of the Residence, and some members of them – though devout in their quest for the true word of Heaven – still cling to some very outmoded definitions of the words "property" and "patriotism". They'll come around,' he added, like an indulgent father. 'But in the meantime, there's no sense in causing trouble by rubbing their noses in what some of the rest of us do here.'

January looked around him, at the single

116

room which comprised the entire lower floor of the cottage. Bunches of herbs and strings of apples hung drying from the rafters which supported the upper floor, draped in ghostly shrouds of cheesecloth. Wide shelves and bins of apples occupied most of the floor and wall space; other shelves contained sacks of meal and flour, barrels of cider and molasses. As they'd crossed through the rows of apple trees, he'd seen at least three other of these small, gray, stone outbuildings, the windows of their upper floors shuttered. *Cider press?* He'd wondered. *Laundry?*

At a guess, they'd started out as ammunition stores.

'Ain't that dangerous for you, sir?' he asked. 'These people come here to live a Christian life, won't they think it's wrong for you to be breakin' the law of the land?'

Broadax chuckled again, his smile slightly at odds with the piercing quality of those pale eyes. 'Well, fortunately for us all, those who come here have their own salvation in mind, to the exclusion of almost anything else. And while in ordinary circumstances I would of course not misuse the power this gives me' – he raised his bushy brows in self-deprecating amusement – 'I do find that in some matters, my authority can be most convenient.'

Spring laughed, and Broadax set on the table the pottery jug he'd brought from the house, and a split-oak basket which proved to contain part of a sausage pie, a small crock of butter, a number of hard-boiled eggs, and half a loaf of

117

fresh bread. The jug contained lemonade, heavily doctored with ginger and cinnamon. 'The one disadvantage of the original property here is that the springs are all a little salt. Nothing harmful, but it does explain how Mr Ott – the man who purchased this property from old Sempronius Teasle's estate – got the place so cheaply.'

The Patriarch blessed the meal, and while they ate together, January asked, 'This Mr Ott is one of your flock, sir?'

'One of the first to join,' affirmed Broadax. 'To the horror of his family, I might add. He left ample property in trust for his sons, but of course that isn't enough for them. Not a week goes by that one or the other of them isn't here pestering him about what he owes them.'

January, who could just imagine what his own mother would say if he were moved to bequeath the house on Rue Esplanade to the Church, inquired cautiously, 'You get much of that, sir? I mean, I'm thinkin' bout how my old master's mama would carry on if he'd left so much as two square feet of a wood lot to anybody but family—'

The Patriarch sighed, and patted January on the shoulder with one huge hand. 'I can well imagine how that lady will carry on about *your* decision to self-emancipate, my friend. Property is the curse of this nation.' He leaned back in his chair, to touch the rail of the stair which led up to the floor above. 'How much property – how much money – does any man really need? We do God's work here, and we live as God instructs us. Thirty

118

families so far have been moved to join with us, giving land and goods, as the early Christians did, for the welfare of all. With what result? We now conjointly own nine thousand acres, and every man knows that he and his family will have a home here, in perpetuity.

'And it's really so simple.' His blue eyes shone with the vision of his Blessed Land. 'Knowing that they have a home – that they will never be in want – there is no striving. Everyone here works, for the good of all. One reason it's taking me so long to translate the Babylonian text of the Gospel of James the Brother of Our Lord, is that much of the summer I've been out in the fields, getting the hay in. The Herald herself wields a hay rake. I wish you could hear her, when she raises her voice to lead the women in song.'

'An' do you live – well – like the Apostles lived, sir?'

'Some of us do. There is a Men's House, and the Women's House, over on the other side of the Residence, for those who seek to dedicate the whole of their energies to God's work. A House of the Children as well. But if anyone wishes to live in the old-fashioned way, with parents dominating their offspring like medieval kings, they are free to do so. And as I said, five families have quarters of their own in the Residence itself. I don't tell anyone how to arrange their private affairs.'

'I expect there's people all over the county,' said Spring, 'who'll call you a heathen and a blasphemer because you don't!'

The pale eyes sparkled. 'Well, the Ott boys certainly do,' he agreed wryly. 'And the family who thought they were going to get Ulee Wellman's farm when he dies. And a dozen others I could name. "All that will live godly in Christ Jesus shall suffer persecution", the Apostle says. And, "Blessed are ye, when men shall hate you, and when they shall separate you from their company, and shall reproach you, and cast out your name as evil . . ."' A kind of serene glee tinged the deep, melodious voice.

'But as with bigotry, and attachment to old bad ideas about who rules over who in the world and why, one day these grabby, greedy families will see how their brothers and fathers have been made pure, and happy, by the way we live here. Those families who have come here together, one day will see the light of truth, and will let go of possession of one another of their own accord. But that's the reason,' he added with another wink, 'that though I don't hide how we live here, I don't go rubbing our doctrines in the noses of the Tappan Brothers, for instance, or the American and Foreign Anti-Slavery Society, who have been . . . quite generous in their assistance.'

He turned back to January. 'I'll have someone bring you across to the Residence as soon as it's full dark,' he promised. 'It should be quite safe. Tonight is a Night of Revelation, when the Herald will proclaim to the whole of our community here – and indeed, to seekers who've come from Albany and even New York to hear her. In a few hours there'll be folk all over the Residence

120

and the grounds. No one will notice another person, more or less.' His smile widened. 'Even one as big as yourself.'

'Might I . . .' began January, diffidence in his voice. 'Would it be possible for me to listen to the Herald as well, sir? What Mr Spring has told me, and now hearing about her from you yourself, sir . . . Well, it's something I'd like to hear more of.'

The Patriarch considered for a moment, then nodded. 'I don't see why not. Mr Spring, would you care to join the Community for supper? I'm afraid, if you remain here, you can't be seen to be going back and forth from the orchard. Just in the interests of not calling attention to these cottages.'

So Spring remained with January in the cottage, until soft northern twilight turned the air to gray crystal, and the clank of bells beyond the orchard wall told of cows being brought in from pasture. In the dimming light, Spring studied the daguerreotype of Eve Russell again, as he had on the voyage up the Hudson. 'It'll be dark in the Great Parlor while the Herald is speaking,' he said. 'But in the dining room I'll have a chance to see peoples' faces.'

They were sitting on the doorstep of the cottage, which faced back towards the woods, eastward away from the Residence.

'Even if they lower the lights in this Great Parlor of theirs,' said January, 'I should get a look at most of them, if I can get into the room early enough. That still sounds like a hell of a risk to run, with families living in the same house.'

121

'You haven't been in the place.' Spring half-smiled. 'You could put five families in the two west wings – they make a sort of courtyard over on the far side – and I'd bet money that the children of those families couldn't find their way around the north or east wings without a piece of string. It's a labyrinth, and every room of it wallpapered in this appalling blue-and-gold pattern that makes you think you've got yourself trapped inside a Christmas package. Hiding runaways there isn't as dangerous as it sounds.'

As the sky lost its light, the two men walked through the orchard trees to the wall that bounded the Residence's immediate grounds, and looked between its palings – with their growth of pole beans and pea vines and tomatoes – at what could be seen of the sprawling building. Now and then someone would emerge from the big front doors, most wearing clothes made of what looked like a hard-wearing blue cotton broadcloth: January had noticed the Reverend Broadax's jacket and trousers had been made of it. Carriages and chaises were already beginning to enter the grounds, the teams led away by children, also dressed in blue. Lamps had begun to shine behind a number of the big house's many windows. Greetings and laughter sweetened the dusk.

January saw nobody who looked like Eve Russell.

'You don't think somebody else in this Community might have lied to her – lured her here – without the Reverend being aware of it, do you? Or that she lied to one of them,

122

and he or she hasn't yet told the Reverend about it?'

Spring considered this for a time. 'I doubt it,' he said at last. 'For one thing, where would they put her? All the Community – nearly two hundred souls – live either in the Residence itself or in the dormitories on its grounds. And at this time of year, none of them could have gone away for the weeks it would have taken to arrange for Miss Russell's disappearance, without being noticed. The Patriarch was in New York with the Shining Herald, but his secretary Mr Teems would have been here, as well as Mr and Mrs Greene, the couple that came out from New York with them. I think Greene had sold property in New York so that the Community could purchase the land immediately adjacent to Mr Ott's original donation. And why would anyone do such a thing in the first place?'

January shook his head. 'I don't know.'

The young preacher nodded, as if at the image that January carried in his pocket. 'I can't imagine what kind of lies she'd have told the Reverend – or Teems, or the Greenes, or any of them. She simply doesn't look like the type.'

'There was a woman in New Orleans six years ago,' returned January, 'named Delphine Lalaurie, who "didn't look like the type" either. She kept slaves tied up in her attic and tortured them.'

Unconsciously, he rubbed the shoulder that had been dislocated in the horror house of Madame Lalaurie's attic. 'I'm sure that woman in Delaware ten or fifteen years ago was perfectly

123

charming, too – the one who kidnapped free blacks as well as runaways, and who'd get the men of her gang to beat the captives so she could watch, because it "did her good". Or that German woman who was called the Angel of Bremen, because she took such devoted care of her parents, two husbands, a fiancé, her brother, her three children and I don't remember who-all else while she poisoned them with arsenic – apparently just for the pleasure of watching them die.'

Was that why, he wondered, that little dark spider of suspicion lingered in his mind, in spite of everything he had seen and heard in this quiet place?

Or was he simply so scarred, after eight years back in the United States – after his earliest years spent as a slave on a plantation run by a vicious drunkard – that he was sliding into hatred of all white men? He hoped he was not, but wondered if he'd be able to tell, to judge his own progress into darkness. Was this simply the soured bigotry that regarded all Protestants with suspicion, not to mention those who claimed to be translating lost books of the Bible . . .?

Men, women, children were now coming from all directions, some of them clothed in simple corduroys or cotton prints, others in that plain hard-wearing blue. Light streamed from the doors as they were opened, brightened across the sunburnt faces.

'Best you go across now, Spring, if you're going to get supper.'

124

As he watched his companion stride off toward the gate that faced the Residence, January tried to imagine what it would feel like, to live without fear. Since the days of his earliest memories, it was what he had always wanted. A home that nobody and nothing could take from him.

Every man knows that he and his family will have a home here in perpetuity.

A home in perpetuity. *It's really so simple . . .*

Like those old New England congregations of seventy years ago, he thought. Was that what they were really seeking, these Children of the Light? These others he had heard about, in congregations and communes that dotted this beautiful world: the world that their parents had grown up in? A world where things were orderly, and people trusted one another, and everyone knew who you were?

A world where people cared?

What *wouldn't* you give, in exchange for that?

Darkness closed in. The dull glow of oil lamps brightened more and more of the windows in the rambling old house. Light appeared, too, away to January's right, deeper into the orchard. Evidently at least one of the other cottages was used for something. He wondered what.

The scents of supper began to drift from the kitchen wing, which stretched to within a dozen yards of the orchard fence. Buggies continued to arrive, and through the chinks in the palings, January studied the faces of those who emerged from the front door to greet the newcomers.

Two riders drew rein before the door, dismounted

125

and pounded heavily on the panels. It was opened by a fair-haired, weedy-looking young man with a thin beard that did nothing to conceal his jawline. He exchanged words with the visitors, then went back inside, returning several minutes later with a barrel-chested, red-bearded man in a wine-red coat and old-fashioned breeches. It was too far to judge their faces, but against the lamps of the porch January saw how similar the old man was to the two younger arrivals. When a violent quarrel broke out between them he deduced that the older man may well have been that Jared Ott that Broadax had spoken of, whose sons objected to the disposal of his land.

In time, the tumult of fists shaken and hands raised to Heaven reached a point when the house doors opened again, and Byron Spring emerged, accompanied by a powerfully built man of almost January's height. Ott – if the old quarreler was Ott – turned on his heel and stormed back into the house, and his sons – if they were his sons – stalked down the steps and mounted their horses again, yelling maledictions at Spring and his companion.

Ignoring them, these two crossed the open ground toward the orchard gate. The taller man bore a lantern, whose bobbing yellow glow revealed a good-natured, gap-toothed face and, though his complexion was almost as light as a Spaniard's, features as African as January's own.

Spring introduced his companion as Hal Shamrock. 'He's the blacksmith in Liverpool,' he explained. 'He'll drive me back to Syracuse tonight, for me to catch the train in the morning.'

Shamrock shook January's hand with a black-smith's powerful grip. 'Pleased to meet you, Ben. And pleased to be of help.' His voice was a light tenor, at odds with his massive size. 'Brother Byron tells me you're going to stay a bit downstairs to listen to the Herald,' he went on. 'You won't regret it. Her words changed my life – her words, and the words she spoke to me from my angel mother, three years ago.'

'So it's true, then?' asked January. 'She does . . . The dead do speak through her?'

'Sometimes the dead,' returned Shamrock. 'Sometimes her Angel speaks – the angel Amorasa that led her to our Patriarch in a dream. But yes, I was sold away from my mama when I wasn't but three years old, back in Virginia. But she knew me. She came to me, when first I heard the Herald speak – my mother. I was a drunkard, and a thief, and a pimp. And my mother came to me across the Veil that separates us from the Summer Land, and called me to the light. I haven't had a drink since that day, and to the best of my ability, I've paid back every penny I ever stole.'

They stepped through the gate, and into the long grass of the open ground between the orchard trees and the house. Another carriage had drawn up, and children – clothed in the plain hard-wearing blue that had made up the Patriarch's garments – led the horses away to the other side of the house.

'Will her Angel speak tonight?'

127

Shamrock grinned. 'You can't ever tell. Sometimes she'll speak of what she sees of the Summer Land, what God inspires her to see – that's what I think the Reverend should write of, when he's done with the translation of the Gospel. Sometimes her Angel will speak through her, or the spirits that have passed before us into the Summer Land, like my mama. There,' he said, pausing in his tracks, and there was reverent delight in his voice. 'There she is!'

A woman appeared in the open door of the Residence, slender and almost girlish in her white frock. Just reaching the bottom of the shallow steps that led up to the porch, January observed the unlined prettiness of her face, the doe-like, dark-blue eyes, the delicate oval bone structure framed in braided loops of wheat-blonde hair. The man who hovered protectively at her side carried himself with the unmistakable, unplaceable reserve of a townsman, despite rather rough country tweed clothing. He too was fair, fairer than she, his baby-fine hair almost flaxen and his features delicate. The lamplight within the house flashed across the thick lenses of his spectacles, like the gleam of insect eyes.

'That's Mr Teems with her,' whispered Spring. 'The Reverend Broadax's secretary.'

Shamrock strode forward, to exchange a few words with them, and January took the opportunity to whisper, 'Did you see anyone at dinner, that could have been Mademoiselle Russell?'

Spring shook his head. 'But not everyone eats up here in the house, not even on Nights of Revelation. There they are,' he added, nodding towards other figures emerging from around the sides of the sprawling house. 'They'll be the ones who had their dinners in the Men's House and Women's House. But pretty much all the Blessed – as well as the visitors – will be in the Great Parlor. If we get there before they turn the lights down, we can have a look at everyone.'

He stepped back out of the way as a sleek dark-red brougham drew up before the doors. A footman hopped down from the back and ran to hold the horses' heads; another opened the door and let down the step, then held aloft one of the carriage lamps as he helped down an oldish man in a very smartly tailored black frock coat that no longer fit him. January had the impression, looking at that sunken face in its unkempt frame of gray hair, of a man for whom the world's sunlight has been snuffed out, leaving him in darkness. A man who has forgotten how to eat, or to care for himself, or to speak to his fellow humans.

January knew the look. He had seen it in the mirror, in the weeks following Ayasha's death.

Spring whispered, 'Good Lord! That's Jonas van Martock!'

And, when January didn't react to the name, he explained, 'He owns blocks of warehouses along the waterfront – one of the richest men in New York. He owns most of the stock in the Utica and Syracuse Railway line, and most of the land around Lispenard Street where David Ruggles lives. Probably owned the steamboat we came up-river on.'

As he said these last words Shamrock returned

to them, and with them, watched the old man escorted by his servants into the house.

'Men of all walks – yes, and women, too! – are called to the Light by the Herald's words,' said Shamrock. 'Rich and poor, white and black. The light shines on all equally. The feast of hope is spread for everyone who is willing to put aside his prejudices, and accept.'

Including a seventeen-year-old girl who had asked all her life why her friend had died? Asked why she couldn't attend school, and why men and women were enslaved, and what happened on Judgment Day, and had only been told, 'Heavens, child, to think of you asking such questions . . .'

Farmers' faces in the lamplight, rugged with sunburn and hard work. Townsmen like Mr Teems, smooth and pale and confident – like those businessmen, January reflected, who would journey two days from New York, to seek spiritual solace.

All of them looking for something. Hungry for a food they'd never tasted, whose name they didn't know.

Eleven

They passed through a vestibule papered in a florid pattern of blue and gold, down a corridor, and through another small, windowless chamber that seemed to serve no purpose but as a gathering point outside the Great Parlor, which itself was larger, January guessed, than the bottom floor of his house on Rue Esplanade. It was also papered in the same gaudy print, and contained, at one end, a piano, a daybed, and a podium, separated by several yards from the multitude of kitchen chairs which filled the remainder of the room.

Lamps burned on small tables around the sides of the seating area. One, with a pierced brass shade which flung a pattern of star-like spots of light, stood beside the daybed. The spindly, fair-haired young man January had seen in the doorway earlier was playing the piano – not very well, in January's opinion, and the instrument was out of tune. Three girls in white dresses stood around it, their voices lifted in the dense gloom of the big chamber with the sweetness of morning birds.

> Awake, our drowsy souls,
> And burst the slothful band;
> The wonders of this day
> Our noblest songs demand . . .

Old hymns, thought January, and comforting, to those living in this new, cold, noisy world. From their inconspicuous corner at the back of the parlor, January studied the faces again, though the light was scarcely better than it had been outside. In a curious way he was reminded of those he'd see in Congo Square back home, when the slaves gathered to dance the dances that spoke to them of an Africa that most had never seen.

131

To taste a world that they knew only from their parents' accounts of what it had been like.

But he saw no round, snub-nosed face framed in light-brown curls. No girl or woman short enough to be Eve Russell.

He saw the Reverend Broadax easily enough. Only Hal Shamrock, and he himself, were taller, and few of the other men were as tall. The Patriarch moved among his followers, shaking hands, greeting this man and that. 'That's Jared Ott,' whispered Spring, and January saw the man who'd been arguing on the porch with his sons. He seemed very short next to Broadax's great height, his red curls fading and what had once been a Cupid-bow mouth turned to granite with the griefs of life. 'The young gentleman at the piano is Dr Hayward. He and his parents, and his two younger sisters, live over in one of the west wings here. That gentleman in the gray frock coat is Matthias Vermeer, one of the wealthiest merchants in New York and one of the Anti-Slavery Society's most generous supporters . . .'

Broadax and the oleaginous Mr Teems both went to greet Mr van Martock – (*And why not?* thought January. *If he owns that much New York real estate, I expect everyone wants to be his friend . . .*) – and Broadax himself escorted the elderly gentleman to a chair centered in the front row. Teems went to the girls grouped around the piano, and at his signal, four others came through one of the room's half-dozen identical doors to join them.

Young Dr Hayward rose from the piano, and

as he and Jared Ott began to move around the big room, extinguishing the lamp flames, the girls began a second hymn, louder and more firmly.

> We will meet you in the morning,
> Where the shadows pass away;
> We will meet, we will meet,
> We will meet over there;
> We will meet you in the morning,
> Where all tears are wiped away . . .

As though the stronger music was a signal, the chatter in the room sank. People took their seats, leaning forward as if to better see across the wide gap between daybed and chairs. Broadax lit a single candle on the podium, turned down the lamp beside the daybed, leaving that end of the room in near darkness. Mr van Martock's two footmen, January noticed, were relegated to chairs at the back, just in front of where he, Shamrock, and Spring stood against the rear wall. The men looked around them with curiosity that had nothing in it of belief, and now and then put their heads together to whisper. This was just part of their job.

Two small doors – demi-portes, such things were called in New Orleans – pierced the wall behind the daybed, and even though that end of the room was now in darkness, January saw when one was opened. The candle on the podium had been so placed that its light touched the white folds of the Herald's simple dress, whispered on her golden hair. A schoolgirl's mouth, soft and a little uncertain, with a short upper lip and a tiny trace of an overbite. The doe-like eyes were downcast as if in shyness or fear.

The little choir of girls filed, still singing, away from the piano, to stand along the walls beside the first row of chairs. Broadax led the Herald to stand beside the daybed. The candle's glimmer framed him and his prophet in a topaz halo, as if they'd been preserved a thousand years before in amber, like some great horn-headed beetle and a gauze-winged moth.

The choir fell silent, and the Herald looked around her at her audience. Her dress, January noticed, though perfectly proper in its cut and wrought of white linen without ruffle or ornament, somehow gave the impression of a nightgown, or a shroud. A garment to veil vulnerability. Her slim hands were bare of rings, her throat, of necklace or pendant.

'Dearest friends, how glad I am to see you.' Her voice was a musical alto touched with a slightly countrified accent that added to the impression of her youth. 'Some of you have come so long a distance, and I'm filled with apprehension, in case this is one of the evenings when the Spirits don't come to me. In case I disappoint you. I never know, you see. I never know what I will see and hear, what visions will come. And if I see nothing, hear nothing . . . Please forgive me. This is not something I can control or command.'

Taking her hand, Broadax said – softly, but his bronze voice carried to the farthest corners of

134

the darkened room – 'You know they understand, ma'am.'

Her lips parted as if she would have said something else, but then she only turned to the audience again, with that shy smile. 'You all know,' she said, 'that the Spirit Amorasa has come on to me in this fashion since I was a little girl. When I was very little I didn't even know what they were. I'd see them, and I just thought they were other playmates, until my mother told me that the people I saw and spoke to weren't there at all. But they were.' Her voice sank low. 'They were.'

'It was this Herald,' said Broadax, 'who appeared to me in a dream, as I lay sleeping in my tent among the ruins of Jericho in the winter of 1836. She spoke to me by name, led me by the hand through a ruined palace, which I had never seen before, and showed me the place where, eight weeks later, I was to find the lost Gospel of James the Lesser, the stepbrother of Our Lord – the book that will change the shape of men's faith as we know it. The book that has revealed the incomparable truth of what this lady – this Herald of the Light – has known all her life.'

He leaned forward, his powerful hands gripping the edges of the podium.

'That the dead live. That only the thinnest of veils separates us not only from those souls, those spirits we have known and loved in this lifetime, on this earth, but from souls who lived other lifetimes, on other earths, other worlds, other times. And from those great,

135

shining Souls who have never been incarnate, the souls which men call Angels. Which in other times, other places, men called gods.'

He held the Herald's hand as she sat on the daybed, then, when she lay down full-length on the pale squabs, covered her to the waist with a dimly figured gray-and-white shawl. 'Seek, and ye shall find,' he quoted, and, taking a taper from the table, touched the flame to three little pots of incense that stood on the piano. '"Knock, and it shall be opened unto you: For every one that asketh receiveth; and he that seeketh, findeth."'

The virgin voices lifted again, in a hymn like a lullaby.

> Lead, kindly Light, amid th' encircling
>   gloom,
> Lead Thou me on;
> The night is dark, and I am far from
>   home,
> Lead Thou me on;
> Keep Thou my feet; I do not ask to see
> The distant scene; one step enough
>   for me . . .

Then silence, as if the big room were cut off from the world outside, where the Erie Canal and the railway lines stretched back to Albany and boats went down to Peck's Slip, and the Roach Guards beat debtors on the dung-smeared cobblestones of Broadway. Where grown men feared to go out on the streets alone in daylight, lest they never see their families again, because

136

of the color of their skins, and people paid fifty cents to see an old woman's body cut up in a saloon. Where young women of intelligence and questing souls were told by their mothers, 'What a question to be asking . . .!'

The scent of frankincense blessed the darkness like the wordless intimation of other worlds.

'I see light.' The Herald's voice, though quiet, easily carried to the farthest corners of the room. 'Trees, flowers – the souls of every flower, every tree, that has perished in winter since the dawning of the world. The souls of every bird and lamb. A land where the sky is only light. There were forty thousand angels, and of them, ten thousand hardened their hearts; Beelzebub and Lucifer, Abraxis and Kimaris, Ifrit and Focalor. They said unto themselves, "We cannot harm the Almighty, save by vexing the lives of those children that he loves. Let us go then and cover his beloved ones in darkness, and lead them astray, and chase them round and round so that they cry out and their cries torment His ears. Thus we will hurt Him, the way all things are hurt, through that which they most love . . ."'

She fell silent again, lying on her couch, her slim hands folded on her breast. One could have heard a needle drop into a china dish, so deep was the silence.

Is Eve Russell here after all? Maybe in that stone cottage in the orchard, where the lamplight burned? Would she avoid this gathering because of the chance that one of those New York businessmen who came to the Patriarch for spiritual

137

solace might recognize her? Might have been a fellow guest at Mrs Winterink's?

Or was he on the wrong trail entirely?

'Isaac.' The Herald moved her head on the cushions. 'Is Isaac here?' Standing at the back of the room, some fifty feet away, January's view of her was obscured, but with his great height he could get a good idea of what was taking place. 'Sarah is here,' she went on. 'Sarah . . .'

And a man somewhere in the midst of the room cried out, 'Sarah!' and sprang to his feet.

And as he did so, January saw – or thought he saw – that the air around the Herald's couch had become suffused with a filmy luminescence. He blinked, strained his eyes, wondering . . .

'Isaac,' she called again. Then her voice changed, deepened, and a trace of German accent flickered on its edges, 'Isaac, I am sorry. Sorry that we never spoke. Sorry that I never came . . .'

'It is nothing!' cried Isaac, his words cracking with tears. 'I was angry, you were right not to come! Are you all right, my beautiful one? Are you happy?'

'So happy,' the Herald whispered. 'Oh, so happy to see you again, to see you so well . . .'

January blinked again, wondering if his eyes deceived him, or if there was in fact a pale form standing behind the Herald's couch. A woman in a white robe, he thought, with long braids down the front of her bosom. She reached out one hand, and put the other to her throat. Isaac cried out again, 'Sarah . . .' and

138

for a moment it seemed that the woman took a step towards him.

Then she was gone.

'Sarah, I love you!' said Isaac. 'I will love you, forever, forever!'

But his voice cried out into darkness, and in the ensuing silence, for a time, only the suppressed choke of his sobs could be faintly heard.

The light – or maybe it wasn't really light – flickered around the Herald's couch, and in a light, small voice like a child's, she said, 'Grandpa? Grandpa, are you there? It's Bethunia.'

A man at the front of the room said, 'Oh, God . . .' and against the light January saw him jerk to his feet as if yanked upright by a rope. Stooped, sunken, the faint reflection of the podium oil lamp traced grizzled hair. 'My child! Oh, my child!'

'Grandpa, it's all right,' said the child's voice. 'Don't weep! I've missed you so. It's beautiful here,' she went on, against the broken sound of his tears. 'I'm so happy, except that I miss you. It's so good to see you! How is Pompey? Don't blame Pompey for what happened, it wasn't his fault—'

'No.' The old man struggled to control his voice. 'No, Pompey is well. We . . . we still have him.'

'I'm so glad! He couldn't help falling . . . Liquorice is here,' said the child. 'He keeps me company, and we play all day – Momma is here, too! Beautiful . . . beautiful . . .'

'She was always beautiful,' the grandfather whispered brokenly. 'Oh, God, oh, my child—'

For a moment January thought again that a dim shape almost coalesced behind the Herald's couch, before the light faded, and the gloom seemed all the more dense. January heard someone nearby whisper, 'God's truth . . .!' He glanced sideways, and could just make out the shadow of Byron Spring's head, and the way he raised his hand to his mouth in wonder and shock.

Then out of the darkness the Herald spoke hesitantly, and said, 'Malek? Is there one here . . . Malek?'

January felt himself turn cold all over.

He didn't speak, and a moment later the sleeping woman spoke again, in French this time, with the singsong accent of Africa. 'Malek, it is thy nightingale. You are in danger – beware.'

He bit hard on his lips, his heart pounding. She was dead, who had called him Malek: a thousand sleepy mornings when the little rooms in the Rue de L'Aube were freezing with the pre-dawn cold. When he'd hold her to him, their cats lying curled asleep by their feet, and he'd smell the scents candle wax, and frankincense in her hair.

To the bottom of his soul he felt it, and had no name for what he felt.

'I rejoice you are well,' she said, after silence. 'I rejoice you have love, and beautiful sons. But flee in the darkness. Know that they lie. They all lie.'

Darkness then, and stillness. After a time she spoke to someone else, a rough young voice, like a young man's, but January was shaking so

140

badly he didn't really hear anything that was said. Nor did he listen when the Shining Herald, the cloudy nimbus around her stronger now, spoke of the Summer Land again, and of how those who dwelt there lived like happy children, following God's simple rules. Once he looked sidelong again at Spring, but the young preacher was concentrating on the doctrines that the Angel Amorasa, now, was propounding to the Herald – listening to the gentle questions that the Patriarch was putting to the Angel, who answered through the Herald's lips.

He felt that everyone in the room could hear the hammering of his heart.

She was here. No one in the world called him – or had ever called him – Malek, save she.

She was here.

Then it was over. The choir sang again; Jared Ott and young Dr Hayward edged around the room, turning up the lamps. When January moved toward the nearest door – everyone else was paying too much attention to the Patriarch and the Herald to notice – Hal Shamrock moved quickly to join him, and Spring, following on their heels, asked, 'You all right, Benjamin?'

'I didn't—' he began.

They all lie. Beware.

Concerned faces, as they stepped with him into the hall.

'Were those . . . How does she . . .?'

'I felt that way,' said Hal Shamrock, 'first time I heard the Herald speak. I was a drunkard and a sinner, but I had to go back. To hear her again. Then she spoke . . . My mama spoke to me through her lips. Told me to change my ways. Told me that beautiful things waited for me, that I could be a servant of the Light, if only I'd give up the drink, and turn my back on the darkness. She saved my life. The Herald . . . and my angel mama, there in the Summer Land.

'Byron' – he turned back to the young preacher – 'they'll save Ben's life as well. Tomorrow night, or the next, you'll be on the road to Canada, Ben.' He put a hand on January's shoulder. 'Can you write?'

January had recovered just enough self-possession to shake his head. 'But I'll find someone to write for me,' he promised, looking down at Spring. 'Let you know I'm well.'

'Five or six of those who've passed through here have done that,' said Spring.

'I wish you would, Ben,' agreed Shamrock. 'The abolitionist societies put store by those letters. 'Course, you can't tell where you are, or how exactly you got across, because they'll sometimes publish those letters. But it helps. Shows others the light.'

Around them, people were talking as they moved away through the several doors that led out of the Great Parlor. The door they passed through, going out, wasn't the same one they'd come in by, but the wide hallway beyond was papered in that florid blue and gold, as the windowless vestibule had been, so it was difficult to tell. The shiny pattern seemed to gleam in the light of the too-few lamps, as men and women moved past them, seeking the outer doors.

142

January shook hands with Spring, and bade him a warm farewell, thanking him as if the preacher were going to be returning to New York. In fact, Spring would be at a farm near the town of Auburn, some twelve miles to the west along the Canal and the current terminus of the railway line. 'I hate to lie,' he had said to January, last night in that seedy Syracuse lodging house. 'But I understand why you want to keep it quiet, and see things for yourself. If the Reverend Broadax does find out I lied about where I was going, I can tell him I got a message from my friend – Ammi Seabright – when I got back to Syracuse.'

More than ever, now, January appreciated his willingness to stay at least reasonably close to the Blessed Land while January pursued his investigations.

They lie. They all lie . . .

But why tell me so?

He wondered how easy it would be to slip out of that 'little windowless cell' in the dead of night tonight, to have a look around.

Can I get out of the house to take a closer look at that cottage in the orchard . . .?

He followed Hal Shamrock's bobbing oil lamp through a door, up a narrow back stair. Down a corridor (still papered in blue and gold) and across a windowless chamber which seemed to have been partitioned off a larger room. The noise of chatter died utterly behind them; this part of the house was silent as a tomb. Thick carpet muffled their steps . . . How much did *that* cost?

143

Something of the incongruity of carpeting the upstairs prickled his nape a little. Or was that just because children lived in the house, albeit in the opposite wings?

You are in danger. Beware.

They passed through another windowless hallway, which smelled of must and incense.

Something was wrong here. Olympe would say, *Something about this doesn't listen right . . .*

But he couldn't put his finger on exactly what.

'Here.' Shamrock opened a door, stepped aside, and let January pass before him into the small chamber beyond. The aromatic scent of peppers and spices filled the cramped space, from the covered dish on the table. 'Goodness knows what Old Man Teasle hid up here – guns, everybody in the county says, to sell to the Iroquois once the war was over.' He set the lamp on the table, which held a covered pitcher as well. A tin cup, a knife and spoon. A narrow bed along one wall, covered with a light counterpane, though the room was stuffy and, being at the center of the house, uncomfortably warm. A screen concealed a chamber pot and a couple of pegs for clothes.

Like the hallways, the little room was thickly carpeted, and eerily silent. Two or three layers of rugs. Was that because, as Broadax had said, not everyone who dwelt in the Blessed Land was entirely in favor of robbing those poor slave holders of their bought-and-paid-for property?

Maybe. Maybe.

In a house this old, floors would creak. Footfalls would echo. January had completely lost his bearings, and for all he knew the room could be

144

above chambers inhabited by one of those families who chose to live in the Residence.

'With luck I'll see you again tomorrow.' Shamrock clasped January's hand again. 'But the Patriarch told me downstairs that one of his conductors is here tonight. He said he'd speak to him, and may be able to sneak you out of here and get you on your way before sun-up.'

He spoke with enthusiasm, and January made himself look eager and interested, though inwardly he grimaced. *Will I have to sneak back here clear from Oswego on the lake shore, and spy in the woods, to get a look at everybody in the place? Or, God help me, from Canada?*

'That would be wonderful!' He tightened his grip on his host's hand and arm. 'I tell you, Mr Shamrock, I haven't had a minute's rest, since I ran from the home place, fearin' they're on my trail. Fearin' what would happen if somebody saw me . . . You know I ain't easy to miss!'

Shamrock laughed. 'Back in my thievin' days I was always in a sweat, 'cause I was so tall. I was near six feet, 'fore I turned fifteen – I was lucky I wasn't catched and hanged!'

'They call you "Gog"?' asked January with a grin, remembering the boys who would taunt him at the St. Louis Academy – as much for his ebony blackness, and his country ways, as for his massive height.

'No, but they was always singin' *Fi, Fi, Fo, Fum* when I'd come down the street. You'll sleep good tonight,' the blacksmith promised. 'You're safe here, to close your eyes.'

'I'm lookin' forward to it.'

'You keep that door locked.' Shamrock produced a key and inserted it on the inside. 'If I, or the reverend, or Mr Teems, needs to come in, we'll knock three times, like this: one . . . one-two. Otherwise, you stay silent as a mouse til morning. There's supper here for you, an' lemonade . . .'

'Bless you,' January said. 'And thank the reverend, with all my heart. I know what a dangerous thing it is for him, to hide me like this. To put me on my way.'

'Like the Patriarch says,' returned Shamrock, 'how else we gonna thank the Lord, for all the blessins He's piled high before our feet?'

And as he turned, and opened the door to leave, a soft puff of air from the empty chamber next door whiffled into the hidden room. And just for an instant, as Hal Shamrock slipped through the door and away, January smelled, on his clothing, the rancid pong of stale wine.

Twelve

There was no mistaking it. January had lived long enough in France – and played piano at enough white folks' parties in New Orleans – to be a judge of that odor. He could tell the smell of red wine from white, sherry from Burgundy . . .

And he knew with dreary familiarity that stale reek that told of a man who'd been drinking.

146

He stood for a time beside the door after he locked it, and heard the door at the other end of the empty antechamber close behind Shamrock . . .

Men did, of course, backslide from vows of temperance – and lie about having done so, particularly in the house of a Patriarch whose teachings they claimed had saved them.

Slowly he took off Mr Barnum's swallow-tailed blue coat and hung it on one of the clothes pegs, hung the plug hat on another, and took off his boots.

But in his experience, men who backslid from being severe drunkards seldom backslid to wine – and to the very moderate quantity of wine implied by the faintness of the scent that had clung to Shamrock's clothing. Hannibal Sefton had described the effects of a drink on him – back in his drinking days: *It's like falling down a well. The first sip, and I completely forgot every time I'd wakened in the gutters of Rue Bourbon in a puddle of my own vomit, or the times I opened my eyes in bed with some woman I didn't even remember meeting. I'd have one glass of anything, and spend the rest of the night hunting for more . . .*

Others whom January had met, had said the same.

Not all men are like this, Hannibal had said. *Thank God. Otherwise humankind would have perished from the earth long ago . . . carved to pieces by their exasperated wives, I daresay. But once a man starts down this path it is very, very hard to turn his steps back. And well-nigh impossible, if some friendly soul persists in thinking that he can drink occasionally, like other men.*

The reflection that Shamrock had lied wouldn't have bothered him, January thought, if he'd met him in New York or New Orleans or on the steamboat. *Just another man who wants me to think well of him. Who wants me to come to the Light.*

The lamp flickered. As he adjusted the wick, January saw that the reservoir contained almost no oil, barely enough for another ten minutes. An understandable precaution, he thought, given – like the carpets – that some in the house might ask questions, or speak of their doubts to plausible strangers they met in Syracuse . . .

Still . . .

It was one thing too many. It was what he'd do, if he wanted someone to fall asleep.

He uncovered the lemonade ewer, took the tin dome from the bowl. Used as he had been, for the past eight years, to the rich flavors of gumbo and andouille, to the savor of garlic and cayenne and the hot chilies of Mexico, he had found the rations which Spring had brought along on the steamboat and railroad – not to speak of what had been served up in the cheap lodgings in Albany and Syracuse – insipid, something he had put up with because there was no alternative. As a slave child on Bellefleur Plantation, he had endured worse.

This was heavenly.

The house of the Patriarch must have someone in their kitchen inspired by the gods.

148

And that, he thought, was also a little odd.

He sniffed the lemonade. In that stone cottage in the orchard – whose upper story had been locked – he had found the drink cloying, stronger than anything he'd encountered even in New Orleans. It was laden not only with lemons and sugar, mint and lime, but with cinnamon, cloves, ginger. Now – offered it again – he thought that this time, there were other scents in it as well.

They lie.

You are in danger.

Did the garlic and cayenne, the cinnamon and ginger, mask another taste? Perhaps the odd, flowery bitterness of opium?

He crossed to the door, turned the key, and, very gently, pushed on the panels.

The door was bolted on the outside.

He felt as a cat does, when its back arches like the Midgard Serpent at something invisible to human eyes.

The lamp flickered again. *Oil nearly gone.*

What the hell is going on?

Is the Patriarch working for slave catchers? The thought was absurd. It wasn't something that could be hidden, not for long. *He's getting money from some of the wealthiest abolitionists in New York and New England, he can't risk even a rumor getting out.*

What, then?

Figure that out later. Whatever is happening, you probably have very little time to get out of here.

He took the lamp, and in the few minutes left of light, examined the walls of the room, and the floor. Above the line of the panels, on a sort of carved dado around three sides of the little chamber, there was a curtain rod: he had to stand on the bed to get a look at it. The carpets, when he crouched, bore the dents of heavy furniture. What looked like a bed or a divan where the narrow truckle bed stood; something that could have been a console or a table along one wall. The free-standing prints of a small table or ottoman. More noticeably, when he knelt to look – the light dimming fast as the last of the oil was drawn from the wick – he smelled, in the carpet, the in-ground sweetness of incense.

Incense? In a hidden room, up here?

Pressed deep into the thick pile he found a seed pearl – which proved to be glass, when he rubbed it against his teeth – and two gold sequins . . .

And in the shadows half-beneath the truckle bed, a slip of paper, a scribbled and much-folded receipt. The clerk's handwriting was illegible in the flickering of the dying lamp, and the letterhead type was small and blurred, but as the lamp went out January distinguished at least that it was from New York.

He crammed the paper in his pocket, hands shaking with tension and shock. He set the lamp down beside the bed, groped his way to the screen, and found his boots. Putting them on, he drew the knife from the right one, then groped back to the bed. He was both hungry and thirsty now, but guessed what was in the food and lemonade.

150

But *why*? What the hell would they want with a black man, if not to sell?

The thought danced absurdly through his head. *Are they building up their reputation as abolitionists, to glean donations from the Tappan brothers and the British Anti-Slavery Society and then selling their 'cargoes'?*

They'd never get away with it. Word would leak out.

And what did any of this have to do with Eve Russell – if anything?

New York . . .

The Patriarch has only had this place for a year, he reminded himself. *Does he plan to decamp at the first whisper of trouble? With all the donation money?*

That would actually, he estimated, be a fairly considerable sum.

All the more reason for them NOT to help Mamzelle Russell come here.

A thought that turned his flesh cold settled like a ghost on the end of the bed, close enough for him to feel its terrible presence, as the darkness lengthened and the silence of the hidden room pressed down around him.

But why would the Herald warn me?

And HOW would she KNOW to warn me?

No, he thought. *No.*

Ayasha had called him Malek. No one else, ever, in his life. It meant Angel, or King.

Hungry as he was, thirsty as he was, in the hot summer stuffiness of the windowless chamber it was hard to keep awake, but he sensed that his life depended, now, on hair-trigger readiness. He dared not even – as he often did, when obliged to wait somewhere with nothing to occupy his attention – mentally play every sonata he knew, or work his way through Dante's *Inferno*, canto by canto, or see how much he could remember of *Hamlet* or the *Marriage of Figaro*. Only silence. Only darkness.

Only those two shades: Ayasha's, and what he thought might actually be going on here.

Sound. Very light. A slurring across that thick carpet. Nowhere near the door.

One of the wall panels slides.

In a smuggler's house, it would . . .

Feet whispered. January sat still.

When a hand touched his arm he mumbled, 'Who dere?' and groped feebly about with his left hand – his right ready, gripping the knife. *If I attack now I'm still locked in this room . . .*

'A friend.' The voice was pitched very low, but there was no mistaking Broadax's velvet bass. 'You come along with me, Ben. It's time to go.'

'Gonna go – that feller with the boat?'

'That feller with the boat, yes.'

January staggered as he got to his feet, and the Patriarch's big hand firmly gripped his arm. There was no mistaking his size or strength, even in darkness. He mumbled incoherently, 'Izzit tomorrow?' and the reply was soothing, gentle – and absolutely unsurprised.

He expected me to be intoxicated.

'It's tomorrow, yes.' January smelled a trace of liquor on the man's breath. 'This way . . .

That's right . . .' He was steered to what felt like a very narrow doorway, and Broadax put a hand on his head, to stoop him through. 'There's a ladder here. Go down carefully, I'm right behind you—'

Heart hammering – he'd be utterly vulnerable in the first second when he reached the bottom (*Would they REALLY kill me in what has to be smack-dab the middle of the house?*) – January obeyed, the wooden rails creaking slightly with the weight of the man descending above him.

His mind raced.

Of course he's never had anything proven on him, of course he's never been caught with runaways, of course they just disappear no matter how many slave catchers are watching the river and the lake. What does he do with the bodies?

And the next second, *That's insane. YOU'RE insane. Your hatred – your rage – at the slave catchers is turning your brain . . .*

His foot jarred on planks and he stepped back at once, away from the ladder. No one grabbed him. He smelled hot brass and the fishy reek of whale oil. *He's got a lamp down here, covered.* January slipped the knife up his sleeve, keeping hold of the hilt. He heard the rustle of Broadax's clothing at the ladder's foot, felt the man brush past him. Then the dimmest whisper of dull-orange light suffused the darkness. Too little, he reflected, for a man whose pupils were contracted with opiates to make out anything. He turned his face away, leaned heavily against the wall – damp earth propped with old half-rotted timbers. Through chinks in the planks underfoot the light glinted on water. In the marshy soil near the river, without planks on the floor the tunnel would be ankle-deep.

He groped about a little with his left hand, as if unable to clearly see, and the Patriarch took his arm. 'This way, my friend.' January didn't dare look him in the face for fear his own features would reflect not only his sobriety, but his rage. But from the set of the man's shoulders, the movement of his body, he could read nothing but the businesslike grimness of a farmer who goes out to cut the throat of a hog at first frost.

Like the slave catchers themselves, he thought. Men who considered destroying a man's life – and the lives of his children and family – all part of a day's work. Worth nothing, when put up against their own desire for the money that man's enslavement would bring.

He'll use a knife. He can't fire a gun unless every single person in the Community is in league with him . . .

At the moment, scalded by bitterness and disgust as well as keyed-up terror, he was only a step from believing that as well.

The tunnel, perhaps two hundred yards long, widened out twice, spaces clearly intended for the storage of barrels or crates. The first of these was empty. The second, not far from a makeshift door nearly invisible in the gloom, was larger, and held a table and a bench. 'Sit for a minute,' said Broadax, steering January to the bench. He set the lamp down, took a step back from it (*He's*

154

getting his knife . . .); 'I have to see if Simmons is out there waiting.'

The lamplight just reached the wall of the niche. There was a little pile of shoes in the corner, 'slave shoes' such as were manufactured cheap in Massachusetts for sale – through New York – to plantation owners from the Potomac to the Rio Grande. His glimpse was only for a moment, in the instant that he saw Broadax move, drawing his knife and reaching for January's shoulder in the same smooth, practiced action.

January bent, spun, and heaved the bench at him like a battering ram, then slapped the lamp from the table. In blackness he flung himself down the tunnel, crashed into the door at the end. The handle didn't respond – it was bolted, and he didn't have the time to grope for the bolt. He aimed a flat-footed kick just below where the handle was, and the door – old and half decayed like the supports that propped the tunnel's walls – gave way with a splintery rasp.

An enclosed space beyond, with boxes in it – January tripped over one – pitch-dark. *He's heard me break the door he'll be here in seconds, lamp or no lamp . . .*

How many of them are in this?

His outstretched hand encountered a wooden wall and he groped along it for less than six feet before he found a door. *Hinges, handle . . .*

Another kick with the whole force of his body, and he was outside, blundering in a tangle of leaves and branches that ripped his face and clutched his clothing. Pitch-dark – the moon was westering but he was in a forest in the fullness

155

of summer leaf. He stumbled on a deadfall, blundered into a tree, nearly breaking his nose. Groped, staggering, wanting only to put as much distance between himself and the shed (*it has to be a shed*) as he possibly could.

He stumbled again over rocks, fell into water with a splash. Pond? Stream? *Stream . . .*

He fell twice more before the running trickle brought him clear of the trees, to the river's bank, and moonlight at last.

Right is upstream. Upstream – eventually – was the lake, and at the lake's far end, Syracuse. He hadn't heard any sound of a dog pack in his afternoon in the orchard cottage, but he nevertheless waded along the shore as far as he could, knowing the water would eradicate his tracks. As soon as dawn brightened enough – as Ayasha used to say – to tell a black thread from a white one, he went ashore, and moved inland into the woods.

He knows I saw him. He knows I wasn't stupefied.

He'll send men, and the river and the lake are the first places they'll search. With luck, he'll think I'm heading downstream, for Oswego, Lake Ontario, and Canada.

But he'll also try to cut me off between here and Syracuse.

God knows what he'll tell them I've done.

So he took bearings on trees, rocks, a snake-rail fence – as he had used to navigate the stagnant bayous in the bottomlands of Bellefleur Plantation as a child, when he and his sister Olympe would hide from their chores in the *ciprière*. From its ribbon around his neck he drew the silver compass that Rose had lent him, to keep from moving in a circle. These woods of beeches and oak, so different from the dark swampy forests of his childhood, were just as thick, and once away from the river it was impossible to judge his way in the iron twilight. The rail fence, and the marks where branches had been lopped – or entire trees cut – told him that this area was inhabited. He was almost certainly still within the nine thousand acres of the Blessed Land.

How long would he have to travel, to get himself out of it?

In the end he took refuge in one of the thickets of witch hazel, that clumped where the land was marshy. He had drunk from the stream before abandoning it, but had nothing in which to carry water; nothing in which to carry food, even had last night's supper not been drugged.

And now what? Try to make it back to Chloë at the Western Empire hotel in Syracuse? He recalled the slave catchers he'd seen on the railway platform, and shivered. They knew that any runaway in the county would have to pass through Syracuse, to reach the border. They'd be watching.

Broadax HAS to catch me. He can't afford exposure. He'll enlist their help, as well as the help of every man in the Children of the Light.

And any judge in the state would take the white man's word over his.

Go deeper in-country, to Auburn, and find Spring? The Children of the Light at least wouldn't be searching in that direction. As a black man

157

– preacher or not – Spring's word would have less influence with the law, and any accusation from Broadax would stick. January had not the slightest doubt that the moment the Patriarch regained his breath and got to his feet, he'd had the last evidence of his victims cleared out of the tunnel.

Would there be enough left of the fugitives' bodies – which had almost certainly been dumped in the river, weighted with stones or with their bellies slit so as not to swell up and float – to prove a word of what January said?

He whispered, 'Damn it.'

And what about the pearl? The sequins? The smell of incense?

He dug in his pocket, pulled out the slip of paper and studied it in the rising light. The clerk's handwriting was still illegible, but he was at least able to make out the date: Monday, the eighth of June. The day Eve Russell had disappeared. And words that could have been King's something-or-other . . . *King's Point*?

And the letterhead, at least, was readable now. It was a travel receipt for a steam packet company in New York.

Thirteen

January saw the first searchers shortly after sunrise. *That was quick. I wonder what Broadax told them I'd done?*

Lying flat among the ferns, he peered over a

158

deadfall log and saw them, Jared Ott and two other men, all armed with shotguns.

You are in danger, she had said.

And, *Malek* . . .

Something twisted inside him, though in the growing light of the morning he knew it had to be a trick, a dodge of some kind. Yet if they knew that about him – if they knew *that much* about him, to use such a trick – what else did they know?

And *how* did they know it?

They passed, but he lay for a long time in his thicket, listening as the sound of their passage faded. Whatever Broadax had told them, it had probably included the words, *Shoot him on sight.*

Mamzelle Russell is there. Or WAS there . . . Remembering that little jumble of shoes in the tunnel, he knew with deadly certainty what a man like Broadax would do if word got to him that the sheriff was on the way.

Byron Spring had given him a rough map of Onondaga County, but it only told him that Auburn lay about seventeen miles west of Syracuse, on the railway line, not anything about the country in between. He dared not follow the line itself, or the Canal. But swinging south of the line, to come to Auburn through wooded country, he might easily miss the little town.

How many men in the Blessed Land *were* in on Serapis Broadax's scheme to get money out of abolitionist donors?

Or did the Patriarch's followers simply obey his every word, unquestioning?

If thirty of them signed their farms over to his

159

Community of the faithful, reflected January bitterly, *they probably WILL obey his every word . . .*

He began to have a certain amount of sympathy for Ananias, who had held out on handing everything he owned over to St. Peter (and had been struck dead for his pains). How *did* you tell the difference between a holy man and a charlatan?

Well, presumably St. Peter was wearing a halo . . .

But he saw again the light that had glowed around the Herald, as she lay on her divan. Eyes closed, speaking to him with Ayasha's words . . .

Why would she tell me I was in danger?

He debated moving his hiding place, but before he came to any conclusion, he heard more voices, and the swishing scrunch of men striding through the undergrowth. One said, '. . . should get the Herald to ask the Spirit Amorasa to find him . . .'

Another voice, lighter and with the accent of New England, replied, 'They did. She laid there in a trance for an hour, tears runnin' down her face, but not a word did she say. Wakin', she remembered none of it, an' couldn't say why she wept.'

'Well,' retorted the first man, 'then they should get ol' Del Pearce to look.'

'That heathen heretic—'

'Pearce used to be the best treasure scryer in six counties. Why, I remember he used to find Spanish treasure buried under the ground, right over in Camillus, it was. He'd put that peep stone of his into his hat, an' clap his hat over his face, an' see that treasure, right through the earth.'

'No heathen,' declaimed the New England man – January could see them, now, a big man and a small one, both roughly dressed with jackets of that same uniform blue, shaggily bearded and both carrying shotguns – 'is capable of scryin' treasure. Scryin' treasure is a gift from the Lord, an' the Lord doesn't go passin' out blessins like that to men who deny His prophets an' turn their backs on His Herald.'

'Well, he does.' The small man scratched under his shirt in a businesslike fashion. 'My great-uncle Marcellus could scry treasure in the earth no matter how deep 'twas buried, an' he was the one walked straight into the New Light church in Skaneateles an' said there weren't no God in Heaven nor no Devil in Hell—'

'Hell, those New Light folks aren't Christians! You could say anythin' about 'em an' God wouldn't care.'

'What I'm sayin',' insisted Shorty firmly, 'is that Marcellus was a heathen right down to his toenails, an' he could find treasure buried in the earth, lookin' in a peep stone, or in a mirror – I once saw him summon the image of a chest of pirate gold buried under Oswego Hill, by puttin' a fragment of my grandma's broken mirror in the bottom of his hat. An' we'd have had that treasure, too, 'cause it had worked its way right up out of the ground, an' was just a-settin' there, 'til it saw us comin'. 'Course, it looked like a rock, but Issachar Grote, who was there, he could tell 'twas real treasure. He saw it in a vision.

161

But there was evil spirits in it, that made it sink back into the ground, 'fore we could reach the place. After that Uncle Marcellus drew magic circles, an' made spells, an' even sacrificed one of Lu Sparger's chickens to the demons what had hid it, an' never could get it to come back up. An' it'd sink right away from our shovels, no matter how much Grandpa an' them others dug for it . . .'

'An' that,' retorted the bigger man triumphantly, 'was 'cause Marcellus Bradley was a heathen, even if he did show up those New Light folks. An' Del Pearce is another.'

'You can't tell me Pearce can't dowse water . . .' The men began to move off.

'Water-dowsin' got nuthin' to do with God,' explained his companion patiently. 'It's all in just findin' the right willow branch. Or the right peep stone, if that's how you're doin' it. My grandma could dowse by danglin' a peep stone from a string . . .'

January wondered who he could ask what a peep stone was.

If all they were doing to find him was drop pieces of grandma's mirror into the bottom of a hat, he supposed he'd be safe enough, once twilight came, to make his way to Auburn. If he went south . . . He looked again at his map. If he swung south-west through the crossroads town of Skaneateles, then west to Auburn, he might well outdistance his pursuers, who would be watching for him on the approaches to Syracuse.

But what he needed first was food.

The hard-boiled eggs and sausage he'd had the afternoon before had been a long time ago, and he could feel exhaustion creeping into his limbs. This was not the time, he thought, to lose his alertness.

It was too early in the year for nuts. The woods all around him were dotted with the bright green leaves and tempting purple-black clusters of elderberries, but his one childhood experience with eating uncooked elderberries had taught him a lesson still unforgotten at age forty-seven.

So as he traveled south-west he kept an eye out for blackberries – he was so hungry by this time he didn't care about the scratching he got from the canes of the thicket – and once found, to his surprised gratitude, the nest of a chicken who was 'laying out' and had three eggs. 'Sorry, Biddy,' he said, as he cracked off the tops of the shells one by one. 'I'll burn a candle to St. Francis for you when I get home.' The hen only regarded him beadily from the branch of an oak tree, too stupid to care whether he devoured her offspring or not.

He heard more searchers shortly after that, ahead of him, and retreated to a spring he'd crossed some time earlier, where two deadfall trees had run up against some boulders near the stream-bed, making a shelter beneath. He emerged after an hour, but not long afterwards heard other hunters, and had to backtrack again. He was not, in fact, entirely certain that these were Children of the Light. They could have been slave catchers, and it was almost twilight

163

before he moved on. He now suspected he was much farther south than he should be, and veered westward, obliged to make another detour when he saw the lights of a farmhouse through the trees. The temptation was strong to approach it and investigate – if, like the Children of the Light, the farmer stored his apples in an outbuilding it would be a gift from the Heavens. But they could just as easily have been something like mangle-wurzels, and January's every instinct told him to avoid people until he reached an actual town . . . And then, to be careful.

'Lead, kindly Light,' they had sung at the House of the Patriarch.

> Lead, kindly Light, amid th' encircling gloom,
> Lead Thou me on;
> The night is dark, and I am far from home . . .

With darkness coming he went to ground, making a rough shelter for himself against a bank of stacked logs cut by some farmer (*The fellow in the lighted house?*) in what looked like a half-cleared field. With his knife he cut more boughs from the surrounding trees to form a bed, reminding himself that he'd have to take pains to scatter them in the morning, lest searchers pick up his trail from there. Then he lay watching the last of the green daylight fade from beneath the leaves, listening to the birds settle in for the night, and the croak of frogs in some marshy pond not far away.

I have to get food tomorrow. I can't be THAT far from Auburn . . .

Ammi Seabright was a Quaker, Spring had said, and had also helped fugitives across the border to Canada. *Not in Auburn . . . 'near' it, whatever 'near' means . . .*

The croaking of the frogs was comforting, like the friends of his childhood in the bayous, speaking to him out of the darkness. Deep burps, and little silver tapping . . . As a child he had given them names.

I will definitely have to ask Ammi Seabright what a peep stone is and how one uses it to find buried Spanish treasure . . .

What the hell were the Spanish doing in upstate New York anyway?

He was waked by the baying of dogs.

No one who had ever been a slave truly liked dogs. Not the big dogs, the hunting packs that county sheriffs would hire to track down runaways. January dreamed of them, just before waking – dreamed of being hunted as a child, and, later, as a man, when he'd sojourned for a time in Mississippi: remorseless, untiring, and unhuman. A neighbor of his old master's had bred and trained a pack, feeding them only when they'd caught prey, teaching them the difference between the smell of a slave's old sweat-imbued garments and a well-fed white man's cleaner linen. Every field hand in Orleans Parish had hated those animals, and even January – knowing as a man that the dogs only did as they'd been taught to do, like men

165

– still wished every one of them, by name, in Hell.

In his dream they were as they'd been to his five-year-old eyes, the one time he'd been late coming back from the *ciprière* and Michie Fourchet had had Old Tranch call out his pack. In his dream they were black and huge, with fire pouring from their eyes and mouths like the spectral hounds of English legend, rangy running shapes of muscle and malice. He remembered, too, his master and Old Tranch howling with laughter as they'd watched him run, sobbing, chest bursting for breath, across the pasture with the pack at his heels.

His eyes jerked open.

The baying didn't cease.

They were close, by the sound. January didn't pause to look behind him or break down his shelter of boughs. He ran, scrambled up the nearest oak tree, picked his way along a branch. There was another tree, an elm, close enough to jump to – moreover, he could see what last night's darkness had hidden from him: the brightness of unencumbered daylight beyond the trees about three hundred yards ahead. Meadow? Pasture? Road? He sprang – carefully – from the oak's limb to the elm's, and was edging along the boughs when the first of the pack reached the tree behind him, swirling around the trunk, howling and jumping. The crown of the elm was thick and January bunched himself up tight among the leaves, unable to tell whether anything of his feet or clothing showed or not.

166

Men came running up from the woods. January recognized the burly and the short hunters of the night before, with Ott and two others. '*Fucken goddam murderin' nigger!*' shouted Ott, his red beard bristling in frustration.

'Climbed the goddam tree.'

'Just like a goddam monkey.'

You'd climb a tree fast enough if those dogs were after YOU . . .

The men looked around and January held himself very still.

'Butch! Wolf! Juno! This way . . . He's got to come down someplace . . .'

The men moved off, the dogs milling around them, sniffing the ground. January waited, heart pounding, as their voices faded into the tangles of laurel and dogwood.

Murderin'. That did *not* sound good. He wondered who Broadax had told them he'd killed, and whether in fact someone *was* dead, to make the accusation look good. *Not Mamzelle Russell. Please, Virgin Mother of God, not that innocent girl.* At the moment, he wouldn't put much of anything past the man.

The trees around the elm were thinner, none large enough to take his weight closer than forty feet away. He slid down the scabby gray trunk, dropped to the ground, and ran for it.

Baying, the pack burst from the foliage behind him. Someone yelled, 'There he is!' and January ran full-tilt for the clearer ground ahead. A shotgun blast kicked a geyser of dead leaves and dirt three yards to his right. He swerved, zigzagged, as another man fired. 'Goddam murderin' bastard!'

Beyond the last of the trees the ground fell away into a twelve-foot drop. Lake water shimmered beyond. *Shit*—

Another gun fired and January flung up his arms as if hit, and pitched down over the cliff, praying that the water was deep.

It wasn't, but it was deep enough that the rocks on the bottom only scraped his arms and back, and he managed to kick free of the sunken tangle of dead trees below the surface. In the split-second before he jumped, he'd seen that a line of brush clung along the toes of the cliff at the waterline, and this he rolled into, his head concealed by the tangled leaves and his body underwater still. He heard the men's' voices above him: 'You see him?' 'Nuthin' . . .' 'I got him. I know I did.'

'God damn. God damn, what we gonna do now?'

'We'll tell 'em back at the House—'

'Fucken ungrateful bastard murderin' bastard—'

The voices faded again. January stayed where he was.

He knew from that map that there was a succession of long, narrow lakes south-west of Syracuse, as if a monstrous tiger had raked the ground with its claws. He had indeed, he deduced, come too far south of the line between Syracuse and Auburn. He guessed himself to be within a half-day's walk of Auburn, always supposing no other vengeful believers appeared with shotguns . . .

Lying half underwater, shaking with fatigue and

hunger, he wanted only to stay where he was. *Or as long as I'm wishing for things, I wish I was back in New Orleans on my own front gallery with Rose . . . Trying to figure out how we're going to get enough money to make it 'til Christmas?*

Eve Russell is back there. If she's still alive.

He dragged himself half-clear of the water, felt for the daguerreotype and remembered that it was in the breast pocket of his coat – of Michie Barnum's coat – back at the House of the Patriarch.

That tears it, he thought. *They'll know I was looking for her. They'll know SOMEONE was looking for her . . .*

It's been twenty-four hours, he thought, *since my escape from the house . . .*

Dread sickened him, at the thought that they'd have gotten rid of her . . . *But why did they want her in the first place?*

It kept coming back to that.

Damn it, he thought, as he pulled himself – cautiously – from the water, and picked his way among the submerged rocks and underwater deadfalls along the foot of the cliff. About a half-mile further along the shore, the ground came down to the water.

He knew he had to go back.

Not if they've killed her already.

He shook his head. *You don't know that she's the one you're supposed to have killed.*

But the logic of the matter was relentless.

Who else could it have been? Who else could cause them trouble, when her parents came looking for her?

Damn it. Damn THEM . . .

The ground leveled out to his right, the cliff descending to a slope thick with honeysuckle. His soaked clothing clinging to him, January stumbled on to firmer ground, rocks underfoot rather than the broken mass of half-rotting branches. He scanned the ground ahead, listening for dogs, for voices. *How the hell am I going to find the Seabright farm 'near' Auburn, if the whole countryside is out looking for me for murder?*

A woman stepped out of the shrubs along the shore. 'Don't be afraid,' she said. 'I've been sent here to help you.'

January straightened. He'd reached a point of mistrusting anything and everything said to him, and calculated, briefly, the distance he'd have to swim back across the lake if indeed this was a trap. About a mile. No effort if he were rested and had had something besides a handful of blackberries and three raw eggs in the past twenty-four hours, and hadn't just fallen over a twelve-foot cliff.

'Is your name Seabright?' he asked.

She shook her head. She was, he guessed, about sixty, her thick, graying blonde hair gathered sloppily under a house cap, her neatly patched gown faded colorless and hanging slack on a body like a fence rail. Her gray eyes seemed deep as sparkling water, and kind. 'Anne Seabright died thirty years ago,' she said. 'I was sent to inhabit her body, to help all those in this world who need help. To lead them – if they're willing to see it – to the Light.'

She held out her hand to him, to help him up the shallow bank, and asked, 'Are you the man who killed Serapis Broadax?'

January said, '*WHAT???*'

Fourteen

The Celestial Comrade (as she introduced herself) lived in a half-ruined farmhouse about a mile from where she met January, on the opposite shore of Otisco Lake. As they crossed the spotlessly tidy yard she introduced him to the three cows and such of the chickens as were present ('I think that must have been Caroline's nest you found – black hen with a bit of gold here on her neck? She's always laying out. I'm glad she was able to help you.').

'Anne Seabright had cousins living near Auburn,' she told him, as she took bread, cheese, and hard-boiled eggs from the cupboard in the kitchen, and a crock of butter from the pottery jar buried in the coolest corner of the big room. 'They're probably the ones your friend is staying with. But word is everywhere this morning, about you stabbing the Patriarch, so it won't be safe for you to go into town.'

'I didn't kill him!' said January.

She set a pottery bottle of cider on the table before him, seated herself on the bench opposite him, and folded her hands. 'Eighty-three people at the House of the Patriarch saw you do so,' she informed him, in her gentle voice. 'Turning yourself in might be the best course for you, since the Children of the Light are beside themselves – shattered – with rage at the deed . . . understandably so, of course. They might very well do you a harm, if they encounter you free.'

'They *saw* me?'

She nodded.

'If eighty-three of them saw me do it' – January fell back on the only rational argument he could think of – 'why didn't any of them stop me? And if all of them were too far away to stop me, at that distance how could they be so sure it was me?'

She considered him with grave interest – her deep calm reminded him of nuns he had met. 'Oh, the description was quite definite. Your height and size are difficult to miss. They all spoke of the darkness of your complexion. You were wearing a blue swallowtail coat and a plug hat – I believe that's what they call those high-crowned hats? – which I assume you've gotten rid of—'

January stammered for a moment at the accurate description of Barnum's coat, then swung around as a shadow darkened the kitchen door. The man who stood there could have been any of the men he'd glimpsed in the half-darkness of the House of the Patriarch, a farmer of the district, medium-sized and stringy, with a narrow forehead and a chin like a coffin framed in shaggy, graying hair and flowing side whiskers. His teeth were a broken horror of stumps, his eyes a pale and intolerant arctic blue.

He held a rifle under one arm, and an ax in the other hand. Two immense dogs – one gray and one yellow – seated themselves just behind him, like good soldiers told to stand guard.

'Spirit,' he said, 'what do we got here?'

'It's the man who murdered the Reverend Broadax,' replied the Comrade, with matter-of-fact calm, before January could speak.

'I can see that.' The farmer came in and set his rifle in a corner by the door. 'But what's he doin' here? Pearce,' he added, holding out his hand to January. 'Delivered Pearce.'

'I didn't kill him,' said January, with the odd feeling of having wandered into a dream.

'Eighty-three people saw you do it,' pointed out Pearce, and turned to the Celestial Comrade. 'You all right here for kindlin', o Spirit, or should I split some 'fore I haul in the cord-wood? I got flour an' salt out in the wagon.'

'Bless you.' She gave him a smile that would have stopped hearts in the days of her beauty forty-some years ago. 'I am running low on kindling, if you would be so good, Mr Pearce.'

'Always a pleasure.' He saluted her with the ax, took a bucket from beside the door, and thrust it into January's hands. January saw that Pearce's hands had been crudely tattooed, as men sometimes did themselves at sea. LORD was tattooed on the fingers of his right hand. DEVIL on the fingers of his left (including the thumb). 'Ben, is it? You might help fetchin' in water.'

173

January followed him into the yard. Delivered Pearce – presumably Delivered-From-Sin or Delivered-From-Evil or something of the sort – picked up his rifle on the way through the door before him; the dogs got up and padded at their master's heel. January repeated, on the way to the well, 'If eighty-three people saw me murder Broadax why didn't any of them stop me?' and Pearce shrugged.

'Myself, if I'd been there an' seen you do it, likely I wouldn't have stopped you either,' he said. 'The fires of sin burn around that man like the smoke that comes off the sun in eclipse an' somebody was bound to do it, no matter what those idiots in the Blessed Land say. They're all burnin' in sin, too,' he added.

There didn't seem to be much to reply to that, so January asked instead, 'You wouldn't be the fellow who finds buried Spanish treasure, would you?'

The cold blue eye slid sidelong at him. 'I am.'

'I heard them speak of you,' said January. 'Out while I was hiding in the woods.' He felt as he had a year ago, when he had traveled in Haiti, on the errands of his wife's family; or when he had stood among the votaries at the voodoo dances on Bayou St. John. Not a dream, as he had thought before, but a land where the rules were not those he'd learned in Paris and London, the science and rationality he'd studied in his medical classes.

Shakespeare had written truly, that there were more things in heaven and earth than were dreamt of in philosophy. Things that couldn't be explained, or whose explanations were doubled: madness on the one hand, and on the other . . .

Something else.

He asked, 'Are all of them in on it?'

Eighty-three . . . and some of them, if Spring was right, ordinary farmers who'd tilled the lands hereabouts, until they'd joined the Children of the Light. Until they'd heard the Shining Herald speak to the dead.

Until they'd heard the dead speak through her.

Rose, he knew, was going to ask him if the Shining Herald came from the same part of Heaven as the Celestial Comrade, and if they had been friends before the steps of God's Throne.

Pearce frowned as he set his rifle down next to the woodpile and kicked a couple of thick billets over to the tree stump that served as a chopping block. 'In on what?'

January hesitated, wondering how much *Pearce* knew. Wondering if Pearce was 'in on it' as well. *I'll be suspecting Spring next . . . and the whole Russell family after that . . .*

He asked instead, 'Where am I supposed to have killed Broadax? And how, with eighty-three people standing around?'

'Oh, they wasn't there when you did it.' The farmer set up a chunk of wood on the block. 'An' they didn't see where you was. Night before last Broadax disappeared. Near two hundred people heard him speak at the Residence – couple of 'em say you was there at the back of the room. That smooth weasel Teems says he saw

175

him go up the stairs to his own quarters. Next mornin' his bed hadn't been slept in, an' Teems an' the Herald searched the whole house an' then the whole of the property. Turns out nobody'd seen him since that time.'

His ax came down with a sharp *clunk* on the wood; he brought it up, wood and all, and smote the block again, splintering the chunk in two.

'Seems the Reverend had some important papers to sign for Teems that had to go to New York right that day, an' Teems was like a maiden lady with a cockroach up her petticoats, flutterin' around lookin' for him. 'Fore noon men was out huntin' the woods – leavin' those with a lick of sense back in the fields to get in the hay. By evenin' not a sign of him did they find.' He split another chunk from the wood, and the Celestial Comrade emerged from the house, with a basket on her arm. January, conscientiously, went over to the well, set his pail down beside it and lowered the bucket, trying to match up times and events in his mind.

The men he'd heard the previous day had been searching for Broadax, not himself. He wondered if they had actually approached this grizzled lunatic about finding the Reverend with a dowsing rod.

'The Herald tried two-three times that day to find where he was. Third time, I hear tell, she woked up cryin', but couldn't say why. That night, when she tried again, three-quarters of them heretic Children was packed into that Residence of theirs, for one of them Nights of

176

Revelation. You seen her,' he asked, 'when she speaks with the dead?'

'I have.' January shivered at the memory of the darkened parlor, the sweet wailing of the little choir and the smells of burning frankincense.

'You see 'em appear?'

January was silent, as he turned the windlass, lifted the bucket from the well. *Had* he really seen those glowing shapes in the darkness behind the sleeping Herald's couch? *Had* he really seen the bluish glow that surrounded the unconscious woman – or seemed to surround her? His recollections after Ayasha had spoken to him – *had* Ayasha spoken to him? – were less clear, but he thought that at least twice more, shining shapes had materialized from the gloom near the couch. But behind the crowding backs of the Children it was hard to be certain.

I have seen things I can't otherwise explain, Ruggles had said.

At length he said, 'I'm not sure what it was that I saw.'

The pale glance sized him up. Then the ax came down with a thwack. 'You a skeptic, sir?'

'I'm not sure of that, either.'

'Sounds to me,' said Pearce, 'like you got some thinkin' to do. Be that as it may, ever'body in the room saw it, when Broadax appeared, dim an' shimmery, as these visions do, an' his face twisted with terror. He raised up his hands to protect himself, an' they saw you – an' at least six of 'em knew you, from seein' you out in

177

front of the Residence – come out of the dark with a dagger, an' bury it in Broadax's chest. Then the Herald screamed, an' the vision disappeared, an' she sat up, weepin' an' screamin', an' the men all grabbed up weapons an' run out into the night to search for you, like idiots, an' been searchin' since.'

He struck another piece of kindling from the block. The dogs rose leggily and went to greet the Celestial Comrade as she emerged from the chicken coops, her basket filled with eggs.

'*I didn't do it.*'

'Then how do you account for the vision?'

'The Devil sent it,' answered the Comrade, pausing between the well and the woodpile to look from one man to the other.

Picking up the pail, January reflected that this argument would almost certainly not stand up in court.

No more, he thought, than *I didn't do it* would stand up, coming from a black man and a reputed fugitive at that.

'Really, Mr Pearce,' added the Comrade calmly, 'why is it that you find it so easy to believe that spirits of light can send visions, and spirits of darkness cannot?'

'There ain't a man in the Blessed Land,' returned Pearce, 'who'll believe that the Devil could swap in a lyin' vision to the Herald, an' steal away the true one. Once they open that door, that'd mean that the visions they seen of their sweethearts, their children, their parents, might have been swapped in by the Devil as

178

well – an' don't think pratin' heretic swine like that Reverend Mason over to Skaneateles ain't gonna be on *that* argument like a cock on a June bug. Nor all the families of them Children, who feel they got gypped out of their land. An' them seekers that comes in from New York on the railroad; it'd mean the ecstasies *they* feel, when Broadax guides 'em into dreams, could be the visions of the Devil as well, sent to lead 'em straight on to Hell.'

He stretched out his left hand as he spoke, with its broken, dirty nails, then curled the powerful, crooked fingers in, so that the Devil's name stood out clear on the backs of his fingers like an omen of doom. 'Which they is,' he finished quietly. 'An' they'll kill him, 'fore they'll let him bring *that* argument to court.'

The woman's calm gray eyes turned to January, and she asked, 'How can we help you, Ben?'

January took a deep breath. 'I have friends in this district,' he said. 'Can word be gotten to them, without anyone learning that the message comes from me? Because if the Children believe in this vision, as you say, my friends may be in danger as well.'

'I'll take 'em word,' grunted Pearce. 'Serapis Broadax was a warlock an' Satan's own imp, an' if you didn't kill him I'd ask you to show me the man who did so's I can shake his hand. But lies won't help you,' he added fiercely, 'one way or t'other. Only the truth'll bring you through to the Light.'

With that he turned, and began chopping kindling again, while January hefted his pail of water, and followed the Celestial Comrade back into her tumbledown house.

She made up a pallet bed for him in the loft, among bins of apples and sacks of potatoes and beans. 'Other friends will be coming later in the day,' she explained. 'They are so kind, to help on this farm . . . Not all of them see the Reverend Broadax as Mr Pearce does. Mr Pearce has farmed in this country since the end of the Revolution, but he came here from Massachusetts. He has no tolerance for the new ways of preaching the Gospel, for the extravagance and enthusiasm which swept over this district like the fire of the Lord twenty years ago. No tolerance for those who see the face of the Lord, and hear the Lord's voice, in any fashion but those that he himself was taught, in cold New England all those years ago. Please forgive him his eccentricities. God is in him, too.'

She brought him, in addition to food and drink, several sheets of paper, ink, a quill, a candle, and a stick of sealing wax. 'Mr Pearce can be trusted not to speak of you to others,' she went on, as she laid these things down on the little stool which was the loft's only piece of regular furniture. 'I'm afraid he was sincere in his praise of the Patriarch's murder, whoever did the deed. The teachings of the Herald, and the translation that the Reverend Broadax had undertaken of the Lost Gospel of James, are to him proof that the whole of the Blessed Land is under the sway of Beelzebub. And in any case, everything that concerns this world has to him

180

been anathema for many years. It is, he says, none of his business what people do with the years God gives them, for nine-tenths of them are going to Hell.'

She smiled, and shook her head. Her love for the old man shone clear and sweet in her eyes.

'Does he include you in that group?' January seated himself on the sill of a low beam, with the stool drawn up between his knees like a desk.

'He claims he doesn't know. That no one knows such a thing of another. But he loved Anne Seabright – the woman whose body I now inhabit – and for her sake I think he looks after me, now that the strength of this body begins to wane. And he – like the other neighbors who are so good to me – helps me in my work.'

'And what is your work?'

She looked surprised at the question. 'To help every soul in the world,' she said. 'To lead them to the Light, one soul at a time. It is a task that will take many thousands of lifetimes – as I, and others like me, have been working at it, many thousands of lifetimes. But we will bring them all safe through the Gate in the end.'

She left him then, and January moved a little along the beam, to where the light was better, near the attic's single gable window. He thought for a time, about what he had seen in the House of the Patriarch. About Eve Russell, and the Shining Herald, and the Reverend Serapis Broadax.

About his wife, his beautiful Rose, reading the letters he'd written her from Havana, from

Charleston, from New York. Rose sitting on the gallery, doing the household books with this same fading sunlight slipping across her spectacles like quicksilver, while Baby Xander crawled in purposeful circles around her chair leg at the end of his little tether. In the parlor, Zizi-Marie explaining to three-year-old Professor John why spiders built their webs but why they couldn't let them do so in the house.

Rose tidying up her laboratory above the kitchen, not only in preparation for the students (three of them!) who would come in October, but for the work she did for John Davis of the Theatre d'Orleans, when he should bring an opera company to the city after Christmas. Rose's long fingers, delicate as she measured chemicals, mixed ingredients: gunpowder, niter, sulphate of potassa. Phosphorous that glimmered in the dusk.

Then he wrote three short letters. One was to Byron Spring, one to Chloë Viellard.

One was to P.T. Barnum.

Fifteen

It was twelve miles to Auburn, fifteen to Syracuse, from the house of the Celestial Comrade. When she came back to the attic at noon, the Spirit told January that Delivered Pearce ('Delivered-Out-Of-The-Hand-of-Iniquity' she explained) had taken his letter to the Seabrights, who had a farm a few miles from Auburn, and had given the other two to a boy named Dark Travis – 'Fear-No-Darkness' she said, and smiled.

'Unlike Mr Pearce, Dark chose that name himself, when he was baptized into the New Land Congregation, over on the shore of Skaneateles Lake. They believe, with Swedenborg, that the Last Judgment has already occurred – that all things now exist in a spiritual state. Unlike the Swedenborgians of the New Jerusalem, the New Land believers abstain from the union of the flesh and from all fleshly things. I think they are mistaken,' she added. 'But they are all of them good, hard-working men and women, living like the Apostles with all their property in common, and who am I to speak ill of the path that they follow to the Light? If Mr Pearce tells Dark – or indeed any of them – that the letters he gives them are in confidence, to be spoken of to no one, they can be utterly trusted.'

As if she saw the doubt in January's eyes – or in his heart – she went on, 'This is a district where belief takes many shapes, Benjamin. Before the Sower of the parable went out to sow his seed, the ground hereabouts was fertilized with strange nutriments. The wheat that grew up from the seed that took root doesn't always look like what we think wheat should. But much of it is wholesome, nevertheless. The Millerites – and there are a goodly congregation of them in Rochester – believe that the Day of Judgment, which Swedenborg said took place in 1757, will be sometime in the fall of 1844. October, I think. Yet they, too, seek for the path of righteousness so that they may be ready for it when it comes. Does that make one man wrong and another right?'

She moved to pick up a sack of flour, and January, rising from where he'd been sitting near the attic's gable window, forestalled her, and lifted the sack himself. She was a strongly built woman, and moved like a young girl still, but there was little flesh on her bones.

She smiled her thanks, unhooked a couple of strings of dried apple slices from the rafters, and led the way down the steep stair, deftly unwrapping the fruit from its cheesecloth shrouds as she descended.

'Some congregations see sexual congress, man with woman, even within the bounds of marriage, as sinful,' she continued, as he set the flour on the scrubbed oak table in the kitchen. 'Others believe that the Lord commands each man to take unto himself several wives, so that all the women of the congregation may have protectors to care for them. Still others say that men and women should be as they were in the garden of Eden, loving freely and each child the child of the whole congregation, not of one man or of one woman only. All have scripture that will support their views. All these congregations include men – and women – who do great good in the world, who are kind, and merciful, and seek only good. And of course' – she took a well-worn dough trough from its shelf – 'all include sinners, and monsters, and the self-deceived as well. There is bread in that box there' – she gestured with a floury hand – 'if you're

184

hungry, and butter and cider down in the jar under the floor, there.'

January shook his head, and checked the big pottery jug on the shelf, to make sure there was water in it still. 'And what about the Shining Herald?' he asked. 'Tell me about the Blessed Land.'

'The Shining Herald began to preach in Rochester, and Syracuse, and as far east as Cooperstown a little more than a year ago,' she said. 'Like many of Swedenborg's followers, she believes in communication with the dead. She speaks with them – brings them across the veil that separates this world from that beyond, so that those who loved them may be comforted by the sight of their faces once again, the sound of their voices. It was through conversation with the spirits of the ancient dead, the priests of Babylon and Judaea, that she directed the Reverend Broadax to the tomb where the Gospel of James was found, and through her – through the spirits that she serves – that he is able to translate the ancient Babylonian in which it is written.'

'And do you believe the gospel is genuine?' asked January, seating himself at the table opposite her. 'If you are a spirit yourself, can you recognize in her a fellow spirit?'

'We are all fellow spirits,' replied the Comrade. Her big hands, strong and sun-browned, worked the flour and yeast in the trough, as he had seen his sister Olympe do, times without counting. 'When I take a human form – as when we all take human forms – there are things that I don't

185

remember about the realm from which I come; it's like looking through a very dirty window. That doesn't mean I don't remember who and what I am.'

'No,' said January. 'Of course not.'

'You don't believe me.' She smiled again, not the least disconcerted. 'Many people don't, and why should they? The world is full of liars – and monsters.'

January thought of the little heap of shoes, in the dark of the tunnel. Of the scribbled ticket receipt.

'As for the Blessed Land,' she went on, 'Mr Pearce remembers it as a garrison fort for the British after the Revolution, when there was scarcely anyone in this country and the British still refused to withdraw their men, even when the peace was signed. When they did leave, everyone said that Sempronius Teasle was their agent, selling guns to the local tribes that he'd bring up through the tunnels from the river. After his body was found dead in the house, the place was deserted for many years. Everyone hereabouts said that it was haunted.'

She smiled at the recollection. 'Ursula Ott asked me if it was true, and was there anything I could do to rid it of ghosts? Jared wanted to turn it into lodgings for the workers, when the Canal was being dug. He was always on the lookout for a dollar, before Ursula's passing. I spent three nights in the place, but saw no spirits there.'

She turned the round, solid loaves on the floured table, her big hands working almost

186

independent of her thought. 'Before that, of course, there had been a terrible rumpus over the land. Liam Harter claimed the pastures across the river when Jared Ott bought the place, saying they'd been a part of his father's land. When Mr Ott signed the whole of the property – and all of his own farm, save for small portions to each of his sons – over to the Children of the Light last year, after the Shining Herald gave him word from Ursula in the Summer Land, Harter claimed the pastures again. The lawsuit is still not settled.'

She set the loaves in the trough, and January got to his feet and carried it for her to the warm corner next to the kitchen's stone fireplace, and fetched half a pail of water from the copper that simmered on the back of the low-burning blaze.

'Did Mrs Ott come from beyond the grave to tell her husband to give the land to Broadax?'

'His sons say she did.' The Spirit sluiced the table's surface with a rag, and a dusting of salt, which in that neighborhood was cheap. 'But in fact – or from what I recall Mr Ott saying to me – he only realized that he had lived wrongly and in sin for the whole of his life, and saw in the Blessed Land the world that he wished to live in. A world where he could help others, and live as the Lord intended that all men live. His sons tried to have the Reverend Broadax arrested – for immorality, I think – but Sheriff Harter hated Mr Ott, and would do nothing, and now their lawsuit over the land is tangled up with his. And in any case the

187

sons are Methodists and Harter a Congregationalist, and so far as Harter is concerned they will all of them burn in Hell. People in these counties take their faith seriously, Benjamin – whether the old faiths, that they brought from New England with them forty years ago – or the new faiths with which men and women seek to cleanse this world and heal their own hearts.'

Chloë, Leopold, and Hélène arrived just before twilight in a rented buggy, led by a youth whom the Celestial Comrade said – as soon as the young man departed – was Fear-No-Darkness Travis. Del Pearce had stopped by in mid-afternoon, to tell January that Byron Spring had been away from Ammi Seabright's place when Pearce had arrived there. 'Says he'll hand him your word when he gets back. Should be back tonight, he said. My guess would be Spring heard somethin' about you killin' Broadax, an' went to find out what he could.'

January whispered, 'Damn it.' Broadax would not only know that January had been planted like a spy in the Blessed Land to find Eve Russell – he would know that Byron Spring had been in on it.

He had spent the day assisting the Celestial Comrade with the endless work of a small farm, disappearing indoors – or up to the attic like a squirrel taking refuge in a tree – whenever one of her many friends arrived, to likewise lend a hand. Evidently this was something most of the neighborhood did on a regular basis, no matter who they thought was currently occupying

Anne Seabright's body. From overheard bits of conversation, January gathered that a number of them believed matter-of-factly that she was what she said she was: an otherworld being come to earth.

Others of them clearly believed that stones which had natural holes in them (*so THAT's what a peep stone is!*) could be used to scry lost objects or buried Spanish treasure; believed that the Spanish had come through this part of New York (*lost from the Armada?*) to either mine silver or bury treasure; believed that Indian sachems had summoned demons from the stars or the earth's core which still haunted the vicinity of certain stones or hills in the woods, and that a specter could be seen walking the road between Auburn and Lake Cayuga on windy nights, searching for something that could never be found. Others spoke of visions they had had, of God, or angels, or shining men who told them of strange destinies; or of seers to whom they had spoken, who preached new revelations; or of stones they had found in the deep woods, graven with signs in strange alphabets, stones which had subsequently vanished (like the Spanish treasure chests) without trace.

It was with considerable relief that January recognized, from the attic window, the uncompromising fair bulk of Leopold at the reins of the buggy as it entered the Spirit's yard, and not simply because it meant he was no longer without support. He had a sense of seeing a signpost that would lead him back to a land of reality.

Hastening down the stairs, he found Chloë on the doorstep, listening with interest to the Celestial Comrade's explanation of who and what she was. 'If you wish to help everyone in the Universe, why not enter the body of someone extremely wealthy?' she inquired logically. 'Why not take over the body of Baron Rothschild when he died a few years ago? Or of the Duke of Bridgewater, who certainly never did anything to help anyone with his money whilst he was alive?'

'I can only assume,' replied the Spirit, with perfect composure, 'that at some point in the future I will have the opportunity, here where I stand, to save a soul, or help a person or a family, who will do incomparable good as a result of my action – something which can be said of us all. Else why would God have incarnated as a common carpenter's son in Galilee? Benjamin' – she turned with a smile – 'perhaps you'd better stay inside . . . Madame Viellard?'

She stepped aside from the doorway, and Chloë rustled in with her whisper of pale-green silk.

'Would you like to go into the parlor? It's a bit stuffy from disuse, but I can then ask your good companions into the kitchen, to have some ginger water, rather than sitting out in the buggy, without them catching a glimpse of Benjamin here. Do they know he is here?'

'I told them only that I'd received a letter,' Chloë replied, 'and would be driving out here this afternoon. I'm sure they haven't heard a word about Mr January supposedly murdering this preacher – Hélène speaks only French and

Leopold, only German. But so many people come through Syracuse on the railway who may very well speak French or German, it's best to be careful. Does that sound acceptable to you, M'sieu January? Oh!' she added, as the sturdy figure of Del Pearce appeared in the yard, trailed by his dogs, and started to cross to the house.

'It's all right,' said January, hoping it really *was* all right. 'He knows I'm here.'

'And just in time,' smiled the Comrade. 'Mr Pearce, could I beg you the favor of taking Mrs Viellard's horse and buggy around to the stable while her companions come inside?'

January retreated to the parlor, which was, as the Comrade had warned, shuttered up and stuffy. His hostess followed him in a moment later with a lamp, which showed that, tiny and cramped as it was, the nearly bare chamber was spotlessly clean and meticulously maintained, smelling of soap and beeswax. Voices in the kitchen – Chloë speaking to her servants, the soft clink of pottery cups. Then Chloë entered, closed the door behind her, and said, 'I thought I'd heard some extraordinary things on the train, and at the hotel in Syracuse—'

'Wait until I tell you about how I committed murder in front of eighty-three people.' January held a rocking chair for her, in which the little lady sat a trifle uncertainly: rocking chairs not being items which the elder Madame Viellard would permit in the New Orleans townhouse. 'And about conversations with the dead.'

He took one end of the stiff oak settle at the left of the cold fireplace, and related to her, first what Delivered-From-the-Hand-of-Iniquity Pearce had told him of the shared vision of the Children, then of what he himself had seen in that darkened, crowded parlor: the unearthly radiance that surrounded the Shining Herald as she slept, the glowing figures he had seen – or thought he had seen – in the darkness behind her couch.

'Rose has used magic lanterns when she works for the opera,' said January. 'Glass slides held before lamplight, and reflected in mirrors from another room. Thinking about it, the hymns that continued after the lights went down could easily have covered the sound of a mirror or a scrim being run out just behind the Herald's couch . . .'

He glanced around, as the Celestial Comrade and Del Pearce came in from the kitchen. The Spirit bore a tray with several pottery cups and a plate of bread and butter, Pearce a softly steaming teapot – half-swaddled in a dish towel – as a priest would carry a relic in procession. The dogs followed behind, savage and scruffy as Viking warriors, and plopped themselves down beside the Comrade as she took a seat.

'But magic-lantern shows, even if you change the slide very quickly, are clearly images, pictures. Even when they move back and forth, the figures themselves don't change. What I saw . . .' He fell silent, trying to express what he had seen . . . or thought he'd seen, in the near-complete darkness, with the Herald's voice sinking to the roughness of a young man's, or transforming into a child's bird-like treble.

Grandpa, it's all right, don't weep . . . I've missed you so . . .

'When they moved, it was the movement of life,' he said. He gestured with his arm, as the dim, glowing shape had gestured, beckoning, clasping hands over heart. 'You can tell the difference. I've never heard of a magic lantern being able to do that.'

'A trapdoor?' said Chloë doubtfully. 'A panel in the wall?'

'House has sure got enough of those.' Pearce set the teapot down on the oak table. 'Old Man Teasle could come and go like wind through a crack. More than one revenue man there was, went into the place lookin' for him – or for his cargoes – and never came out, nor was never accounted for again, the Tory bastard.'

January said, slowly, 'The floor in the parlor was carpeted. But there was a gap of ten or twelve feet, between the chairs and the podium. And the room was quite dark. It's true I was in the back of the room—'

'And those heretic heathen imbeciles wouldn't notice if ghosts in white bedsheets was let down from the ceilin' on ropes,' growled Pearce. He handed January a cup of tea. 'Not if there was initials embroidered on the sheets an' the imposter's feet hangin' down under the hem in bed socks.'

'Just because I don't understand what I'm seeing,' continued January, 'doesn't mean I think it's magic . . . or a miracle. When I traveled in Italy I saw statues of the Virgin Mary which were supposed to have wept blood – and I saw the blood on the statues—'

'Scarcely the same thing,' remarked Chloë, who had, like most wealthy New Orleans girls, been raised in a convent.

'I'm sure my wife – or indeed, Madame Viellard' – he nodded to Chloë – 'could explain how the trick was worked, or *could* have been worked . . . if it was indeed a trick. The fact remains that the Reverend Serapis Broadax attempted to kill me in the tunnel under his house, and I have reason to believe that the reason the runaway slaves he assists are never caught on their way to Canada is that he kills them, and sinks their bodies in the river. So I'm inclined to think that what I saw – and what the witnesses to my "crime" saw – was a trick of some kind, done I don't know how. But I need to take another look at that house.'

'Good luck with that.' Pearce flipped a fragment of buttered bread to his dogs.

'And whatever else is going on,' January went on, 'I found this.' From his pocket he withdrew the ticket receipt, signed – illegibly – by the clerk on the eighth of June.

Chloë studied the scrawl intently – the words that might or might not have been King's Point – and raised those huge aquamarine eyes to his, behind their slabs of spectacle lens.

'It proves nothing,' he said. 'Whether Mamzelle Russell is there or not, he has to get rid of me – he knows that I know there's something amiss in that house, and that's information he can't afford to have noised abroad. Not if he's going to go on having wealthy New York businessmen come to him to have their burdens lifted – and

194

I daresay their purses lightened. So I assume he's still alive, and this spectral dumb show was designed to encourage his followers to shoot me on sight.'

He looked across at the Celestial Comrade, sitting quiet on the other settle across the empty fireplace, her long fingers tangled in the larger dog's mane, her gray eyes sad. Something made him say, 'I'm sorry.'

'You're certain of what you saw in that house?'

'I saw about a dozen pairs of broken shoes,' said January. 'Slave shoes, the kind that planters buy – and good Massachusetts merchants sell them, however much money they contribute to the abolition societies. And Broadax did attempt to drug me and kill me. Beyond that . . . Maybe the man does actually help people to escape to Canada. Maybe the Shining Herald is actually in mental converse with Babylonian priests who are helping to translate a lost gospel. Maybe the spiritual advice he gives to these wealthy gentlemen from New York is good, and genuine, and well intentioned. Maybe one of his followers just happened to be crossing from King's Point to New York on June the eighth. I don't know. But I think I need to find out.'

'I don't imagine M'sieu Broadax's antecedents will be terribly difficult to trace,' remarked Chloë thoughtfully. 'Given the amount of sugar the Viellard family ships through the big New York importing firms, I'm sure there will be someone happy to assist me in my inquiries. When we return—'

January shook his head. 'I won't be going back to the city with you,' he said. 'I don't know how Eve Russell fits into all this, but I'm pretty sure she's still there. And if Broadax is the one who's supposed to be dead, there's a good chance that Mamzelle is still alive.'

'She won't be' – Chloë smoothed the receipt and handed it back to him – 'should Broadax conclude that whatever she's worth to him alive doesn't outweigh the danger of her being found in the compound.'

'Which brings us – yet again – to what he thinks Eve Russell is worth to him alive.'

'Y'er mighty sure the old limb of Satan's alive yet,' remarked Pearce.

'Aren't you?'

The old man's pale eyes glinted. 'I'm sure of nuthin' in this mortal world,' he said. 'But I purely wouldn't bet against it.'

Sixteen

'This isn't the place,' breathed January. The little hay barn stood a dozen yards from the river, whose black water glimmered faintly in the light of the sinking moon.

''Tis one of 'em,' retorted Pearce. 'And the one I know. There's a wharf down there where the bank curves and the water's deep enough to bring a boat to shore. Old Man Teasle had more'n one way into that house of his, and more'n one

196

way out. This tunnel leads to one o' them cottages in the orchard, and I'd rather come up there than in the middle o' the house itself where we'd be bound to meet God-knows-who. Them cottages been empty for years.'

January looked towards the house. The moon was a day past full, and its light touched the erratic roof line with threads of silver above the inky cloud of the orchard trees. He and Pearce had left the Celestial Comrade's farm just before sunset, January concealed beneath a load of hay in the old man's wagon. It was after midnight, now.

Despite his exhaustion he had slept uneasily last night. He would wake with a jolt, at the skitter of a mouse along the attic beams over-head, or the screech of an owl in the trees beyond the open gable window, and for a moment he would be back in the stuffy darkness of that windowless room in the Residence. Or he would be standing in the earth-smelling black of the tunnel, seeing the lamplight flicker for one terrible second over the jumble of shoes along the wall.

The smell of that hidden room came back to him, the unearthly silence, and the ground-in whiff of incense.

Incense?

And the way the thick layers of carpet sank beneath his foot. A fraudulent pearl, two cheap sequins . . .

Only when they were inside the barn – redolent with cut hay – did Del Pearce light the candle he carried, in the old-fashioned way, with striker, tinder and flint. By its wavery light the old man advanced three paces from the door, and knelt. 'Still here,' he said. 'Used, too, by the look on it. Reach me that pole there by the door, will you, Ben?'

A couple of hayforks hung near the door, and beside them, two twig brooms and a six-foot stave with a small, blunt metal hook at one end. It looked like some kind of agricultural implement, but January, born on a plantation, had never seen such a tool. He handed it to Pearce, who hooked the metal end into a small hole – like a knothole – in the puncheon floor, twisted it, and pulled.

A whole section of floor came up, three feet by seven, a shallow ramp running down into darkness.

'Tunnel forks about forty yards along,' the old man informed him. 'Left-hand fork'll take you into the cottage nearest the house. Along to the right'll take you up into the house itself, where the east wing comes out past the kitchen and into the garden near the orchard. I'll close up this trap and sweep away the sign that it's been used, an' I'll give you warnin' if I can, if any comes in here. Brutus' – he added, snapping his fingers to the dogs – 'Mars: guard!'

The dogs lay down, on either side of the door. It had been understood that Del Pearce would guide him to enter the house, but had no intention of accompanying him inside. As January checked the loads on the two old-fashioned pistols Pearce had lent him, he asked, 'Is that likely, at this hour?' and the farmer shrugged.

'Like you said, that heretic rabbit-sucker is up to something. And he'd not go about his ill deeds in daylight – 'specially if he's convinced his followers he's dead. Like as not he'll be found alive, the minute *your* body is swinging from a tree. He'll have a few bandages on his breast and some piteous tale of lyin' unconscious in a cave someplace.'

'Splendid,' sighed January. 'Just what I need to hear. And meanwhile, he's coming and going from this place' – he held the lantern close to the fresh-scuffed mud of the tunnel floor – 'so I get to meet him on my way out.'

The old man stooped to peer at the smears. 'Could be,' he agreed. 'Myself, looks to me the rumor's true, about his women.'

'His women?' January's brows skated up his forehead.

'Oh, not the good wives of Onondaga County.' The discolored teeth gleamed in an evil grin. 'Now an' now, I've heard rumor before, more'n one skiff-load o' muslin been seen at that river landin' yonder, where the path comes up. From Rochester, I'd say, to keep talk away.'

January remembered the childlike face of Eve Russell in the daguerreotype, and he felt a chill anger clench around his heart. 'And that's the rumor, is it?' he murmured. 'And how often do these visitors appear?'

'Beats hell out of me.' Pearce shrugged. 'House is big enough for all them secret rooms to conceal any kind of goin's on. Myself, I've wondered if *that's* what those wealthy gentlemen from New York come to seek – if it's true.'

Grimly quiet, January felt in his pocket, and touched the tiny pearl. 'I'll let you know.'

As he moved down the ramp, shielding his candle flame against the slight draft that moved the air around him, he tried to piece together a picture of the house in his mind. Two wings, Broadax had said, formed a courtyard on the western side. A 'Men's House' and dormitories for women and children beyond. Five families in those wings . . . *He must keep the doors locked, that lead from that area of the house into the main block, and his own wing.* His recollection of the relationship of the Great Parlor to his own 'secret room' was less clear, owing to the dimness of the oil lamp that Shamrock had carried, and the disorienting sameness of that lurid wallpaper.

Pearce was right, he reflected, about the size of the maze-like house concealing all manner of *goin's on.*

The recollection of those shoes returned, the awareness that he was dealing with a man who could, and would, kill as casually as a farmwife wrung the neck of a chicken, her only thought the dollar the dead bird's meat would bring on the market.

How dare you? He recalled the men and women – children, too – that he'd helped on their way to freedom: men he'd concealed in the storerooms beneath his own house on Rue Esplanade, women he'd smuggled to the packet boat landings in the dead of night, their babies wrapped in blankets to silence them. The children he had held, whispering to them to still their fears. *How DARE you treat people so?* Thought of Hannibal, cheerfully forging passes and freedom papers in whatever grimy whorehouse attic he was inhabiting that week, well aware that if he'd been arrested for the crime of slave-stealing he almost certainly wouldn't live to stand trial. Of David Ruggles, printing warnings to men who had every legal reason to believe themselves safe – warning them that they were not. That they never would be.

Fugitives came here, trembling with excitement to be on the last leg of their brutal journey, ready to walk through the gate that led to Canada, where no slave catcher could follow. Where they would be truly free.

How DARE you?

Eve Russell . . .

The smell of incense in the secret room, the cheap spangles, such as might fall from a whore's dress. *Looks to me the rumor's true . . .*

Rage, disgust, and hatred of the man filled him, turned him momentarily sick.

Spiritual counseling my arse.

He took the left-hand fork of the corridor and climbed the ladder a dozen feet further along. The trap at the top opened into a cellar: beams, boxes, shelves of bottles in the candle's darting light. A trestle table . . .

And the smell.

Blood.

Beyond any mistaking.

Blood, and the wastes that a corpse will leak after death.

Rats and black beetles scurried for cover from

201

his light. The trestle table was empty, the gore on it, fresh. A head wound, and one in the chest or back. The blood was tacky-wet, only hours old.

He felt as if his heart contracted in his chest. *No . . .*

As if he had been present, as if he had witnessed it, January saw Byron Spring ride up to the door of the Residence. Walk through those blue-and-golden corridors, up a flight of stairs. Tap at the door of Broadax's office. *I heard rumors about Ben, about the Reverend Broadax. What happened?*

God damn it, no!

More scurrying, when he approached the split-oak hamper in the corner. But all it contained were sheets that had been draped over the table, gummy with blood. Searching the room for clothing, he found only that the bottles on the shelf contained some of the most expensive brandies on the market: Courvoisier, Martell V.S.O.P. Others held laudanum, or similar powerful tinctures of opium; others, syrups that would disguise that bitter, flowery taste. Smaller packets, unwrapped, exhaled the earthy, slightly fruity, and absolutely unmistakable odor of hashish.

Bitter enlightenment smote him. *No wonder those tired New York gentlemen leave here looking 'soothed'!*

On the lower shelf, pottery jars held dates, raisins – carefully sealed against rats – smaller pots of the expensive spices, like ginger and cinnamon, that had cloyed the lemonade.

He almost laughed out loud, seeing this confirmation of Pearce's 'rumor'. Hashish. *They probably don't even realize that it's not all a dream. No wonder Ruggles said they radiate 'integrity' and 'probity'* . . .

And if they suspect, I'm sure they don't want to know.

His eyes went back to the blood on the table. His mind, to the shoes in the other tunnel. This was no matter for even bitter mirth. *The boys throw stones at the frogs in jest,* Bion of Borysthenes had said, centuries before the birth of Christ. *But the frogs do not die in jest. They die in earnest.*

Another short ladder let him into the cottage above. The trapdoor was weighted overhead rather than locked; it took all his great strength to push it enough to slip his hand through, but he found when he did so that it was simply the leg of a table, resting on the boards that formed the trap. This he pushed aside, wincing at the scrape of the wood on the floor, and then folded back the cover. Like the trapdoor in the barn by the river, this one was nearly invisible in the boards of the floor, marked only by a small notch, like a knothole. The hooked rod that fit it stood in a corner.

By the candle's light he saw that Pearce had been mistaken about the cottage's disuse. The little square room was clearly in use, and not as a storage place for apples. Heavy draperies swathed the walls, mounted – he held the candle up to the length of his arm to see – on a rod set just under the low ceiling, like the curtain rod that had been in his own hidden chamber in the Residence. The dark, cheap fabric reminded him of the backstage curtains at the Theatre d'Orleans, that were hung to absorb light. At one side of the room was a sort of divan, such as the Shining Herald slept on to receive her revelations. At the other, the table that he'd moved held a lamp, and a box containing a goblet.

Both Ruggles and Spring had spoken of the men who came seeking spiritual counsel, who received guidance from the Patriarch in dreams. *Take hashish down here in a dark meditation chapel, seem to dream elsewhere in incense-laden Paradise . . .*

The chamber was about three-quarters the size of the ground floor of the cottage in which he'd spent Monday afternoon. Its draperies covered the door, and whatever windows there might be. Feeling through the heavy cloth, January found the door almost at once. It was firmly locked, not with a latch but with a brand new Chubb lock, which looked excessive to protect a table, a lamp, and a divan. He continued around the curtained walls, and found three windows, old-fashioned sashes latched from the inside, the shutters that protected them latched from the inside also. At the fourth wall, as he worked his way around the room, the curtains gave before his touch like sheets on a clothes line. Pushing his way through, he found that they concealed a stairway to the story above.

The trap at the top was locked, with padlock and hasp.

Presumably, thought January, *the trap door to Paradise.*

Descending, he returned to the windows. These proved easy to open, and he blew out his candle – first making sure that he did indeed have his little tin of lucifers in his pocket – and slipped through into the rustling darkness outside.

The full moon had passed its zenith: pale brilliance spangled the deep grass under the apple trees. The smell of barns, and of outhouses, oriented him west towards the Residence, stronger even than the luxuriant sweetness of drying hay that seemed to fill the night. An ordinary farming community – even one that believed its leaders conversed with the spirit world – was, he knew, asleep not long after full dark, particularly during haying. But though it was well after midnight, he mistrusted his luck, and it wouldn't do to pop up through the trap-door into the house itself only to find the Patriarch going over the books . . . or half the Children gathered around the Shining Herald, frantic to hear her revelation concerning the whereabouts of their missing leader's murdered body.

I wonder how she explains the fact that she can't locate ME simply by going into a trance . . .

Malek, she had whispered. *You are in danger* . . . Ayasha's soft inflections, how could she have known? He shivered.

What do I do if she can find me?

The gate in the orchard wall was locked. A smaller man would have been hard-put to

205

scramble over it, but January's height and strength worked in his favor. He got his elbows over the top of the wall, fearing the hinges would rattle under his weight, and looked toward the dark bulk of the house. And yes, there were lights burning in two of its windows on this side.

Someone translating the Lost Gospel of James, perhaps?

Or adding up the contributions from the wealthy Tappan Brothers, from church groups and believers all over the East Coast? From the Anti-Slavery Societies of America and England who marveled that no slave Serapis Broadax had helped had ever been captured? From wealthy gentlemen who had received spiritual soothing in the warmth of astonishing dreams?

Maybe writing a letter purporting to be from Byron Spring, apologizing to his congregation in Seneca Village and explaining why he wouldn't be returning to them . . .

Would they be holding Eve Russell in one of those windowless chambers in the main house?

He looked back in the direction he thought the other cottage had been, the one where he'd seen light Monday night. *If Broadax knows I'm still at large he'll have her moved into the main house. How likely is it—*

Shouting from the direction of the house, loud even at that distance in the stillness of the night.

Pearce . . .

He was about to pull himself further up on the fence when lanterns bobbed, thrashing, around

206

the corner of the house, and he lowered himself to just the level of his eyes.

No dogs, he thought. *Can't be Pearce . . .*

More lanterns (*not coming this way, at least . . .*). Dim shapes emerged from the dark of the porches. A confusion of voices, those of women rising above the bass growl of the men. Anguished cries. Lights blossomed in the front of the house, wavering in the windows, and shadows blundered across their glow. More men emerged. A horse, tied to the porch railing, flung up its head with a neigh of fear. Men raced to the clump of outbuildings north of the house, came back with a wagon and team as more and more people crowded around the front. Lamps and candlesticks waved aloft. Shouts that January couldn't understand at that distance.

When the wagon moved off at a rattling gallop, everyone followed, dressing gowns and nightrails clutched up around their thighs for better speed. The house was left in darkness.

January had no idea what was going on, but understood that this was his chance, if anything was. The lamps on the east wing of the house had been quenched. *Not much time.* He slipped back through the cottage window, blundered through the curtain and fumbled with match and candle.

It drove him frantic to take the time needed to close and latch the window behind him, to run his bandana around the table's leg so as to pull it back into an approximation of its original position, almost on top of the trap. *God knows when they'll return. Saint Joshua, who sneaked into Jericho and safely out again before blowing down its walls – watch my back . . .*

He guessed that the longer branch of the tunnel would lead into the Patriarch's private quarters, and found that he'd guessed right. The ladder up was a long one, up to the house's upper floor. By the cold brick of the walls around it, he suspected it was built into the side of one of the many chimneys. He pressed the panel at the top – *I'll have to leave this one open behind me . . .*

He'd expected the darkness of the room beyond to smell of the fishy nastiness of whale oil, but it didn't.

It smelled of blood.

Seventeen

Byron Spring knocking on the door of the Residence.

Byron Spring being shown up to the Patriarch's study – by the lanky, flaxen Orion Teems? By solid red-bearded Jared Ott? *I've heard rumors – outrageous, they have to be untrue! – about Ben . . . about Ben doing harm to the Reverend Broadax . . .*

They couldn't POSSIBLY have killed him in this house!

But he remembered the house of Delphine Lalaurie. Big as it was, it was considerably smaller than this one, and evidently neither her daughters nor her husband had been aware of what was going on in the attic . . .

Then, too, if Spring had come that afternoon, everyone would have been out in the woods looking for the 'missing' Broadax. *They'd be safer murdering him then, than I am at the moment . . .*

The room he entered was clearly the Patriarch's office. Papers littered the huge desk, strewed the table beside the open cabinet. Even the upholstered divan was covered with them, where, presumably, the Shining Herald lay – or was supposed to lie – so that the spirit Amorasa could translate the Babylonian script in which the Lost Gospel was written.

The blood on the carpet – wet, just soaked in a few hours ago, like the blood in the cottage – lay between the desk and the door. Droplets had splattered the papers on the table and the divan. A violent blow or blows. January stared at them in the candle's wavery gleam. If everyone was out searching, it would be an easy matter to carry Spring's body down the long ladder to the escape tunnel, to take him to the cellar of the cottage . . .

He could easily have missed a blood trail, hurrying by a single thread of light.

Had Eve Russell been one of those dressing-gowned women, with their long hair hanging down their backs, who'd gone streaming after the wagon, lamps upheld in their hands?

Or is she somewhere in the house still?

The study door was locked. Poking through the keyhole with a rolled-up quill of paper proved useless. The key had been taken.

Damn it . . .

He went back to the desk, opened the upper drawer and found half a dozen keys, strung together on a ribbon. His silver watch was there, too, taken from his coat – or more properly Mr Barnum's coat – that had been hanging behind the screen when Broadax had come for him. With them was the daguerreotype of Eve Russell. Beside it was another picture of her, an ivory miniature done – by the look of her – a few years ago, when she must have been twelve or thirteen.

How the hell would they have laid hands on THAT?

She's here. She must be here.

He picked the miniature up, turned it in his fingers. He felt shocked and angry, but not really surprised.

This was more than the girl running away. This theft – *by a servant? From her mother's luggage, or her mother's handbag on some shopping expedition?* – made it clear.

She had been targeted.

WHY???

Even as his mind turned at the puzzle, he was trying keys in the study door, and yes, one of the larger ones worked. He tied a loose end of ribbon around it, to identify it in a hurry, and taking up his candle, moved down the hall again, trying to recognize the way he'd come Monday night. He found the back stair up which Hal Shamrock had led him, but the hallway, despite the identical, ubiquitous wallpaper, didn't look familiar. He opened a door into a small room draped, like the cottage, in black curtains, and smelling, like his former prison, of incense.

There was a divan here, too. A lamp, and a goblet on the table, but the floor underfoot was thick with carpet.

The same room, altered? He felt along the curtains and found a door, which let him into another room, windowless also, but festooned like a stage-set in colored curtains that glimmered faintly in the glow of his candle. Plaster pilasters circled its walls – he was reminded again of the Theatre d'Orleans – and between them postured some of the most indecent statues he'd encountered this side of Paris. The room smelled of incense, of sex, and of stale perfume.

He thought, *Ah*. In a sense, it *was* a stage set. An artificial Paradise.

Hashish, houris, someone you trust telling you it's all a dream . . .

A dream you paid for, of ecstasies you'd never have touched in your pious and prudent waking life.

His suspicion – and Del Pearce's rumor – was confirmed, but the solution solved nothing.

The world is crammed with whores. But Hannibal was right: why kidnap – or seek out and lure – one specific girl whose parents you know will cause trouble?

Time to go. His heart was pounding. They could be back – *Heaven knows what took them out of here in such a rush . . .*

Or is this the night that Broadax 'returns from the dead'?

211

Can't be. January paused in the corridor, trying to get his bearings among walls that all looked the same. *He's not going to make his reappearance until I'm dead.*

Maybe someone found Spring's body, in some artfully contrived setting, with a note from me in his pocket announcing my intention to murder the Patriarch.

I wouldn't put it past him.

He locked the study door behind him, but kept the keys. He guessed, now, what he'd probably find in the locked upper story of the cottage he'd been in tonight, if he had time to look. Another 'paradise chamber' where a wealthy gentleman could have his dreams come true.

The Old Man of the Mountain in legend has nothing on the Reverend Serapis Broadax.

He paused by the littered work table, his eye caught by a tattered, smoke-stained brown scroll. Unrolling it a little, he saw that it was written in some unknown lettering. The papers next to it bore a man's firm, scrawling handwriting: 'And the Lord said unto Peter, "Nothing shall be lost, to those who Believe; no, not even the very gates of Death. For know you, that . . ."'

He unrolled the scroll a little more. The rest of it was blank. The four other scrolls, tied up with faded ribbons, were, when untied, also blank.

He felt no surprise whatsoever.

He slipped through the panel in the wall by the fireplace, and gently pulled it to behind him.

And the courts won't believe a word of it, he reflected, descending the long ladder to the

212

tunnel again. *Who knows? The local judge may be one of those gentlemen believers, who come to the Blessed Land to be 'soothed' with a couple of spoonfuls of hashish and some amazing dreams of being serviced by beautiful houris in a silk-draped room . . .*

Or perhaps experiences less conventional. And less innocent.

He could just hear the local sheriff: 'There's no crime being committed . . . and aren't you the feller they saw murder the Reverend Broadax?'

But what I CAN do, he reflected angrily, *is get them to drag the river close to that barn in the woods where the other tunnel comes up. Ten to one they dump the bodies of the runaways there, with their bellies slit and their feet weighted so they won't float.*

He can get rid of the shoes, but he can't hide the bones.

His steps slowed as he approached the outside end of the tunnel, and he slipped his hand into his trouser pocket, to reassure himself that his box of lucifers was within reach. As he did so his fingers met with the stiff rectangle of the daguerreotype, the smooth small shape of the miniature of Eve Russell as a young girl.

Where would they have gotten that miniature? Were they watching her family – dogging them – from the moment they came to New York?

What was it about them – about *her* – that drew their attention? Or did they steal it *after* she started coming to the lectures, started showing how drawn she was to the messages from the

213

Other Side? Did *she* give it to them? And if so, why?

Is she their victim, or their accomplice?

He stood still for a time with one hand resting on the half-rotted wooden tunnel prop beside him, listening. Listening for his life.

Silently – and for all his great size, January could move like a cat – he edged forward again.

The ramp sloped up. He would have wished to enter the haybarn unbeknownst to Pearce – or anyone who might have surprised Pearce, disposed of him and replaced him – but the old man had told him he would close up the trap and sweep dirt and straw over it again. That way, if anyone did enter the barn, he – Pearce – could hide, and it wouldn't be obvious that someone had entered the Residence that way. Had something happened to Pearce, he doubted he'd have heard the dogs barking, while he was in the house.

He pushed up the trap, which must have been counter-weighted, for it moved easily.

Candle gleam flickered above. January put his head over the edge. The eyes of the dogs glowed in the dim light like demon mirrors, but neither made a sound. Del Pearce whispered, 'Ben?' and emerged from behind a support post.

'I hope so.'

'You see what went on? I heard one hell of a commotion, 'bout three-quarters of an hour ago: shoutin' an' clamorin', an' I feared it all had somethin' to do with you.'

January emerged from the trap, which he then lowered into its place again. Pearce stepped from the shadow, fetched the twig broom, and brushed straw and dirt over the cracks, while January held both candles and stood halfway to the door, listening. 'Nothing to do with me – I hope,' he said grimly. 'The whole population of the Blessed Land, it looked like, got stirred up like hornets, and I took that as a sign from Providence that it was time to have a quick look in the Residence itself.'

As they made their way back to the wagon, January related in a whisper what he'd found in the few minutes he'd stolen within the old fortress: the scrolls, the hidden chambers, the blood that spattered the study's heaped papers and soaked its carpet. 'We need to get the sheriff,' said January. 'Quickly, while Spring's body will still be recognizable. Before they can clear away the blood-soaked carpet in the study – the amount of furniture in that room will slow them down. They can get rid of the trestles in the cottage cellar . . .'

'And who'll testify?' demanded Pearce. 'You?' The late moonlight glinted on his snowy hair. 'Sheriff Harter's hand in glove with the slave catchers. Has been for years, for all his readin' the Bible in Church every Sunday. Judge Bale may listen to your story and even swear out a warrant, but little good that'll do you if Harter claps you in jail for the murder, and the blackbirders just happen to come through and recognize you as a runaway from South Carolina that they just happen to be lookin' for.'

January was silent. The man was right, and he knew it. He climbed into the hay wagon, standing undisturbed where they'd left it, the team hitched to the back of a long stack of cord wood such as he'd slept under – had it only been Tuesday night? Kindled a lantern, and held it while Pearce slipped the bits into the mouths of the horses again, and backed them on to the narrow trace that the woodcutters had left.

'Myself,' grunted the old man, 'I say we wait, 'til that little gal of yours gets back from the city an' tells us somethin' useful about that godless heathen heretic. If that Russell girl is still alive at this point, she's like to remain so while they thinks they're safe. You put your nose out of hidin', they'll spook. Who's this Old Man of the Mountain you spoke of?'

January took the reins while Pearce sprang, with surprising lightness for his seventy-eight years, to the box beside him.

'The Old Man of the Mountain was a Mohammedan preacher, back in the old days of the Crusades,' he said. 'According to legends – which may or may not be true – he would train his followers as assassins, and reward them by giving them a "magic potion" which transported them to Paradise, where they'd be entertained by spirits in the shape of beautiful young women. In reality, of course, what he'd give them was a dose of hashish and put them in a secret garden, to be entertained by beautiful young women in the shape of beautiful young women. And, when they came out of it – feeling very good but rather tired, I daresay – he'd tell them that only he could transport them back there. They had sworn vows of celibacy, but because it was

216

all a dream and the beautiful young women were only spirits, everything was all right and they hadn't broken any vows.'

'Tcha! Just like I said – heathens!'

'How much do you suppose men would pay,' asked January softly, 'for "beautiful dreams" of doing things, perhaps, that they wouldn't want to admit to themselves that they wanted to do? Or things that they admitted they wanted, but didn't dare seek in New York?'

Pearce said, 'Tcha!' again. 'So it's true about them girls he brings in from Rochester.'

'Maybe not always girls,' murmured January. 'And maybe not always adults. Considering he got the house and the land free, and add that to what New England abolitionists are donating to him, and what people give him to translate the Gospel of James – with supernatural assistance, of course – and what people pay the Shining Herald to chat with the souls of the departed . . .'

Malek . . . whispered a voice at the back of his mind, and he thrust the thought away.

'More'n enough,' growled Pearce, 'to hand over fat Christmas presents to Sheriff Harter, for damn sure. An' he'll ask you – as he's shovin' you in the cells – even if it's all true, what laws have been broke in all that, give or take a Commandment or three?'

'Murdering my friend,' said January quietly. 'And tricking and kidnapping an English girl who thought she was finding answers to her life.'

Though both men were exhausted, they drove until almost dawn. They stopped finally in a

217

woodlot near Marcellus to sleep for a few hours, big gray Brutus and squat yellow Mars keeping watch under the wagon bed. January dreamed uneasily of the corridors of the Residence, multiplied endlessly in a maze of gaudy wallpaper and locked doors, behind one of which – but he didn't know which one – a girl was crying. He knew – and he didn't know how – that Ayasha was somewhere in the Residence also. *I have to find her*, January kept thinking, *before I leave.*

Maybe if I find her, I can bring her back with me . . .

Then he would wake, to hear the wave of first birdsong passing like wind through the trees. The metallic *breet* of the night hawk, the sweet coo-coo-coo of the cuckoo, answered distantly the shrill alarm of first cock crow in the yard of some farm.

Chloë won't even be leaving for New York until this morning, he thought, as he sank back into the hay. He tried to remember when the last train stopped at Syracuse, and how long it would take for a buggy to reach the town. A day from Albany down to the city, two days to return. Add to that whatever time it would take for her to learn whatever might be learned, to Serapis Broadax's discredit – given that his name probably wasn't really Serapis Broadax. He tried to put together how many days that added up to.

They know Miss Russell is a liability to them. How many days, until they lose their nerve. . .?

Dark Travis was in the dooryard of the Celestial Comrade's tumbledown farmhouse when the wagon drew up before the haybarn there. The young man looked surprised at the appearance of a wagonload of hay at this early hour, but January – concealed under the load – saw the Celestial Comrade speak to him, explaining – *Do spirits tell fibs? And if so, how well?* Whatever she said, it served to distract him, for he turned back to her, and continued speaking as she counted out eggs for him to put into his basket. Pearce meanwhile unharnessed the team and led them to their stable, the dogs padding at his heels hopeful of breakfast, and January remained under the hay, struggling not to fall asleep again in the morning's growing heat.

Hunger kept him awake. It had been a long night.

At long last the young man departed – with two covered kettles of milk and a basket of eggs – and the Spirit crossed the yard, and held out a hand to steady January in climbing down.

'What happened last night?' she asked.

January shook his head. 'I learned something of what's going on in the Blessed Land,' he said. 'There's been murder done there, but I'm afraid that if I go to the sheriff—'

'Sheriff Harter's already on his way there.' Her gray eyes were dark with concern. 'Had you not driven into the yard just now – and Mr Pearce gone about his business as he always does – I would have feared that they'd found you, either the sheriff or Mr Teems and his followers. Dark Travis says, the Children are angry enough to do you mischief, and not wait

219

for what Mr Harter says. They are searching every barn and farmhouse in the county. I'm not sure now that you could get across to Canada, or indeed that you could make it to Syracuse—'

And, when January looked at her in puzzlement, she said, 'They've found the Reverend Broadax's body. And Dark says, that they're saying that the tracks all around where he lay could have been made by no one, save a man of your size.'

Eighteen

The Children of the Light arrived an hour and a half later.

January had by that time helped Del Pearce return all the hay to the loft and put the wagon away. From the hollow bed of a broken-down cart in the barn – a cart whose false floor made him wonder whether it had originally been acquired from the enterprising Mr Teasle – he watched Jared Ott and three other men poke around in the bins of oats and corn along the far wall, while Orion Teems stood awkwardly in the doorway. The other men wore expressions of grief and rage, but Ott, it seemed to January, was only quietly grim, like a man hunting rats. Once, when the other two searchers had gone up to the loft, Ott glanced around, as if to make sure he was unobserved, and crossed back quickly to Teems. January didn't hear what he said to the gray-clothed secretary, but Teems returned sharply, 'Now isn't the time!'

'When, then?'

'This afternoon. Before dinner. Come up to the . . . come up to the study, and I'll show you.'

Ott grunted, that Cupid mouth set like a beaver trap and his eyes narrowed, but he went back to his searching without further words.

January wondered if he had asked Teems about what was going to happen to the land that was held – supposedly – by the Community, now that the Patriarch was allegedly dead? And if Teems was nervous because Ott hadn't been the only one of the Children to ask?

Or does Ott, too, suspect there's something amiss about this 'corpse' they've found?

And how is Teems going to explain the blood in the study? Presumably, that's what he's going to 'show' Ott.

To prove what?

Teems turned quickly to speak to someone outside, his face smooth and grave. 'There is absolutely no question that you would knowingly shelter a murderer, m'am, but I'm afraid we're going to have to search the house as well.'

'You'll search the house when you show me a warrant—' began Del Pearce's harsh voice, and the Celestial Comrade overrode him.

'A warrant won't be necessary, Mr Teems. Of course you and your friends may search.'

Teems inclined his head, morning light flashing on the small, oval lenses of his spectacles. Looking at his well-cut town jacket and unsmirched trousers, January remembered Spring

221

telling him that Teems had been Broadax's secretary on that expedition to Mesopotamia. January supposed that appearances could be deceiving, and that the stooped, slightly balding man could be tougher than he looked.

But in Paris, he had talked to men who had actually been to the ruins of Babylon. And whereas it was possible to picture the powerful Broadax scrambling around desert ruins and marshy oases haunted by the kind of banditti these men had described, he couldn't picture Teems dealing with heat, thirst, sandstorms, and nomad tribes who would kill Christians under the impression that doing so would please Allah.

For one thing, now that he saw him in daylight, Teems' alabaster complexion had clearly never encountered the violence of the desert sun – certainly not less than two years previously. For that matter, now that January cast his mind back, neither had Broadax's. His strong hands had been without calluses, and for all their hairiness, lily-white as a lady's. The hands of a man who had never done manual labor. The face of a man who has not spent months in blistering sun.

Was that why I was so ready to disbelieve?

The men left the barn. He heard their voices in the yard, and slithered from the false wagon bed to peek through the crack of the door. Teems was standing by his horse's head, apologizing to the Celestial Comrade and to Pearce for troubling them. 'He will be buried on Sunday,' he said. 'Men and women are coming from as far away as Rochester and Utica, to pay homage to one who was, perhaps, the most remarkable human soul that I have ever known.' He bowed his head, as if struggling to control some grievous emotion.

'I would like to be able to tell them, when his earthly body is laid to rest, that his murderer has been brought to justice.'

'And *he* can't tell you where the man is?' jibbed Pearce.

Teems just managed not to glare at him, though his back stiffened as if he'd been goosed. 'I think everyone in the county,' he said after a moment, 'has heard how he appeared in a vision to his followers on the night after his death, showing us all – eighty-three people! – what had become of him. Last night he came to the Herald in a dream, telling her where his body could be found, at a crossroads in the woods about a mile from the Residence.'

The old man looked about to make some other acid observation – the one that sprang to January's mind was *And if it was lying at a crossroad how did they miss it in the three days they've been combing the countryside?* – but the Celestial Comrade casually stepped on Pearce's foot – hard – and asked, 'Might I, then, come to pay my respects?'

Teems bowed deeply and said, 'Of course, m'am. We would be most honored.'

He glared at Pearce again, mounted, and, trailed by his posse, rode away. Pearce's dogs, standing behind the Celestial Comrade's skirts, barked at them as they left.

In the gate of the yard they passed a rider coming in – tall, powerfully built, and stocky – who removed his shabby tweed cap with a flourish to bow to the Comrade and revealed the amiable, round, and still slightly discolored countenance of P.T. Barnum.

'Do I address the Spirit called the Celestial Comrade?' asked the showman, as Teems and his party disappeared around the copse of trees which hid the road.

'You do, sir.'

'My name is Phineas Barnum.'

He dropped from the saddle, bowed, and glanced at Pearce, who said gruffly, 'Del Pearce,' and thrust out his hand. 'Ben January'll have wrote you?'

But January was already striding from the barn, his hand held out and a smile of relief seeming to fill the whole of his body. Barnum grinned back and returned his grip.

'Lordy, you were right when you said you were a man skilled in choosing the moment to fly! The whole district is up in arms! So you've gone and done for the Shining Herald's mouthpiece, have you?'

'I have not!' January was laughing in spite of himself, as the Celestial Comrade smiled, and beckoned them both to follow her to the house. Pearce took the reins of Barnum's horse ('I could get ten cents a head exhibiting him as half-horse, half-snail,' the showman remarked a little later), and came into the kitchen after a few minutes, as the Comrade was pouring out cider for her guests.

January rapidly narrated his experiences in the Blessed Land, both on the previous Monday and last night, while Barnum nodded at the account of frankincense, hashish, and shimmering curtains in hidden *sancta sanctora*. 'That all sounds very like the set-up a confidence trickster named Callan was running in Philadelphia a few years ago,' he said. 'Callan was a big fellow, too – I went to some of his lectures – with a tremendous mane of brown hair, and blue eyes. He had a great following among wealthy men, mostly churchgoing elders who would drown themselves rather than ogle a shapely . . . um . . . *ladybird*' – he substituted a more refined term, with a quick, shy glance at the Comrade – 'much less put a foot across the threshold of a disorderly house.'

January smiled a little to himself. A Spirit sent by Heaven – and presumably on good terms with the creator of human bodies and human souls – would probably not be shocked by anything a mortal man could say.

'They'd go to him for "mystical visions" and evidently had visions of experiences beyond the dreams of . . . well, beyond the dreams of anyone but Samuel Taylor Coleridge and the average fourteen-year-old boy.'

Sudden anger flickered in Barnum's dark eyes. 'I'm a humbug, Benjamin,' he said. 'I'll be the first to tell you I'm the King of the Humbugs. I'll admit to the world I collected twenty-five cents a head for people to gawk at George Washington's old mammy – as I'm sure your friend Mr Spring told you . . .'

'He did,' said January, rather grimly.

'Well, I did the poor old lady no real harm, for all that. She'd have been worked a good deal harder – and at her age, too! – had Lindsay and Bartram sold her to some gentleman who wanted a baby nurse or a sewing woman down South. And I did *not* have her teeth pulled so she'd look older – they were rotted to the root and she was in pain.'

He glanced across at January, as if expecting him to contradict, but January said nothing.

'I can promise you she ate better, and slept warmer, as my employee, than she would have had she been "given her freedom" and turned loose on the Philadelphia streets because she was no use to anyone anymore. And I did no harm to those who paid twenty-five cents to see her – every one of whom, I daresay, suspected in his heart that he wasn't really seeing George Washington's mammy. Except of course the children.'

He relaxed, and smiled. 'And they were thrilled. I could have stood a man up in a little cotton nightshirt with a slingshot in his hand and advertised him as King David, and the children would have been just as delighted. And they would have taken no harm from it any more than they take from believing that jolly old Santa Claus comes bouncing down their chimneys on Christmas Eve with his sack full of toys.

'But dosing a man with hashish, unknowing, so that he'll be free of his own hard-held scruples long enough to do what he's chosen all his life – for whatever his own reasons – *not* to do, under

226

the impression that it's all a dream . . . Faugh! Broadax – if it's the same man – is lucky none of his "spiritual clients" has yet picked up a dose of' – he glanced again in the direction of the Celestial Comrade, calmly holding out a plate of bread and butter to him – 'um . . . picked up a cold in the head from one of those "visions". And if what you say is true about his methods of getting money from philanthropists like the Tappans . . .'

January said quietly, 'I think it is. I won't be able to prove anything until the river is dragged, opposite where that tunnel comes out. He'll have gotten rid of whatever evidence there is in the house or the tunnel, by this time.'

'You think his death is a fake?'

'Of course it is. It's his quickest way to make sure that his followers kill me.' January shivered at the recollection of the dogs bursting through the foliage of the woods, of the long drop down the cliff into the lake waters, not knowing what rocks might lie beneath the surface.

'I suspect that "vision" the Children had Tuesday night was a stopgap, for him and whoever he's working with – certainly Teems, probably Hal Shamrock – to find someone who's enough like Broadax for his body to pass for the Patriarch's. With men coming and going through Syracuse to work on the railroads, it couldn't have been hard. I'll bet you a quarter that the body they found was dressed in Broadax's clothing, but the face was too mutilated to be clearly identified. After I'm dead, he'll turn up saying he doesn't remember a thing about what happened—'

'Or that he was temporarily taken up to Heaven,' suggested Barnum, with a grin, 'and that he now has revelations of his own to impart.'

Pearce exclaimed, 'T'cha!' at this blasphemy.

'I wouldn't put it past him. *Could* he fake that vision? Dozens of people saw it.'

'Of course.' The King of the Humbugs looked surprised that he'd ask.

'My wife works for the opera,' January explained. 'Backstage, making colored fires and clouds of smoke and mist. She's worked magic lanterns, but a magic lantern slide is static—'

'They have a new type of light,' said Barnum. 'I've read about its use in London, and on the Paris stage, but it hasn't appeared in America yet, not even in New York.'

'Limelight,' said January. 'Calcium light, from burning quicklime. I think I've even seen it in use—'

'It's a very intense white light,' agreed Barnum. 'It's easily strong enough to carry the reflection of a living person through a couple of mirrors, into a darkened room. Did you happen to get a look at the ceiling of that parlor where they hold these conversations with the dead?'

January tried to sort his memories of a very crowded evening.

''Tis beams,' growled Pearce. 'Bare beams, an' all dark with smoke.'

'Beams the length of the room, or the short way across?'

'Short way across.'

228

'I thought as much,' said Barnum briskly. 'That would hide the supporting rods for the pane of glass that they'd run down behind the podium and the Herald's couch – there was a space between the chairs and the couch and podium, wasn't there?'

'About twelve feet.'

'The room where the figure actually stood – or where the white light was reflected from, to shine around the Herald's couch – would be actually underneath the parlor, or to one side of it . . .'

'I thought it might be something like that.'

'Who wouldn't?' Barnum shrugged. 'Except of course people who aren't used to asking if what they're seeing is really what they're seeing.'

'Pah!' Del Pearce's fists tightened, the names of God and the Devil rippling below his knuckles as if readying for Armageddon. '"The children of this world are wiser in their day than the children of light," the Lord says, but they'll be damned to the flames of Hell all the same.'

'Yet they do come up with some very ingenious devices,' murmured the Comrade, fascinated and at the same time, January thought, rather sad.

'They have a sort of choir singing,' he recalled. 'That would cover whatever noise the mechanism would make.'

'Well, there you are. You have a room nearby in darkness, except for a couple of these calcium lights and a large, angled mirror to throw the image on to the glass. If, as you say, you were taken from your prison room just as you stood in your shirtsleeves, nothing would have been easier than for them to dress someone in your

229

coat – or *my* coat, I should say . . . the garment seems to be having more adventures than I have, since I left my lodgings in New York last Saturday . . .'

'That'd be Hal Shamrock,' pointed out Pearce. 'He's near to Ben's height, and if he put boot-blacking on his face, there's not one man in ten in this county who'd see anythin' but, "There goes a great big black nigger who's blacker'n Shamrock".'

'And how many other giant blackamoors are there running at large about Onondaga County?' demanded Barnum rhetorically.

'That's actually very clever,' remarked the Spirit. She settled with her hands folded around her pottery tumbler of lemonade. 'Even should Ben go to Sheriff Harter – even were Sheriff Harter an honest man, which I fear he is not – Harter could not but arrest him. Once he's in jail, I fear there are enough men in this county who believe in Broadax – who believe that the Shining Herald speaks the truth – that Ben might very well come to grief in the jail, before anything can be proven one way or another. Mr Ott, at least, and Raleigh Shadwell over in Auburn, are quite capable of storming the jail. And there are others in the county as well. And even if the matter comes to trial, a judge might well not draw a line between what men say they saw in a vision, and what they can actually have been proved to have seen with their own eyes.'

'More than that,' said January quietly. 'Your adventuresome coat, Mr Barnum, wasn't just the thing they used to identify me. By the

230

daguerreotype that was in the pocket – the daguerreotype I found in Broadax's desk – they now know that I was sent to find Eve Russell. Which means there's a good chance that, whatever their reasons for luring her to them in the first place, they'll have to get rid of her, the minute they sense they're in danger. A judge – or your Sheriff Harter – may not believe me. But they'd believe her. And Broadax knows it.'

The Celestial Comrade said, as if it were a matter of retrieving a pair of gloves dropped at Church, 'Then we'll have to go back.'

'And it had better,' said Barnum, 'be tonight.'

It rained in the afternoon, thunder rumbling over the wooded hills. January ate, and slept, while Del Pearce returned to his own farm – which he shared, January learned, with a niece and her husband – and Barnum assisted the Celestial Comrade with bringing in the cows to be milked. In this he was aided by two women from the New Land Community ('Oh, we're always glad to help the Spirit . . .'), and a man who belonged to the Swedenborgian congregation in Auburn. Waking a little after noon in the tiny attic, January heard their voices rising dimly from the kitchen as the rain drummed on the shingles, talking of Heaven and God's will for humankind and whether it was Peyton Shadwell's dog that had gotten into the New Land hen roost, or a fox. ('It ain't the first time Goliath's gone after chickens, but the bites on that hen don't look big enough for Goliath . . .')

The storm had ceased, and the air felt fresh as

if new-laundered, when Del Pearce returned with his team and a small wagon. A layer of empty apple boxes filled the back. 'Which I'll say as I'm taking to Duncan Turner, who thinks his orchard's gonna crop heavy this year,' said the old man. 'If any asks.'

'It's always best,' agreed Barnum, 'if one looks like one has a perfectly legitimate reason for doing what you're doing . . .'

'So say the children of this world,' sniffed Pearce, and gave the Celestial Comrade a hand up on to the wagon seat. But when Barnum asked him about treasure scrying ('What *were* the Spanish doing, burying treasure hereabouts?'), and how to make demons tell you where gold was hidden, and the dark thing that was said to dwell at the bottom of Lake Cayuga that the Indians wouldn't talk about, he loosened up. 'Young Joe Smith, over to Monroe County, that later founded his own religion and moved on to Illinois with the whole tribe of 'em – now, *he* was a prime treasure scryer in his day . . .'

The Celestial Comrade, leaning over the back of the wagon seat, added her experiences and recollections, and, sitting on the floor beside Barnum's feet, January once or twice caught a glance, when Pearce looked over his shoulder at the tall, thin woman in her faded frock, that told him that what she had said was the truth. Pearce had loved Anne Seabright, and thirty years later, loved still the woman she had become after her illness.

'Where does Broadax get his information?' asked January. 'Or does the Herald get hers?

What I heard Monday night sounded very specific, names and ages and incidents—'

'I daresay he buys it from servants,' put in the Celestial Comrade unexpectedly, exhibiting a degree of familiarity with the ways of the world that would have surprised many preachers January knew. He had been right, he reflected, about how thoroughly spirits sent from Heaven might have been briefed before their descent. 'It's what professional blackmailers do, isn't it?' She looked inquiringly at Barnum. Behind the wagon, Brutus and Mars darted into the woods along the roadway at the sight of a squirrel, to return, panting and muddy, to their places.

'There's men in town who broker such things,' agreed the showman, his brow again growing dark. 'Men – or women – who let it be known they'll pay good money for letters or trinkets or cooked account books, with the understanding that they know what to do with them, and the servants in wealthy households don't, really. Or Broadax can have stooges he works with regularly, who move from household to household. This Callan fellow in Philadelphia was supposed to have a wife who was a hairdresser – fat little woman named Katy – who picked up all kinds of information for him.'

'There's a voodoo in New Orleans,' said January slowly, 'who dresses hair – white ladies' hair – and knows every secret in the town.' He remembered, too, how his sister Olympe would do favors for slaves, uncrossing them when they found their shoes had been cursed, or making juju candles or love drops,

233

with the understanding that if they ever found any interesting bits of information about their owners, that they'd pass those items along to her.

'As for the Herald,' Barnum went on, 'I'd say it's a combination of being a good guesser, and being able to read people. Or maybe Mrs Callan – if Broadax and Callan are the same person – is still in the picture someplace. But some people can simply do that. Can tell, looking at a man, if he's lost his wife or his child or his brother. When I saw the Herald a few years ago in Rochester – and I'm pretty sure it was the same woman, though she went by Molly Skeritt then – she'd start in with things like, "I see a woman standing behind you . . . her hand is on your shoulder . . ." and eight times out of ten the mark'll cry out "Elizabeth!" or "Matilda!" or whatever her name was. I will say, young as she was – and at that time she was barely a girl – Skeritt was good at leading marks – *clients'* – he corrected himself, a little self-consciously – 'from one thing to the next. She worked the towns along the Canal for about two years, before she hooked up with Broadax last year and started preaching as well – not to speak of translating ancient Babylonian texts.'

He frowned again, looking out into the soft-falling twilight beyond the trees that bordered the road. 'She wasn't doing any real harm in those days, you know. And I think she comforted many people, who could not face the thought of never speaking to their loved ones again.'

And Pearce said, 'Bound for Hell, the lot of

234

'em. Folk should read their Bibles and trust in the Lord, rather'n running to lying heretics. Serve 'em right, if they're robbed.'

They reached the haybarn beside the river at full dusk, and Pearce once again opened the trap in the floor. 'We shall stay at the back of the Great Parlor,' promised the Spirit quietly, 'close to the door that leads into the east wing.' In her dark, plain gown, too large for her thin frame and thirty years out of date, she could have been any farmwife, bound for church.

'If they have a limelight set-up,' added Barnum, 'the best place for it will be in a cellar directly under this Great Parlor of theirs. Or a room immediately adjacent to it.' He touched a match to the flame in the dark lantern which Pearce brought out from beneath the wagon seat.

'That close to the river,' said January, 'did the old fort *have* cellars?'

'Aye,' growled Pearce. 'Shallow ones, like those under the cottages, though the fort was built on a fair spur of firm land. There's a cellar below that Great Parlor of theirs, right enough.'

'Meaning the floor – carpet and all – is hinged, unless the limelight apparatus – valves and cylinders and hoses – is in a room to one side or the other. That would make it easier for us to find . . .'

'Easier for us to show the Children of the Light what's going on as well,' said January. 'And if we can catch him in there, so much the better.'

'Don't even imagine it, dear boy.' Barnum held

his lantern high, and looked appraisingly down at the slanted floor of the tunnel. 'Do you think even one of them would believe you, even when presented with the evidence of their own eyes? They'd say it was all a trick – *your* trick – murder you where you stand, and welcome him back to life with tears.'

'Take this.' Pearce held out to January one of the pistols he had lent him the previous night. 'If there's trouble, we'll make for here. No goin' back for anybody 'til dawn. No sense blunderin' about in the woods missin' each other.'

January noticed that the old farmer's coat pocket sagged with the weight of the other pistol of the pair, and wondered if the Celestial Comrade was aware that her friend was armed. Barnum's ragged corduroy jacket – actually his own – he noticed, hung lopsided as well.

'Whether or not they believe me,' he whispered, as the trap settled down behind them with a leathery creak, 'at least I'll have a white witness to whatever we might find.'

'My dear Benjamin, you don't think anyone in New York would believe a word *I* say?'

January paused, and held the lantern down close to the muddy floor. The scuffs and marks in the mud there weren't more than a few hours old – and certainly more numerous than they'd been the previous night – but he doubted even his friend Shaw of the New Orleans City Guards would have been able to make anything of them.

'How many people would have to be in on this?' he asked softly, as they resumed their progress.

'If Broadax and the Herald are up top doing their act, someone has to be operating the lime-light apparatus – lowering the floor, moving the mirrors into place. And someone else has to be the actual specter with a sheet over his head. Mr Spring mentioned a couple named Greene, who came here with Broadax and Orion Teems last year. There's Hal Shamrock, who by his own admission comes from town. Would he have others?'

'Not if he's smart, he won't,' murmured Barnum. 'Unless you're running what's called a Big Store set-up – a confidence trick in which *everybody* is in on the game, to target a single, extremely wealthy, mark – every extra player, means one more chance that somebody'll peach on you. He's probably got others – including a child, or a midget – in New York . . . What's up there?'

'One of the cottages,' whispered January. 'I was in it last night – and in any case I'm virtu-ally certain they'll have Mamzelle Russell in the main house . . . if she's still alive. A dead body lay there sometime yesterday,' he added quietly. 'Spring's, I think. Of course he'd come here, when he heard of Broadax's "murder". He trusted Broadax. Believed in him implicitly.'

Barnum was silent for a moment. Then he said, 'That's his skill, you know. Broadax, or whatever his name really is. Like a singer's voice, or a writer's way with images and words. The ability to make people trust him. Some people have that, you know.'

January said, very quietly, 'Yes,' thinking of

all those people who'd paid twenty-five cents – the price of food for a family, down in the Bowery – to see George Washington's mammy.

Thinking also of that tall, lanky quadroon who'd come out of a nameless saloon on Perdidio Street, to drape an arm around a young black sailor's shoulders and smile, 'You look like you need a guide 'round here, friend!'

'I can't imagine all those farmers,' Barnum went on, 'who formed the "Community" so that the place would be isolated and under Broadax's control, would be in on it. Certainly the poor saps who pay for spiritual advice and amazing visions wouldn't be. You can get your boots waxed, even with incense and silk curtains thrown in, if that's your fancy, back in New York, without coming all the way out here. There are places in town sufficiently discreet about it, if you're willing to admit *to yourself* that that's what you want.'

January recalled the specialties of some of the brothels in Paris, and New Orleans, and felt a sour taste in his mouth. 'And a nice little investment for Broadax,' he murmured, 'if he wants to go in for blackmail later on.'

They climbed the ladder to the second floor, closed the slides on their lanterns. Listened, barely breathing, at the panel, before January gently pushed it open and they stepped once more into the darkness of Broadax's study.

After the uncanny stillness below the ground, the hymns that floated up from the Great Parlor seemed very clear. Barnum looked around him at the confusion of papers, piled now not only

238

on the desk and the worktable, but on the floor as well. 'Good Lord . . .'

'I thought last night the place might have been searched,' whispered January. 'It looks as if someone came in and finished the job.'

'Or someone else came.' Barnum risked pushing the lantern slide wider, held up the light. 'And did it more thoroughly.'

January remembered Ott's sharp, low-voiced question put to Teems that morning, and the secretary's sharp reply: 'Now isn't the time!' Softly, he said, 'I can guess what they were looking for.'

'Not for evidence of Testamentary Fraud, I daresay.' Barnum touched the scrolls on the table. 'Although I suppose Broadax would claim that the letters appeared and disappeared from the paper – that's been done before. It's surprising how many people believe in that kind of thing. The murder was done here.'

January nodded, and crouched to move aside papers which had fallen over the now-crusted bloodspot on the carpet. No effort had been made to clean it up, or to wipe away the spots on the desk. The blood-spattered 'translation' had been half-covered with a stack of notebooks.

Barnum moved his light, the glow falling across more notebooks, opened and stacked on one another. 'Looking for the accounts?'

'Or the contracts. With Broadax "dead"' – January stepped over to peer into a cabinet, empty, its contents spewed on to every nearby table and surface – '*I'd* certainly want to know the status of my farmland vis-à-vis the Blessed

239

Land. I had less of a light last night, and I was in a hurry, but I'll swear the mess wasn't nearly this bad. Look,' he added, his lantern glow traveling to the cold fireplace, where notebooks, ledgers, and papers had been stacked carelessly around a couple of chairs and a table, the only pieces of furniture in the room not piled with records. 'Two people. It wasn't like this last night.'

The light slithered across the round sides of a bottle of V.S.O.P. brandy, and two glasses.

'Mighty cool.' Barnum crossed to join him. His voice took on a mocking lower-class accent: 'I say, we've just burgled the place, let's have a little spot of something . . .'

January had picked up one of the glasses and sniffed it, the heavy sweetness of the liquor all but hiding that deadly bitter whisper underneath.

He handed it to Barnum, and sniffed the other glass.

Brandy alone, or so little laudanum as to be undetectable.

The bottle, when he smelled it, remained untainted as far as he could tell.

Barnum set down the glass with the drugged remnant in it, his face sober. 'You're sure?'

January shook his head. 'As I said, I was in a hurry. I had no idea when they'd be coming back. But I think I'd have noticed the two chairs being clear if everything else was in this much disorder. And I'm pretty sure,' he added, holding the untainted glass close to his lantern, 'that the dregs of the brandy are fresher than the blood.'

'This afternoon,' Teems had said. 'Before dinner. Come up to the study, and I'll show you.'

As they stepped into the corridor the music drifted up some nearby stair in the darkness:

> Ye fearful saints, fresh courage take;
> The clouds ye so much dread
> Are big with mercy and shall break
> In blessings on your head.

Yet another 'Night of Revelation' as well as a service for the corpse? January wondered if Broadax himself would appear to his followers, to urge them to find his murderer – though in that case, how would he then resurrect himself after January had been found and killed?

Does he even intend to?

How many of those families who had signed over their property to the Blessed Land had been sufficiently skilled in the language of contracts to make sure that they said what Broadax told them they said? 'It's all so simple,' the Patriarch had explained . . .

And what could be simpler, after Benjamin January had 'murdered' him, than for him to simply remain dead, and quietly carry through the sale of the properties as he'd all along intended to do? The farms, the houses, the investments, in land skyrocketing in value as the railroad followed the trade route of the Canal . . . those had been the real kill. The money from abolitionist groups, and devotees of the newly translated Gospel of James, and those who'd paid to hear the Shining Herald give them word

241

of those they loved . . . Not to speak of wealthy gentlemen seeking spiritual solace and dreams of what they'd dare not admit in waking life . . .

That was all window dressing.

'This is the stair I came up Monday night,' he breathed, and Barnum nodded. The Great Parlor lay just below, and a faint reflection of its lamplight outlined the shut doors at the bottom of the stair. The two men closed the lantern slides again, crept down, step by step, feeling their way along the gaudy blue-and-gold wall.

> Blind unbelief is sure to err
> And scan His work in vain;
> God is His own interpreter,
> And He will make it plain . . .

So Broadax will appear to them, thought January, *clearly visible in this new 'limelight' reflection in the darkness, and tell them all that now's the time to contribute all they have. Maybe even promise, 'On the third day I will rise again'* . . .

There was a second door, small and inconspicuous, beside that which led into the Parlor. Putting his lips close to Barnum's ear, January whispered, 'Could the apparatus be in there? On the same floor?'

'Could,' murmured the showman. 'It's a little close for my taste, but it could be done.'

It would certainly be easier, reflected January, for him and Barnum to lead Broadax's victims into that room, rather than trying to herd them all down into a cellar, to reveal how they'd been tricked. It was hard to believe that, faced with

242

such evidence, they wouldn't turn against their Patriarch . . .

He nudged open the door.

Two candles burned at the head of a black coffin, mounted like a martyred emperor's on a trestle table that was draped around the base with a black velvet pall. January glanced at the wall that separated the little parlor from the great room next door. It was heavily curtained, so there was no chance of a telltale flicker of lantern light through a door crack advertising their presence. Neither was there any sign of stage apparatus, mirrors, gas cylinders or hose-pipes or burning calcium.

But the air was heavy with the onset of decay.

He walked up to the open coffin.

Serapis Broadax lay on a bed of white satin, his beard combed carefully over his breast, a white satin cap, like a turban, on his head.

January moved it back.

His skull had been split with an ax.

Nineteen

January whispered, 'Jesus,' as he and Barnum slipped back through the narrow door into the dark vestibule at the bottom of the stair. *I guess the business about 'on the third day I will rise again' is out . . .*

'Well, at least we don't have to worry about him surprising us,' the showman whispered back,

243

and fumbled a silver flask from his pocket, his hands shaking. 'And I expect there isn't a man present who'll listen, should you point out that the vision showed you stabbing him with a knife rather than hitting him over the head with an ax.'

He took a drink, and passed January the flask. In the dim slit of the dark-lantern glow, his eyebrows stood out blackly against flesh pale with shock.

Though he had killed men in battle, and in fighting for his own life, January didn't feel terribly steady, either.

'The man's been dead less than three days,' January said softly. 'If he'd actually been killed Monday night, as hot as it's been, he'd be blown up like a balloon. There'd be fluid tracking from his mouth and eyes, and I'm not even going to go into the subject of maggots.'

'Please don't,' murmured Barnum. 'And how are we going to phrase our argument, when the mob is closing in on us with pitchforks and hatchets? Please observe the absence of fly larvae in the split in his—'

He broke off, and flung up his hand – unnecessarily, because January had felt it, too.

The slightest, the barest whisper of a vibration in the wall against which they stood.

As if a door were opened. Or a mirrored trapdoor, thought January, such as would be used in the glen scene in *Der Freischutz*, or during Orpheus' visit to the underworld, if the promoter of the opera wanted to cause the audience to gasp at what were obviously apparitions rather than extras dressed in rags and flour.

At the same instant a man's voice cried out in the Great Parlor beyond, and January heard the scrape of a chair, and the Herald's voice, sweet and soft as a child's.

Very gently, he thumbed closed the last half-inch of the lantern slide, and touched the door into the parlor.

'I'm here, Grandpa,' said the Herald – said the child, the softly glowing shape of the young girl, as she stretched out her hands towards the white-haired man standing barely visible in the darkness. 'I'll always be here, whenever you need me. Please, please be here, when I need you!'

'My child!' The old man's knotted fingers trembled as he reached for her in return, across the yards of darkness that separated his chair in the front row from her glowing shape. 'My little, little one!'

And at his back, January heard the intake of Barnum's breath. 'Good *lord*!'

January stepped back, and pulled the door soundlessly to. He, too, felt chilled all over as he drew Barnum back toward the stair.

Barnum whispered, 'I don't believe it!'

'Don't believe what?' It was Barnum, after all, who'd told him how the trick was worked. They'd both felt the shiver in the walls, as the trapdoor was opened to cast the reflection from whatever hidden, darkened room lay beside or below or above the parlor . . .

245

The showman sounded a little strange as he managed to say, 'That's Bethunia van Martock!'
'*WHAT???*'

Part of January's mind was yelling at him, *We don't have time to stand here talking . . .*

But part of him had to know. '*WHAT???*'

He drew Barnum back up the stairs, and around the corner that would baffle both sound and light.

'Bethunia van Martock,' said Barnum, visibly shaken. 'Her portrait is on the wall of her father's bank, I've seen it a dozen times. And he used to pay to have an engraving of her printed in the *Herald*, on the anniversary of her death . . .'

'This?' January fished in his pocket, for the ivory miniature he'd found in Broadax's desk. He felt curiously dazzled, as if stepping into daylight from shadow for the first time in three weeks.

Barnum held the picture close to the lantern. 'That's her,' he said. 'The flowers at the tops of her pigtails are in both the portrait and in the engraving, I gather it was—'

January produced the daguerreotype of Eve Russell, and held them side by side.

Barnum stammered, 'Well, I'll be . . . But this girl's older—'

'This is a picture of Eve Russell.'

Barnum stared at him, then back at the pictures.

'When did Mademoiselle van Martock die?'

'The year of the cholera. She was thrown from her pony, and broke her neck. That was . . . eight years ago. I was still publishing a newspaper and running a store in Danbury, Connecticut . . .'

Grief pinched January's heart, like unexpectedly stepping on a piece of broken glass. Ayasha lying dead on their bed in the late, hot, afternoon light, her long black hair trailing over the edge into a puddle of dark vomit. *Malek . . .*

Could I be deceived about Ayasha's face and form, after eight years?

Or about her voice?

Part of him cried, *Never!* But the other part – the part that had been educated in Paris, the part that had watched men and women who came to him for healing, or in the hopes that he'd bring them justice in circumstances which practically precluded it – asked, *In a limelight reflection in a dark room? With the same style of hair, the same dress, speaking across the distance between the living and the dead?*

How good is that poor old man's eyesight?

And then anger hit him, as if he'd been struck in the face. Anger at Broadax, at the Shining Herald, at all humbugs who tricked and contrived . . .

His neutral tone sounded like someone else's voice in his own ears. 'If you look closely, you'll see they aren't twins, though the superficial resemblance is strong. They're both young, they both have that wide forehead and wide-set dark eyes, and both have that round chin. If a portrait of Mamzelle van Martock hangs in her grandfather's bank, it would be simple to have a dress made up in the same style – I noticed the one she's wearing this evening is the kind a schoolgirl would have worn in the late 'twenties or early 'thirties. And the hair is the same, the pigtails

247

with the flowers at the top. How could he *not* think it's her?'

Barnum was silent for a long time. Then, from the bottom of his soul, he said, *'Bastards!'*

A moment later his dark eyes shifted, calculating. 'Broadax has got to have a stooge somewhere in the girl's social circle . . . That certainly isn't unheard of. Another point that it could be Callan – and Callan's wife Katy. Polite society's full of hangers-on who need money. You said she's English? Just visiting this country?'

'They arrived in April.'

'So Broadax hears from someone – someone who keeps his or her ear to the ground in New York society, and I'll bet it's a *her* – that there's a girl who looks like old van Martock's granddaughter, and here's our chance to get *him* to sign into the Blessed Land set-up and take him for everything he's got.'

'And *she* – whoever *she* is,' continued January, 'a servant or a hairdresser – drops the hint to Eve or Eve's cousin that it would be great fun to see the woman who can speak to the spirits, who converses with angels. If she'd been of another sort of mind,' he added drily, 'they'd have run in some handsome young man. Or a plausible preacher or abolitionist, probably Broadax himself. It's the Old Man of the Mountain game, all over again.'

'Only the dream is different.' Barnum handed the pictures back, and tiptoed down the stairs again, and down a short corridor, listening at doors before cautiously opening them. 'I wonder what they told her?'

January, thinking of the occasions upon which 'slave catchers' had tried to coax him into having a drink with them or accepting employment at some house distant from town, answered grimly, 'Whatever they thought she wanted to hear.'

'Hmph.' Barnum made a soundless sniff. 'That's just what people say about the Devil.'

Two more windowless rooms, inky-black and cluttered with anonymous-looking furniture, and a small parlor at the end of a garishly papered corridor with a single window. The smell of cooking, which disappeared when they tried to follow it back into the corridor (or was it a different corridor?). 'There'll be a stairway to the cellars from the kitchen, anyway,' said January, and Barnum nodded. 'At least we know the girl is still alive.'

'And now we know why they kept her so. Good heavens, what a labyrinth – no wonder he can get houris in and out of the place without anyone meeting them on the stairs,' murmured the showman. 'God, what I could do with this place! Twenty-five cents a head, and exhibits in every room! Ghosts, too . . . people love a haunted house! Makes one wish for a ball of twine, except somebody would see it.'

'Makes *me* wish for a sledgehammer and a compass, to knock a path straight out through the walls,' returned January, a trifle exasperated at his companion's enthusiasm. 'Only someone would see *that*, too. This one goes up' – he'd opened what appeared to be a cupboard door to

249

reveal a stair as narrow and steep as a ladder – 'but not down. Here's the gallery . . .'

He turned back at a door flanked by two narrow windows, which showed a porch, though he couldn't tell on which side of the Residence. He tried the knob, but the door was locked. No key was in the lock on their side. Peering through the glass, January could make out dim moonlight on trees in the distance, but nothing more.

'I think the Great Parlor would be that way . . .' Barnum pointed uncertainly back along the hall.

'In a house this size,' said January, 'there has to be more than one way down to the cellar. Smugglers couldn't always be back tracking through the kitchen. Ah,' he added, opening a door to show a long dining room, the gleam of polished wood and of open-front china cabinets, and a table that could easily have seated twenty. 'I wonder if there's more than one dining room? This one looks small, to seat even half of the—'

One of the two doors on the opposite wall opened. January and Barnum shielded their lanterns and dropped into the black tangle of shadows at floor level behind the table. There was a long pause, and peering through the carven slats of one of the chairs, January could see the dim yellow of an oil lamp in the room beyond. Then Orion Teems' firm, light voice said, as if continuing a conversation, 'It's what he would have wanted, you know.'

The light moved. Prim as ever, his spectacles

flashing in the lamplight, Orion Teems emerged from the doorway, looking back to speak to the girl who followed close at his elbow.

'Then the Community will go on?' she asked.

'Of course it will, child. It must. The Reverend made arrangements for all that.' Teems prodded his glasses more firmly on to the bridge of his nose. 'This Blessed Land was his lifelong dream. Just because he's . . . uh . . . no longer among the living' – he fumbled a little at the words, as if trying to think of a way not to come right out and say, *dead* – 'not living with us here, I mean – doesn't mean he won't . . . uh . . . guide and direct us. Think about how Jesus Christ is always with the Christian Church.'

Though crouched behind the table, January got a glimpse of them, Teems looking down earnestly into the face of the girl.

Eve Russell looked exactly like she did in the daguerreotype, despite the fact that she was dressed in a schoolgirl's white frock and her hair had been slicked with pomade and braided, each plait topped with a little cluster of flowers. January only had a brief glimpse of her face, but there was uncertainty in her voice as she asked, 'Has he . . . Do you know if he's spoken to the Herald? Has he said what we're to do?'

'I know he has visited her,' said Teems, more confidently. 'But . . . uh . . . he told her not to reveal . . .'

The door closed behind them.

Barnum's lips almost touched January's ear. 'I'll follow them. You find the cellar.'

251

'Meet back by the barn by the river.'

Barnum nodded, patted January's shoulder, and – slipping open his lantern slide once again, just enough so as not to fall over the furniture – crept to the door Teems and Eve Russell had gone through. January crossed to the door through which they'd come. He listened for a moment at its panels, then opened it and slithered through. He was back in the library – which he would have sworn was on the other side of the Great Parlor – and there was another door (*or is this a different library?*) which opened into one of those baffling little interior rooms, outfitted, like the one in the cottage, as a sort of meditation chapel. *Probably with a paradise chamber above it. Drink the 'magic potion' down here, lie on the divan and go into a 'trance', and wake in the arms of a houri – or a rent boy – telling you this is all a dream and you can do whatever you please . . .*

A stairway led down. January edged the lantern slide back a little more, wary in the confined space of the stairwell. 'Please be here when I need you,' Bethunia had said – the Shining Herald had said – to the wealthiest man in New York.

No wonder they kept her alive.

At this very moment, beyond a doubt, January guessed that Teems would be offering the grief-laden Jonas van Martock the opportunity to commit himself as a member of the Blessed Land. All his material wants would be provided for, and he would see visions of his grand-daughter, his blessed child, holding out her hands to him, smiling at him, speaking to him through the medium of the Shining Herald.

And of Eve Russell.

Speaking of things in their past that Broadax's informant – quite possibly Broadax's wife, if Barnum was right – would dig up from gossip or servants' recollections or newspaper articles back in New York . . .

All he had to do was sign the papers Teems would give him.

And the trustee for the Children is none other than . . .

Broadax?

But Broadax is dead.

And by my hand, according to eighty-three people upstairs . . .

He listened at the door at the bottom of the stair, then pressed the old-fashioned handle, and pushed it cautiously. It was locked, which didn't surprise him. And if this was the room where the illusion was generated, it would be directly under the Great Parlor, so simply kicking in the door wasn't a good idea, though there was almost certainly a thick layer of something in the floor that separated the two rooms.

Does Eve Russell even know why she's asked to perform the actions she performs? Know to whom she holds out her arms, for whom she smiles with joy?

Silently he reascended the stair.

The door at the top was locked.

Twenty

Shit . . .

Panic zipped through him like an electric shock.

Teems stopping in the doorway, as he and Barnum ducked behind the table.

He must have glimpsed us then.

Teems fumbling for words, like a man trying to carry on a conversation – trying to maintain a convincing lie – while thinking what to do . . .

Why don't you go on up to your room by yourself, Eve, dearest, I've just remembered something I've forgotten to do . . .

And the next moment, what? Lock every outside door to the house and call up the men who were 'players' in the game – Hal Shamrock and this Mr Greene from New York, maybe Jared Ott – while they tactfully herded the faithful outside?

Or crash into the Great Parlor crying, *Our Patriarch's murderer has returned!*

Either way, January knew there was no question of his seeing the sunrise or being allowed to present his side of the story to the sheriff.

Did he see there were two of us? Have they got Barnum already?

Have they got the Spirit and Pearce?

The cellar stair was steep. He made a run at the door, and the impact, at so awkward an angle, nearly threw him back down the stairs. *Damn it . . .*

The top step was barely seven inches broad, there wasn't even room to brace his feet.

With the light speed that belied his size, he darted down the stair again to the door at the bottom, and stood for a moment, listening. Not a sound from above. *No help for it*, he thought. The game was up already, and his only possible chance to survive depended on getting out of the house and away into the darkness within the next few minutes. The door yielded to a flat-footed kick next to its lock plate, and yes, this was the place where the illusions were generated. But instead of the square wooden box of a 'magic lantern' that January knew from backstage at the opera, was a more complicated array of mirrors, blowpipes, gas cylinders and bellows, and a small metal bowl which contained the half-molten waste of burned quicklime; January stepped back quickly from its acrid fumes.

The room was stiflingly hot. A lead chest stood near the door, in which the lime had undoubtedly been brought. *The whole illusion would be impossible*, he reflected, *before the railway line went in. They bring in the quicklime and the gas cylinders through one of the tunnels, store the stuff in one of the cottages . . . And the people in New York whose house is used for smaller gatherings has to be part of the group as well. And others there. Broadax was lucky he didn't manage to burn the house down during one of the Herald's 'visions'.*

The door on the other side of the big cellar was also locked. When January kicked his way through, his lantern showed him a long, low chamber half-filled with a jumble of boxes and barrels. Stores for the kitchen?

There has to be a way up. Do NOT get trapped down here . . .

The silence was eerie. *There must be a layer of something like sand or shells, in the floor beams, which would make sense if the British stored their powder down here . . .*

How many men can Teems call on? How long will it take him to get the rest of the believers out of the house, especially if they're hoping to have a revelation from their Patriarch?

Is Teems going to find some actor big enough to pass for Broadax, put him in a fake beard and hope for the best?

How many minutes do I have?

He flashed his lantern beam behind a stack of boxes, saw only the crumbling plaster and coarse brick of the wall. Another line of boxes seemed to him to stand out from the corner. He strode to it, flickered the light across the brick-work, then jerked back as a dozen rats poured out of the inky shadows that surrounded what looked like a crate half-hidden by loose boards.

There was no mistaking the smell.

Spring . . .

He didn't want to, but had to be sure.

Rats would flee. He knew from long experience that ants didn't care about light or a threat or anything, and there were ribbons of them, creeping from the wall to the crate.

He lifted the boards aside, and shone the lantern light down into the narrow black rectangle of darkness.

The rats had been busy, but the body folded up inside hadn't been dead, January estimated, for more than a day, and it wasn't Byron Spring's body. The hand, lying uppermost on the dead man's thigh, was white, and furred with coarse reddish hair.

January moved the lantern closer, and saw the heavy, snub-nosed features of Jared Ott.

He didn't even really feel surprise.

Come up to the study, and I'll show you.

Show you the contracts, probably, but it didn't really matter.

Like the Devil, Teems merely offered whatever Ott wanted to hear.

Let's talk this over like civilized men. Have a drink, Jared . . .

He reached down, and lifted the thick-muscled wrist. It came easily. Because of the rats it wasn't easy to tell, but it looked like the man had been dead only hours.

And hours, he guessed, was how long it had been since the opiated brandy in Broadax's study had been drunk.

One glass tainted, the other clear.

Papers piled everywhere, as if someone were searching . . .

January's every instinct shrieked to find the way out and leave the place at once, but he bent closer, held the lantern inches above the dead man's shoulder. Above him, around him, the Residence was silent, but he could almost feel the quiet rush to and fro. *Lock up the doors, watch the windows, get everybody out of the place before we search . . .*

Ott's body cached in the cellar would severely limit the number of men Teems would call on to search.

Jared Ott had been garroted. The mark of thin cord stood out red on his neck. But neither the skin of his throat, nor the flesh of his fingers, bore any sign that he'd clawed at the noose as it was twisted tight. Nor was there bruising on his wrists, as if he'd been tied as he was strangled, the way the Spanish Inquisition would bind victims into a chair to tighten the horrible tourniquet. Nothing under the fingernails except farm dirt. Neither the skin and blood of his killer, nor the hairs of his own red beard that would speak of a frantic effort to wriggle a hand beneath the inexorable rope.

January bent even further forward, to sniff the dead man's lips. A lingering wisp of V.S.O.P. brandy, and the faintest bitterness of opium.

The echo, in fact, of the cloying lemonade he'd been offered Monday night. *You come along with me, Ben. It's time to go.*

Bastard. His mind echoed Barnum's heartfelt, furious disgust. *Bastard . . .*

So was Ott Broadax's killer? Or did Teems kill them both?

Depends on who gets title to the Blessed Land . . .

Light.

He jerked around, whipping his knife from his boot, and saw a white figure behind him, small

258

and curiously sturdy in her schoolgirl dress and flower-decked pigtails.

She had an oil lamp in one hand, its flame turned very low. The other hand was pressed to her mouth, her eyes stretched with shock at the sight of what was in the crate. And no wonder, given what the rats had done so far . . .

January put one finger to his own lips and met her eyes. *Please* . . .

At that she seemed to gather herself together, and nodded, though she was trembling and looked about to burst into tears. She beckoned, and led the way to a door at the far end of the room, hidden from his view by an angle of the wall.

'They're searching in the woods all round the house,' she whispered. 'Was there somebody with you?'

'Yes.'

A back stair snaked up from the smoke-smelling cavern of the kitchen. Through the inky glass of the kitchen windows January could see lights bobbing in the darkness, like far-off fireflies, appearing and disappearing among trees. Swift footfalls passed in a nearby hallway. A man's voice.

Eve led the way up, closing the stairway door behind them. Saying nothing, as they ascended four flights, the last of these only a ladder in darkness, such as were found in church steeples. The space at the top, like the room in which he'd originally been hidden, had been carved out of other attics, a tiny cupboard half-filled with crates which contained – January saw – old

259

Brown Bess muskets, thick with dust and grease. There were no true walls, only the ceiling rising to a peak in the center.

'All the secret rooms here use the same type of key.' Her voice was barely a breath. The floors of the house below vibrated with purposeful, angry strides. 'They keep them in a drawer in . . . in the Reverend Broadax's office.' She gulped a little over the name. 'Did my father send you?'

'Yes, mamzelle.'

She took a seat on one of the boxes, motioned for January to do the same on another, and set down the lamp at her side. 'You were the one who had the daguerreotype of me? I saw it in the Reverend's study, after . . . after he was supposed to be dead, but he wasn't. I couldn't imagine . . .'

She broke off, listening, then asked, 'You're the one they all said killed him? They said he was a man of your color, a big man—'

'Benjamin January.' He held out his hand to her. 'At your service, Mademoiselle . . . Russell? And doubly so, in gratitude.'

Her cold, short fingers touched his, briefly, and she nodded.

'The Children of the Light will almost certainly kill me if they find me. You know that?'

She closed her eyes briefly, as if at momentary pain. 'I . . . Yes,' she said. 'Yes. Did . . . did Father ever actually get either of my letters? At the time I got his I was just so glad that he understood – that he would be sending me money, so I wouldn't have to be dependent on the Reverend and the Herald. He said the door was always open, should ever I write him a wish to return home, though I couldn't imagine ever doing that . . .'

His voice was as gentle as he could make it. 'He wrote no such letter, mamzelle.'

'No,' said Eve, and sighed softly. 'I . . . I guessed that. Not at first, but when I thought about it, I realized that the paper was wrong. The paper it was written on, I mean.' Her eyes opened again: her mother's, brown and bright and intelligent. 'Mother's horribly finicky about notepaper. She won't have anything but French or Dutch linen paper, and just despised American paper.'

'My sister's that way,' said January. 'And my mother. I knew American paper was different from what I used in France, but that was eight years ago, and I've never thought much about it, one way or the other.'

And the girl smiled; perhaps at the thought of her mother, a smile of kindness mingled with exasperation. 'You're not a young lady being taught all about the social niceties of corre-spondence with one's aunts.'

She went on, more steadily, 'So even when I got Father's letter – or what was supposed to be Father's letter – I did notice that it wasn't on the paper we use at home. Mother brought about two quires of it with us, and they'd have been using it in New Orleans. It was browner than the linen paper, too. In fact, I realized that it was the same kind of brownish paper the Reverend Broadax used . . . but then when I

261

looked for Father's letter to compare them, in the drawer where I'd put it, it was gone.'

She was silent, looking down at her hands as she folded and refolded a crease in the girlish sash of her dress.

January, sitting on one of the crates opposite her, said nothing.

'That's when I . . .' She paused again, with a gesture of her hand half-made, as if to shape a thought that she couldn't quite bring herself to say. 'It sounds so . . . so mad,' she said. 'And there have been times when I wondered if I *was* going mad. Or if I'd been mad all along. But it crossed my mind that since coming here I'd felt . . . I hadn't felt like myself. Sort of dreamy and . . . and everything they said to me sounded so reasonable and right. And I remembered that since coming here, I hadn't drunk any water. Only lemonade, or cider. The Herald told me the well here was brackish – like the salt springs all around Syracuse. The water was perfectly wholesome, but it tasted foul, she said.'

January said, softly, 'Ah. That's what they told me, too.'

And her gaze, meeting his, changed a little, as she saw that he understood.

'Then Wednesday night – after I saw the Reverend Broadax, crossing the yard in the moonlight – and I found myself thinking, *Oh, this must just be another dream* . . . I . . . I poured out the lemonade, and started drinking the water they'd leave in my bedroom pitcher to wash my hands in. And it tasted perfectly all right.' Her eyes glimmered momentarily with tears of shame. 'I was drunk, wasn't I? I have no idea what it feels like to be drunk—'

'Probably what was in the lemonade was hashish,' said January. 'That's why they have to spice it so heavily. I'm guessing they'd use laudanum from time to time, if they wanted you to be sleepy for some reason.'

She made a face, and a sound like, *Euhh* . . .

'They tried to drug me, too,' said January softly.

'How horrid! This was all right before they moved me from the cottage in the orchard into a room here. I think it was a day or two ago. It's hard to tell, because of there being no windows. I managed to steal a key,' she went on. 'They just leave them in the locks of some of the secret rooms. And I sneaked down to the Reverend Broadax's study, and saw the daguerreotype Father had done of me in New York. So I knew somebody had come here from him.'

She looked away into the dusty corner of the attic, tears shining in her eyes. 'And I knew I'd been fooled,' she continued, keeping her voice perfectly steady and conversational. 'But I can't imagine *why*. It isn't as if Father's rich, or we're important, or anything.' Her gaze returned to him. 'Do you know?'

'Have you been hurt?' he asked. 'Forgive me for asking, mamzelle, but have you been molested in any way? I'm a physician,' he said. 'A doctor, in New Orleans.'

Her expression brightened. 'So you can become doctors here? Men of your race? I'd heard there were some, in New York . . .'

January grinned. 'In New Orleans, I have to play the piano at parties to make ends meet.'

'Oh, *shame*!'

'And give music lessons. And,' he added, a little grimly, 'undertake expeditions to find missing persons. Family friends put your parents in touch with me, when Mrs Winterink's letter reached them about your disappearance.'

Her eyes flooded again, with mortification as well as sorrow. 'I did write to them,' she whispered. 'And, no, I haven't been . . . been hurt in any way. In fact I've barely seen anyone, since I came here. The Reverend Broadax told me that one has to spend three months in a sort of . . . purification, praying and meditating in complete seclusion and reading all sorts of things: the Bible, and Saint Augustine, and something from Ancient Egypt, I think, which were all very interesting. That's why I was kept isolated in the cottage. The Reverend himself, or the Herald, would come and talk to me, and Mr Teems or . . .' She hesitated, and shivered. 'Or Mrs Greene . . . would bring me food and clean clothes and things. They were the only people I saw.'

She was silent again, and the house below them, now, was silent as well.

'Mr January,' she said at length, 'what . . . what *happened*? To poor Mr Ott, to the Reverend . . .? And what *is* happening? The Herald . . . She *knew*, she spoke to . . . to someone I knew, as a child, who had passed across . . .'

'What did they tell you?'

She said nothing for a long time then. At length

she drew a deep breath, let it out, and asked in a voice like a saddened child, 'It's all been a lie, then, hasn't it?' A tear stole down her face. 'Everything they told me?'

'From what I've learned about Broadax,' returned January softly, 'I think so. Yes.'

She wiped the tear aside, and took a small handkerchief from her pocket and blew her nose. 'I feel so *stupid*.'

'Stupid, nothing, mamzelle,' said January firmly. 'You were smart enough – even half-dopey on hashish – to figure out that you were being lied to and drugged, and to do something about it. And I think – I suspect – that you were entrapped by your own will to do good. What did they tell you was going on?'

Eve opened her lips to reply, then turned her head quickly, listening. She got to her feet, walked with silent delicacy to the trap in the floor and crouched beside it, straining to hear something – or the lack of it – in the house below. After a moment January joined her, lying flat on the floor – something he was only able to accomplish by bending his knees around the old rifle crates – and pressing his ear to the boards. He heard nothing.

Barely breathing, the girl murmured, 'One of the downstairs windows was open. I think they thought you'd got out that way and were headed for the road or the river.'

January sat up, looked at his watch. It was nearly midnight. 'How long will they look, do you think?'

'Most of the men hereabouts are farmers,' she

said reasonably. 'They have to be up early, because they're still getting the last of the hay in. I should think we'll be safe enough.'

January nodded, and with gingerly care opened the trap.

Twenty-One

'As you said, I was only trying to do good.' Eve gathered her childish skirts around herself, and slipped down the ladder into the absolute darkness of the larger attic below. January fetched his lantern, opened the slide the tiniest crack, and blew out the lamp that the girl had carried, leaving it where it was beside the old gun crate. The last thing they needed would be someone seeing a moving light through one of the windows of the house.

'It's hard to explain what it's like,' she went on, her voice barely more than a cautious whisper. 'I don't know how much you know about what it's like, in a family where your father is a banker and your mother is related to a baronet just closely enough for her to think of herself as a member of the aristocracy. Did you ever hear those fairytales, about the elves kidnapping babies out of their cradles and swapping them for fairy babies? I always felt like one of those poor fairy babies. I love my mother, Mr January, and I love my father. Truly I do. But . . .'

She spread her hands helplessly, then took the lantern that he handed down to her.

He descended, closed the trap above him, came down to her side. Quietly, he said, 'It isn't my place to say so, mamzelle, and please forgive me if I'm stepping over the line here – but I've met your father, and I've met your mother. You don't need to explain anything.'

'Well.' She led the way, with silent care, across the attic to the back stair. 'It was as if I'd finally found my way to the people that were my . . . not my real family, but people who believed and thought and looked for what I was looking for. After the Herald spoke to me . . . After . . . after my friend Belle spoke to me . . . Mr Teems came up to me, and told me about the Blessed Land. About helping runaway slaves escape, and receiving new revelations, true revelations, un-polluted by the ignorance of churchmen and apostles over the centuries. I expect you know something about all that, if you've talked to my father, and probably to Lucy and Mr Grislock and all of them.'

'I have.'

'It was like . . . It was like I'd been groping my way through a cluttered house in twilight, and *finally* coming to a door into a garden . . . rather as we're doing now,' she added, with a gleam of shaky amusement. '*Finally* seeing light. And I . . . I couldn't let them go away back here, and me never see them again. I just *couldn't*. Not when I knew they had the answer.'

The stair creaked, very slightly, under her foot,

and she froze. January whispered, 'Keep close to the wall, mamzelle. Less creaking.'

Her breath was almost a chuckle. 'You sound like you've done this before.'

'More times than I want to think about.'

'Well, I asked Mother, could I stay on in New York? Mr Teems met me on the steam packet back from King's Point, with a change of dress and a pair of tinted spectacles and even some flour to comb through my hair, to change its color. The first thing I did when we reached Albany was write to Mother and to Mrs Winterink, telling them where I was and begging them to let me do this. To let me seek the life that was calling to me. Mr Teems never sent them, did he?'

He shook his head.

'But *why*? I mean, my parents can't pay thousands of pounds in ransom. If they were going to kidnap somebody, why not Georgiana Ganesvoort, or Aemelia Drew? Aemelia's silly enough to go off with a preacher . . .'

'I'll get to that,' said January. 'What did they tell you about this?' He gestured to the short dress she wore, the white roses tucked into the tops of her childish pigtails.

An expression of unhappiness crossed the girl's face, of uncertainty. 'It sounds so . . . so *fishy* to me now, but I can only think it's because of that horrid lemonade. I believed a lot of things they told me . . .'

'They're people who know what they're doing, mamzelle,' said January, as they slipped through the door of the back stairs, crept along the hall

268

through near-pitch darkness to the stairway to the floor below. 'It's their profession, to get people to believe them.'

'Oh,' she whispered. 'Oh, dear. But I suppose if he didn't seem so kind and understanding and *good*, he'd have had to get himself a real job, wouldn't he? It was the Herald who asked me . . . But I expect the Reverend Broadax came up with the story.'

She halted at the bottom of the stair, put her ear to the panels of the narrow door there, and listened. January, who had slid the lantern completely closed, leaned his forehead on the wall beside the door, straining to make out anything in the space beyond.

Not a murmur of sound. Not the vibration of a footfall, or the creak of a stair somewhere in the night-filled labyrinth of the old fortress. Nothing, save the pounding of his heart.

She pushed the door gently open, and January cracked the lantern slide, the barest thread of light. He wondered if it was Barnum who'd left the window open as he'd escaped, and if the mob of enraged believers had caught him.

If Pearce and the Spirit aren't at the wagon, what do I do? Search the cottages in the orchard for them and for Barnum?

No, he thought. *Before anything else, I have to get this girl to safety.*

'The Herald told me,' whispered Eve, 'that for some people – for many people – hearing the voices of their loved ones isn't enough, you see. Some people need to *see* them. Need it desperately, and it isn't always possible. She

269

said that sometimes the spirits appear – as my friend Belle genuinely did – and sometimes they don't. For the good of all, for the good of everyone, she said, sometimes a . . . a show is needed.' She turned her face aside from him again as she said this, and he guessed, had there been a little more light, that he would have seen her blush. 'After she told me that I did sometimes wonder if the figure I saw was real, but the voices are always real, she said. The spirits are always there. But they have . . . They have an apparatus . . .'

'I've seen it.'

'Oh.' She seemed a little disconcerted, that what to her seemed marvelous and unique turned out to have been a commonplace stage trick. 'Oh, of course. If you were in the dining room, you must have seen the door we came out of . . . It was for their greater good, the Herald said. For their greater faith.' They moved like shadows through another room done up as a black-draped meditation chapel, with cup and couch, and into the hall – yet more blue-and-gold wallpaper – beyond.

'Belle told me things – said things – spoke of her mother, and her sister. What I would be doing – the Herald said – wouldn't be specific, just a . . . just a spirit of welcome, like a picture on a wall. One can't expect an infant to stand up and walk about on her first try, the Herald said. She needs a baby walker, so she can strengthen her legs and learn her balance. Later, she'll walk – and run – and dance, on her own.'

'Did she say who this "show" was intended for?'

270

Eve looked at him in surprise. 'For . . . for those not yet able to believe, she said. All I had to do was to hold out my hands, beckoning and welcoming. What they would see would be a . . . a spirit on the threshold of the Blessed Land, the *real* Blessed Land, while upstairs she would speak what the spirits told her, of what it was like, of the welcome all living souls receive there. What I saw in Mr Rankin's house in town was . . . wasn't the same thing . . .'

From his pocket, January drew the miniature of Bethunia van Martock, and held it close to the splinter of lantern light.

Eve stared for a moment, her hand flying to the rose pinned above her right braid.

Quietly, January said, 'This is Bethunia van Martock.'

And he could tell, by the way her eyes flew to his face, aghast, that she knew who that was. 'Bethunia . . . Oh, *no* . . .'

'And while you were smiling and beckoning in the cellar, the Shining Herald was telling poor old Jonas van Martock how much his granddaughter misses him, and how she'll always be there waiting for the Herald to open the curtain that hangs between them . . .'

She flinched, and looked away again, and he could see by the hunch of her shoulders the agony of her mortification and shame. Had she been of his own color he would have drawn her to him for comfort, but of course that was unthinkable.

Gently, he said, 'What I'm pretty sure they wanted – and in fact may have gotten him to do

271

this evening, if they weren't interrupted by the alarm for me – was to sign over his property to the Blessed Land . . . Only I'm also pretty sure that Mr Teems, who I'll bet is a lawyer rather than a secretary, made sure that the Blessed Land is a limited trust under New York law, with the sole trustee being—'

'Oh!' This time when she swung back around her face was flushed with anger, dark eyes snapping like fire. '*Oh!* That *scoundrel*! That poor old—'

She broke off, frowning. 'But he's dead,' she said.

'That doesn't mean there aren't other beneficiaries to the trust – including Broadax's wife – who're going to pocket the lot and disappear, as soon as they've liquidated every asset that's been signed to them in the past twelve months. That—'

He whirled at the noise, more felt than heard, at the far end of the upstairs corridor where they stood. He pushed open the door of the nearest room, barely stopped himself from grabbing her arm and pulling her after him. 'In here—'

The shot was like a thunderclap in the labyrinthine dark of the house. Eve gasped, clutched the sudden blotch of red – virulent in the lantern glow – spreading on the white of her dress, dropped the lantern, and fell.

January flattened back into the dark room behind him, as footfalls creaked down the hall.

Hal Shamrock's voice said, 'Shit, man, you didn't have to kill the bitch!'

'Didn't I?' Orion Teems knelt swiftly to right the dark lantern before its oil reservoir could leak. The flame had, fortunately, gone out at impact. At the same moment Shamrock slipped open the slide on his own lantern, and caught Teems' wrist as he reached for his bullet pouch to reload. 'And what do we do with the girl if I don't, Hal? Take her with us? Let her go? Get Molly to tell her that she's had a communication from Drake's spirit that the three of us are supposed to go to Canada *and here's six dollars for your fare back to New York, it's been wonderful knowing you*?'

He tore the paper off the cartridge with his teeth, spit it out, and poured the powder down the barrel. Shamrock only stood looking uncertain. But all he could find to say was, 'I don't like it—'

'And I don't like the idea of spending the next fifteen years in the New York State penitentiary after Little Miss van Martock here spills the beans to the police. How the hell did she get out of her room anyway?' he added, dumping the ball in after the powder and adding the wadded-up cartridge paper. 'If she's done *that* more than once, God knows what she's heard and seen. We'll be lucky if we can keep Ott's boys out of our hair long enough to get the farms sold and van Martock's property liquidated. He's already asking why he has to stay in one of the cottages instead of here in the house like Drake promised him.'

Shamrock had a knife – January could see it in his belt – and a cudgel in one hand, and the

273

way Teems stood over Eve's body, he would have seen movement in the darkness of the room where January crouched.

'That silly bitch Maria Tarwell's already giving me enough trouble, over why *her* family had to be moved out, and how Molly would *never* have given her permission for it. Even Hayward's been asking questions—'

Molly must be the Shining Herald . . . and Drake would be Broadax . . .

He had a vague recollection of young Dr Hayward, with his weedy yellow beard, playing the piano for the choir . . .

'Where is Molly?'

'Where do you think?' snapped Teems. 'In her room with a bottle of laudanum, trying to "open the gate" to have a chat with Drake . . . By God, I'll be glad to be out of this business and away from these lunatics. Damn it,' he added, as footfalls clumped distantly downstairs.

His fingers stuck on pulling the ramrod from beneath the pistol's barrel and he looked down to unclip it, and in that second, January lunged from the darkness of the room and smote him a blow on the chin that lifted his feet from the floor. His body crashed back into Shamrock – who did, as it turned out, have a gun in his pocket, but who didn't have the sense to catch his balance before he pulled it out and fired. The ball buried itself in the ceiling, voices yelled downstairs, and Shamrock shouted, 'Up here!' at the top of his lungs. He grabbed Teems's pistol and tried to fire that, too, as January scooped up Eve's body into his arms. She cried out in pain, and the pistol ball – which had not been tamped into place – fell out of the barrel when Shamrock tried to fire.

Feet thundered on the stairs, men's voices shouting. January ducked when Shamrock slashed at him, first with the pistol butt and then with the cudgel, which nearly broke his shoulder. His arms full of the bleeding girl, January flung himself back into the room behind him, slammed the door with a kick, and braced the first piece of furniture his groping hand could touch under the handle – it felt like a chair. He laid Eve down, shoved something else that felt like a daybed against the door, struck a match, and dug a candle from his pocket.

The door jerked against the makeshift barricade and January drove his hand into Eve's pocket. *All the keys to these secret rooms are the same . . .*

He shoved the door closed against Shamrock's pounding, thrust the key in the lock and turned it and yes, Eve had been right. The whole wing was shaking now with men thundering up the stairs. January lifted Eve again, carried her – awkwardly, because of the candle, fearing every moment that he'd light her dress on fire – through the door to his right. Silk curtains swathed the walls and framed the bed in the chamber beyond. He laid her on it, locked the door into the hall and the one through which he'd just come, and pulled open the door, more than half-hidden by the curtains, that communicated with the next room along.

A dressing room for the houris, with a door into the hall and, thank God, a window. He locked the hall door, shoved the cheap pine dresser against it, and dashed back to where Eve lay. God only knew what Shamrock – and Teems, if he'd recovered yet from the blow January had given him – were telling the men, or how many of them knew what about Broadax's schemes. He tore down a bed curtain, wadded it into a pad and bound it (more bed curtain, thank God they were gauzy and easy to handle) over the wounds. Front and back, the bullet had gone clean through the girl's body just below the clavicle, shattering her left shoulder blade on its way out. Blood was pouring out and her face had gone chalky in the candle glow.

Damn them, thought January, *damn them* . . .

Teems would blame him. He knew it. And Shamrock would back up Teems' story.

He'd be lynched or clubbed to death, Eve would be safely tucked up into bed somewhere in the house and either the bandage would come accidentally loose in the middle of the night or someone would quietly put a pillow over her face, and who'd be the wiser?

He looked again at her waxen face and knew he'd have horsewhipped anyone who had so much as suggested moving a patient with such a wound.

Much less carrying her out a window and down a makeshift rope made of silken curtains down the side of a building . . .

He put his head out the window. In the hall-way he could hear crashing and shouting, the

276

splintering of a door, the bumble of men shoving at the barricade. He knew they had only seconds.

Damn it, damn it . . .

As he'd feared, they were in the central block of the house, on the third floor. A good thirty-five feet to the ground. Torch light threw reflections on the wall of the orchard, he could hear men shouting. *They won't even hear me if I yell that Broadax was swindling them, that they'd signed their property over into his name . . . Not with Teems and Shamrock, men they know . . .*

They won't even hear me if I tell them Ott's body is in the cellar . . .

He was already back in the paradise room, yanking gauzy lengths of silk from the walls (cheap silk – he'd been married to Ayasha long enough to know one grade of silk from another and some of this was simply cotton gauze shiny with sleaze). He caught up a chair which looked sturdy enough to brace against the window frame and take his weight and Eve's – strode to the window again, to gauge how far he'd have to run across open ground to the orchard wall (*better take some of this fabric in case I need a makeshift rope . . .*)

And saw torches, coming over that wall.

Damn it . . .

Fighting despair, he looked in the other direction. Men were milling in the darkness, the jerky glare of lantern light jolted by, held by a man running. *If I can get to the woods . . . circle around to the barn by the river . . .*

She'll never survive it.

He turned his head back towards the door of

277

the paradise chamber, the white form on the
bed. The girl who'd only wanted to find a life
beyond what her parents thought was good for
a well-bred girl. *Damn it . . .*

He was aware that the furious pounding on the
doors had stopped. Voices yelled down below,
and, from the yard and the orchard, the sound
of shots.

Twenty-Two

She'll die if we stay here.

*I'll be blamed for her death if she dies in the
escape, and hanged or beaten to death for
Broadax's murder if I stay.*

He knotted the curtains even as he thought, made
a loop of them fast around the frame of the
chair. The corridor outside was silent. Braced
the chair against the frame of the window, then
strode back to the bedside. When he pressed his
hand to Eve's throat he felt the pulse there weak
and thready; when he touched her hands they
were cold, though sweat beaded her face.

*Virgin Mary, protector of women, help me.
Save this poor girl who only sought truth . . .*

He unlocked the door of the paradise chamber,
pushed it open a crack, and his own heart turned
cold within him even as he drew back into the
room, coughing.

Smoke.

DAMN it . . .

278

The house below was on fire.

He ran again to the window, and yes, yellow reflections whipped and danced on the ground beyond the corners of the house. The crazy light illuminated the orchard wall, the edges of the leaves beyond. More shots, and men's voices shouting in rage. As he watched two men came running around the corner of the house, carrying blazing branches. These they hurled through the windows of the house, smashing the glass. Then they ran away.

Looks like somebody besides Mr Barnum finally thought to ask exactly what they'd been talked into signing . . .

He knew he'd never be able to find his way out of the house in darkness and smoke. If the lower floors were in flames, he'd almost certainly suffocate in a stairwell. On the other hand, chances were now good that nobody would shoot him as he descended on his makeshift rope.

He checked the blood-soaked pad that he'd bound so tightly over Eve's breast and shoulder, moved her gently to the floor beside the bed, then stripped off the coverlet and sheets. The sheets seemed stouter, so he knotted one of them into a sling, wrapped Eve in the coverlet and laid her inside, tying her there against the remote possibility that she would regain consciousness and try to struggle free. He'd now need a double length of rope, and tore down the rest of the curtains around the wall – thanking heaven for the theatrical Oriental décor – tore the sheet in two and added both lengths to what he already had, giving himself a clumsy line of about eighty feet.

Eve was light as a child, as he carried her into the dressing room. He passed the free end of the line beneath the knots in the sling, and he prayed all his knots would hold and that the cheap gauze of some of those draperies wouldn't come to pieces with the burden halfway down. Slowly, he played out the free end of the rope, lowering Eve down the wall in her sling. He held his breath when the sling passed over the first knot in the rope . . . So far, so good. Now if . . .

Smoke billowed suddenly into the room and he heard the door slam open behind him. He was half-turning when Orion Teems cannoned into his back, and felt the man's knife slash his arm. Thrust him away with all his strength and drove his elbow through the glass of the window sash, but had to struggle and kick as he was attacked again. There wasn't time to untangle his pistol from his pocket; he fended Teems off as he cinched the free end of the rope through the broken mullions in a makeshift knot before turning to strike at the secretary's tall, lean form.

January's eyes burned with the smoke that now filled the room. He heard Teems gasping, and then the man came at him again, armed with a chair this time. January felt the blood soaking into his shirt and knew he'd taken at least a couple of slashes, but he was scarcely aware of pain. He made a feint at the man, but dared not get far from the window; dodged a brutal swipe with the chair, caught the rungs in one hand and twisted it from Teems' grip.

He has to kill me, cut the rope – Eve falls to

her death and then he climbs down and takes credit for trying to save her . . .

Teems jumped back, cut at him again, having evidently learned the first rule of knife fighting: *you don't lunge in and stab your opponent. You cut and leap back, cut and leap back, like a bullfighter, until your man bleeds out.*

Which would work, thought January, if the building weren't burning beneath you and if you kept yourself from the desperate urge to finish it and run before you all roasted together . . .

He saw the sweat rolling down the lawyer's thin face, the panic terror in his bespectacled eyes. He strode in on him, swinging the chair, in a blow that knocked the spectacles from the man's face. In the moment of Teems' panicky disorientation January deliberately trod on the delicate glass, and in the same instant swung again with the chair, catching Teems on the side of the head with a force that sent him sprawling. January pounced on him, kicked the knife from his hand, and with brute deliberation, as the smoke thickened in the room and he saw through the door the reflection of flames in the corridor, broke Teems' right arm at the shoulder.

Then he flung himself back to the window, untwisted the rope and looked out, to see men clustered in the yard below, shouting and pointing. They bore rifles and torches, and even as Eve's body neared the ground, four men came running from the direction of the barns, carrying a long ladder.

Good, thought January. *About time I had some help . . .*

He fought for breath, dizzy from the smoke and from the blood that trickled from his slashed arms and back. *I do NOT want to climb all the way down on these blasted curtains . . .*

The firelight in the yard brightened as the flames took hold. By it he recognized the frail Dr Hayward, among a group of men which included Del Pearce, helping to raise the ladder. With them, her long graying hair straggling from its cap, was the Celestial Comrade.

January was sorely tempted to leave Orion Teems where he was, especially when the lawyer clawed and bit him – feebly enough – as he picked him up and carried him to the window. 'You want me to leave you here, I will,' he said wearily, and the lawyer responded with a spew of verbal filth that would have choked a Parisian fishwife. The ladder only reached to the windowsill of the Residence's second story, but January wasn't certain he could have made it all the way down on the curtains, even though Teems had stopped kicking at him. As Pearce and Hayward reached out from the top of it, to relieve him of Teems' weight, the lawyer sobbed, 'He shot her! He shot that poor innocent girl! And then he broke my arm, and was going to leave me to burn . . .'

'Until what?' demanded January sourly, as he edged on to the ladder himself. 'Until you talked me into saving your life?'

'. . . leave me to die,' Teems continued to gasp, as they descended the ladder. 'Going to leave me to die . . .'

282

'I'm not going to leave you to die,' rasped one of the men who stood gathered at the ladder's foot. He was broad-shouldered, pock-marked, with a round face and Cupid-bow mouth that marked him clearly as a son of Jared Ott. Another man, shorter, stood behind him, Ott's face again in a frame of curly red beard, a rifle in one hand and a torch in the other. The taller son continued, 'Not til you tell me what happened to my father—'

'He killed him!' Teems pointed shakily to January. 'He did it!'

'Your father's body is in the cellar under the kitchen.' January leaned, gasping, against the ladder. 'By the look of the body he was drugged and strangled late this afternoon or early this evening. Please,' he added, turning towards the group gathered around Eve, 'could someone please bring a litter, and blankets – is there a place we can take her?'

More and more men were gathering in the open space between the house and the orchard. Farmers, by their clothing. Most carried guns. Many bore torches as well, and their weather-beaten faces were grim with rage in the wild topaz light. Other than young Dr Hayward, January saw none of the Children of the Light, at least none that he recognized, either by face – from Monday night – or by garments of that characteristic blue. Someone held a torch down close and the Celestial Comrade, kneeling beside Eve with her hand to the girl's throat, said, 'She lives.'

'I'm a doctor,' said January. 'Please. Is there something that can be used as a litter?'

'The Women's House is closest,' volunteered Hayward, panting. 'Someone, please – we have to save the scrolls of the Gospel! We can't—' He broke off, looking down at the girl before him. 'But surely that's . . . that's . . .' He peered at her in the torch light: the chalk-white face, the girlish braids with one rose still tangled in the rumpled brown hair.

'Her name is Eve Russell,' said January, feeling infinitely tired. He knelt, turned back the coat that someone had already bundled around the unconscious girl, gently checked the bandages. *Warmth*, he thought. *Stillness, until the bleeding stopped with the pressure . . .*

'She was tricked into impersonating Bethunia van Martock, to get her grandfather to sign over his property to the Community . . .'

'The way my father was tricked,' shouted the younger Ott in a voice like the grinding of stones. 'And Ulee Wellman. And you, too, Monroe . . .'

Hayward stared at him, eyes wide with shock and grief. 'No,' he said softly. 'No. The Herald . . . she would not lie. I saw the light shine holy around her. And the Gospel scroll . . .'

As if he'd accidentally stepped on a piece of glass, a fragment of words returned to January's mind.

The Herald . . .

Damn it. Shit. Damn it . . . No . . .

He said, 'She's still in the house.'

They all looked at him, even the men running up with a shutter fetched from one of the barns.

January rose from Eve's side. 'The Herald. She's

still in the house. Teems said so. She's unconscious, she drank laudanum in her grief . . .'

Ott said, 'Let her burn.' As the fire took hold in the house the light dyed his face like gold and blood.

January looked from the flames pouring now from the roof of the east wing, to young Dr Hayward. 'Where's her room?'

'In the tower. On the third floor. Where the east wing joins the north.'

'"Thou shalt not suffer a witch to live." Her lies dragged our father into death. Got him to rob his own sons—'

January ignored Ott's interpolation, looked from face to face of the men around him. Giddy and sick from the wounds in his back and arm, the last thing in the world he wanted was to go back into that house again, but he knew, as surely as he knew his name, that if he said, 'Some of you have to go in and get her,' they would only look at him, then at one another, and each come up with a good reason why he shouldn't and couldn't . . .

Flame blazed in every window of the west wing, ran in threads up the kitchen roof.

'Do you know the way up there? Could you lead me?'

Several of the men faded back into the darkness at this. The young physician's eyes stretched with fear. 'I . . . I think I probably—'

'I think you probably would get yourself roasted in the first three minutes,' snapped a farmer in a calico shirt. 'You're the only doctor we got here, Monroe. Shadwell's been shot—'

'I'll go.' The Comrade stepped forward calmly, tucking up her skirts into her belt.

'Damn it, no!' Pearce grabbed her wrist.

'I know the house,' she said, as if fire could not burn her, and smoke could not kill. 'The fire hasn't taken hold in the north wing where the Greenes had their quarters. We can get in on the second floor with the ladder—'

'Don't be a fool, Annie!'

She regarded him with those infinite gray eyes. 'Are not all mankind fools, Del? Benjamin is needed here—'

January glanced from Ott's face to those of the men around him. Only Hayward was looking towards the house, his face twisted with anxiety and shock and tears now pouring down his cheeks. A stiff wind, he thought, would blow that fragile young man away. He'd collapse, and then January would have two to get out of the place . . .

Dizzy as he felt, from smoke and bloodloss, he knew there was a chance that *he'd* collapse . . .

Some of the men who remained looked horrified at the idea of simply leaving the Herald to burn in the house, but in their eyes, as well as their genuine horror, he could see their resentment and their fear – fear of what was going to come when the legal battle started over the Blessed Land, now that its Patriarch was dead. (And several of them, January was aware, were looking sidelong at *him*, as the Patriarch's murderer. *Just what I need . . .*)

One man asked, with gruff hesitance, 'So is it she, now, that owns all our land?'

The men looked at each other, glad that someone had asked. Then looked at the burning fortress again.

'I'll go,' growled Pearce. 'I know the house.'

'I can—' the Comrade began.

'Don't argue with me, woman!' roared the old man. 'You can stay here and help *them*. Help Hayward with the girl. Get the stock out of the barns if they catch. You're as stubborn now as you were when you were—'

He broke off, unable to frame the next words. January wondered what they were.

When you were sixteen?

When you were Annie?

When you were sane?

He snarled to January, 'Let's go, before the poor bitch roasts.'

Men enough – guilty at their thoughts – were willing to manhandle the ladder around to the north wing. Pearce snapped, 'Somebody give me a crowbar,' and someone else handed January a coil of light rope, which he slung around his shoulders. Behind him he heard Hayward directing others to put Eve gently on the shutter, and get her to the small outbuilding where women of the Community had lived and worked.

'Please,' he called to January, 'please, if there's any way you can do it, please save the scrolls . . .'

January hadn't the heart to tell him they were blank. Somebody thrust a couple of soaked bandannas into his hand, and he heard Orion Teems cry out in agony as someone got him to his feet. Heard him sob, 'Oh, God, *please*—!'

The air on the north wing's second floor was baking hot, and the dense haze of smoke flung back their lantern light as he and Pearce clambered through the window. Even with the bandanna tied over his mouth and nose January felt suffocated, and every question he wanted to ask – what had happened? How had Ott's sons learned of the swindle? Was it Ott who'd killed Broadax (*secure in the knowledge that I'D get the blame for it, damn him . . .*)? – strangled in his throat.

Time enough to ask if we live to get out of here.

Pearce had a lantern in one hand, and a huge hunk of white chalk in the other. With this he marked the vivid wallpaper every few feet, enormous Xs that would have been hard to miss even in near-total darkness. They passed a narrow door which, even shut, seemed to give off a blast of heat: January saw that the metal door handle was so hot it charred the wood around it. A back stair, he thought. Which would now be a chimney, to the flame from below. Between violent coughing, Pearce cursed, though whether this was at Old Man Teasle, at Broadax, at his own faulty memory of the way, or at Anne Seabright, January couldn't determine.

The door that led from the north wing into the main block of the house was locked. January felt the handle, hot but not burning, and though smoke wisped beneath and above the door it wasn't pouring in rivers. At a nod from his companion he kicked the lock, twice, the second time smashing the panels. The heat was worse, the smoke an impenetrable wall. It was like standing in the doorway of Hell.

Pearce snapped, 'Run!' and they strode, coughing like consumptives, down the short corridor and up a narrow flight of stairs, to a locked door at the top. Pearce wedged the crowbar in the door and January flung his weight on it, and they stumbled through into the dark.

There was barely more than a haze of smoke up here, but the heat was horrific. January leaned against the door jamb, unable to get his breath; the floor, for a moment, seemed to sway under his feet. He was aware that two of the cuts on his back had opened up again but barely felt the pain, through the panic pounding of his heart. *Don't you DARE faint now . . .*

The room itself was large, square, and cluttered with expensive furniture: not the stage-set orientalism of the 'paradise' rooms, but the extravagance of a young woman who has been poor, and suddenly has a great deal of money at her disposal. A canopied bed in polished blackwood, too many dressers, too many carved tables, costly little knick-knacks and lace-trimmed scarves and runners on everything. Like the houses of dozens of wealthy American families he'd entered in New Orleans, to teach their children to play their brand new gleaming pianos.

Even through the heat and the smoke, the heavy sweetish stink of spilled laudanum clogged the air.

She lay on the bed, fair hair spread over the pillow, her hands folded on her breast in an

289

attitude reminiscent of the one she'd take when in a trance. Maybe she *did* want to put herself into trance, he thought. Maybe she actually wanted to speak to her partner in crime. To get his advice and guidance.

Perhaps even his love.

Her breathing was labored, the plain white gown she had worn earlier in the evening rising and falling with the stertorous gasps. She looked – as she looked when speaking in trance – beautiful and innocent, like an angel sleeping. He saw now that her hands were the hands of a woman who has done no manual labor in the whole of her life.

All she had lived by was trickery, he thought. Tricking Eve Russell. Tricking Jonas van Martock. Tricking Jared Ott and the other farmers who had believed, and all those people who'd contributed money so that she could miraculously translate a new Gospel from ancient Babylonian. Harvesting them, like so much standing wheat that she was entitled to take . . .

And people called his sister, and Marie Laveau, witches . . .

He gathered her up into his arms. Like Eve, she was light as a child.

'Let's get out of here.'

Smoke nearly smothered them as they descended the stair. Coughing racked January's body; barely able to see, nearly unable to breathe. He couldn't tell whether it was hotter now than it had been minutes ago, or if it was the smoke or the blood he'd lost, but his head began to swim and the floor started moving again, like the deck of the *Marengo* as they'd plowed northwards from Havana. *Rose*, he thought . . . For a moment he seemed to see her, washing up the teacups on a blistering-hot New Orleans morning, sunlight gleaming on her spectacles.

Then through the nearly impenetrable murk he saw the reflection of flames beyond the doorway to the north wing, and Pearce cursed as only a man raised on the Law and the Prophets can.

'This way—'

The old man tested the handle of the nearest door, then pushed it open. The air was cleaner in the windowless room beyond. January cursed anyway. He was heartily sick of Old Man Teasle's architectural crochets.

'Here . . .'

The door to their right was locked, but the key was in it (*No wonder Eve was able to steal one so easily . . .*); the room beyond had a window, as well as a dresser and an armoire easily heavy enough to serve as an anchor. January stumbled to the window, laid the Shining Herald on the worn rug and threw open the casement. 'You got enough rope there?' asked the old man.

Trembling, January leaned into the clear air, pulled down his bandana and still couldn't seem to fill his lungs. 'We're above the kitchen,' he managed to say. 'Unless there's another room that's only one-story high—'

'There's not.'

He could see smoke fuming up from the shingles of the roof that lay twenty feet below, and the glare dyed trees of the orchard beyond as the blaze, like some monstrous animal, devoured the house. January felt a curious calm. *Just what we need. For the kitchen roof to burst into flame as we're scrambling down it . . .*

'Can you carry her?' Pearce's voice seemed to come to him from a great distance away, and he was a little surprised to see the man still close at his side.

He shook his head, knowing he hadn't the strength. 'You go down first,' he said. 'I'll knot the rope around her and lower her to you.' *And thank God she only has about half a bottle of Hooper's Female Elixir in her, instead of a bullet.* 'You'll have to wait for me. There isn't enough rope to go across the kitchen roof and to the ground.'

'I'll wait.'

Flames were coming up through the kitchen roof by the time January had lowered Pearce, then the Shining Herald, to its sharp downward slant. He himself was so giddy from the heat and the smoke and exhaustion that he wasn't at all certain he could make it to the ground alive. *The rafters must be eaten through, they'll collapse under us . . .*

But when he slithered to the roof below, Pearce shouted something to him – he couldn't understand what – and the old man half-carried him down to the roof's edge. There he saw, rather cloudily, that a ladder had been set up against the section of the kitchen wall not yet in flames, and Barnum stood at the top, reaching out to steady him down. He heard the showman yelling, as they reached the ground, 'Somebody get a sheet, wrung out with water . . .'

Pearce carried the Shining Herald, Barnum put a shoulder under January's arm, and they retreated from the swelling inferno of the Residence, toward the wall of the orchard, and the moist darkness closer to its trees.

The noise and the milling crowd were gone. January whispered, 'Where's Mamzelle Russell?'

Barnum replied, 'In the Women's House, with that young doctor fellow. Here,' he added, helping January to sit on a woodpile near the orchard wall. 'Good God, man, what happened to you?' he added, as he carefully stripped January of his shirt.

'Teems.' He raised his head as the Celestial Comrade appeared, her dark skirts tucked up to her knees, carrying a willow basket that dripped water. From it she unfolded a wet sheet. January flinched as they draped it over his bare shoulders, but the coldness seemed to leach away the burning pain in his flesh.

'You're going to have a prize set of blisters in the morning, Ben. I'll see if that young man – what did you say his name was? – can leave Miss Russell and take a look at those cuts.'

'I have calendula at the house,' said the Comrade, drying her hands in her skirt. 'I can make up a paste of it.' She turned away, and hastened to where the Herald lay, on a pile of men's coats.

'Will Mamzelle be all right?'

'No idea. The Spirit says she can drive her to Dr Wellburton in Liverpool, as soon as it's safe to move her.' Barnum spoke briskly over his shoulder, as he took another wet sheet from the Comrade's basket and handed it to Pearce. The old man snatched it ungraciously, flung it around himself like a drippy toga, and stalked to the Comrade's side. As he did so, the Spirit turned her head and met January's eyes anxiously.

January sighed. Though he wanted nothing more than to stay where he was and if possible fall asleep there, he got to his feet, picked up the basket, and staggered to the unconscious Herald's side. Her breathing was still labored – *that will be the smoke* – but her pulse felt stronger. The Comrade had loosened her collar, and bathed her face.

'We should wrap her in a sheet as well,' said January. It took him three breaths. 'The heat alone in there was enough to burn her. I think she'll be well, if we can keep her away from – were those Jared Ott's sons?'

'Two of them,' returned the Spirit. 'Cain and Saul. I gather that when the vision of the Reverend Broadax's murder manifested itself to the believers here, Mr Ott went to Mr Teems and demanded, who would take his place as the head of the Community? Cain Ott says that he spoke to his father on Thursday, and his father said that Teems had put him off. He said that they'd all been swindled – that the words of the contract had been changed after it was signed. He – Mr Ott – was going to speak to Mr Teems about it. Early this morning, Cain says that his

294

father returned to the Residence to help in the search, saying he'd be back this evening. That was the last he saw of him.'

January said softly, 'Ah,' and looked back toward the Residence, now merely a scaffolding around a core of flame a hundred feet high. He wondered if the cellar walls would protect Ott's body sufficiently for anything to be identified once the ashes finally cooled off. Not, he guessed, with the quicklime that close.

Then he glanced around him, noting again how still the night was. No figures, now, darted around those blazing walls.

'We may need to keep a guard on the – er – Shining Herald.' He laid the young woman's uncallused hand down, and moved back. Even in New York state, it wouldn't do for anyone to be able to say, *That black man laid a hand on a white woman* . . . 'I take it the men with the Ott boys were locals with their own grievances against the Blessed Land?'

'Half the county had 'em.' Pearce squatted beside him. His dogs had joined him, tongues lolling as they looked across at the holocaust of the burning house. 'The half that was related to them who'd signed their farms over: the Wellmans and the Tarwells and the Vermeers. But there's no need to worry,' he added. 'They hightailed it the minute the fire took hold. The sheriff'll be here—'

'And nobody in the county,' predicted Barnum cheerfully, 'will have seen a thing.'

Except those of us who're left here, holding the bag. January considered making a break for the trees, but the thought of even standing up made him flinch, much less spending the remainder of the night dodging deputies in the woods. 'What about Teems?' He tried to recall just when he'd last seen the lawyer, and in whose company. He couldn't. Amid a confusion of darkness, flame, choking smoke and the urgent need to make sure that Eve Russell would be cared for, he had only the dimmest recollection of Cain Ott saying, '"Thou shalt not suffer a witch to live."'

Of turning away from Teems who had sunk to the muddied gravel of the yard—

Of hearing him cry out as he was lifted. *Please*—!

'Teems is dead,' said Pearce briefly. 'Died of his injuries.'

'Died of his— He had a broken arm, for God's sake!'

'Not to fratch yourself,' grunted the old man. 'A dozen people saw you carry him down from there alive, includin' a couple who'll even be willing to say so in court. He died later, in one of the barns.'

January stared at him, shocked. But not, he realized, terribly surprised.

And as if to give the lie to the old man's reassurance, at that moment four men came out of the darkness – giving wide berth to the inferno whose heat parched January even by the orchard wall – and crossed to the little group. 'You're Ben?' asked the man in the lead, broad-shouldered and slightly stooped, with a mouth whose sensual shape, beneath a drooping black mustache, was weirdly at odds with the harsh expression of someone who has felt no joy for decades.

Pearce shoved his long, white hair from his eyes. 'Don't you might have better men to look for, sheriff?'

Sheriff Harter gave him one cold glare. 'Like yourself?' He turned back to January, studying him in the wildly flaring light like a man comparing what he sees with a description.

January sighed. 'I'm Ben.'

He felt no surprise whatever when informed that he was under arrest.

Twenty-Three

Barnum accompanied January to the Syracuse city jail in the small hours of Saturday morning, and gave his name to the sheriff as Ananias St-Chinian. His sister, Chloë Viellard, he said, was Ben's owner, and would return from New York City on or about Thursday. 'Ben's my brother-in-law's valet,' he explained, slipping the deputy a few coins that, frankly, January was rather surprised that he had. 'I'll be back tomorrow with a doctor, to see how he does. My sister-in-law would *take on something terrible*' – he emphasized the words – 'should any harm come to him.'

The deputy looked sour, but Sheriff Harter said, just as meaningfully, 'He'll be fine.' And glared at the deputy.

Barnum beamed. 'I'm sure he will, sir.'

January was in the Syracuse city jail for six days. He knew, intellectually, that there was little chance that Harter would let the slave catchers take him – Barnum came in every day, to 'cheer him up' as he said. But he did not sleep well, and when he did, his dreams were fearful. Twice in the first two days, slave catchers visited the jail, escorted by Harter or by the deputy, whom January privately christened Flimrap, after one of the less pleasant characters in one of his favorite books. The blackbirders would turn up within hours of the arrest of any man of color on any charge whatever, and they invariably recognized the prisoner as a runaway.

'God damn you, I'm Larry Mason from Schenectady!' screamed one young man, clinging to the bars of the cell. 'Ask anybody who I am! Send to Schenectady and ask Walt Carmody, he's my boss—'

One of the plug-hatted ruffians smashed his fingers with the cudgel he carried, while another struck him a crippling blow over the kidneys. Harter, looking on, shook his head. 'Say any damn lie, niggers,' he mourned, and followed them out. January, in his own cell at the end of the narrow brick hallway, said nothing – dared not. But he was shaking all over, hating himself for not stepping into a situation which would only end in his own enslavement, possibly his own death.

Larry Mason. Walt Carmody in Schenectady.

He remembered the men who'd slipped away into the darkness at the suggestion they help rescue the Shining Herald, and felt the sting of shame.

When Barnum came the following day, January gave the information to him, to send to Mr Carmody at once. But he suspected that even before it reached him, Larry Mason would be in some anonymous barracoon in Maryland, or on a steam brig headed for New Orleans.

In his dreams that night it was he who was dragged away, screaming, while every white person he knew stepped back into darkness and vanished.

On that first Saturday also, when the doctor had taken his leave (after trying unsuccessfully to get January to take a concoction of laudanum and camphor), Barnum stayed with him, sitting on a bent-willow chair in the corridor, for which he'd paid Flimrap five cents. He'd brought pen and ink, and January wrote letters, to Chloë Viellard and to Paget Russell in New York. On that first day it was all he could manage to do. For twenty-four hours he did little but lie on the narrow bunk in the end cell – a luxury for which Barnum also paid the obliging Flimrap – and alternately cough and sleep. 'How is Mamzelle Russell?' he asked, looking up from his writing, and the showman shook his head.

'Unconscious still – and pretty well dosed on laudanum.' Barnum, too, looked haggard, and January tried to calculate whether *he'd* had any sleep . . .

'She's at the Comrade's farm, and the Liverpool doctor's been out to see her. It's not that I don't trust that young Hayward fellow – who swears that everything was a plot by Jared Ott to discredit the Herald's teachings. But Pearce is staying out there, too.'

January sighed, which felt like having the lining pulled out of his lungs. He said, 'Good.' He handed Barnum the letters, and drifted off to sleep almost at once.

He woke late the next afternoon, his skin raw to the touch and blistered on his neck and hands, but feeling better. When Barnum arrived, January asked after the Shining Herald, and Barnum's wide mouth turned down at one corner.

'Nobody seems to know. Or at least nobody admits to knowing.'

The sound of church bells drifted through the window at the end of the jail corridor. The sound brought back to him the Sabbath bells as he'd trodden the platforms at Schenectady, Utica, here in Syracuse, the reminder of how long it had been since he'd knelt in the cathedral at New Orleans.

Byron Spring had been beside him.

He closed his eyes, between anger and grief and despair. *I need to write to Ruggles . . .*

It was like contemplating climbing the Alps.

'And I'm not the only one nobody's talking to,' Barnum went on. 'I journeyed to the Blessed Land this morning with Harter, and he told me he can't get word of any of them. Not the Shining Herald, not these Greenes, and not half a dozen of the Children, either. Hal Shamrock's smithy is locked up . . . Of course,' he added, lowering his voice, 'Harter may be lying as well.'

'Did they find Jared Ott's body?'

300

'We found *a* body. Two bodies, in fact, and right where you said they'd be. There wasn't much left of either, and Cain Ott got into a hell of a flap with Harter about whether you'd be able to give evidence in court about his father's identity. Harter wasn't in favor,' he added drily.

'Probably afraid of what else I'd say.'

'The ashes are still hot as Hell's doorstep.' Barnum passed a satchel through the bars – shaving things (January wondered how much he'd paid Flimrap to let him bring in a razor) and clean linen – and skootched his chair closer. 'Young Dr Hayward accompanied us. I gave them all the grand tour of the pit that used to be the cellar. It's amazing, how much more sense that house makes, when you can see the bare foundations laid out like a map . . . and there's little more of it left than that. But the remains of the mirrors are there, and enough of the mechanisms that moved them, and the sheet glass, into place when the lights went down, to make it pretty obvious where those "apparitions" were coming from.'

'How did Hayward take it?'

The showman shook his head wonderingly. 'He came up with three other things they might be used for, instead of illusions to hoax the faithful. But these weren't terribly convincing, and I could see Harter wasn't terribly convinced. It was actually sad, in a way.' The wry smile returned. 'Of course, there were also those hundreds of laudanum bottles to be accounted for, dozens with the labels still more or less readable. Poor Brother Hayward was hard put to come up with good reasons for that kind of wholesale consumption.'

January soaped his face – wincing at the blisters – and wondered if Barnum had enough bribe money left to cover water for him to wash all over, and if so, how he could tactfully request it.

Instead he asked, 'You found Broadax as well, then?'

'Cremated in his coffin.' Barnum's wide brow puckered and he shook his head again, but January had the suspicion that he harbored a touch of unwilling admiration for a fellow humbug who operated on such a scale. 'The parlor he was in was directly above the chest where they stored the quicklime. It must have been like the heart of a blast furnace when it all went up. But the skull was intact, and visibly chopped open, not split with the heat. I think it was then that Harter began to believe there was some kind of jiggery-pokery about that "vision" that eighty-three people had of you stabbing the man.'

'Thank God for small favors.'

'A very large favor, my friend. Nobody likes to think he's been made a fool of. And Heaven only knows what Miss Russell will be able to tell him when she comes round.'

January turned from the small mirror which he'd hung on the bars of the window. 'And how is she?'

Keys rattled at the far end of the corridor, and Flimrap – standing guard at the end of the corridor – said in his nasal New England yap,

'Yeah, he's down there at the end.' January and Barnum both looked toward the outer door, and January almost gasped.

It was Byron Spring.

Byron Spring ashy with fatigue, his right arm in a sling and an old-fashioned jacket around his shoulders, of the kind January had seen on some of the Celestial Comrade's friends from the New Land Congregation, when they'd come to muck out the cowshed.

'I just heard this morning, that you'd been arrested.' He thrust his left hand through the bars as Barnum shifted his chair out of the way, grasped January's in a hard grip.

Then he turned to Barnum, took his hand in turn. 'And God bless you, sir, for helping Ben in this mess. I misjudged you, and I am heartily sorry for anything I've said of you.'

'Lord, Mr Spring, it's my chosen profession to get people to believe I'm something I'm not,' grinned Barnum. 'You can't be blamed for doing what I try to get everybody to do. I'm just delighted to see you on your feet!'

'What happened?' asked January, and Spring shook his head.

'I think you were right, in that letter you sent me,' he said slowly, and fished it, unhandily, from the pocket of that shabby, full-skirted coat. 'Which I didn't get until today, by the way.'

'Did you go to the Blessed Land to ask about me?'

Barnum had risen from his chair, and at his gesture the young preacher sank gratefully down on to it. 'Thank you, sir.'

Barnum waved the gratitude aside. 'Good Heavens, man, you look like ten miles of bad road. Can I get you anything from that extremely venal specimen of the *genus miles gloriosus*?' His eyes moved to indicate Flimrap, still guarding the door, and Spring smiled at the Latin insult.

'Thank you, no, sir, I'm well. Just . . . tired.' His glance returned to January. 'Yes, I went to the Blessed Land as soon as Ammi Seabright told me that the Reverend Broadax was supposed to have been murdered by a runaway slave he was sheltering – that every believer had seen the vision of you stabbing him. This was . . . Wednesday. This past Wednesday. I reached the Residence late in the afternoon, and Mrs Greene – one of the very good ladies who lives in the Residence with her family – told me Mr Teems was out in one of the cottages. She was standing in the main doorway talking with Mr Ott, who was in a fearful taking about something.'

'If I'd signed my land over to a religious community whose leader had just been murdered,' said Barnum reflectively, 'and was trying to get some information about just who, in that case, was going to control the Community's lands from then on, I think I'd be in something of a taking, too.'

This was clearly something Spring hadn't thought of, but his brows plunged down immediately as he saw the implications. 'Was *that* it?'

'It's what makes the most sense.' January

304

wiped his razor on the towel Barnum had brought. 'Go on.'

The preacher considered for a moment, then nodded slowly. 'It makes sense of what happened, doesn't it? Mr Ott and I walked out to the orchard together. When Mr Teems opened the cottage door and saw us he looked shocked – horrified, in fact. Mr Ott tried to push his way in, demanding that Mr Teems explain something to him about the Community – I don't remember the exact words but realize it must have been something about the land holdings. He said something about, "You're not going to put me off any further," or "You're going to give me some straight answers". Mr Teems barely looked at him. He was looking at me, looking almost stunned, as if he'd been taken completely by surprise by something important . . .'

'They thought you'd gone back to New York,' said January. 'And once Broadax – or Drake, as another of his names seems to have been – found the daguerreotype of Eve Russell in my coat pocket – Mr Barnum's coat pocket, actually – he'd have known that the game was up. If you'd introduced me into the household, it meant you knew whatever I knew – which meant that he had about a week to get Jonas van Martock to sign over his assets, sell off the Community lands, pack his bag, and get across the lake to Canada.'

'And all of a sudden' – Barnum spread his arms like an actor calling in a chorus of supernumeraries – 'there you were, offering yourself on the doorstep like a sacrificial lamb. He must have been hard-put not to shove poor Ott out into the road!'

Spring grinned in spite of himself, and very gently touched the back of his head. 'He grabbed my arm as if he thought I would run away – I can see why, now – and practically begged Mr Ott to wait for a few minutes, which of course Mr Ott was unwilling to do. Mr Teems pulled me inside, sat me down at a little table there, said, "Oh, wait, I've forgotten to tell Mr Ott something," and went towards the door, which was behind my back. I turned in the chair just in time to see him swing at me with a cosh . . .'

'Oh!' cried Barnum. 'Clumsy! The man was hopeless as a ruffian—'

'He did well enough,' retorted Spring ruefully. 'It cracked my shoulder – broke the clavicle, Mr Earth told me later, when I came to at the New Land Congregation. I fell, and his next blow caught me on the back of the head. Why he didn't simply shoot me—'

'Not with half the Community milling around in an uproar a dozen yards away, he couldn't,' pointed out January.

'You're lucky he didn't have a knife on him,' pointed out Barnum. 'Like I said, the man was no proper ruffian.'

'Well,' Spring went on, 'he bent over me and I kept my eyes shut. I was too stunned to do much else, really. I heard him go to the door, open it, call for Mr Ott, who didn't answer. Then he went out.'

'Probably going to fetch Broadax from the house,' said January. 'Another mistake. Broadax

306

was still alive at the time,' he added, seeing the young preacher's surprise. 'If this was Wednesday afternoon. By the look of Broadax's body, I don't think he could have been killed much before Thursday evening. We'll get to that.' He reached through the bars, and gripped his friend's wrist. 'Go on. You know Teems is dead, too.'

'That's what I heard.' Spring rubbed his head again. 'God rest his soul. There's not much more that I remember clearly. I managed to stumble out of the cottage and I must have made it to the woods. I knew they were going to kill me; I couldn't imagine why, or why Mr Teems hadn't done so already.'

'I can,' said January. 'Other people saw you at the Residence Monday evening. Teems couldn't get you out of the cottage by himself – he wasn't a very strong man – and a shot would bring thirty people on the run. Teems had no idea who you might have talked to. With Broadax still hiding in the Residence itself, they couldn't risk more questions.'

'And of course,' corroborated Barnum, 'poor Broadax couldn't leave the Residence to help Teems carry you away because it was still daylight and there were too many people about between the Residence and the orchard fence.'

'Or because Ott went right back across to the Residence,' surmised January, 'to have a look at Broadax's study . . . and possibly ran into Broadax himself.'

There was silence, broken only by the sound of the church bells, and the rattle of a buggy driving by. January recalled the disheveled mess of the study, searched and then searched a second time. The oozy wetness of the blood on the carpet, only a few hours old on the Thursday evening.

'Awkward,' murmured Barnum. 'Awkward all around. Blew up whatever plans Broadax might have had for a quiet getaway . . . No wonder Teems didn't get back to the cottage in time to stop *your* getaway. Wonder what Broadax told Ott to keep him quiet?'

'What would *you* have told him?' inquired January drily, and returned his glance to Spring. 'Go on.'

'I can't,' said Spring. 'Not really. I have vague recollections of staggering through the woods, of dusk coming on. I do remember being terribly thirsty, and trying to drink from a stream.

'After that' – he shook his head – 'nothing, until I came around – well, my head cleared, they tell me I'd been in and out of consciousness all the previous day – on Friday, in an attic room at the New Land Congregation's farmhouse. Mr Earth – the Congregation's Speaker – told me I'd begged incoherently for them not to tell anyone, not *anyone*, where I was: "They're all in it together," was what he said I'd said. He said that otherwise he would have made inquiries at the Blessed Land, since he thought that I was a runaway and guessed that's where I'd been headed. It was the next day – yesterday – before I was able to be moved. But I asked them to get word to Ammi Seabright at Auburn. Ammi drove most of the night, and reached the New Land this morning, with the news that the Residence had been burned to the ground by Mr Ott's sons and other disgruntled members of the Community. He said you'd been arrested – I knew by the description it had to be you – and that Mr Teems was dead. They said also that you'd carried the Shining Herald to safety, as well as a "girl in a white dress" . . . Miss Russell.'

'Mamzelle Russell,' affirmed January. 'Whose testimony – when she's able to give it – will, I hope, make sense of the rest of this story. It had better,' he added grimly, 'because as it stands, neither your word nor mine is likely to hold up against the word of white men in court.'

Twenty-Four

'Danged if I ever saw any nigger hold court the way you do,' groused Flimrap the deputy on the following day, as he unlocked the door of January's cell, and led him out to the watch room where Harter and the deputies had their desks. 'Here's half the damn county, come to make sure you're feelin' better.'

He looked put out, as well he might. A free black carpenter from Auburn had been brought in drunk yesterday afternoon while Spring and Barnum were still present, and had given his name and the names of his white employers to Barnum, who had promised to let the employers know that same evening. January tried hard not to look gratified in the deputy's presence.

The men now seated in an assortment of rough wooden chairs (including two borrowed from Harter's desk and that usually allotted to the deputies) were the three sons of Jared Ott, and two other men clothed in the frockcoats and top hats of professionals. The older of these Cain Ott introduced as his lawyer, William Galway. The younger, brisk and bespectacled and in his thirties, was, Ott said, Dr Julian Thatcher. Flimrap rather ostentatiously took a shotgun from the rack on the watch-room wall, and went to stand guard at the street door, presumably in case January made a break for it.

In his gravelly growl, Cain Ott said, 'Sheriff Harter tells me you saw my father's body in that godless hell-trap of Broadax's, Mr January.'

'Before some *person or persons unknown*,' added Galway with deliberation, 'maliciously or accidentally burned the place down Friday night.'

January's eyes went to the silver-haired lawyer's, then to Cain Ott's stony face. The young man had his father's large, round head and the features of a disagreeable putti who has been whipped every day of its life.

'It was a terrible thing,' he said calmly. 'I was hoping that there might be witnesses who saw me carry M'sieu Teems, Mademoiselle Russell, and the young woman called the Shining Herald to safety from the flames.'

'There were indeed,' responded Galway at once, with the air of a man happily conceding

310

a point in negotiations – which indeed, reflected January, was exactly the case. 'Quite a number of the neighboring farmers, attracted by the blaze, came on the run to help put it out, though by that time the flames had taken too strong a hold. Several of them – as well as your master's friend Mr St-Chinian, and Mr Pearce – are prepared to vouch for your heroism, as well as for the fact that Mr Teems was alive and spoke to them after you carried him out of danger.'

'Thank you.' January inclined his head in gratitude, though he wished he could ask openly that this be put in writing. 'I understand poor M'sieu Teems passed away later that evening—'

'It was very sad,' agreed the lawyer briskly. 'Dr Thatcher' – he nodded to the physician – 'examined him and said that the smoke and the exertions were too much for his heart.'

Evidently nobody was going to mention the broken shoulder. January did his best to look grieved. The Brothers Ott, sitting in a row in their hard chairs, didn't even make the attempt.

The youngest brother – slender and straight-haired in contrast to his rough-hewn, wide-faced brothers – spoke. 'Tell us about our father, if you would, Mr January. There . . . there wasn't much left of his body after the fire. You're sure it was him?'

January said firmly, 'I'm very sure, sir. I'd been introduced to M'sieu Ott on Monday night, when I arrived at the Blessed Land—'

'*Blessed Land*,' growled Cain. 'Blasted Land, I say. And blasphemy to name it Blessed.'

Galway opened his mouth to silence him, but

311

January met the young farmer's eyes and said quietly, 'I'm not sure you even know half the evil that went on there, m'sieu.' He turned his glance to take in Saul, and the younger boy, even as the lawyer, his face brightening with a professional satisfaction that bordered on delight, whipped out a notebook.

January described Ott's body, as he had found it in the cellar; Dr Thatcher was also taking notes. 'For twelve years I was valet to a surgeon in New Orleans,' he explained, very conscious of Flimrap standing by the door. 'My master – Dr Gomez' – he named the free, colored surgeon who had in fact been his teacher – 'taught me a great deal about the progress of the physical symptoms of mortality in a corpse. I don't believe your father had been dead more than a few hours. His flesh was cool, but the muscles had not yet begun to stiffen. I lifted one of his arms, and was able to turn his head, even, which is where rigor first sets in. Also, though there were – please excuse me for speaking of this, m'sieu – though there were rats, their depredations were not, to my judgment, more than a few hours advanced.'

Saul Ott, the middle son, turned his face away as his expression crumpled in horror and grief. He fought sobs, while his older and his younger brothers listened unmoved.

'I saw him that morning,' said Cain Ott, 'when he left for that cursed Hell pit.'

'And I saw him,' said January, 'a few hours before noon, at the farm of the woman they call the Celestial Comrade. She will also attest to the time. M'sieu Ott had a brief altercation with M'sieu Teems – no more than the exchange of a few words – but M'sieu Teems said, "Let's talk this over in the study after dinner", or words to that effect.'

'Your master taught you very well,' remarked Dr Thatcher, gesturing with his notes.

'Thank you, sir.' January inclined his head again, annoyed as always that he had to pass himself off as a surgeon's valet instead of a trained surgeon himself. But nobody with any political or economic clout, he knew, would go looking for a free, colored surgeon if such a man happened to go missing. They *would* go looking for a valet who would have cost them over a thousand dollars.

He held his tongue.

He went on to describe the condition of the body, the marks of the garrote, the absence of any sign of struggle, the smell of laudanum that had lingered in the man's whiskers, and the finding, in the library, of two glasses, one tainted with the drug. Again the middle brother pressed his hand to his eyes to hide his weeping, while the older and the younger wore the faces of men of stone.

Cain Ott said, 'Pa came to my house Wednesday night, angry like, but quiet.'

Galway began again, 'Mr Ott, it might be better if you kept your observations—'

'Don't turn lawyer on me, Galway, this's the truth and I don't care who hears it.' He turned those hard, coal-dark eyes on January. 'When he come by my place that afternoon he was hot-mad, sayin' as how he'd heard in town that that weasel Teems was here in Syracuse, askin' on the quiet about sellin' up the land of that heathen gang he was so set on. I'd told him it was against Family, for him to go sign over his land to those folks, even if he did give each of us a hundred acres. What the hell is a hundred acres, these days, with corn at fifty cents a bushel, and a man's family to feed?'

'Job told him, too.' Saul spoke for the first time, deep and gruff, hoarse like the bark of a dog. He nodded toward the youngest son.

'Job told him two-three times,' rasped Cain, 'how he should read that contract he signed, make sure it said what that Broadax bastard said it said, and how did Pa know *for sure* that all those in the Blasted Land would have a place to live an' be looked after in their old age? Job's slick.' He thumped his youngest brother on the shoulder. 'Job reads law with Mr Galway here.'

'I thought it might be something like that, sir,' said January quietly. And, when Cain swung around on him like a half-wild horse about to kick, went on, 'My friend Mr Spring was at the Residence Wednesday afternoon when your father was there, demanding to speak to Mr Teems.'

'And where might we find this Mr Spring?' Galway's voice scintillated with contained eagerness.

'If there's a hotel in town that caters to men of color, that's where he'll be staying.'

January almost laughed to see the lawyer's face fall. But an instant later Galway's eyes took on a slightly distant look, calculating how to deal with a witness whose testimony, though legal in New York State, might be discounted by some of the jurors, on account of his race.

January added, 'I believe he came into town with Ammi Seabright.'

Galway sighed, in relief and recognition. *I can make something of that local connection . . .*

Cain Ott grunted, 'That's why Pa was there Wednesday. I thought he'd go back to that godless hellhole but he didn't. We'd gone to bed – Saul, and my wife and me, and all of us – when Pa came knocking on the door, asking for bed space. He was quiet, angry-quiet, like he was thinkin' something over. Thinkin' what to do. He didn't go back to their Blasted Land that day, but stayed at my place, choppin' winter wood while Saul and I got in the hay.'

'He was a rare hand with an ax, Pa,' offered Saul, bringing out the memory of his childhood, like a schoolboy producing a toy. 'He could cut a cord of wood as fast Cain or I could fill the kindlin' box.'

Job added, his fluid tenor at odds with the animal growls of his brothers, 'You wouldn't think it, a little man as he was. He built the whole of our house, when we were boys, just with an ax. Cut the pegs for the roof beams, smoothed the floorboards, even carved the forks and spoons in the kitchen, just with that one tool. He said cuttin' helped him think.'

'So it did.' Cain shifted his weight in the sheriff's big chair. 'Wednesday was first time I seen Pa look like he had in the old days. Not sayin'

315

much, but with that far-off look in his eye, like he'd get when he was schemin' on how to turn a bargain, or outfox the revenue men if you want the truth. Before Mama died an' he got religion that first time.'

'Pa got religion, first time, with the New Covenant Methodists,' explained Saul earnestly. 'Right after Mama passed. Then he got in some row-de-dow with the preacher, and last year he heard how this Herald lady spoke to the dead, an' he went—'

'A witch,' spat Cain viciously. 'And the New Covenant preacher's a heretic and a servant of the Antichrist.'

'I suspect,' said January, 'that Wednesday afternoon, when my friend M'sieu Spring was being murderously assaulted by M'sieu Teems' – they all looked astonished at that, but January went on – 'that your father crossed back to the Residence, and searched the Reverend Broadax's study.' He hesitated, fitting the times together in his mind: what Broadax must have offered Ott, to keep him from telling the world that the Patriarch was still alive. What Ott must have guessed about what that offer was actually worth.

But he knew better than to voice his suspicions about who had whacked Serapis Broadax over the head with an ax, and said instead, 'I think he found evidence of some kind that either M'sieu Broadax or M'sieu Teems had altered the contract he'd signed, or worded it in such a way that it gave control of all the Community's lands to M'sieu Broadax alone. Did your father go back to the Residence the next day?'

316

'Just at sunset.' Ott stroked his rufous beard. 'He had rooms in that big house, an' keys to get in. But he always said, nobody was let into the east wing, where that lyin' scoundrel Broadax had his quarters. We thought Pa'd stay there Thursday night, Saul an' my wife an' me, but he come back, just after we'd gone to bed. The moon was just past full, an' the night fair for ridin'. Then early, Hal Shamrock rid over, with news that they'd found Broadax's body, layin' in the road.'

January's glance flickered from Cain Ott's face to those of his brothers. Saul had looked away again, prey to another wave of grief. But January saw the slight frown that pinched Job's brow, and the uncertain glance that the youth gave Galway, presumably, like Barnum, wondering how Broadax's body could have lain in the road for over three days – surrounded by the tracks of a big man's feet – without any of the searchers who had combed the countryside for him, and later for January, stumbling over it.

January made himself frown, and asked, 'Was there blood on your father's shirt when he came back to your house Thursday night?'

Startled at the question, Saul asked, 'How'd you know?'

Galway looked like he could have struck him. *He guesses, too . . .*

'Your father had a cut on the side of his wrist,' lied January convincingly, and pointed to the spot on his own right wrist where blood could have splattered on to his sleeve, in more or less

317

the place that it would splatter had, for instance, he struck another man in the head with an ax . . . 'Not a big one, but it looked nasty.'

'Oh, yeah,' agreed Saul, nodding. 'Blood on the front of his shirt, too.'

Galway ground his teeth, and remained ominously silent while January went on to describe to Dr Thatcher, in accurate, medical detail and without any sort of speculation whatsoever, what he had observed of Broadax's body. If Cain and Saul drew any connection between the nature of the wound which had killed him and the blood on their father's shirt when he had returned from the Residence Thursday night, or between the usual progress of decay in a corpse and the state of the Patriarch's remains as of Friday night when he'd seen the body, they gave no sign of it. Dr Thatcher and Job exchanged several glances, and cast inquiring looks at Galway, who smiled and nodded blandly. 'Shocking. Very shocking.'

'I was certainly shocked,' January attested, hand upon his heart. 'As was M'sieu St-Chinian, who saw the Reverend Broadax's body that night as well. And the light, as I've said, wasn't at all good. I was seeing all this by the glow of a single candle' – he turned apologetically back to Thatcher – 'so I'm afraid my observations might not be accurate. And as my old master said, there's so much variation from one . . . er . . . body to another, depending on things like the heat of the day and the age of the deceased, I'm afraid that what I've told you might be of very little use, to you or to anyone.'

Galway relaxed visibly, and beamed, not only at being handed this means of obfuscation about who might have wielded the fatal ax, and when, but also at the presentation of a white witness who could be instructed to say whatever was necessary. 'To be sure.' He rose and held out his hand. 'And where might we find Mr St-Chinian . . .? Ah, excellent. And you may rest assured, Mr January, that in case there's any question about . . . ah . . . what caused Mr Teems' unfortunate demise, we do have a dozen witnesses as to the fact that he was alive when you so heroically bore him from the house.'

January stood also, bowing them from the watch room as if from his parlor at home. He almost felt that he should walk them to the door.

'Mamzelle Russell,' he said, 'will bear me out in all particulars about Mr Ott's body. She saw it, too.'

And God knows what else . . .

'Miss Russell, yes.' Galway nodded, and his brow clouded a little, either in genuine sympathy or with vexation over a white witness who might not be able to testify. 'We hope, indeed, to have her testimony to corroborate yours. But . . . well . . .'

Damn it, thought January, remembering the childlike face, the small hand gripping his arm. *Damn it . . .*

As they were crowding and sidestepping to leave, Job, the slender changeling of the brothers, stood and stepped forward. 'Mr January,' he said quietly, 'do you remember how my father was dressed when you saw his body?'

319

January shut his eyes, calling back the horrible scene. The gnawed mess of flesh, the eyeless sockets, the milling ants. 'Old-fashioned, wine-colored coat,' he said. 'Fustian, I think – I felt the fabric when I picked up his arm. My wife – my first wife – was a seamstress . . .'

His voice stumbled a little at the thought of her, as if he heard her whisper again, *Malek* . . .

The breath of intimation, that all was not yet over, nor was all as it seemed.

He shook the thought aside. 'Steel buttons,' he said. 'Old-fashioned, fall-front breeches – light gray-brown wool, as far as I could tell, dark as the room was. Wellington boots, I think. Plain waistcoat – I think the buttons were copper basketwork.'

'Like these?' Job dug them from his pocket, dark with charring and soot. With them were a few steel coat buttons, and the cracked pieces of the horn buttons from a man's fall-front flies.

January said, 'Like those.'

Job nodded. 'Thank you.' Gently, he put his hand on his middle brother's back, as he steered the weeping man to the door.

Twenty-Five

'Ott did it, didn't he?' remarked Barnum, when he came to the cells later that afternoon.

January nodded, and glanced down the corridor toward the door that led into the watch room.

But Flimrap, bored or bribed, had abandoned his post. *Where's Barnum getting his bribe money?* wondered January. *Has he located Thomas Jefferson's bootblack, and is now exhibiting him for twenty-five cents a peek?*

'I don't think we'll ever know for certain,' he said. 'But I think you're right: when Ott went back to the house Wednesday afternoon, while Teems was dealing with Spring, he encountered Broadax himself while he was searching the study. What could Broadax do? The man could have cut and run the minute I escaped – the minute he knew the game was up. But he hadn't yet gotten van Martock to sign over his lands. He needed one more Night of Revelation. One more vision.'

'A fact,' said Barnum quietly, 'which probably saved Miss Russell's life.'

'And cost Broadax his.' January leaned back, and folded his hands around his drawn-up knees. 'But once Ott had seen him, what could he do? Ott had only to shout to bring half the congregation racing up the stairs. All Broadax *could* do,' he went on, 'was promise Ott a cut of the profits if he kept his mouth shut . . . A promise Ott clearly didn't believe.'

'Under the circumstances I'm surprised Broadax thought he would.'

'Broadax was desperate by then,' said January softly. 'And I suspect he was one of those men who believed himself smarter than anyone he met. Did van Martock sign, do you know?'

'He did,' said Barnum grimly. 'For all the good it did anyone, since the contract went up in flames

321

along with everything else. When the hullabaloo
started they hustled him – slightly befuddled
with opium – into his carriage and sent him on
his way. I spoke to his coachman before the lot
of them got on the train for New York Saturday
afternoon, and I gather that the intention had
been for him to spend the night at the Residence.
So you probably saved his life as well. By
the time the carriage reached Liverpool and the
nearest hotel, they had to carry him indoors.
The poor old man was unwakeably asleep and
if he'd stayed, would have roasted in his bed.'

January was silent, remembering the complaints
of the families who had lived in the Residence's
west wings, summarily moved out during Teems's
final few days of trying to hold the hoax together.
Their lives, too, had been saved.

In time he asked, 'Does he know that his
visions of his granddaughter were a hoax?'

The showman's broad, good-humored face
seemed to darken. 'He was told,' he said. 'Raleigh
Shadwell – one of the men who had a lawsuit
going against the Blessed Land – went to van
Martock's hotel Saturday morning and told him
that the whole thing had been a fraud. Shadwell
says – I spoke to him this morning, he's one of
the men who "just happened to be present" when
the Residence burned down – that van Martock
at first refused to believe it. Shadwell offered to
take him out to the ruins and show him the
remains of the mirrors and the gas cylinders –
everyone in six counties has been out there by
now. He said Miss Russell was at the Celestial
Comrade's farm and the Spirit would almost

322

certainly let van Martock see her. Van Martock said he wanted to hear no more of it, and would not see the girl. He left on the train for New York and, I am told, has offered a reward of five thousand dollars for information leading to the capture of the Shining Herald or anyone else connected with the hoax.'

'And I expect,' said January drily, 'that his lawyer will turn up in town in time for the trial . . . if there *is* a trial.'

Barnum spread his hands. 'Who would they try?'

Who, indeed?

'Eighty-three people saw a vision of you stabbing Broadax Tuesday night – an event which supposedly took place twenty-four hours before that. Three times, in the chest, with what looked like an ornamental dagger. But I – and apparently over a dozen Children of the Light who helped carry his body back to the Residence in the small hours of Friday morning – can testify that he died of being struck in the lower back, from behind, with an ax, and then having his skull split open.'

'Thursday evening,' said January. 'When Ott returned to the Residence – having worked out that if eighty-three people saw *me* do the deed, nobody was going to ask him what *he* was doing on the night of August the sixth.'

'Sounds as if he thought that the contract simply gave Broadax a claim on the land and that if Broadax was killed, he – and everyone else – would be in a position to get it back. Obviously a man who'd never dealt with corporations and trusts.'

323

'Maybe,' January replied. 'Or maybe he had, and killed the Patriarch simply out of rage and revenge. He may have been trying to get Teems alone, when he spoke to him on Friday, with the intention of killing him as well. I don't know.'

'Or he may have been trying to lay hands on the contracts. It would account for the room being searched a second time, probably when he got there Thursday. Or he may have wanted to find out what Teems knew – though I can't imagine anyone believing a word the man said.'

'This afternoon,' Teems had said. 'Before dinner. Come up to the study, and I'll show you . . .'

'As you said,' pointed out January quietly, 'sometimes people want to believe. Need to believe. And thousands of people,' he added, 'believed *your* story about Joice Heth being a hundred and sixty-one years old.'

In New Orleans, in Texas, in Paris – in Mexico and Washington City – Benjamin January had at one time or another unraveled the circumstances of murders, logically tracing killers by the signs they had left and by the times when they could have been nowhere but with their victims. He had sought out information, pieced together blood spots on clothing and the stiffness of a corpse's wrists or neck, or the dark mottling of *livor mortis* on a dead man's face or back, to assemble a picture of how and when death had occurred, seeking the only explanation that could cover *all* those tiny elements.

So for the remainder of that day – Monday, the tenth of August – and all throughout the next, when he had a few hours alone in the sweatbox of his cell in the Onondaga County jail, he assembled those mosaic pieces of what he knew, what he thought likely, and what he surmised. It was like a mental game of Patience, to keep his apprehensions for his own safety at bay.

He did not have many hours of uninterrupted reflection, however, because he was visited three times on Tuesday by Barnum, twice by Byron Spring, once by the Celestial Comrade and Dark Travis – each with small tales and details of the events that swirled in the backwash of the downfall of the Blessed Land. A handsome, quietly dressed woman from Rochester had arrived in town Monday evening, whom Travis (rather shyly) said that the local grocer had identified as a woman of ill repute. Since the train had also contained (said Barnum, the following day) four very pretty, very young ladies in extremely colorful dresses and two extremely pretty boys as well, one could guess that news of events had not yet reached Rochester. The quietly dressed woman had asked for the Reverend Broadax, and when informed he was dead, had asked to speak with his lawyer.

'I'd give a lot,' January remarked, 'to have been present for *that* meeting . . .'

Two elderly gentlemen from New York, continued Barnum, had arrived late Tuesday afternoon with the same request, and had seemed profoundly shocked and disconcerted at the news.

Spring, coming Tuesday forenoon (and looking

a great deal better), recounted the descent, by every farmer who had joined the Children of the Light in the past year, upon the town's lawyers, in quest of information about the contracts they had signed.

'And I foresee,' sighed January, 'a wholesale exodus of legal clerks on the Albany train tomorrow, to have a look at the actual deeds in the recorder's office. And good luck to them.'

Spring also reported that the Oswego River had been dragged that morning, where it ran close to the charred ruin of the Residence. It had so far yielded seven male, and four female bodies, and the remains of six children whose sex was harder to determine. There were, Sheriff Harter had surmised, probably others.

Close by them, its blade not even rusty, had been a small hatchet, of the sort used to chop kindling.

The Celestial Comrade, when she came Tuesday, spoke with profound pity of the quietly pious Boston gentleman with the haunted eyes, who, when shown the remains of the mirrors and limelight apparatus in the pit of the Residence, had sat among the blackened stones and wept.

Eve Russell, the Spirit said, had regained consciousness, but was still very weak. She had asked after him, and after her parents. Mostly she slept.

Knowing how easily pneumonia could set in on the heels of injury or infection, January could only pray for her. He had no idea what Chloë Viellard would learn – or had learned – in New York, or whether or not it would support all these fragments of information that he gleaned or surmised. He could only wait.

There was still no word of the Shining Herald.

The lawyer Galway – who had clearly also been apprised of these various arrivals – visited January's cell Wednesday morning, bringing a clerk with him to take down shorthand accounts of his observations. By his questions, January gathered that the sharp-eyed, old gentleman had been retained by eleven of the thirty families whose property had been entangled in the Blessed Land, in addition to the Otts. He also brought assurances that affidavits had been collected from a number of 'chance' eyewitnesses, who had 'just happened to pass by' the burning Residence in time to see January emerge from it with a perfectly healthy Orion Teems on his back.

'Thank you,' said January, and meant it. 'Let me know how I may assist your own investigations.'

While Galway was there, four other lawyers put in appearances, all asking the same questions about what he might have seen or heard.

Patiently, January replied that he had seen no contracts in the few minutes he'd spent – by the flickering light of a single dark lantern – in the Patriarch's study. 'I could make a fortune,' sighed Barnum, visiting late that afternoon with a picnic supper of cold chicken and potatoes, 'by forging contracts, returning the land to its original owners – all with the understanding that they'd be proved to be forgeries the minute all those clerks get back from Albany with true copies of the originals. I wonder what the actual terms of the trust were? And who were the other beneficiaries?'

'If any.' January unrolled the battered copies of the New York *Post* and the *Western State Journal* that he'd also brought across the foot of his pallet. 'I'm sure we'll find that out in time. The way I'm sure we're next going to be visited by the lawyers of the Tappan Brothers, and everybody in New England who donated – or invested – money towards the translation of the Lost Gospel of James. To say nothing of the representatives of the American Anti-Slavery Society. I'll let Spring and Ruggles handle those. All I want to do is get out of here, and go home.'

He almost flinched at the sound of voices in the outer office – *not more of them!* – and Barnum grinned like a schoolboy. 'It's the price of fame, my friend.'

'And here I am only forty-seven,' January grumbled. 'Think how many will come when I'm a hundred and sixty-one.'

And Barnum replied gravely, 'It's why I'm only charging two cents a head for them to see you now.'

The door at the end of the little hall opened, and Flimrap's voice said, 'He's down the end.'

Boots thumped on the planks, and Paget Russell's voice said, 'Ben?'

Chloë must have briefed him, thought January, *to remember that I'm supposed to be a slave . . .*

At the door, Flimrap said to someone outside, 'You prob'ly shouldn't—'

'Oh, get out of my way,' Rachel Russell

snapped, 'you tiresome little man!' and came flying down the corridor in a frou-frou of skirts.

Barnum was already on his feet, bowing, as January said, his eyes meeting Russell's, 'You remember M'sieu St-Chinian, sir? Madame Viellard's brother?'

'Ananias,' assented Russell with a smile, clasping Barnum's hand and not even glancing back at the deputy standing beside the door. 'Your sister will be here tomorrow or the day after. She said there were things she needed to finish up with, in New York.'

But his wife was already at the bars of the cell, gasping, 'Have you seen her? Is she all right?'

Carefully, January replied, 'I haven't seen her, m'am. I assume they're still holding me on the outside suspicion I had something to do with M'sieu Broadax's murder. But she's being cared for by friends, at a farmhouse out by Lake Otisco. I spoke to the woman yesterday, and she said your daughter is improving, though still very weak.'

'What *happened*?' Her small, lace-mitted hands gripped the bars. 'You said she'd been injured . . .'

January had written simply that Eve had been hurt, but had not included details, guessing that whatever he could tell about the events of Friday evening would serve only to frighten this woman with shadows and maybes. He had said, *She is in good hands and I have every confidence of her recovery*, a confidence he wished he felt now.

'There was gunplay,' he said quietly, 'in getting Mamzelle away from the scoundrels who had lured her to their compound. Mamzelle was injured—'

Mrs Russell let out a stifled cry, and sagged suddenly against her husband's arm, her head lolling; Mr Russell dug in the pocket of his coat and produced a bottle of smelling salts.

In the same quiet voice, January continued, 'But before that happened, sir, I had her assurance that she had sustained no other injury—'

The Englishman's eyes met his sharply, over his unconscious wife's bonnet feathers.

'And by her demeanor and what I know of the circumstances, I believe she was telling the truth. She said she had not been molested or interfered with in any way, as I wrote to you, except that she had been drugged – not heavily – with hashish over a period of about six weeks.'

For a long moment Russell held his gaze, before he yielded his wife to Barnum's steadying grip. As the showman helped her to sit on the wooden chair, Russell said softly, 'Thank you, Mr January.' Then he turned, rather awkwardly, back to his wife. From his end of the corridor, Flimrap watched the whole proceeding with great interest.

'I want to go to her,' gasped Mrs Russell, and pushed aside the vinaigrette Barnum was holding to her nose. 'Where is this Lake Otisco? Paget, please, we have to—'

'It's a twelve-mile drive,' January warned. 'It will be well past dark by the time you reach the place—'

'Take us! Please, take us! I can't . . . Not all the way until morning . . .' She reached out to her husband, and when he took her unhandily in his arms, clung to him and began to weep. 'Please, please!'

Barnum handed the smelling salts to Russell, said quietly, 'I'll see if Sheriff Harter can be bribed into accepting a bond,' and moved off down the passageway to the watch room.

Harter was at dinner at Florrie's Tavern, across the street from the jail, but Barnum returned to report that he was willing to release January for twelve hours on a hundred dollars 'bond'. By the promptness of the transaction – with nary a mention of a judge – Russell and January both suspected that this sum would go straight into the sheriff's pocket. But the Englishman accepted, and then paid another exorbitant sum to the owner of the local livery for the rental of a horse and buggy that weren't likely to be returned until midnight, if then. To January's surprise, Barnum rented a saddle horse and offered to ride ahead, to inform the Celestial Comrade of the late-arriving visitors. 'As kind as she's been, and with the trouble she's taken, it would be poor thanks to knock her up in the middle of the night. Although,' he added, 'I perfectly understand that Mrs Russell isn't in any case to think of these matters.'

When, later, after a four-hour drive through the narrow trails and byways south-west of Syracuse, January mentioned his surprise to Del Pearce as he led the rented horse to the stable, Pearce chuckled grimly.

331

'Where did he get the money?' January remembered the showman's impoverishment on the steamboat and train. 'The same place he's been getting the money for all the bribes he's paid to bring me better food and shaving facilities, I assume . . .'

'Him?' Pearce glanced towards the lights of the shabby little farmhouse, upon whose porch Barnum was introducing the Comrade to the Russells. 'Huh. First day, 'fore the ashes was even cold, he set up railin's around the ruins out at the Blessed Land. Hired Josh Muchmore's three boys for fifty cents a day, an' these five days, been chargin' ten cents a head for them as want to come see the place. Been makin' ten-fifteen dollars a day.'

January sighed. 'Of course he has. I trust Mamzelle Russell is doing better? Yesterday' – it seemed like a week ago, since the Comrade had visited him in the jail with her bits of news – 'the Spirit said she'd regained consciousness . . .'

'Aye, she's done that.' The old man stripped the harness from the horse's back, and slung the mass of buckles and straps over his shoulder. 'Take the lantern an' fetch me some oats from the bin, would you, Ben? An' water from the well, if you would. This poor lad's had his work this evenin' . . . Thank'ee.'

Brutus and Mars padded out of the darkness, and sniffed the harness suspiciously, as if to make sure there was nothing harmful about it.

'I'd been thinkin' I'd need to get my shotgun, to keep them lawyers off the place. Started turnin' up on the Sunday, 'fore she ever opened her eyes.' He dumped the measure of grain into the manger, while January moved the lantern closer, and fetched a rag to rub the harness sweat from the animal's back. 'Though I did tell that feller Galway that I didn't think the Lord ever forbade shootin' lawyers on the Sabbath.'

'I can see no reason why He would,' agreed January gravely. 'Or on any other day, for that matter.'

As they crossed the dark yard toward the dim glow of the house, Pearce added, 'Girl's lucky Mr Barnum ain't chargin' twenty-five cents a head for them as been here today, wantin' to come see *her*. He'd do it, too, I reckon, 'cept I told him I'd take out an advertisement with his face on it, if he so much as thought about the idea. He's afeard some of them slave catchers in town might be workin' also for the feller he owes money to back in New York. Not, I don't think, that he really would,' added Pearce grudgingly, glancing toward the showman's burly shadow against the light of the farmhouse door. 'He is a son of Moab and slick as snot on a doorknob, but in time he may prove to be among the saved, for all that.'

'God works in mysterious ways,' January agreed.

Barnum's voice came softly from the dark of the porch. 'Ben? Miss Russell is asking to see you.'

The big room that January guessed had been the Comrade's own chamber had been converted into a sickroom. The Spirit herself greeted him

333

in the kitchen, with outstretched hands and a smile. At the table, a cup of tea steaming gently before her, Mrs Russell wept very softly with a look of such peace, such happiness on her face that January felt his own eyes fill. Her husband sat beside her, tea before him and a plate of bread and butter between them. His long arms were wrapped around her shoulders, but his eyes were closed, his face fifteen years younger than it had been in the jail, or all during the long drive through the woods in twilight and darkness.

A lamp burned beside the narrow bed in the room beyond. Eve Russell looked up from the heap of rolled blankets and folded bolsters – topped with a solitary pillow – and whispered, 'Mr January,' in a thread of a voice.

She looked like the dried skeleton of a flower, as if the reunion with her parents had drained what little strength she had. January said, 'You should sleep,' and she shook her head.

'I will. I'm much better, really I am.' A slight motion of her fingers beckoned him to the stool beside the bed. 'Mr Pearce and the Spirit tell me that you saved my life. I had to thank you.'

'It's all right.'

'And that it was Mr Teems who shot me.' Her brow creased as she tried to recapture the events of Friday night. 'I don't really remember. He's . . . he's dead, they say. And the Residence is burned down—'

'And every lawyer in New York State is on his way here,' said January, 'to sue each other over the Blessed Land's property.'

In spite of herself she gave the breath of a chuckle. 'Oh, dear . . . I shouldn't laugh, those poor people . . .'

Illness had wasted her firm sturdiness; she looked like a wraith, with her light-brown braids lying on the pillow and her hands like little bundles of knotted grass stems on the simple coverlet. Two of the Comrade's many cats made furry lumps at the bed's foot. 'What about the Herald?'

January shook his head. 'No one has seen her.'

'Mr Pearce says you got her out of the building . . .'

'I did. But I was arrested immediately after that—'

'Arrested!'

'At this point,' said January, 'I think it's more to keep me from running away. They still believe I'm a slave, and we are within a few miles of the Canadian border. But it means that I have no idea what happened to the Herald, whether she was gotten away by the faithful, or whether—'

He looked at her ghost-white face, and stopped himself from voicing his other speculation as to what could have become of the Herald that night. The possibility that she, like Orion Teems, had 'succumbed' to some unspecified 'exertions' in the darkness of one of the barns wasn't one that Eve Russell needed to know about right now. Enough time for her to work it out – as he had – that the Shining Herald might well be one of those who had claim on whatever property the Reverend Serapis Broadax legally owned.

Were that the case, her death could easily leave

335

the congregation's lands without anyone to fight for them in court.

He tried to look as if none of this were going through his mind.

'I'm sorry.' Eve folded her fragile hands. 'She was so kind to me. I know now she was a scoundrel,' she added, in a matter-of-fact tone. 'But she didn't lie to me the way . . . Well, the way Mr Teems did, and the way I know the Reverend Broadax must have been doing all along. Because I'd see people from my window in the cottage, you know. I used to sit in the window of my room there, when I was supposed to be reading or meditating, I'm afraid, and I'd sometimes see people coming and going from the other cottages. Mr Teems, and Mrs Greene, told me I was dreaming, and since I was still drinking that awful lemonade I thought, maybe I *was* dreaming. But the Herald said, No, people would come from far away, to meditate through the night in the other cottages, and have visions.'

Visions indeed. The Rochester madam who'd turned up in Syracuse Monday came to his mind, with her girls and her rent boys . . .

'Did you ever see Mr Ott?'

'Oh, yes. He'd come to the orchard, and speak to the Herald there, or to the Reverend Broadax. I'd see them from my window. I was a little afraid of him. He looked so hard and grim. I had to tell myself that if he was there in the Blessed Land, he must be a believer like myself. I think he must have had someone speak to him, someone reach out to him, through the Herald, from the *real* Blessed Land, the land where it's always summer . . .' Her voice stumbled a little, as if she saw herself in a gown that she now knew had been copied from a dead girl's portrait, in order to deceive an old man into signing away his property, and tears gathered in her eyes.

She brushed them quickly aside. 'He had a most fearful row with Mr Teems, on the Wednesday afternoon. That was the day after the vision everyone had, of you stabbing the Reverend . . . Mr Teems had come out to break the news to me, and I was almost ill with grief and shock. That vision must have been made the same way the visions of me were done, wasn't it?'

January nodded.

She was silent then for a time, her face averted. She wiped quickly at her cheeks again and in a voice that trembled with an effort to sound matter-of-fact, she said, 'That must have . . . have been Mr Shamrock, who impersonated you . . .'

'I think so, yes. He's disappeared too, you know.'

She swallowed hard, not saying what January guessed was in her mind: that the comfort she had taken in hearing the voice of her own dead friend had been just as false.

After a moment she went on, in a calmer voice, 'I heard them arguing in the orchard. I looked down to see if the Herald were coming to see me – which Mr Teems said she would – and I saw Mr Ott striding away toward the house.'

Her brow creased again, with some inner pain. 'It was that night,' she said, 'that I saw the

Reverend. I was still waiting for the Herald to come – hoping she'd come, to comfort me . . .'

That same night, thought January, that he had slept in the Celestial Comrade's attic for the first time, among the sacks of apples and potatoes. Had slept, he realized, with the soundness of a tired child, for the first time since he'd left New Orleans, the white moon blazing in through the gable window to print a square of light on the floor so bright that, waking, he had thought for a moment that Rose had dropped her scarf there.

'The moon was full,' Eve went on, 'and I saw him, crossing from the farthest cottage to the gate in the orchard wall. As I said, I thought it must have been a dream, the way Mr Teems was always telling me that I'd dreamed this or that. But when I told Mr Teems about it . . .' Her frown deepened at the recollection. 'He said I was imagining things, and that my room was to be moved, that I would be staying in the main house. That's when I started to wonder – that's when I looked for the letters Father had written me, to look at the paper again . . . and I realized that they'd been taken. That they must have searched my room. They always left a pitcher of that lemonade in my room, in case I got thirsty, and that was in the new room in the Residence also. But that's when I stopped drinking it, and drank the water in the wash pitcher instead. And I realized they'd lied about that, too.

'I felt ill after that,' she continued after a moment. 'Not feverish, or pain, but . . . I can't describe it. It grew, during the day, while down below my window – which was on the same side as the orchard – I could hear the voices of the people coming and going as they looked for you. My head ached, and I felt a kind of awful grief, and . . . and restlessness, as if I couldn't keep my hands and feet still. I think that must have been the drugs in the lemonade.'

January nodded, with a kind of awe and admiration, that this young woman had been – and still was – able to reason so clearly, after everything that had gone on.

Wherever she went from here, he thought, the mere furbelows of 'polite society' would be wasted on her. He hoped her parents knew it, now.

He hoped *she* knew it.

'I went to the window, thinking if I got some air I'd feel better. It was evening, then – it was dark, but the moon was up, as it had been the night before. And I saw Mr Ott come along the little path that led from the woods, through the orchard, towards the house. Walking fast, and carrying a lantern – the kind my father always called a bull's-eye, with a slide to cover the light – and a satchel, the sort I'd see him carrying his tools in, when something needed repair.'

Twenty-Six

When Flimrap came into the cells on Friday with the news that January had yet another visitor, he looked so cheerful – and so dazzled – that January guessed that it had to be Chloë Viellard and that she'd tipped him well. He was even more certain of it when the deputy unlocked his cell and escorted him out to the watch room – though on their walk down the corridor between the barred gratings of the other cubicles, January reviewed in his mind how he'd make a break for the outside door if, in fact, his visitors turned out, instead, to be particularly well-paying slave catchers.

But in fact, it was Henri's wife who was seated at Sheriff Harter's desk, exquisite as a Meissen china shepherdess in her gown of rain-flecked pale-green lawn.

He felt as if iron bands, locked around his chest and skull, broke and fell away. As if, after an endless fall, he had landed safe and unhurt on his feet.

'Madame,' he said, in French, 'were we not being observed, I would fall down before you and kiss your shoes. Which of Hercules' labors do you want me to perform for you, in thanks for the mere sight of seeing you here?'

'The Golden Apples of the Sun,' she replied promptly, 'when you have time. I've always been curious about whether those were really apples, or oranges, or some unknown phylum, and Henri would simply love to write up a study of them for the *Journal of Gardening*.' She turned her head as Flimrap bowed deeply to her and left – the older deputy, whom January had christened Skyrep, dozed in a corner over the New York *Sun*. Outside, rain pattered on the roof of the porch. Hélène, straight as a ramrod, worked at her embroidery on the bench just inside the door, and paid not the smallest attention to anything that transpired in the room.

'Looking for Sheriff Harter, m'am?' inquired January, with a glance after the departing deputy.

'For the local judge,' she returned. 'To release you into my custody.'

'I really will kiss your hands and feet, m'am,' said January. And, seeing the slight pucker of concern that darkened her pale eyes, he added, 'In truth, your "brother" Ananias took very good care of me. Brought me food and clean linen, and made sure the local deputies didn't sell me to the blackbirders behind the sheriff's back. He usually comes in around this time with dinner – I gather he's been selling tickets to the ruins of the Blessed Land, and within a week I'm sure he'll be able to pay off the moneylender who chased him out of . . . Ah!' he added. 'And here he is.'

Barnum paused in the doorway, in the act of shaking the rain off his umbrella, and began to remove his hat to Chloë. She crossed the little office to him with a dazzling smile and cried, in English, for Skyrep's benefit, 'Ananias! *Dear* brother!'

For a man who'd never laid eyes on Chloë Viellard in his life, Barnum made a split-second recovery, beamed in return, and held out his arms. 'Chloë, my dear! Let me look at you!' He met her eyes, behind their round slabs of spectacle glass, caught her hands in his, held them out so that he could admire her frock of celery-green lawn, then kissed her fingers in a brotherly fashion.

Hélène paused for one half-second over her stitchery, either at her mistress' *soi-disant* relation's shabby corduroy coat and tweed cap – she knew perfectly well that her mistress was an only child – or at this unmerited display of kinship, but she said not a word.

'Thank you, dear brother,' Chloë said, 'for taking so much trouble to make sure Ben was all right! Did M'sieu Russell—'

'They arrived the day before yesterday.' Barnum conducted her back to Sheriff Harter's big chair. 'They went out to the Comrade's cabin on Lake Otisco that night, and have been there since. And I hope,' he went on more quietly, 'that the experience will give them a better idea of who their daughter is, and what it is that she needs out of life, poor child.'

'And how is she?'

'Recovering,' said January, 'so far as I could see when I was furloughed Wednesday to guide the Russells out there.'

'I was there yesterday, and this morning,' said Barnum. 'I won't say the roses have returned to her cheeks, but there is a definite sparkle to her eyes.'

'Then our work here is almost done.' Chloë sighed. 'Which is a fortunate thing, because poor Henri is being driven demented by his mother, who is also much better, under the ministrations and flattery of this Dr Fiedler. He has assured her that her ailment is *not* gout, but in fact "traveling spavins", and has prescribed compresses of fresh ginger, and his own personal tonic, which so far as I can tell consists of cherry juice, sugar, and cider vinegar. She has purchased a crate of it, and has put in an order for regular deliveries henceforth, at ten dollars per dozen bottles, plus shipping. It does not smell,' she added, 'as if it contains either laudanum or alcohol, so there is little likelihood it will be stolen en route. Ah!'

She turned as the door opened, and Flimrap re-entered – rather damp from the rain – followed by Sheriff Harter, who bore a paper in hand.

January stepped back respectfully to let Barnum perform the introductions. Chloë smiled graciously, took the bond, studied it, then paid over the two hundred dollars (for which she made Harter sign – January had been right in his suspicion that Paget Russell would never see his own hundred again), plus a dollar *douceur* for the sheriff. 'Do you mind that I've taken a servant's room for you at the Western Empire?' she asked – reverting back to French – as they descended the jail's steps, with January holding Barnum's umbrella over Barnum and Chloë, and getting rained on himself. Hélène followed proudly through the lessening drizzle as if proclaiming that dryness was for weaklings.

'Madame,' said January feelingly, 'I will sleep on a towel in the hallway, to be out of the cells.' Though the blackbirders hadn't been through for four days now – and though he was fairly certain Galway and the other lawyers would never have tolerated his disappearance at this point – the jail smelled of old vomit and old piss, and his cot was infested with bedbugs and fleas. He found himself counting the seconds until he could have a genuine bath, and clean clothes.

In company with Byron Spring – and Byron's friends the free black couple who ran the livery stable and bathhouse – January had his first decent supper in two weeks at an eating house near the depot, while Barnum escorted Chloë down to dinner at the Western Empire. They reunited in Chloë's private parlor later that evening, to find, on the marble-topped parlor table, half a dozen neat stacks of notebooks and papers in the glow of the gasolier overhead.

'Ah!' cried Barnum in delight, as he entered the room in January's wake. '*Éclaircissement* at last!'

Spring bowed as he was introduced to Chloë. 'Not so much *éclaircissement*,' he said with a half-smile, 'as the putting together of pieces, like those dissected maps they make to teach geography. Thank you for letting me join you this evening, m'am.'

She tilted her head a little to one side, considering him with her usual detached calm. 'You were duped as much as anyone,' she said gravely, 'if you introduced this Reverend Broadax into antislavery circles, which I understand that you did.'

The preacher nodded, and January saw the muscle harden in his jaw. How many of those seven men, four women and six children, he wondered – and others besides whose bones were yet undiscovered – had Spring advised to seek refuge in the Blessed Land? Had he led there?

344

'It was his business,' Chloë went on after a moment, 'to get people to trust him. You were far from the only one. He was very good at it.'

'He was, madame.' Spring didn't look as if that knowledge were any comfort to him.

Rain pattered on the parlor's curtained windows. Hélène, stitching in a corner, looked as if she'd rather pretend that this entire event were not taking place.

No tea was served. January didn't know whether to be vexed or amused at this manifestation of the American protocols, of who could be seen consuming food or drink with whom.

Chloë took her seat at the table, and Barnum drew the gasolier down closer to the marble surface. 'It took me a few days,' Chloë said. 'And I had considerable help from a detective officer in the Sixth Ward named Mr Sullivan. But I think we'll find this illuminating.'

This proved to be an understatement. As January had suspected, the Reverend Serapis Broadax – also known as Henry Drake, also known as Henry Callan, also known as Professor Enoch Hogan and Father Burnwell Aiken – had a back trail decades long of fraud, imperson-ation, confidence games, and blackmail, with occasional forays into forgery, pimping, and the 'slave catching' of people who hadn't originally been slaves.

'Apparently this wasn't M'sieu Drake's first occasion of playing Old Man of the Mountain.' Chloë thumbed through one of the several memorandum books in the stack. 'In Philadelphia in 1832, under the name of Callan, he advertised

345

himself as a "nerve doctor" specializing in treatment for "overwrought gentlemen".'

'Aha!' cried Barnum. 'I thought so!'

'At his rural headquarters beyond Germantown, they'd have an "electric bath" consisting of mild electrical shocks, followed by a dose of "soothing draught" and a night spent in a specially constructed "atmospheric concentration chamber" which produced, I am given to understand, quite extraordinary dreams. The gentlemen in question very quickly discovered they couldn't do without these—'

'I can well imagine,' interpolated Barnum. 'And all concerning things they wouldn't have conceived of doing in what they believed to be their waking lives?'

'I expect he had to choose his clientele rather carefully.' Chloë turned over several pages. 'All M'sieu Viellard would wish to dream about, for instance, would be new species of *blatta orientalis* or *formicidae* – at least, so far as I know – and this M'sieu Callan would be hard-put to conjure visions of those. Or perhaps,' she added thoughtfully, 'Henri would dream longingly of an afternoon spent without his mother. Poor Henri.' She frowned. 'Then again, I suppose those who wanted dreams about orphanhood or cockroaches wouldn't have returned for second treatments – or third, or fourth, or seventeenth . . .'

Her brow puckered as she selected another page. 'At any rate,' she continued, 'this "Professor Drake" – and the description of him is *very* like this Broadax – departed from

Germantown without paying his rent. I could find no record whatever of the Reverend Broadax – or anyone else who sounds in the least like him – undertaking an expedition to the ruins of Babylon in 1837. Rather, Drake and his wife Katy – a hairdresser – and one Tristan Parnel – a lawyer whose description sounds very like Mr Teems and who made his living forging documents for the shadier Democratic politicians of New York – were running a series of blackmailing schemes in that year. Madame Drake let it be known among servants in the wealthier households that she would buy information, and then either brokered it to other blackmailers, or turned it over to her husband for use. As a hairdresser, Madame Drake herself had considerable contacts—'

'Wait!' exclaimed Spring, startled. 'You don't mean – there's a woman named Katy Callan who dresses hair for half the ladies in society! Three women in our congregation in the Village work as housemaids – for the Drews, the Livingstons, and the van Santvoords – and all of them have mentioned seeing her.'

'"Woman in her forties",' Chloë read in her notebook, '"small and stout of stature, dark hair, prominent front teeth, slight cleft in the chin" . . .'

'Yes! The teeth and the chin, anyway . . . If this Mrs Russell was staying with rich friends, she must have had this woman work on Miss Russell.'

And heard all about poor little Belle Martin, reflected January, remembering Eve's tears, as

347

she realized that the reassurance she'd had of her friend's love and happiness had only been bait, a little piece of rancid bacon that concealed the hook. *And she'd have heard about Eve's craving for meaning in her life.* He had seen his sister Olympe, and the voodoo queen Marie Laveau, speaking to clients, drawing them out, listening for the timbre of voice, the hesitations over certain topics; watching for the fidgeting of the hands . . .

It would have been like taking a toy from a child. Or luring a miser, greedy for gold, into a trap.

Where would such a man, such a woman, spend the rest of eternity, in Hell? Anger flashed through him again, so that he only half-heard Spring say, 'Ran for it, I should say, when she heard of Broadax's death . . .'

And Barnum: 'Are you joking, my boy? She'll be in Albany even as we speak, putting in her claim on the property . . .'

Somewhere in the stinking sewage of the Eighth Circle, January reflected, remembering the Boston man the Comrade had told him about, weeping among the burned ruins of the Residence, weeping with horror at the memory of dreams which had not been dreams. *Or stumbling among the blind fortune tellers . . .?*

What penalty would a just God mete to those who'd turned poor old van Martock's vision of his precious granddaughter to the sour ash of mockery and theft?

To those who had murdered the hopeful, on what they thought would be the threshold of freedom?

Dante had reserved the lowest circles of Hell, where even the air was frozen to powder, for traitors.

'In 1838, however,' Chloë went on, 'the Reverend Serapis Broadax appeared at Niblo's Garden on Broadway, presenting a young woman whom he called the Shining Herald – purportedly a visitor to this world from what he called "The Realms of the Ineffable". So far as I can tell, a young lady of her description named Mary Skeritt had been preaching in a small way in Steuben County, in the back end of nowhere. She would fall into a trance in her aunt's parlor—'

'That's her!' cried Barnum. 'She'd preach about Heaven and Hell, and later claimed she had no recollection of what she'd said. She wasn't the only one doing that, either.'

'An angel, she said,' reported Chloë, 'put the words into her mouth. She would also, upon occasion, say that she saw and spoke to the spirits of the dead.'

'And I'm guessing' – Spring's voice was bitter with the gall of his own betrayal – 'she charged a tidy fee for the service.'

'Not at first, I gather.' Chloë tucked a finger into the notebook. 'She came to the attention of the authorities for stealing her stepfather's savings from the family sugar jar, and running away to New York with it. She later claimed – to the police – that that gentleman had beaten her for "blasphemy" – he was the local Congregationalist minister, which I should imagine was why she would have her visions at her aunt's rather than at home.'

'Perhaps,' said January, 'she was a better preacher asleep than *he* was awake.'

'In any case' – she returned to her notes – 'as Molly Skeritt she was arrested twice in 1836 for picking pockets and once early in 1837 for public lewdness – cursing at a minister, I gather.'

Spring exclaimed in disgust.

'I understand that Jonas van Martock has offered a reward for her capture . . .'

'Five thousand dollars,' affirmed Barnum. 'And from what I saw at the train station this afternoon, every Dead Rabbit and Shirt-Tail and Roach Guard in New York are spread out along the route of the Canal, from Albany to Buffalo, watching for her.'

And with any luck, thought January, the hunt for the Shining Herald would distract the local slave catchers for long enough to let every runaway in the district get safely across the border.

It was the least the girl could do, to atone for the mess she had helped to cause.

But even so, he wondered if anything would ever atone for the grief of betrayal.

On the drive out to Lake Otisco the following morning, Barnum remarked speculatively, 'You know, without the railroad, Broadax could never even have undertaken his schemes.' Far in the rain-washed morning distance, the whistle of the train sounded, bound for New York.

'Nor could he have,' pointed out Chloë, 'before the development of koniaphostic light – this

350

"limelight" that was strong enough to make an image clearly visible through several reflections. I daresay most of the people who attended the Shining Herald's demonstrations didn't know that there *was* another explanation, other than a supernatural one. Nor, I suppose, did it occur to any of those poor gentlemen, who had probably never felt the effects of hashish in their lives, that what they were experiencing might *not* have been a dream.'

'Particularly not,' said January quietly, 'if they were told by someone they trusted that it *was*. And if they wanted very much to believe that that is *all* that it was.'

'New crimes for a new age,' said Barnum.

'An old crime,' January pointed out. He leaned around from the driver's box, where he sat next to Leopold, to address those in the back of the wagonette. 'I'm fairly sure Broadax originally meant the Blessed Land to be just another version of his Old Man of the Mountain game. The railroad just meant that he'd be less likely to be investigated by any police that knew what they were doing.'

'But his wife's information could still reach him easily,' agreed Barnum. 'As could his clients.'

'And the clients were the same. All the men who, quite literally, dreamed of having experiences in the bedroom that their scruples, their upbringing – their faithfulness to wives or families or beliefs or simply common decency – would never permit them to seek. Longings they'd held in check all their lives.'

Chloë frowned, as if such longings were

something she'd heard about – like unicorns – but had never really believed existed.

'What a pity,' she remarked after a time, 'that the Reverend's account books went up in flames with the Residence. I should be extremely curious as to how much money he accrued in donations from this form of phantasmagorical procuration. But once he established the Blessed Land, the temptation to profit further must have been overwhelming. And I don't suppose any of the farmers who believed in the Herald's "revelations" even thought to make sure that they got their own copies of the contracts they signed.'

'Why would they?' said January. 'Why would anyone who believed in Life Everlasting doubt that the souls of those they loved could return? We all believe – or want to believe – that love does not die.'

'And apparently will pay almost any amount,' sighed Barnum, 'to have our hopes confirmed.'

In the darkness of his mind, January saw again the glowing shape of a girl with flowers braided into her plaits, holding out her hands . . .

And like the breath of wind that stirred the leaves, he seemed to hear a voice whisper, *Malek* . . .

January sat for a time in the late-afternoon sunlight, smoking a cigar on the rough bench beside the Celestial Comrade's door. Brutus and Mars dozed contentedly at his feet, now and then whining as they pursued savage prey in their dreams. Barnum was still inside, gleaning

352

from Del Pearce further details about Spanish treasure and the monster that was supposedly seen in the waters of Lake Cayuga – presumably intending to capture and exhibit it at ten cents a head. Rose, thought January, would demand of him every fragment of information about these matters when he got home, but for the moment his blisters still hurt, his half-healed back still smarted, and he wanted only to rest where he was.

He had taken his leave of Eve Russell, had both her parents clasp his hands in thanks. Much as he disliked the thought of being mercenary, he was deeply glad for the amount of the draft Paget Russell had given him on Thelwell's Bank, which he was well aware would be joyously accepted by any financial institution in Louisiana. (*Jesus of Nazareth was a working carpenter – I'm SURE He'll understand . . .*)

It was time to go home.

Del Pearce emerged from the house behind him, crossed to the rented wagonette. Pillows, quilts, and sheets were rolled up beneath its seats: the Russells would be remaining in the Celestial Comrade's house for some days yet, until their daughter was well enough to be taken back to town. January rose to help him and Pearce waved him to stay where he was. 'They'll come for their truck in a minute,' he said. 'No look-out of yours.' He coaxed the bits into the mouths of the team, stroked their heavy-muscled necks. 'And best you do get shut of this country. Else you'll have every lawyer in the state at you lookin' for affa-daveys about that Residence of Broadax's—'

'I understand Madame Viellard is having M'sieu Galway write up a single, blanket statement, for distribution to all lawyers concerned.'

'Huh.' The old man checked a buckle. '*Lawyers*. She's smart, that girl. Too smart.'

'Smart enough to learn the truth about the Reverend Broadax from police records,' January pointed out. 'And it doesn't do to speak ill of smart women. My wife is a smart woman.'

'Nuthin' good came of smart.' Pearce turned back to him, his hand resting on the horse's shoulder, the blue letters of the Lord's name faintly traced on the fingers. 'Men and women both, the stupid of the world cause great evil, but it's the smart that get away with it, and go on to spread it. Like that Reverend, and that Herald witch.'

He paused, and watched as Barnum and Mr Russell emerged from the house, and crossed to the wagonette to get the quilts.

'Children of this world,' growled the farmer, though January wondered if he meant Broadax and Mary Skeritt, or the jovial, curly-haired showman now carrying pillows back to the house. 'Wiser in their generation than the Children of Light. Like monkeys, they is. 'Twas a reason the Lord forbade them in the Garden to eat that apple. Knowledge of good, an' knowledge of evil . . . better they'd stayed away from 'em both, and trusted God instead.'

He snapped his fingers for his dogs, who came

354

scrambling to his side. Knowing neither good nor evil, reflected January, but only love.

'You keep safe on the road.'

The old man stumped off toward the barn.

Turning, January saw the Celestial Comrade, standing behind him in the doorway of her house. Watching her friend go, with smiling eyes.

'Do you believe him?' he asked softly, and her eyes warmed still further. Her smile the smile of a Spirit who has come to the world to help those in need of it, the children of this world as well as the children of light.

'I have no more idea than you do,' she said, 'why God gives one man brains like a threshing machine, and another a heart like the ocean and the sky. I think he's angry because in his way, Mr Barnum is a little like the Reverend Broadax. Both were gifted with that understanding, to read people's dreams. To know how much people will pay for wonders.'

January said, 'We all need wonders.'

'More than ever, now,' she agreed. 'With the railroad, and the factories, and the steamships that can bring poor people from one land to another, fleeing from one set of horrors to find themselves in another . . . It is a world that none of them were ready for. Poor Del – and I'm sure, Jared Ott and Ulee Wellman and Monroe Hayward and Dark Travis and all the others in this land over which the Lord's fire has passed. Freed from darkness to a wider world, with no advice as to where to go in it. They remember the land the way it used to be, and want to go back there. And they can't go back, any more than they can take off their adult bodies and run about naked and innocent as children again. But everyone wants to remember how it felt.'

January opened his mouth to remark that he had never felt innocent, never felt free of care . . .

And then remembered chasing through the dark swamps near his master's plantation, playing hide-and-seek with the other children. For a time not knowing that they could be sold away from their mothers without notice, any more than they knew they could die of snake-bite, or drown in the bayou. Life was the way it was, and at that time, the evils they feared were the spook-tales old Auntie Jeanne would tell, about the platt-eye devil that lurked behind trees to devour little black boys and girls, or the witches that waited in the darkness to ride the unwary, ride them to death until daylight. Coming home in the twilight, he remembered making up names for all the different frogs whose multifarious cries pierced the dark-green gloom, and listening for the fiddle of Compair Lapin, the trickster rabbit, who could use music to dance the Devil out of Hell.

'People need wonders,' said the Comrade. 'Just because he has grown to man's estate doesn't mean a man no longer hungers to remember what the world looked like in the light of new morning. Wonder makes men vulnerable, as love makes them vulnerable. Opens them to evil or to good.'

Twenty-Seven

'Where will you go?' asked Chloë, when the wagonette pulled up just in view of the first glowing lamps of Syracuse, to let Barnum spring down.

He had kept them all entertained, on the long drive back to town, with tales of the confidence tricksters he'd known in New York, and the adventures of low-life gamblers in such Bowery haunts as the Hurdy-Gurdy and the Arcade, and how three putative 'Spanish Dancers' had managed to rob the Five Points moneylender Camphene Shea of an entire month's profits through one of the oldest tricks in the book. But as they'd approached the town he'd grown quiet, and glancing over his shoulder at him in the dusk, January wondered whether his silence betokened concern about precisely Chloë's question, or the uncomfortable reflection on how narrow was the line which separated the Patriarch's toxic chicaneries from his own.

'Boston, most likely,' he said, rousing himself. 'Or Philadelphia. Maybe back to Danbury for a time. Anywhere to keep ahead of Uncle Geogehan's hired thugs. I wasn't jesting, when I said every ruffian and slave catcher in New York are prowling the Mohawk Valley.'

He dropped from the wagonette to the long grass beside the roadway, a big, sturdy, curly-haired Yankee in January's decrepit corduroy jacket. Mellow sweetness softened the evening air, an echo of a world where things had been simpler, and it was more possible to believe in Spanish treasure and communities that would care for you for life. 'Half of them may have seen Miss Skeritt on stage, at some point in her career – and Heaven only knows how many of them could recognize me as the man who owes Uncle Geogehan a hundred and fifty dollars.'

Or the man who sold the right to gawk at a poor old black woman for ten cents a time . . .

Still, there was genuine concern in January's voice as he asked, 'What will you do?'

'Oh, I'll turn my hand at one thing or another until I have enough of a stake to return to New York. I've heard the Scudder family – old John Scudder took over what used to be the old Tammany collection of curiosities back, oh, years ago – I've heard they're looking to sell: curiosities, menagerie, dioramas, building, the lot. If I can find a backer . . . The place is run down and has never been properly advertised. I'd make it hum!

'People want to be entertained,' Barnum went on, eager and serious as any backwoods preacher. 'Not just lectures about Lost Gospels or some preacher's trips to the Holy Land, and not just girls prancing about showing off their drawers, either. People want wonders and marvels. New York is growing, and people want someplace where they can take their families on a Sunday afternoon. Someplace where they can forget their troubles and be amazed. Everyone needs their dreams.' And his whole face brightened, with that dream of his own.

'Give me six months running the American Museum, and I'll be able to pay old Geogehan off with interest . . . even at *his* rates. And I must say, I've made a decent start.' He slapped his pocket. 'Ten cents – one thin dime – to look at a burned-out ruin? Think what I can do with a proper museum, with a theater attached! I wonder if I can get Del Pearce to come and show off his skills as a treasure scryer?'

January grinned. 'I think he'll see you in Hades first.'

Barnum's eyes shone. 'Hades . . . I wonder if I can put together a diorama of Dante's journey to Hades? Now *that* is something people would come for miles to see!'

'And *I*' – Chloë reached down to shake Barnum's hand – 'shall look forward to seeing it, when next my mother-in-law demands to be taken to consult Dr Fiedler – while we're talking of hoaxes and humbugs!'

Barnum laughed. But he was right about one thing, January reflected, watching the tall, stocky form move off into the summer twilight with no more than the clothing he stood up in. On the following day, at every town along the Canal – Rome, Utica, Little Falls – January saw men on the railway platforms: Bowery *b'hoys*, Celtic toughs with their soap-locked hair and plug hats, or with stripes sewn down their trouser legs, blue for the Roach Guards, red for the Dead Rabbits. Men watching for the Shining Herald, but, he was fairly certain, for Barnum as well. Byron

359

Spring pointed out others as blackbirders from town, slave catchers, out to make a little extra cash.

January and Spring were careful never to get off the train alone.

Spring, like Barnum, at first had little to say on the return journey. 'This isn't something that can be hushed up,' he said at last, as the 'Jim Crow' carriage jolted and swayed along the narrow track toward Albany. 'New England provides funds not only to help runaways, but to pay lawyers, and fight the courts on behalf of those accused of sheltering fugitives. Money to print accounts of those who've escaped from slavery; to organize lectures, in all these little towns that we can now get to on the railroads. Money to tell people that it isn't just "slaves" we're talking about, like the Israelites in Egypt or the people who had to serve the Romans dinner.'

And his face, for a moment, was like Barnum's, bright with the contemplation of *his* dream. 'With the railroads, with advertising, with printing, we *show* people who've never thought about it before: "Here is a man who used to be a slave. Here is a woman who saw her children sold away from her. Here she is: look her in the face, and tell her that the Bible says her condition is God's will."'

He sighed. 'This scandal's going to hurt. Some of those people are going to ask, "What if this next request for a donation is going to go to some other lying grifter who has no intention of helping a soul? How would we know? And why should we give?"'

'Anger is building.' He turned his eyes to the peaceful landscape, the fields and woods that seemed to be another world, from the squalid hive of New York . . . the slave pens of New Orleans. 'Building against those who demand the end to slavery. Building too against a government that does nothing. Building against the Underground Railroad, and against the men who hold slaves and twist the laws to maintain the right to do so. Building against a change that must come. Then I see the abolitionists and the Colonizers and the "gradual emancipationists" all quarrelling among themselves, and men getting what they can out of those who're trying to change the way things are . . . and I don't know what people will do instead. Sometimes I wake in the night as it is, wondering, *Where is this all going?* And I'm afraid.'

They spent Sunday night in Albany again, again at the North River Hotel. January, who had not written to Rose from the Syracuse jail lest he worry her to no purpose, debated whether to send a letter now, but knew that, with luck, it would arrive in New Orleans at the same time he did. By the time he reached home, the first of Rose's students would have arrived, a young lady named Germaine Barras, whose father was a planter near Mobile. In October, the bankers and brokers and even some of the families of the planters would be returning to town. At home, he had a list of piano students whose lessons would begin before the first frost.

He would lie at Rose's side again, and breathe the perfume of her hair. He would see his sons.

This was in his mind when he and Byron Spring rode in the back of a porter's van with the luggage down to the quays, where the boats were loading for New York. He kept close behind Chloë as tickets were purchased on the dayboat to the City, uneasily aware of the number of ruffians who seemed to be everywhere: not working, as had been the case on his arrival there. Just watching.

Watching for the Shining Herald, or for Hal Shamrock, or the Greenes, he assumed. Watching the upriver boats and those going down.

But he was aware of the way their eyes followed him – and followed Spring – as if marking him down for future reference, or for an idle moment if they had the chance . . .

And he was fairly certain this wasn't because of the superficial resemblance he bore to Hal Shamrock in height and size.

Chloë handed him his ticket. 'The *Galileo* boards in half an hour,' she said, and propped her spectacles on her nose. 'Over there by the ticket offices, the one with the red signboard on the stern. Leopold is seeing to the luggage.'

January was scanning the walkway along the quays looking for the second-class waiting room when he saw her.

And there was no mistaking who she was.

She'd dyed her hair – the two smooth locks visible on her forehead, and the clusters of curls above her ears, were a sort of odd, dusty dark-gray (*flour on top of black dye*, he thought) – and

362

she'd acquired a pair of tinted spectacles from somewhere. But the frock was exactly as described by Lucy Palmer in New York. Light blue, the black-and-white cloverleaf braid on the sleeves and back unmistakable. The bonnet with its distinctive ruffles as well.

He wondered if that was Eve Russell's portmanteau she was carrying.

She passed between two Five Points toughs as she hurried up the gangplank of the *Clarendon*. Bound upriver, the signboard said, to Schenectady. Men were already casting off the ropes.

They didn't give her a glance, but one of them, January noticed, looked at him, and nudged his friend with a comment.

Damn it. Damn it, damn it, damn it . . .

He said to Spring, 'I'll meet you in New York.'

He had just time to buy a ticket, dodge through the gate, and sprint up the gangplank as the stevedores manhandled it aboard. One of them cursed him, for being late and making them wait.

The *Clarendon* was a small boat. From Schenectady, if he recalled correctly, Molly Skeritt – also known as the Shining Herald, black hair, tinted spectacles, and all – could take a railcar to Saratoga Springs, and disappear into its leisured crowds.

Toughs – Dead Rabbits, by the red stripe on their trousers – were well in evidence on the lower deck of the boat. January followed the blue dress along the narrow port side deck toward the paddle, walking as swiftly as he could without drawing attention to himself, hoping to catch her before she reached the stairway to the

'Ladies' Reading Room' on the forbidden purlieux of the upper deck. She glanced around her, as if conscious of how many people in New York might well recognize her even under her disguise. How many thousands came to her lectures? How many hundreds, to those 'private gatherings' where the wealthier of them – those who'd been checked in advance by Mrs Drake/Callan/Broadax – had received personal messages from those they had loved in life?

She would know him.

She had spoken to him, personally, though he would have sworn she hadn't seen his face as he'd stood at the back of the gloomy and very crowded Great Parlor of the Blessed Land.

He wondered if there were an officer of the police on board – someone who could make an arrest and might even give January part of the reward instead of trying to lure him into having an opium-laced drink . . .

At least I can keep an eye on her, and learn where she goes . . .

She reached the stairway, halted at the bottom. A man stood at the top, slightly less disreputable than the Dead Rabbits and slave catchers who'd been watching for her on the quays, though January could smell his green-and-black checked suit from where he stood. Hard little eyes in fleshy pouches turned idly down toward the Herald and she stepped at once through the nearest doorway, as if that had been her goal. January followed her through.

It was a stairway leading down to the luggage hold. He had only to turn back, climb halfway up the steps to the upper deck, and hail the smelly white man with the cigar and the checkered suit. *The woman you're looking for is down there . . .*

Yes, sir, the dame in the blue dress.

Instead, he descended in her wake.

She was at the farther door of the luggage hold, digging in her portmanteau with frantic urgency by the dim light leaked through the transom over the door.

It must be locked . . .

She spun as his shadow blotted the light of the stairway. Panic-stricken, she tried the door again, then faced him, drawing herself up with cold hauteur and terror in her eyes. Quickly she pulled the tinted spectacles down from her forehead, where she'd pushed them the better to see in the semi-dark of the hold.

'What do you want?'

January said, 'Mrs Skeritt?'

'I have no idea what you're talking about.' Her voice shook. 'And I shall scream,' she added, flattening back against the door, 'and tell them all you tried to rape me, if you come one step nearer.'

'There's no need to scream, m'am,' said January. 'If you'd like that gentleman in the checked suit to come down here, I'll go call him. And those gentlemen from the Dead Rabbits who're on the foredeck, too.'

She bit her lips, and her hand tightened on the handle of her valise, as if readying herself to hit him with it.

He made no move, only regarded her in the

365

semi-dark, thinking of what Chloë had told him Friday evening, when she'd reviewed all she had learned of Broadax and his cronies. Fleeing from one preacher who beat her. Cursing at another.

'Who are you?' she asked at last, when he did not speak. 'And what do you want?'

'The Reverend Broadax knew me as Ben,' he said quietly. 'A runaway who took refuge at the Residence on the third of this month. I'm the man who was supposed to have murdered him.'

She said, 'Oh,' quickly, and a moment later turned her face away.

He said nothing, and made no move. After a long time she asked in a tiny voice, 'Was it true what I heard – the rumor I heard . . .? What he did . . .'

'It was true.'

She drew a quick little breath, as if she would say something, then let it out. Still not able to look at him, she said at length, 'I didn't know.' Only then she met his eyes. 'You don't believe me and I don't blame you, but I . . . I knew Harry took in runaways, and got money from the abolition societies. But I didn't know anything else about it. What he did with them. To them . . . It was the same way he got money from all those people who wanted that silly Gospel translated – and from his New York gentlemen. I didn't think it was . . .'

She broke off, pressed her gloved hand to her lips.

He said nothing further. But he kept a watch

on her face, in the dim light from the gangway behind him, from the transom over her head. Her face, and her hands in their mended gloves – too large, probably, to wear Eve Russell's gloves. If she had a pistol in the valise he could have reached her in two steps and wrested it from her hand, but the moment he laid a hand on a white woman he knew she *would* scream, and would be believed.

And laying a hand on her was not what he wanted to do.

'Those people I spoke to' – her voice stammered on the words – 'about their relatives and . . . and friends, about what the angels told me . . . They came to no harm . . .'

'Except the ones who signed their property over to the Blessed Land,' he said quietly. 'Thinking they'd be able to speak to their loved ones again. I take it Mrs Drake – or Mrs Callan or whatever she called herself – would report to her husband, and to you, on who they were and who they wanted to talk to?'

Molly Skeritt nodded. It was the closest he had ever been to her. Even behind the dark lenses of her spectacles she was beautiful, her face absurdly young in the frame of that glaringly iron-gray hair. 'She fixes hair in town,' she said, in a tiny voice. 'Sometimes she works as a maidservant or a dresser. She has a lot of very good references. Lino Greene writes them up, and Etta Greene's the one who'd go out to meet with the ladies who'd want to hire her, or sometimes Jeannie Rankin. Hal Shamrock told me once that Lino and Etta pay other servants in other houses for information. But most of the people donate, or sign over property – they can afford to pay, you know. Those farmers – they have plenty of land. Plenty of credit. They're people who've never been hungry in their lives.'

January asked softly, 'How do you know?' and she was silent.

At last she said, 'Please don't call those men.'

'I won't.'

She looked up quickly at him, startled. For a moment he saw tears glisten in her eyes.

'Do you have money, m'am?'

She swallowed, and nodded, which told him another thing he needed to know. Had she been lying, she would have come up with a different tale.

'Enough to get to Saratoga Springs, and across the border into Canada,' she said. 'Old Mr van Martock . . . I hear he's a hard man, and . . . and mean. He's not going to call off the hunt for me for a long time. Or rest, 'til I'm locked up.'

'Maybe that's because of how badly he was hurt.'

A shudder went through her, and she could not meet his eyes. 'I . . .' she whispered. 'I didn't . . . Well, I did. But I've . . . I've heard about how things are, at the state prison . . .' She shivered again. 'Please,' she said. 'Please don't . . . don't call those men. Please don't tell them. I have enough to keep me going for a while. My Aunt Tilda used to tell me, to buy things that would pack small and that I could sell again.

I've never forgot her advice. I'll find something to do,' she added. 'Not this . . . But I can sew, and fix hair. I won't starve.'

From the deck outside January heard the voices of a couple of men, and a girl's shrill laugh. No, he reflected, a girl as pretty as Molly Skeritt wouldn't starve.

She evidently heard it, too, for her face hardened, nerving herself against both memory and fear.

He stepped back out of the doorway – far enough back, that she could see that he was beyond grabbing distance. Ducking her head, she started to brush past him, then paused, said, 'Thank you. I don't—'

January shook his head. 'You saved my life, m'am,' he said. 'I owe you. But I would like to know why, and how you did that.'

Unless she was a consummate actress – *and she might be*, he reflected wearily . . . *and I might be as much of a fool as poor Jonas van Martock (and to hell with what Father Eugenius would say . . .)* – her expression of startled bafflement looked genuine. 'I've never seen you before,' she said. 'I've never met you . . .'

'The night I came to the Residence,' he said. 'The night Broadax "disappeared". You told me then to beware. You said, "They all lie." Why did you warn me? And how did you know to speak to me?'

'I didn't . . .' She hesitated, her lips again caught between her teeth. Trying, he thought, to frame words for something that she herself didn't understand. Then she said, 'I don't always make it up. Sometimes they do speak to me. At least that's what Aunt Tilda told me, because I don't remember what I say – what *they* say. It's as if I wake up a few seconds later, and truly can't remember.

'It doesn't happen often,' she added, into January's shocked silence. 'Not but once every few months. Aunt Tilda told me' – and here she managed a shaky, rueful smile – 'that I should never take money for preaching, or . . . or telling the words that come to me. Harry – Mr Drake – the Reverend – said that was stupid. But she said, when I started to work for him, that they'd get angry, and they'd get even. And I'd sure say that it looks like they did.'

'Considering the ways they could have got even,' said January, 'I think you got off easy, m'am.' He stepped before her up the short flight of steps to the port-side deck, and looked up the stair to the reading room above. 'He's gone,' he said. 'You be careful.'

She whispered again, 'Thank you,' rustled past him, and was gone.

'And you believe her?' asked Rose, when he told her of the conversation, in the tepid dawn of their first waking together after his return. As usual, Rose had gotten up before first light, to open the shutters and the French doors that looked out across the shade of the gallery on to Rue Esplanade. The last mosquitoes of night hummed outside the tent of pink gauze that covered their bed. From the tree-shaded neutral ground down the center of the wide street, the voices of the draymen and the familiar creak of harness came from the wagons that hauled goods from the wharves to the Canal basin. But these were distant, like birdsong or the piping of frogs in the evenings. Like the whisper of the afternoon rains. They didn't disturb the silence of the house.

His house.

Their house.

I rejoice you have love, Ayasha had said. The Shining Herald had said, in her humbug aura of manufactured light . . .

'Yes.' He had thought he'd feel silly, and a dupe, and for that reason had almost not told Rose of the whole business. But when he said it he found it wasn't the case.

He did believe her.

And the wreckage of quicklime and gas cylinders and sliding panes of glass in the burned-out basement didn't change that belief.

'I wish I knew how that worked.'

A little surprised, January began, 'Barnum said . . .'

'No, I don't mean how the fake was worked. I would like to know what spirits are, and how they . . . how they exist. I would like to know why some people can – apparently – see them, and hear what they say. Is it some part of the brain that some people have and others don't? Some organ in the body? I know animals are supposed to, but my sister-in-law down on Grand Isle had a lapdog who snored at her feet the whole of one night she slept in a friend's house where there'd been a double shotgun murder,

371

and evidently didn't notice a thing. Or do they just not care about human ghosts?'

She folded her hands on her nightgowned breast, studying the swags of mosquito bar above their heads in the half-light, her brows drawn slightly together. 'It was reprehensible,' she added, 'no matter what Mademoiselle Skeritt said about it, to fool people as she did. To hoodwink their hopes. Like making fun of the maimed or the dying.'

'I think she knows that now,' he said. 'Or will learn it in time.'

'We need truth,' she said. 'And there's too little of it in the world.'

Rose, he reflected, smiling, would be a skeptic and a scientist, even about what lay beyond science.

But what is truth?

In time she slipped from beneath the netting, found her spectacles, wrapped herself in her robe and padded to the little rear bedroom where the boys slept. He heard Xander's sleepy clucking as she checked his diaper, and overhead, the creak of feet in the attic. Zizi-Marie waking, and Gabriel. And at the other end of the house, the fainter stirrings of the girls getting out of bed, Germaine Barras and Cosette Gardinier, the first of the fall's students.

Would I sign over everything I own, he wondered, *if by doing so I could be assured of speaking with Ayasha again?*

What would I do, if I learned that all my dreams were false?

What if I received assurance they were true?

True or false, as Barnum had said, everyone needs their dreams.

And dreams, he supposed, could help those in pain as much as Spirits who came down from Heaven, to do what they could.

Through the French doors came the distant clang of bells from the steamboat wharves, the town stirring to life. The creak of shutters elsewhere in the house, as Gabriel opened them to the morning light.

Over the roofs of the low pastel city, the cathedral bells were ringing for morning Mass.

Author's Note

The Blessed Land, and the people and events described in connection with it, are based on no particular cult or sect of the dozens active in the western counties of New York State in the first half of the nineteenth century. The so-called 'Second Great Awakening' in the early 1800s swept the then-frontier district with repeated waves of religious revivalism and religious enthusiasm, to such a degree that it came to be called the 'Burned-Over District' – seared, they said, with the fires of the Lord.

The result was that the whole area became a hotbed for both radical religious and social movements, and the home of numerous communities more reminiscent – to modern perception – of Marin County in the late 1960s, than of Victorian America.

Actual religious movements which began there include the Church of the Latter-Day Saints (the Mormons), the millenarian Millerites (who evolved into the Seventh Day Adventists), the Jehovah's Witnesses, and numerous small, short-lived cults (including the Bullerites, who lived in the woods, wore nothing but leather and bearskins, didn't bathe or shave, and practiced polygamy). The area also saw a revival of the Shaker faith; the modern development of the Spiritualist movement; the first organized conventions of modern feminism; numerous utopian social experiments like the Oneida and Skaneateles communities; and widespread involvement in the Underground Railway.

The folk beliefs I have described were actually held in that place at that time.

P.T. Barnum and David Ruggles are, of course, historical personages.